MW01155557

DAMIAN'S WORKSHOP

Deborah Kaminski

Dear Susan,
May there be a
Memex in your future!

Debbi Kaminski

This book is a work of fiction. Any resemblance of characters to actual persons, except historical personages, is purely coincidental. Incidents, places, names, and institutions are either the product of the author's imagination or are used for the purposes of fiction, with no guarantee of accuracy.

Cover design by Christopher Kaminski

Copyright ©2014 by Deborah Kaminski
All rights reserved. No part of this book may be reproduced or retransmitted in any form or by any electronic or mechanical means without permission in writing from the author, except by a reviewer, who may quote brief passages in a review.
www.deborahkaminski.com

ISBN: 1502478595
ISBN: 9781502478597

LCCN: 2014917120
CreateSpace Independent Publishing Platform
North Charleston, South Carolina

"Life is either a daring adventure or nothing at all."

Helen Keller, *The Open Door*

DAMIAN'S WORKSHOP

Deborah Kaminski

To Chris,
whose love has sustained me through many trials

CONTENTS

I

OF MICE AND MEMEX

If Brooke Laforge had known how important mouse 116 would be in her life, she might have examined him more closely that morning. But it was just another day in the lab, and she was following a monotonous routine. She grasped the mouse by the base of the tail with one latex-gloved hand and by the scruff of the neck with the other. As she lifted him, he pawed futilely at the Plexiglas floor of his cage, engaging in a ritual of resistance that involved twisting, squirming, and attempted biting, but Brooke was well practiced in handling rodents.

"Don't worry. I won't hurt you," she murmured. She checked his eyes and ears for signs of discharge, palpated his belly, and examined his fur. All healthy. The ear tag labeling him as 116 was in place and not irritating the surrounding flesh. Brooke released the mouse into the cage and he scampered into a corner, huddling near his cellmates. Adding a small cardboard tube as a chew toy, she closed the lid and made a notation on her iPad.

The mice were housed in five foot tall racks that lined the west wall of the lab. Brooke slid 116's cage into place at the top of the last column. The rack resembled a filing cabinet with transparent walls, but Brooke preferred to think of it as a mouse hotel, complete with exercise treadmills and room service. If she were honest with herself, the place was more like Alcatraz than a posh hotel, with the inside of each cell exposed to view and its residents stripped of freedom.

"Well, that's the last of them," she said to Robert Chen, who was doing homework at a desk in the corner. "The mice are all fine." Robert was Brooke's labmate, a fellow graduate student who had joined the research group a year later than Brooke. He was a slim man with close-cropped hair the color of wet bark. His large, wide-set eyes were obscured behind an oversized pair of dark-rimmed glasses.

"Great," said Robert. "Maybe we can start the real testing soon."

"That'll be a relief." After years of preparation, Brooke was alternately excited by the great promise of her invention, the Memex, and worried about its possible shortcomings. Memex was short for "Memory Excitation Device," a machine that was designed to stimulate the brain to recover forgotten memories. They had been doggedly testing effects on mice to ensure safety, but only human testing could reveal the invention's full potential.

The Memex was housed near the back windows, its rack of electronics stacked on a wheeled cabinet topped by two 18-inch flat screen displays. At the end of a long jointed arm, a white plastic helmet hovered over a padded chair that bore a disturbing resemblance to a dentist's chair. A tube just big enough for a mouse, one end swathed with electric coils, rested on the cabinet. The mice seemed perfectly unmoved by their experiences on the machine, at least most of the time. Occasionally they would wriggle within the tight tube, trying to escape from a threat that existed only in their minds. But there was no permanent damage. Perhaps they were remembering a harrowing encounter with a cat, or a sibling crushed beneath the steel jaw of a mousetrap. Of course these were laboratory animals who had never run free or seen a cat, but Brooke didn't want to think about that. The benefits to human health outweighed the horror of their stunted lives.

The Memex operated on the principle of Transcranial Magnetic Stimulation. Coils of wire within the helmet produced a magnetic field that penetrated the brain and induced electric currents. By aiming the field precisely and using the right waveform in the coils, Brooke planned to stimulate memory centers deep in the cortex. She hoped to help people afflicted with amnesia, stroke, and Alzheimer's disease.

The door opened and Prof. Hunter stepped in. As usual, she had not stopped to put on a lab coat or hair covering. Brooke noticed the gray roots at the base of her dull black hair, which covered her head in scattered curls. Prof. Hunter was wearing one of her long plaid skirts with a dark knit top that accentuated her tall, overly thin form.

Brooke was always careful about procedure and resented the professor's casual disregard for the rules. She knew that if she had not suited up properly, Hunter would let her know. Getting ready wasn't quick and easy, either. Brooke normally wore four or five rings, and had to remove them every time she put on latex gloves. Her long, thick, auburn hair did not fit well inside the hair covering and was always escaping under the edges. At least she didn't have to remove her earrings. Brooke adored earrings and had a large and unusual collection.

"I just got the results from the University Review Board," Hunter said. "They rejected our request for testing with human subjects. They wrote four pages of comments on issues they want us to address."

Brooke was stunned. She had thought the request would pass easily and could not understand how this had happened. None of the mice had experienced any problems after using the Memex. She had been careful to include a large sample of mice and to run a full battery of tests. Prof. Hunter had been very optimistic about the request being accepted.

"What did they complain about?" asked Robert.

"They say we haven't done MRIs on the mice, so we don't know what's happening to their brains. There could be inflammation, restricted blood flow, tumors, any number of things. Since we don't have an MRI set-up, we'll have to test for a longer period of time and then sacrifice the little beasts."

"The mice don't show any symptoms of disease," protested Brooke. "Blood and urine are normal and they do great in the maze. No memory loss."

"We wouldn't know if they had headaches." Hunter turned a page and squinted down at the report. "They also want us to document the possible psychological effects of the Memex. Are the mice depressed, manic, or aggressive? Do they sleep well? Do they play nicely with their cellmates or do they huddle in a corner afraid to face life?"

"I spend time every day watching them," said Brooke. "They're always active and lively. We haven't seen any hint of depression."

"Yes, but we have no formal documentation. The board wants a forced swimming test."

"That test is bogus. We thought about it and decided it wasn't worth doing."

"What's a forced swimming test?" asked Robert. He had not worked on the request for human subject testing and was unfamiliar with the details.

"You put the mouse in a plastic container filled with water and let it swim around," explained Brooke. "The mouse can't get out no matter how hard it tries. After letting it paddle helplessly for fifteen minutes, you rescue it. The next day, you put the mouse back in the water. If the mouse hesitates before swimming around, that's supposed to be an indicator of depression." She crossed her arms. "I don't believe it. I think the mouse has figured out what's going on. He knows he can't get out and sees no point in trying. Or else he's waiting for the experimenter to save him." Brooke also thought the test was cruel and unnecessary and wanted no part of it.

"I agree with you," said Hunter. "But we have to bow to the wishes of the Review Board. Prof. Urbanowitz, the chair, has an ego as big as Texas.

He'll never change his mind. With the extra testing time and the new tests, we'll have at least a four month delay." She flipped the stapled pages of the review back into a neat pile and handed it to Brooke.

"Four months! Can't we get it done sooner?" asked Brooke.

"I don't see how. Those mice might die of old age by the time the board is satisfied. Take a look at the board's comments, and we'll talk strategy at our next meeting."

After Hunter left, Brooke read through the report. She sat hunched over in her chair with her chin in her hand and her facial muscles wound up like a clock. She turned the pages listlessly, skipping from one part to another. Since middle school, she had dreamed of becoming a scientist. It was her calling in life, a core value that defined who she was. Now this setback could ruin everything. Without human testing, there would be no doctoral degree and no future as a scientist. There wasn't much time left before her fellowship ran out.

The last section of the report dealt with the human volunteer consent form.

"Robert, listen to this: 'The subjects must be informed of the possibility of reawakening repressed memories. In addition, memories from early childhood may compromise one's view of one's parents.' There must be a Freudian on the Board."

"I had a friend who joined the Peace Corp," said Robert. "When he was in Ethiopia, he got into a terrible automobile accident. He said he couldn't remember anything that happened in the hours before the impact."

"I guess we would have to avoid memories like that," said Brooke. "Unless someone wanted to remember, say for a court case or something. But I don't know how we're supposed to tell what memories a person will have. We'll never figure that out by just testing mice."

She continued leafing through the board report. It was too much to take. She didn't feel like reading the whole thing just then. She knew she would have to go through it in detail sooner or later, but she didn't have the heart to do it at the moment.

"Are you interested in getting something to eat at the Union? I want to get out of here," said Brooke.

"Sure," replied Robert. "Let's go."

The campus of Brackett University was at its most beautiful on that early spring afternoon. The saucer magnolia trees were covered with delicate pink blossoms and the grass glowed with a vibrant new green.

The air was warm with a light breeze and the sky was a deep azure. Brooke and Robert walked along a curving path on the west end of campus.

"I can't believe the Review Board rejected us," said Brooke. "I was counting on getting a lot of testing done this summer. Despite what the board said, I don't think we'll learn anything by more experimenting on the mice." The beautiful weather annoyed rather than pleased her. How could the world be so cheerful when she was so distraught?

"I guess we'll just have to start in the fall. It won't be the first time we've been delayed."

"It's different for me, Robert. My fellowship runs out next spring. My doctoral degree is at risk. Without data, I won't be able to write my thesis. I need to have all my data collected at least three months before I plan to defend. It takes a long time to get all the data and put it down on paper."

"Well, there's nothing we can do about it," said Robert.

Brooke was silent for a while. A thought was forming in her mind, but she wasn't sure what Robert would think of it. They walked along companionably past the ivy-covered upper-class dorms. A flock of birds rose en masse from a giant oak tree. Giving up on her research was like giving up on life. It didn't seem fair. She had done everything Prof. Hunter has asked of her, and her degree was still at risk. Brooke had always obeyed the rules, complying with the system no matter what craziness it asked of her. She had put in long hours of sweat and toil and trusted the university to do its part. Now they had left her in a hopeless position, like a mouse in a forced swimming test. Well she was no lab animal. She had options.

"I could test the Memex on myself," she said.

Robert looked at her, startled.

"You can't do that. What if you get hurt?"

"I won't get hurt. None of the mice were affected. Why should I be? I was willing to recruit volunteers to a testing program so I should be willing to undergo the test myself. We have enough data. I've been watching these mice and I know they're healthy."

"But you won't be able to use the data you get on yourself in your thesis. We have to use a large randomized sample of volunteers."

"If I test it on myself, we can work out the bugs. We can get an idea of how to adjust settings so that we can home in on particular memories or times in a person's life. Knowing that will help us a lot when we start the real testing program."

"Prof. Hunter will never let you," said Robert.

"I don't intend to ask Hunter. I'm just going to do it."

Robert raised his eyebrows and his eyes opened wide behind his black framed glasses. He frowned in concentration and shuffled his backpack higher on his shoulder.

"What if she finds out? Will they kick you out of school?"

"They won't kick me out. Besides, if they do, will it matter? If they kick me out, I won't get my degree. If I don't start testing, I won't get my degree. I've worked so hard for this degree. I won't give up on it just because a Review Board is overly cautious."

"You can't do it alone. You need someone to operate the equipment while you're being tested."

Brooke looked at him steadily.

"Oh, no. You're not dragging me into this. I have a wife and baby girl. I can't afford to get kicked out of school."

"Nobody's going to kick us out of school. I'm not doing anything unethical. I'm the only one taking a risk and I'm completely willing to take it. I'm more fully informed than anyone else will ever be."

"But why put yourself in such a position? Why not wait till we're more sure it's safe?"

"My fellowship ends next spring. I have to be done by then. My family can't pay tuition or help with living expenses. If I don't finish this year, I'll never get my degree."

"Maybe there's another way. Why don't you go talk to Prof. Hunter? Maybe she can find you another source of funding."

"I don't know…" But Brooke could see that Robert needed to be convinced. She would never get him on her side if he thought that she could get funding from Hunter.

"OK, I'll go to Hunter's office tomorrow. In the meantime, promise me you won't mention this to anyone."

"I won't. You can be sure of that."

———

Brooke waited patiently outside the door to Hunter's office. The professor was just finishing up her last meeting, which was running over by fifteen minutes. Brooke had been rehearsing what she would say when the door opened and three students gathered up their belongings and filed out of the office. Hunter waved Brooke in.

"Have a seat. I'll be with you just as soon as I send this email." The gray roots had disappeared overnight and Hunter's hair was now inky black. Every horizontal surface in the room was piled with messy stacks of papers, some on the verge of toppling over. The equations and diagrams on the blackboard next to the desk had not been erased since Brooke had started as a graduate student. Brooke wondered where the professor had found the long paisley skirt that she wore—it looked about thirty years out of date. It fit in with the scuffed and worn black shoes.

"Now what can I do for you?"

"My fellowship runs out next May and I'm not sure we can get all the testing done in time to finish my degree. The Review Board has really delayed things. I wanted to explore alternative funding possibilities."

"Well, I did submit a proposal about six months ago to NIH on this research," said Hunter. "It was rejected. The reviewers wanted preliminary data before they would agree to fund the work."

"But how are we supposed to get data if we have no funding?" asked Brooke.

"You have a point. This is just the way science works. Some researchers already have data, because they've been working in an area for a long time and can use the results from their last grant to make the proposal for their next grant look good. When the reviewers are faced with two proposals, one with supporting data and the other without, they often pick the one with supporting data. This makes it hard to get money for creative, but unproven, ideas."

"They also complained that we didn't have a centralized animal care facility supervised by a veterinarian. That's easy to do if you're Mount Sinai or MIT, where many research groups can pool their resources to support such a facility, but Brackett is a small university. Policies like that serve as much to protect established researchers as test animals."

Before Brooke could point out how well she treated the mice, the phone rang and Hunter picked it up. She got into an involved conversation with the person on the other end, leaving Brooke wondering if she dared pull out her cell phone. Deciding not to risk antagonizing the professor, she scanned the walls aimlessly. A diploma read "Louise Hunter, Doctor of Philosophy, Electrical Engineering, Carnegie Mellon University." Hunter was in the department of Cognitive Science, a relatively new discipline where the professors were drawn from many established disciplines. There was also a plaque with a "Best Paper Award" and another for an "Early Career Research Award." There were no awards for good teaching.

The phone call finally ended and Hunter returned her attention to Brooke.

"Now where were we?"

"You were telling me about the rejected NIH grant. What about a teaching assistantship? I know it'll be more work since I'll have to grade papers, but at least I can finish my degree."

"The department doesn't have a lot of slots for teaching assistants. I already have one for Chad Morgan and I doubt they will give me another. Chad still has at least two years to go." Hunter glanced at her watch, which hung loosely from her thin wrist.

"There is another possibility," said Hunter. "You may want to apply for an internship with a local company. These usually run for about six months and may lead to a permanent job. You can work for the company by day and complete your degree in your spare time."

Brooke thought about this. She imagined spending every day at the office and every night and weekend at the lab. The image was not appealing. After seven years in college, in which she had studied hard to get top grades, she was hoping for a lighter workload, not a heavier one. Worst of all, if she left, the chances she would finish her degree were slim. Too many outside pressures could get in the way.

"I'll think about it," said Brooke. "Thanks for meeting with me." She picked up her backpack and left the office.

⸺∞⸺

On Friday night, the Wilson building was deserted. Only the most devoted or desperate students were still at work. Brooke met Robert in the Memex lab.

"I'm still not sure this is a good idea," said Robert. "I don't know how I let you talk me into it."

"It's all going to work out fine," said Brooke. She threw her jacket on a nearby chair and didn't bother to put on a hair covering or lab coat. If she was going to be a rebel, she might as well go all the way. Besides, she wasn't going to touch the mice tonight, and the precautions were mostly to ensure their health.

Robert turned on the electronics and booted the computer. Then he opened a tall cabinet containing wiring harnesses.

"We'll have to instrument you before the test. Maybe you want to put these patches on yourself." There were at least twenty wires that needed to be attached to her body in various places. Some measured heart rate, others measured breathing and muscle tension. They came with self-adhesive patches.

"I'll need help," said Brooke. "Start with my face."

Robert attached a probe next to each eye. This would pick up any rapid eye movements to see if she had entered a dream state. He also pasted probes on her chin to detect jaw grinding. After that, he appeared hesitant. The next probes would go on Brooke's chest.

Brooke turned her back and unbuttoned her shirt. "Well, here's something we didn't think about when we wrote up the test procedure," she said. "We'll need some private place to instrument the test subjects. See, we're already learning something."

She removed her shirt. She was glad she had worn her new red bra; might as well look good. "Add the probes to my back," she directed.

Robert complied. His hands were cold and a little damp. "I'm not sure I should tell my wife about this," he joked.

Brooke was alarmed. "Don't tell your wife about any of this testing. She may tell her best friend, who will promise not to tell, and the best friend will tell someone else, who will also promise not to tell. You can't keep a secret if more than two people know about it." Brooke was also thinking in the back of her mind that Feng, Robert's wife, might convince him not to help out.

"You didn't tell her what you were doing here tonight, did you?" asked Brooke.

"No," said Robert. "I just said I was working late at the lab."

"Good."

When Robert was done with her back, he paused. Brooke turned around and took the wires. "I'll do my front." She pasted probes over her left breast and under it, as well as on her side. When she was finished, she put on her shirt and buttoned it. A profusion of wires dangled from beneath her shirt and face. Robert helped her gather them up into a bundle and wrapped a Velcro band around them.

By now the computer was up and running. Brooke settled into the padded chair next to the Memex and adjusted the headrest to her liking. Robert lowered the helmet over her cranium and positioned it to stimulate both the hippocampus and the amygdalae, important memory centers within the brain. He plugged the various wires into a switching box.

"Are you ready?" he asked.

"Yes." Brooke clasped her hands tightly together in her lap and crossed her ankles. She wondered if it would hurt.

Robert checked the settings for duty cycle, pulse height, and frequency on the monitor and activated the signal.

"Do you feel anything?" He glanced at her face.

"Nothing," said Brooke. "Maybe we need more power. After all, the level should be higher for humans than for mice." She bit her lip.

Robert cautiously adjusted the input power and the pulse height rose. He waited to see how Brooke would respond.

"More," she said.

Robert raised the power another small notch. Brooke felt her scalp tingle, but no memories were awakened. As Robert increased the voltage further, a faint knocking sound came from the machine. The tingling intensified and her scalp grew warm, but she didn't stop him. These were expected side effects of TMS, nothing to be concerned about. He went higher still, and a muscle in her right cheek started to twitch. The knocking grew louder and a slow burn spread across her cranium.

"That's high enough," she said. "Let's try a different frequency and a lower voltage."

Robert had been methodically keying data into a spreadsheet during the testing. Although it slowed them down, it would be worth the trouble in the long run. He now adjusted the frequency a little higher and repeated the test.

Brooke began to squirm in the chair. She endured the tingling and the noise stoically, pushing herself to go as high as she dared. No memories floated up, but at least her fear had given way to impatience. She was certain the Memex would work once they found the right settings. Three hours later, Brooke had a mild headache and both researchers were tired and discouraged. She sat up and started to remove the wires.

"I'm ready to pack it in," she said. "We can try again tomorrow."

∞∞∞

Saturday night was stormy and Brooke arrived late at the lab. She opened her soaked umbrella and set it down near the door to dry. Water dripped off the points of the umbrella's frame and puddled onto the floor. Robert was already busy at the Memex, reviewing his notes from the previous night. He pushed his glasses, which never seemed to fit comfortably on his face, higher on his nose.

"I'm not sure this is a good idea," he said.

"Why not?"

"We don't know what the Memex might do when I raise the voltage higher. What if you pass out?"

"I won't pass out. If we worry about everything that might happen, we'll never get anything done. What if the roof leaks in this storm and water drips on the machine? It could short out."

Robert looked up apprehensively. "Do you think that might happen?"

Brooke sighed. "No, I was just posing a 'what if.' You can always think of something that might go wrong, but you can't let thoughts like that paralyze you. Besides, would it be better to have a trusting volunteer sitting in the chair instead of me? I'm the one who most wants to know what the Memex can do, so I should be the one to try it first."

Robert still looked unconvinced.

"Maybe we should take a new tack," said Brooke. "Don't exceed yesterday's highest voltage and try new duty cycles. That should minimize the risk."

"I guess so," said Robert and he turned toward the console to begin the set-up. Brooke began to wire herself up for the test. Robert helped her finish and got her settled into the chair. He adjusted the Memex helmet to fit properly around her head. After fussing a bit, he was finally satisfied. With a few taps of his fingers on the touch screen, he applied the signal. As he adjusted the settings, a bolt of lightning flashed outside, turning the tall lab windows into bright slabs. A jarring clap of thunder followed. Brooke wondered if they would lose power. She felt no effect from the Memex.

Robert altered the signal and a creepy itchy feeling ran over her scalp. The Memex thrummed in counterpoint to the drumming of the rain on the roof. Brooke remembered that seizures were a rare side effect of TMS and a wave of fear coursed through her body. She mastered her feelings and said nothing to Robert, not wanting to make him jumpier than he already was. After a while, she grew accustomed to the tingling and the knocking and the warmth, but memories eluded her. What would she do if the Memex didn't work? Resigning herself to a long and probably fruitless search, Brooke began to daydream. Robert continued to make adjustments, working through the possibilities methodically. A half-hour passed as the thunder and lightning kept up a sound and light show outside.

Abruptly, the lab disappeared and Brooke found herself walking down a strange and unfamiliar street...

II

WHERE AM I?

All around her, men strode purposefully to unknown destinations. At first Brooke thought they were Arabs from their skin tone and black beards, but their clothing didn't seem right. They wore long tunics belted at the waist in drab browns and grays, often patched or tattered at the hem. Their legs were bare and their feet were shod in sandals, some with straps that snaked up their calves. No one paid her any heed as she traveled among them. Brooke was certain she had never been here before. Puzzled and curious, she absorbed every detail of her surroundings.

A donkey cart piled high with cabbages clattered by, and the crowd reluctantly parted to let it pass. The driver snapped his whip just above the head of the plodding beast, who was unfazed by the loud crack. The wheels of the cart were made of wood, not rubber, as if she were in ancient Rome.

In contrast to the evident poverty of the people, the roadbed was paved with slabs of marble two feet on a side, lustrous even under the onslaught of thousands of feet. Brooke could understand cobblestones, but marble? She had not traveled much, due to lack of funds rather than lack of interest. The only time she had been out of the northeastern United States had been on a week-long trip to Italy. But she had never imagined that there might be marble streets somewhere in the world.

Involuntarily, she reached up to scratch her face and felt a beard. Her hand was large, with tufts of hair on the fingers. Good lord! She was in a man's body. Brooke had no control over the body's movements. It carried her along as a silent passenger on a trajectory of its own. This had to be a dream, but it all seemed as sharp and detailed as real life.

Although the streets were crowded, there were few women. Those she saw wore long robes and covered their heads with scarves and their faces with veils. Blocky two- and three-story buildings with square windows and flat roofs, painted in neutral tans and whites, lined the sides of the street.

A child no more than seven years old sat on the edge of a roof with his legs dangling over the side and Brooke worried that he might fall. Behind him, two children ran about on the rooftop shrieking in delight, but Brooke's host did not seem alarmed and continued past at a brisk pace. She wished she could look behind her, but could not. It was like being in a movie, where the camera defined what you could see.

They came upon an open square with a small fountain at the center. Water issued from a carved stone flower, dribbling off the petals into a broad basin. The wind blew some spray onto Brooke's face, which she felt as a welcome coolness. A blind man was led by his dog through the square. The mutt didn't look like any guide dog Brooke had ever seen. It was no larger than a terrier, with coarse brown hair and a black spot surrounding one eye. The blind man felt the edge of the fountain with his hands, dipped a bucket in, and carried the water off.

Brooke's host turned a corner and proceeded down another street, which was lined with shops. Through the windows she could see bowls, bolts of cloth, hammers, and household goods. At the next intersection, her host turned right and walked up a gentle hill. Stopping at a wooden door, he removed a leather thong with several keys from around his neck and unlocked it. The workshop within was clean and tidy, with a long wooden table flanked by three stools. A large collection of tools covered the walls—hammers, tongs, chisels in various sizes, picks, files, and other items that Brooke could not identify. Bypassing the workbench, the man ascended a staircase and called out a word that Brooke didn't catch.

A young woman appeared and spoke to the man in a strange language. They conversed for some time in an easy and familiar way that suggested a shared life, and Brooke guessed she was his wife. The woman was attractive, with long, brown hair parted in the middle, a straight nose, and generous lips. Her complexion was light compared to everyone else Brooke had seen in this place, and suggested ancestry in northern Europe.

The man sat down at the head of a long table laid out for dinner. The room was rapidly becoming dark with the onset of evening. Religious paintings hung on the walls, icons of the Virgin Mary with child and the baptism of the adult Jesus in the river Jordan. A small vase containing a single red rose flanked by two silver candlesticks occupied the center of the table, which was covered by a hand-embroidered linen cloth. Two children, a girl of about ten and a boy of seven, ran into the room. Brooke's host smiled at them and took the boy in his lap, hugging him tightly. Brooke did not understand the words but the warmth came through loud and clear. Last to arrive was an aged woman propped up with a cane.

13

After the family were all seated, a serving girl set down a platter of warm, fragrant, bread and a small bowl of oil mixed with herbs. She poured drinks from a flagon into their goblets, water for the children and wine for the adults. The family entered into a lively conversation, with much laughter and joking. The young girl spoke often, sometimes flicking her long blond hair over her shoulder. Her pale skin and coloring were unusual in this city. She must have taken after her mother. The bread, warm from the oven, dipped in olive oil and rosemary, tasted like heaven.

The young boy wriggled in his seat and his mother scolded him. He settled down temporarily. He had short black hair, a thin mouth, and a long scar upon his cheek. When he was older, the scar would make him look rakish rather than disfigured.

The next course turned out to be a sort of porridge mixed with nuts and dried fruit, followed by a platter of pungent cheese. At the end of the meal, the children were dismissed and led off by the servant while the adults remained at the table for what seemed like hours.

Brooke woke up. She opened her eyes and saw the ceiling of the lab, covered with pipes and ducts. She sat up and removed the helmet from her head, relieved to be back in her familiar space and rescued from the strangeness of her experience.

"Why did you leave me under so long?" she asked. "I thought we agreed on one minute for our first experiment."

"What?" said Robert. "Did something happen?"

"You didn't notice?"

"I was figuring out the next few settings to try. I just cut the power. It was only on this setting for one minute."

"Really? It felt like I was under for three or four hours."

"Did you remember anything?"

"I'm not sure what happened. I was in a strange city. Whatever I felt, these weren't my memories." Brooke started to fill Robert in on the details of her experience, but she cut herself short.

"Just a minute. I have to get a record of this." She slid into a chair by the desktop computer and opened a new document. Tapping furiously, she tried to capture all the details of her experience before they skidded away.

Robert stood behind her reading over her shoulder. When she had finished, he said, "I wonder if it was a dream."

"I don't think so. It was so vivid and detailed. Not disjointed as dreams usually are. It felt real."

Robert turned to the Memex monitor and checked the recordings of Brooke's physical reactions during the time she was under. "There were no rapid eye movements. That rules out an ordinary dream. Heart rate and breathing were normal—no sign of stress. What city do you think it was?"

"I don't know. It was clearly not in modern times, but I can't place it. It was a European or Middle Eastern city, not Asian or African. I couldn't tell what language they were speaking. It was totally unfamiliar to me. What settings were you using?" she asked. "I want to add them to my notes."

"I superimposed three pulse trains, each at 700 Hz. The duty cycles were 4.22%, 8.44% and 16.88% and they were in phase. I tried a lot of things and this just happened to work."

"That's odd," said Brooke. "We used a single pulse train of 400 Hz with a 36% duty cycle for the mice."

"Are you going to try again?" asked Robert.

"Yes," she said, "but not tonight."

Sunday morning was perfect for hiking. Chad Morgan enjoyed being outdoors and pushed himself into the climb. The Adirondacks weren't rugged like his beloved Rocky Mountains, but they had their own special charm. The forest was lush and leafy with occasional shafts of light penetrating the dense canopy. He drew in the fresh air, fragrant and clean.

The trail rose steadily through old growth forest, with occasional switchbacks on the steeper portions. Most of the time, though, the path led straight upward despite the grade, as if Eastern hikers were too impatient to meander back and forth. Chad realized he had gotten a little ahead of his friends, and decided to hold up a bit. He turned around to look down the trail, but saw no one. Pulling out his canteen, he took a generous swig of water. He removed his white Stetson and ran his fingers through his hair before replacing the hat.

Soon Brooke would catch up with him, and he yearned for a glimpse of her as a castaway yearns for a sail on the horizon. He wished he could put her out of his mind, but each time he saw her expressive face and lively green eyes, he felt a pang of longing. She wasn't interested in him. He had to accept the fact. When he had first joined Hunter's lab a year ago, he had asked her out. She had been gentle in her rejection, telling him that she thought it best not to get involved with men at the workplace, but it had stung all the same.

He never should have let her talk him into this hiking trip. She was always organizing excursions to get them all outdoors, approaching the topic with great enthusiasm. He knew he should stay away, should distance himself from the unattainable, but the temptation was too great. She had a hold on his heart, and he didn't know what to do about it.

A moment later, Brooke appeared from around a bend in the trail. She was charging along at a steady pace, breathing heavily. Chad had the impression she wished she could keep up with him. Truth to tell, he was in pretty good shape, and Brooke was not far behind. Even though they were in the wilderness, she wore long dangling earrings that bounced as she pumped her legs up and down.

"We're making good time," said Chad. "We should be at the summit by two."

"Great," Brooke replied. "There should be a good view from there, especially in this weather. Let's go on."

Chad had the impression she didn't want to show weakness by taking a break.

"I think we should wait for the others. Don't want them to get discouraged."

They shared a seat on a large flat rock, tilted somewhat from the horizontal, but the closest thing to a bench they could find. Chad offered Brooke a bag of trail mix and she emptied some into her hand.

"It feels good to be in the woods," said Brooke. "Most of the time, though, I'm looking at my feet so I don't stumble on a root or stone." Chad involuntarily looked at his own feet, shod in well-worn cowboy boots.

"Well, now you can just sit and enjoy the sights for a bit," he said.

After some time, Robert Chen and his wife, Feng, trudged up the trail. They paused frequently to catch their breath. Robert was carrying his five-month-old daughter, Emily, in an infant carrier on his back. The little girl was trying to jump up and down in the backpack, her round face grinning happily, and Robert struggled to maintain his balance.

"You're almost here," called Chad.

When they arrived, Chad stood and gave his seat to Feng, who lowered herself wearily. Robert carefully removed his backpack and lifted Emily out.

Brooke raised her arms, saying, "Give her to me." The group rested companionably while Brooke played with the baby.

"It's nice to get outdoors," said Robert. "This is what I needed after a tough week."

"What happened this week?" asked Chad.

"Oh, didn't Prof. Hunter tell you? The Review Board denied our request for human subject testing."

"I see," said Chad, frowning. This was bad news.

"They wrote a long list of complaints. It will be months before we can sort it all out."

"Well, I guess there's nothing we can do about it," said Chad. "We'll just have to persevere."

Robert glanced at Brooke who met his gaze. Chad had the impression he wasn't getting the whole story. Robert looked down.

"Yeah, we'll have to persevere," said Robert.

The Review Board decision was disappointing, but Chad didn't see what they could do other than more testing on mice and more work on the consent form. It would be a delay, but delays were a natural part of research. He had overcome many of them to get this far, and he no doubt would be faced with many more. He had another two years before he was supposed to graduate, and that distant date stretched out into a future that hardly seemed real.

"I think we'd better get moving," said Chad. "We'll get stiff if we sit here too long. Brooke, why don't you lead the way?"

Brooke complied and started up the trail, which had become steeper. They ascended past a stand of beeches and hiked alongside a bare rock outcrop. Chad enjoyed walking behind Brooke. Her long, thick auburn hair, which usually flowed in loose curls over her shoulders, was today tied back in a ponytail. She looked good in a pair of jeans.

"Do you like to collect things?" asked Chad.

"You mean like stamps or coins?" replied Brooke.

"I was thinking more of mountains. There's a group who call themselves the 46ers who have climbed all of the highest 46 mountains in New York State."

"I know about them. I've climbed six of the peaks. If we make it up Giant today, that'll be seven. How about you?"

"I haven't hiked much here in the East," said Chad, "but my dad took me up a whole passel of mountains in Colorado."

"That must have been nice. My family wouldn't think of tackling a mountain. My dad is a plumber. He used to come home from work, wolf down dinner, and settle into the sofa for the evening. The TV was never shut off. Once in a while, we went on a picnic on Sunday, but other than that, I never got much exposure to the great outdoors."

"Sounds tough," said Chad. "I grew up on a farm, but the hard physical labor never seemed to stop my dad. We went fishing, backpacking, snowshoeing, cave exploring—you name it."

"Have you ever tried bushwhacking?" asked Brooke.

Chad glanced at the thick growth on either side of the trail. The steep, uneven ground covered with underbrush was tough to navigate. It was ankle-breaking terrain.

"Not here in the Adirondacks. It looks like a challenge."

"Some of the top 46 peaks are trail-less. Robert, Feng, and I tackled Macomb last year. Half the time, I wasn't sure where we were. But it was exhilarating to finally come upon a landmark. It felt like being rescued or finding a hidden treasure. Now that they have a baby, we stick to the well-trod path."

Chad was tempted. Should he offer to take her on a hike up a trail-less peak? Just the two of them? If she wanted that, she would have to ask. He wasn't setting himself up for rejection again.

The trees were getting shorter as they approached the summit, and they occasionally glimpsed the land far below through a break in the foliage. The last stretch to the top was across bare rock, heavily lined with cracks and spotted with lichen.

When Chad reached the top, he took off his hat and tossed it into the air like a Frisbee. Brooke turned to him with a wide grin. Chad was in the land of the gods, with the world unrolling in a dense green carpet below him. Jagged peaks marched off to the horizon, each more distant peak a paler shade of blue. Life was good, and no research setback was going to interfere with that.

<hr>

The next day, Brooke was eager to try the Memex again. She was of two minds on how to proceed. She could pursue the odd vision that she had happened upon a few days ago or keep searching for a way into her own memories. She didn't want to forget about the unknown man whose memories she had accessed. It wouldn't be the first time a scientist had been expecting one thing and found another. Besides, she was curious. She had searched the internet for cities with marble streets, and come up with Dubrovnik and Zadar in Croatia and Ephesus in Turkey. The first two were old cities that were still occupied today, but they didn't resemble the place she had been. Ephesus was a ruin. So much was missing that she couldn't tell if it was her mystery destination. Clearly more data was needed.

When she arrived at the lab, Robert was already at work.

"Are you sure you want to do this?" he asked. "After your last experience, I'm a little worried. You were like on a drug trip or something."

"It was nothing like a drug trip. I was in my right mind—just not in my right body."

"Maybe we should talk to Hunter about it."

"No way. She'll just tell us to wait out the four months. Look, I'm perfectly fine. No aftereffects at all. This is safe. I'm sure of it." As he gazed at her with a stolid expression, she knew she needed to make some kind of concession. "You were worried about the voltage. Why don't we try a lower voltage today?" He grudgingly agreed and helped her get wired up.

She settled into the padded chair of the Memex, wriggling as the helmet enclosed her cranium. Robert faced the monitor, removing his glasses and chewing on one end. He returned them to his face and stared at the screen.

"Let's try a pulse height 50 mV lower than last time," he suggested. "I'll leave the other settings the same." Brooke concurred. At this voltage, the side effects would be less intense. As the machine came on line, she felt only a mild tingling on top of her head and heard only a gentle knocking. She closed her eyes.

She found herself sitting on a stool at a long bench in a workshop. She recognized it from her previous visit. A belt buckle made of gold was clamped into a jig in front of her. Holding a small hammer in her left hand and a pointed metal rod in her right, she tapped at the malleable gold piece to create a pattern of stars and swirls. It felt odd to work with her right hand. Her host was patient, and had a delicate touch.

The front door swung open and two men entered. The taller one wore a long robe the color of butterscotch held at the shoulder with a silver clasp. His black hair and beard were neatly combed and coiffed. By contrast, the shorter was dressed like most men Brooke had seen, in a simple gray tunic. The dagger stuck into his belt marked him as a bodyguard. Although she listened attentively to the conversation that followed, she could not make out a single word.

Brooke's host pulled out a small, leather covered book and opened it. Brooke could see that the words were in Greek letters, with odd symbols next to them. So this was a Greek city. Brooke itched to have her computer in front of her so she could do some searching, but would have to wait. No wonder she didn't understand anything.

Her host wrote something in the book and put it away. The visitors seemed satisfied and departed. Brooke's host continued his methodical work on the belt buckle. After many minor adjustments, he released it from the jig and flipped it over. An upraised pattern had been formed on the front side due to his careful tapping. The design was well-executed and appeared smooth and symmetrical, but the goldsmith shook his head and returned the piece to the jig. He selected a metal rod with a smaller diameter and a finer tip and continued his craft. His progress was excruciatingly slow.

A young girl ran into the room and sat down across from Brooke's host. She looked like the younger sister of the girl that Brooke had seen on her last visit, with similar blond hair and facial features. She smiled and Brooke saw that one front tooth was missing—she was perhaps seven years old. The girl chattered happily with her father as he listened tolerantly, continuing all the while with his work. Then Brooke picked out a word—he called her Julia. She felt a surge of happiness at having at last understood something. Brooke wondered why Julia had not been at dinner the other night. Maybe she had been sick.

Brooke's host picked up the belt buckle and walked over to a sturdy cabinet. He opened the door and revealed shelves filled with golden items that gleamed in the morning light. He selected a small ring and returned to the workbench. Julia had not stopped talking and seemed to require little in the way of response from her father.

Julia's mother entered the workshop, balancing a toddler on her hip. With a few gentle words, she took Julia by the hand and led her away. Brooke noticed a scar on the toddler's cheek. These were the same two children she had seen last time, but they were a few years younger. How odd.

The goldsmith worked on the ring while Brooke mused. The Memex was designed to stimulate memories. It was not surprising that it might pick up memories from different times in the man's life. But who was he and why was Brooke seeing his memories? They didn't feel like memories at all, but rather like a complete re-living of the experience.

Brooke was back in the Memex lab. She sat up and saw Robert's reassuring presence at the computer.

"Welcome back," he said. "How was the trip?"

"I saw him again. He's Greek. But I was there about three years earlier than last time."

"This is really strange. Did you read a book or something about a Greek guy that might have lodged in your mind?"

"No. This is totally unfamiliar. I wish I could place him better. I wanted to figure out what year it was, but there were no calendars on the wall. Actually, I didn't see any numbers at all."

Robert just shook his head. Brooke resolved to return.

Robert had homework due on Wednesday and couldn't help her on Tuesday night. She burned with impatience. She slogged through her routine at the lab, testing the mice and taking care of them. She subjected a mouse to the forced swimming test with her newly-constructed apparatus, watching anxiously as the little creature struggled. She even found the strength to start work on the new consent form.

At this point in her education, Brooke had finished her course work. All she had left was her thesis, and while it seemed that this should make life easier, it didn't. It was difficult to focus on only one task, day in and day out. She was often distracted, especially at times like this, when her work was delayed by circumstances beyond her control.

Brooke thought about sending an email to Prof. Hunter, admitting to using the Memex. Hunter rarely answered email and would probably ignore it. Then Brooke could claim that she had in fact informed Hunter about her illicit testing. On the other hand, with Brooke's luck, the professor would read this one email and tell her categorically to stop. Brooke didn't want to stop.

When Robert was available to work again, they decided to lower the pulse height on the Memex signal yet again. Brooke hypothesized that she would find the man younger still. Given how little they understood, it might not work, but it was worth a shot.

As the Memex signal activated, Brooke found herself seated in an outdoor arena. Below her was a long oval racetrack covered with sand. Horses galloped around the track, drawing chariots behind them. The arena was immense, rising up in tier after tier of white stone, with thousands of bodies packed together in noisy celebration. Brooke counted thirty tiers in all. Directly across the arena, a privileged group rested upon elaborate chairs in an isolated box, flying banners of state. Burly guards with two-headed axes hanging from their belts protected their masters.

The day was mild and wispy clouds spread across the sky. Next to Brooke sat a giant of a man, his coarse features screwed up into a scowl and his beefy hands spread over his wide thighs. He was engrossed in the show below, eyes tracking the lead chariot. He towered above her, and then she realized that she was in the body of a boy. Her prediction was right. This was an earlier point in her host's life, and she was pleased.

Four chariots vied for position on the field below. Each driver wore a bright tunic in a different primary color—red, green, blue, or white. At the moment, the green driver led the field, his horses rushing forward in a show of graceful strength. Their tails were bound up in multicolored ribbons that streamed behind in their wake. The driver leaned forward, whip in hand, as the spectators in one area of the stands cheered him on. The red team, drawn by four roan horses, was gaining gradually, and looked like it might challenge the green. The other two contenders were far behind and had no chance.

The green driver whipped his team around the final bend, his wheels inches from the inside edge, still losing ground to the red driver, who chased him recklessly. It looked like they might collide, but it was hard to tell through the cloud of dust that enveloped the two contenders. Once back on the straightaway, the horses of the green team saw the finish line and put on a burst of speed, outdistancing their rivals and winning the race. The crowd burst out in a ragged cheer and many rose to their feet.

The man beside Brooke uttered a single syllable in disgust. A fellow one tier lower in the arena turned around with a smile and held out his hand. Brooke's neighbor reluctantly reached into his purse and dropped a few coins into the outstretched palm. As Brooke watched, the man barked something at her and she lowered her eyes. An adolescent girl on the other side of Brooke pointed into the distance and from what she said to him, Brooke caught a name—Damian. Her host was named Damian.

Pleased with herself, Brooke sat back mentally and relaxed. Her over-sized neighbor was probably Damian's father, and the young girl his sister. The arena was almost as large as the Saratoga race track, and had much more seating. The long meridian between the two sides of the track was filled with monuments and sculptures of various sizes and shapes, arranged haphazardly. A marble column of entwined serpents sent a chill down Brooke's spine. An obelisk five stories tall, engraved with hieroglyphics, dominated the center of the arena. It all felt Roman to Brooke.

They stayed for three more races. A food vendor wandered by with little golden buns and roasted nuts, and the father purchased some, but only for his own consumption. The hard marble seat was becoming increasingly uncomfortable as the day went on. Damian's father had a cushion to sit on, but Damian did not. The father lost more races than he won, and appeared to be in a foul mood.

As the sun sank low in the sky, the last race ended and Damian rose to leave along with his father, mother, and two teen-aged sisters. The family pushed their way through the crowd, which was exiting the arena through an archway that had become a bottleneck. A tower atop the exit was crowned with a sculpture of four prancing horses of gilded bronze. Their manes were cut short and their mouths were slightly open. They looked vaguely familiar to Brooke, although she couldn't say where she had seen them before.

Past the gateway was a broad plaza paved with marble. Directly ahead, an imposing building rested on top of a low hill. It was wider than it was tall, with a large central dome and several smaller side domes. The structure had a graceful elegance and Brooke was disappointed when Damian turned aside and headed up a broad avenue.

The roadway that stretched before her was a vision of ancient times. On each side, colonnaded buildings flanked a broad marble-covered street. At the entrance to many of the buildings, the columns supported a roof, providing a covered walkway for pedestrians. Merchants laid out their wares, from fine silks and fragrant spices to fresh-baked breads and sparkling jewelry. As the family made their way up the street, Brooke saw a captive bear, with fur matted and mottled, doing tricks for the amusement of the crowd. A talented juggler was tossing balls for tips. Beggars and homeless people dressed in filthy tatters huddled under the protection of the walkways, calling out to passersby.

They turned a corner, and the crowds began to thin out. The light was fading rapidly and there was a chill in the air. Weaving through the city, they came upon the now familiar facade of Damian's workshop and entered. So Damian had been here a long time, Brooke thought. He must have grown up here.

To Brooke's surprise, everyone except Damian went upstairs. Moving to the fireplace, he removed a broad metal cover from the center, revealing hot coals. He blew upon the coals to coax a flame to rise and used it to light an oil lamp. Settling down at the workbench, he began to work on a silver plate. He hummed as he applied himself, apparently in a good mood after the day's festivities. The oil lamp provided scant illumination, and long shadows stretched into the dark corners of the room. Damian frequently readjusted the work piece, tipping it this way and that to get a better view. This work would have been better done by daylight. Weariness set in and Damian's shoulders slumped ever lower.

Brooke heard the older man descending the staircase with a heavy tread. He stopped at the workbench and examined the silver plate carefully. He spoke to Damian in a harsh tone, and Damian replied calmly. The man was not satisfied and launched into a long invective, working himself up into a fury. Brooke could feel the adrenaline coursing through Damian's body, the fear palpable. Damian made an attempt to placate him, but it was clear that the man had ceased to listen. He grabbed Damian by his shirt front and pulled him, babbling and struggling, to a corner of the room. Brooke, terrified and helpless, wanted this nightmare to end. She thought it was too soon for her to be yanked back to the lab, but maybe she was wrong.

The man fumbled around for something in the dim light. When he had it, he dragged Damian back to the center of the room and bent him over a low stool. He shouted something at Damian and Damian stopped struggling. He ripped off Damian's trousers, exposing his backside. Brooke was aghast.

The first blow fell with a loud crack and pain exploded in Brooke's mind. The second blow left a fiery trace across Damian's backside, and Brooke felt it across her own. Fear, verging on panic, had now overtaken her. She had never felt anything like this before. Damian started to squirm and tears leaked from his tightly closed eyes. At the third blow, he cried out, unable to contain himself any longer. He sobbed and struggled, but was tightly pinioned by the brute above him. Brooke wished desperately to get out of here—shouldn't she be returning to the laboratory about now? With the fifth blow she lost capacity to think clearly and became a mass of pain, no longer able to feel distinct blows or to count them.

At last, the attacker let up and exited the room, leaving Damian to fend for himself. Damian, his face drenched with tears, struggled to his feet. Blood dribbled down the backs of his legs. The pain did not stop, but continued in a burning torment. Damian drew his trousers up, then thought better of it, and let them puddle around his legs. He stepped out of the trousers and retired to a corner of the room where he huddled on a bed of straw. He sobbed, curling into a fetal position. Brooke prayed for deliverance. The pain had eased slightly to a throbbing presence, but it was still almost unbearable. She felt delirious, with images of home flashing in her mind. She didn't think she would ever sit down again.

Damian huddled in the dark on his rough mattress for an immeasurably long time. The oil lamp flickered out, leaving the room in unrelieved darkness. Brooke wished for a light, something, anything, to distract her from the terrible ache. It was frustrating to be unable to do anything. She wanted to apply a soothing ointment, get an antibiotic, go for help, just walk around, do something. But Damian did none of these things. He merely endured.

Brooke felt trapped and helpless. To make matters worse, she began to feel hungry. Damian was apparently not getting any dinner that night. What had he done? He must have made some error on the silver plate that infuriated his father. Brooke had not noticed one, but she was hardly an expert in metalworking. The stinging pain went on, making it hard to think. She thought about the chariot race, and how the father had lost money. She guessed that Damian had done nothing wrong, but that his father had taken out his frustrations on his unfortunate son. Hatred burned in her heart. Hours passed with little relief, and the hunger pains intensified. Damian could not find the sweet release of sleep in his poor stricken body.

Brooke opened her eyes and saw the familiar ceiling of the Memex lab. Relief flooded through her. She sat up and looked for Robert.

"My God, why didn't you bring me back earlier?" she asked.

Robert looked puzzled.

"I brought you back at the agreed-upon schedule. Are you OK? You look shaken."

Brooke was shaken, but she was recovering. The pain had disappeared and she was no longer desperately hungry.

"Couldn't you tell that I was in trouble?" asked Brooke.

Robert frowned. "No. You just laid there looking asleep and peaceful. There was no sign that you were in trouble. What happened to you?"

Brooke hesitated. She wasn't ready to share this particular experience with Robert.

"I sprained my ankle," she lied. Inwardly she cursed herself for coming up with such a lame excuse. Brooke had always thought of herself as a truthful person and somehow, she was slipping into a persona that she was not proud of. First, hiding her experiments from Prof. Hunter and from Chad, whom she liked and perhaps should have trusted, and now telling Robert, her faithful supporter, less than the truth. A slippery slope indeed.

"How does it feel now?" asked Robert innocently, looking down at her feet.

"Oh, there's no trace of the pain anymore. I just wish I could signal you when I want to come back. When the mice are on the machine, they sometimes struggle and squirm in their plastic tubes. I thought there would be some outward sign if a human was in trouble."

"I guess humans are not mice."

III

SECOND THOUGHTS

The following evening, Chad arrived at the Memex lab in a mellow mood. Saying hi to Robert, who was hunched over a computer at his desk, he tossed his cowboy hat on a table and put on his lab coat. He covered his hair, still damp from an after-exercise shower, with the regulation white bonnet and drew on a pair of blue latex gloves.

Fully suited up, he picked up the iPad with the latest data on the lab mice. Prof. Hunter had authorized the purchase of additional mice in order to satisfy the Review Board, and the work required to feed, tend, and test them had increased proportionally. Chad saw that Group B was due for attention, and began to systematically clean out their cages.

Earlier in the evening Chad had poured himself into a hard-driving karate class. He loved the feeling of being totally absorbed in the present moment, his mind and body stretched to their limits as he attempted to perform the required moves. Nowhere else could he scream at the top of his lungs and pound a punching bag full force, working through his frustrations in a socially acceptable way. Best of all, he never thought about Brooke while he was in class.

The high point of the evening had been the sparring. Chad had been paired up with Sensei Nakamura, the head of the club. He had been pressed hard, and the fight had begun to seem real to him. Sensei landed a front kick to Chad's belly and followed it with left and right jabs. Chad blocked the jabs, but lost ground. Sensei continued the attack with a roundhouse kick to the head, which Chad parried.

At this point, Chad's automatic self-preservation instincts took over. He was not in a gym practicing; he was defending himself from a real attack. He attempted several middle area punches, but Sensei swatted them away as one would swat away a fly. Then Chad saw an opening, and landed a punch to Sensei's face. He instantly regretted it. The face was not an acceptable target, but Chad's punch had been on autopilot, a visceral response beyond his conscious control. Sensei responded by redoubling his efforts and soon retaliated with a punch to Chad's face. Chad didn't mind. It was only fair.

As he thought back on the bout while he tended the mice, Chad smiled. Sensei was a 4th degree black belt and Chad was merely a brown belt. He had gotten past Sensei's guard, and that gave him a warm feeling of accomplishment. How many brown belts got to say that they had hit a high level black belt in the face?

The mice in Group C were due for testing on the Memex. Chad readied a transparent plastic cylinder that would serve as a restraint while the mouse was on the machine. He opened a cage and lifted an uncooperative mouse out of his lair. He directed the mouse's snout to the open end of the cylinder and the creature scurried in willingly. Chad snapped the cover closed, trapping the mouse, who now seemed quite calm. The cylinder was punctured by a series of slots to give the mouse air.

Chad snapped the cylinder into its holder so that it was positioned correctly within the coils of the Memex. He checked that the mouse's brain was centered to receive the signal from the machine. He booted the computer and clicked on the testing program, which was set to store the last values used and pull them up automatically. That was odd. The settings were completely unfamiliar to him. The duty cycle was all wrong and the pulse height was way too high.

"Robert," asked Chad, "did you notice these unusual settings on the Memex?"

Robert walked over to the computer and examined the screen. "Uh, they don't look right," he said.

"You can say that again. Everything is wrong—the frequency, the duty cycle, and especially the pulse height. And why are there three superimposed pulse trains? I wonder if the last batch of mice was exposed to these extreme conditions. Have you done any testing today?"

"No," said Robert. "I was working on my homework. My daughter cries a lot and I can't get anything done at home. Feng says that she's teething and it will get better."

Chad flipped through the most recent notes on Memex testing. Everything appeared perfectly normal. According to the records, the mice had been tested according to plan.

"Well, that's strange," said Chad. "I wonder if Brooke knows anything about it. Brooke, you, and I are the only ones authorized to use this lab. You didn't see anybody else, did you?"

"Of course not," replied Robert.

Chad sat and thought for a moment, finally shrugging his shoulders. Apparently no harm had been done. He changed the settings and began the test regime. The mouse appeared to fall asleep, as usual. Chad saw that he was supposed to leave the mouse in for ten minutes.

Chad continued testing twelve more mice, without incident. This batch had never been exposed before, and there was always the chance that one would react badly. But so far, he was in luck. Each mouse fell into a deep sleep with no apparent problem. It was not like ordinary sleep, in which a mouse might shift position. It was creepy, more like watching a breathing corpse than a living creature. Chad began to feel skeptical about this work. What was going through the mouse's brain? Would he ever know?

———

After Chad left, Robert called Brooke.

"He noticed the settings on the Memex," wailed Robert. "You were so upset after your last session. I got distracted and forgot to reset them. I think he suspects."

"Robert, let's talk it over. Can you come to my apartment?"

Robert glanced at the lower corner of his monitor to check the time. "Sure, I'll be there in twenty minutes."

As Robert walked through the deserted streets, he assured himself that he was going to call it off. True, he was curious about what Brooke would discover, but the risk of getting caught was eating at him. Worse, he was not sure what would happen if they did get caught, and that made him uneasy. Brooke was a good friend and he wanted to support her, but he had his family to think about.

Robert had not been to Brooke's place before and it took him a while to find it. It was a third floor walk-up in a once elegant section of town. The area looked clean and safe, but peeling paint and missing fence slats marred the beauty of the architecture. The doorbell chimed to a jazz riff. Brooke opened the door and welcomed him in.

The living room had an air of casual warmth, despite the worn sofa and mismatched chairs. A tennis racket leaned up against the scarred coffee table, which was strewn with books and magazines. The end table was covered with framed photographs—a camping trip, two girls standing arm in arm, and a family group—Brooke with her parents and two younger brothers. The walls were hung with posters in bright confusion from many periods and styles. The piece that caught Robert's eye was an old European church that had been turned into a surreal art gallery. The paintings in the gallery, which covered every square inch of the wall space and extended to the highest reaches of the church, depicted ancient buildings—paintings within paintings.

Brooke noticed Robert examining the print.

"That's one of my favorites," she said. "It's by Panini, a Renaissance artist."

"Is it a real place?" asked Robert.

"No, it's all in the artist's imagination. Churches are supposed to have art of saints and martyrs, but this one is given over to ancient Rome. It's sacrilegious, and I'm surprised he got away with painting it. I got the print on my trip to Italy."

"It sure captures your attention," said Robert.

"Would you like something to drink? We can talk in the kitchen."

Robert settled down at a small round table while Brooke brewed tea. Once the water had fully boiled, she poured it into two sturdy mugs and added loose tea leaves in the Chinese style. Brooke wore enormous gold hoops in her ears. Robert imagined them catching on something and winced.

"I'm nervous," said Robert. "What will happen if Chad finds out about our testing?"

"I don't know," replied Brooke. "I don't think he'll find out. We'll have to be more careful in the future."

"We should quit. Wait till the official testing starts."

"Robert, we're learning so much. This is like archeology of the mind. I don't know who Damian is or when or where he lived, but I intend to find out. The more we learn now, the easier it will be later when we have all the volunteers."

She had a point. He had searched the web to try to pinpoint the city she described, but nothing definitive came up. The pull of discovery warred with the fear of detection in his mind, leaving him miserable. He sipped some tea, and felt more relaxed.

"I have some theories to explore," said Brooke. "I think we must be in the eastern Mediterranean in ancient times. The olive oil and bread I ate are typical of that area. So are the chariot races. Greek was widely spoken throughout the eastern Mediterranean thanks to Alexander the Great. If we just get more data, we could figure this thing out. Once I start to under-stand the language, I'll get more clues."

"Could this just be something you made up, maybe unconsciously?" asked Robert.

"I don't think so. I couldn't have come up with the details of what I saw and did on my own. I'm convinced that I'm accessing some outside source of information, not my own mind."

Robert considered. Brooke was level-headed and reliable, not given to wild fantasies. He had always admired her intellect and looked to her for guidance in his own research. Even now, she approached these bizarre experiences calmly and rationally. If you had asked him a month ago whether Brooke was reckless enough to try the Memex on herself, he would have said, 'no way.' But her drive to persevere in her research had overruled her natural caution.

"Robert, it's for science," said Brooke. "Throughout history, scientists have had to buck the system to make great discoveries. The Review Board could string us along for God knows how long. We have to keep going."

Under the force of Brooke's arguments, Robert's resolve wavered. Maybe she was right and nothing terrible would happen. They were smart enough to avoid getting caught, and besides, he was as curious as she was.

After Robert left, Brooke cleaned up the tea things. Although she had convinced Robert to go on, she wasn't sure she had convinced herself. She was scared. The last session had been a horrific experience that she never wanted to repeat. She had gone home that night and stood naked before the full length mirror in the bathroom. She turned around and looked at herself over her shoulder, expecting scars and finding none. She knew it was irrational, but the feeling was irresistible. She had been there and had experienced every blow.

If only she had someone she could confide in. Her roommate, Claudia, was great for lively conversation, but she had a sharp edge and Brooke didn't think she was patient or empathic enough to be a comfort. Or was it just that she was ashamed to tell anyone about the clandestine tests? They might talk her out of it or tell her that she was crazy to risk her health. She wanted someone to support what she was doing and wasn't sure that anybody would.

On the other hand, Brooke was not about to give up on her degree. Waiting until she had official sanction would effectively kill her chance of finishing the research before her money ran out. She desperately wanted to break into the professional world of scientists. Her family couldn't help her with tuition or other expenses. The meager stipend from her fellowship was barely enough for her to live on. She scrimped on groceries, eating Raman noodles and baked potatoes several times a week. If she never finished her education, she was destined to be poor all her life.

Her childhood had been a restricted time, when she longed for stimulation and got boredom instead. Her family lived in a small apartment building in Worcester, Massachusetts built before the Second World War. The back yard, which had to serve six families, was barely the size of a tennis court, with packed dirt at its center and crabgrass and weeds struggling to maintain a foothold around the edges. It had been Brooke's play space for her entire childhood. At least in college she could take advantage of the great outdoors, exploring the mountains, forests, and lakes that were finally accessible to her.

Brooke wanted to roam further and travel to the exotic corners of the world. She remembered in great detail her trip to Italy, where she had packed a lot of living into a narrow slice of time. The first part, at least, had been fabulous. It was only the last few days that she would rather forget. Despite the problems, she hankered for more foreign travel. She dreamed of seeing France, Norway, South Africa, Dubai, Thailand, Australia, just for a start. Certain cities called to her—Timbuktu, Kathmandu, and Mumbai.

But most of all, Brooke could not see herself living the life her mother had lived, slogging through a boring job from eight to five every day, watching the clock and dreaming of going home. The degree would be her ticket to a more fulfilling life and she would do whatever she had to.

After the last Memex test, she had carefully examined the records of her heart rate, muscle tension, and breathing while she had been under. She did this when Robert wasn't around, so he wouldn't realize how worried she was. None of the measurements hinted at the torment she had been feeling. The third session was not in any way different from the first two, as she had thought it might be. Maybe she could think of a new measurement to add to the regimen, perhaps brain wave activity. Surely if the brain were battling demons, something would show up.

Brooke told herself that she had to be rational about this. An appeal to rationality had always been a comfort to her in times of stress. In fact, she was not injured. Despite what she had felt, there was no damage. Her life and person were not at risk. Brooke had learned about irrational fear during a ropes course training session at grad school orientation. She had made her way slowly and precariously along a rope path high in the trees, all the while protected by a harness attached to an overhead support line. If she had fallen, the rope would have saved her from plunging to the earth. Especially difficult were the transition points, where, clinging to a tree, she unhooked her carabiner and switched from one section of the ropes course to another. In that one moment, she was truly unprotected.

The course culminated at the top of a massive pine tree. A small wooden platform had been nailed into the tree to provide a jumping off point for the zip line that followed. A guide, whose job was to encourage reluctant climbers to jump, sat casually on the platform. When she arrived at the platform, she clipped herself onto the zip line, smiled at the guide, and without thinking much about it, launched herself into space. As she swooped toward the ground, she let out a wild yell. The whole course was fear-inducing, but, in fact, it was safe. The Memex was like that—fear-inducing but safe. She might feel intense pain, but no injury. If she could just be mentally strong, she could continue with her experiments. A lot was at stake and Brooke was not a quitter.

Brooke gave herself a few days off before braving the Memex again. She used the time to hunt up the equipment for an EEG to detect brain waves. It wasn't hard to convince her friend, Jose, that she needed one, although she didn't tell him the real use she intended. Graduate students in cognitive science used EEGs all the time, so her request raised no alarms. The prep routine was a little longer this time, since Robert had to paste electrodes on her head. Her thick hair was an impediment, but not insurmountable.

"Are you sure we need this extra test?" asked Robert.

"Absolutely," replied Brooke. "If one of our test subjects encounters a big problem, we need to pull them out. I think an EEG might help. In addition, let's try for a really quick trip to decrease the risk. And let's choose a pulse height very close to the first session." Brooke wanted to be in the big, strong, healthy Damian and not in the vulnerable child.

"Boy, that sprained ankle really got to you," said Robert. "Good thing it wasn't something worse."

Brooke wished he hadn't said that, but held her tongue. She sank down into the deceptive comfort of the Memex chair and prepared to immerse herself. She clasped her hands tightly together across her stomach, crossed her ankles, and waited. Her scalp tingled as Robert applied the voltage.

Damian was making his way through a driving rainstorm, cloaked in a thick rough garment. His vision was partially obscured by a hood. Directly ahead, Brooke saw something familiar, the stately building across from the arena that she had glimpsed on her last trip. It was well proportioned, with a massive dome, and seemed like a government center. She was pleased that she might get to see it up close.

Damian climbed the gentle hill and entered a majestic doorway. He wove through two hallways with high ceilings before coming upon an immense open space. To Brooke's surprise, it was a church. The nave was breathtaking, with two rows of pillars, one atop the other, rising along the sides. The imposing altar at the front was covered by an undulating canopy of silver and gold. Small windows abounded, letting in a gentle light on this rainy day. There were even windows in the dome, just around its periphery where it rested upon the supporting walls.

The effect was soothing. Brooke felt tiny in this gigantic church, a fitting house for an all-powerful God. The walls shimmered with brilliant mosaics of martyrs, saints, and apostles, each tiny stone piece contributing to the overall effect of vibrancy and harmony. A rendering of the Virgin with Christ Child nestled high up in the apse. The style reminded her of mosaics she had seen in Ravenna, Italy that dated from the year 800 or so. These mosaics were of a similar type but much more extensive.

Damian stood calmly at one end of the church, apparently waiting for someone. There were not many people about, just a man and woman worshiping at a small side altar, and two men wandering about and pointing. Brooke suspected they were pilgrims who had traveled from afar. They wore rough robes unlike the usual manner of dress on the streets of the city and had short beards. Brooke estimated that Damian had been in the church for half an hour, doing nothing. Why wasn't Robert bringing her back? At least she was enjoying the artwork.

A cleric dressed in a long black robe with a heavy silver crucifix on his chest approached Damian. Most of his hair was hidden under a covering that looked to Brooke like something a nun might wear. An amiable face framed by a neatly-clipped white beard smiled at her. After a short conversation, Damian followed the cleric through an archway and down a high-ceilinged corridor. The cleric stopped at a door, drew out a large steel ring bristling with keys from under his cassock and unlocked it. He ushered Damian into the chamber. Brooke had never seen so much gold before in one place and the effect was stunning. She saw gold chalices, candlesticks, reliquaries, platters, and other sacred items. The cleric drew out a small wooden box and lifted the lid. Inside, a long sliver of bone rested on a silken wrapping. Damian took out a small measuring stick and proceeded to lay it near the bone fragment.

At that moment, Brooke returned to the Memex lab.

"How was it?" asked Robert. "Did it go all right?"

"It was fine. I visited an amazing church. But why did you leave me there so long? I thought this was supposed to be just a quick look?"

"As soon as I saw that you were under, I killed the signal. How long did it seem to you?"

"It was about sixty minutes. Must be a time lag. It looks like once you get started, you have to stay at least an hour. That's bad news." There would be no quick escape from a painful situation.

Brooke swung her legs over the edge of the chair and stood up. She and Robert removed all the wires and probes from her body, and she fluffed out her hair as best she could. Curious, Brooke examined the EEG trace, even though she had not been under any stress on this trip. Delta frequencies predominated, typical of "slow wave sleep," a non-dreaming state. She had expected to find indications of REM sleep, but did not.

Brooke took a chair in front of a desktop computer and brought up a search engine. She typed in "ancient church Greek dome" and perused the results. No immediate hit struck her eye, but she checked out the first five choices. Typing in other combinations of key words, she explored the web. It only took ten minutes before she found what she wanted. The image on the screen was unmistakable.

IV

DISCOVERY

C had shifted into third gear and accelerated up the hill in his scratched and dented Toyota pickup. The odometer had crossed 150,000 miles yesterday as he was driving home from the airport. Visiting his folks in Colorado had been a welcome break from the research routine and time working on the farm with his dad had been rejuvenating. They had repaired a leak in the solar collector together and changed the air and fuel filters on the tractor.

The entire family, which now numbered more than thirty, got together for a barbeque on the Fourth of July. He caught up with his cousins, most of whom had stayed close to home. Brent, the cousin he had played with most often during his childhood, was now a ski instructor at Aspen Highlands. They didn't have much to talk about anymore. Sally, his youngest cousin, was already married and expecting a baby in the fall.

Chad had decided to return a few days early. It had been two months since the Review Board declined their request to allow human testing and he chafed under the delay. Before his trip, the endless testing on mice had left him bored and frustrated. Now, refreshed by the break, he was ready to resume, feeling newly hopeful and ready to blast through this phase of the work.

He swung into the parking lot of the Wilson building and snagged a spot close to the front. With the undergrads away for the summer, parking on campus was much easier. The sun, which was high in the cloudless sky, beat down on the tarmac. The brim of Chad's white hat protected him from the intense rays as he made for the entrance.

Chad unlocked the door to the Memex lab and stepped in. He took in the tableau at a glance: Robert, head turned toward the door, eyes wide and mouth open, and Brooke, inert in the arms of the Memex, a thick braid of wires emanating from her heavily instrumented body. A pang of fear coursed through Chad's body.

"What the hell?" Chad advanced on Robert and scowled. "What do you think you're doing?"

Robert rose to his full height. "What are you doing here?" countered Robert. "You weren't due back till Monday."

"Good thing I came early. Get her off that thing."

"It's not time yet. She has three more minutes."

"I don't care how many more minutes she has. She shouldn't be on it at all." Chad moved toward the computer but Robert stepped in front of him.

"It's Brooke's decision. You have no right to interfere."

"I don't have time to argue, she could get hurt."

"Brooke has done this hundreds of times. She's fine."

Chad halted. "Hundreds of times?" he repeated. His anger dissipated and turned into a feeling of foolishness. Brooke and Robert must have been doing this behind his back for a long time. He never picked up on it.

Chad advanced to the chair and examined Brooke. She had a vacant look on her face, so unlike her. Her eyes were closed, as if in sleep, and her mouth was slightly open. Brooke was a beautiful woman, but under the Memex, she looked dead. Chad's unease increased upon seeing her in this state, as if her soul had been stolen from her body. He stuffed his hands into the pockets of his jeans and turned his back. He settled himself in a chair near the cages and sulked.

At the appointed time, Robert shut down the signal and Brooke stirred. She opened her eyes and prepared to hoist herself out of the chair. When she caught sight of Chad, her face reddened.

"I can't believe you did such a stupid thing," he said. "The Memex is dangerous. What were you thinking?"

Brooke's blush deepened, but there was fire in her eyes. "It's not dangerous. Maybe you think it's dangerous, but it's not. I'm fine."

"It's dangerous enough that the Review Board won't let us test it on humans."

"Oh, now you're siding with the Review Board. For the last two months, you've been talking about how idiotic they are. When did you change your mind?"

Chad wanted to shout at her, but he restrained himself and said calmly "Brooke, be reasonable. They know best."

"I'm completely reasonable. It's you and the board who haven't got the cojones to get on with the testing."

Chad's temper jumped up a notch, but he suppressed his reaction. This was getting out of hand. He needed to quench this argument and placate Brooke.

"Brooke, I'm only worried about you. I don't want you to get hurt."

Her expression softened and she said. "I'm sorry about the last comment. It was uncalled for."

"Besides, if they find that we're misusing the equipment, it might delay the whole program. We all have to get our degrees."

Brooke's eyes narrowed. "So what really worries you is that your research will be delayed." She began to tear off the probes that still bound her to the machine.

"You're twisting my words," said Chad. "Of course your health is the most important thing." But he had lost her. Brooke removed the last of the wires and refused to speak with him further. He glanced at Robert, but Robert was studiously examining his monitor.

Brooke left without another word, and Chad decided to stay a while, to give her a chance to get away. If she and Robert had been testing for two months, they must have learned something. But with Brooke in a snit and Robert pretending to be deeply involved in something, it wasn't likely he would find out what. Despite himself, he was curious and a little jealous. How was he supposed to carry on with the dull mouse testing routine while they were making all the discoveries? What if they got so far ahead that there was nothing new for him? Bad enough that they didn't tell him what they were doing, even worse if they ended up with all the credit. His anger was returning, and it took an effort not to lash out at Robert.

Chad wasn't going to get any testing done today.

⊶∞⊷

The next day, Chad found Brooke at work feeding the mice when he arrived at the lab. They exchanged stiff greetings, and she continued with her work as if nothing more needed to be said. For once Robert was not at his desk. Chad consulted the iPad to see where they were on the rotation, and saw that Group F was due for the forced swimming test.

"Do you mind if I begin the testing on Group F?" he asked.

"Be my guest."

Chad slid out the first cage and dropped the mouse into the plastic tank filled with water. As the little animal paddled around fervently, Chad wanted to rescue him. Instead, he stared at the stopwatch on his phone, watching the digits flicker past. This test just seemed mean and Chad hated doing it.

"How was your trip?" asked Brooke.

"It was fine. I got a lot of sun."

"You look tanned." Brooke continued her work, seeming to devote a lot more attention to it than it usually required. After a pause, she asked, "Are you going to tell Prof. Hunter?"

"No."

Brooke's shoulders relaxed. "I appreciate that. Honestly, I didn't want to jump the gun with the testing, but I was in a bind. I have to get some data or I can't graduate. I'll run out of money by next spring."

So that's why she did it. It didn't excuse her deception but it did shed light on things.

"It's a big risk. It's a shame they put you in that position."

"But it has been interesting, not at all what we expected."

Chad couldn't help himself. He said, "What did you find out?"

Brooke tilted her head and seemed to consider. "Actually, it may be best if I don't tell you. We could use an independent assessment of the situation."

"What do you mean?"

She pulled out the next cage and set it on the lab bench. Turning towards him with a faint smile on her lips, she said, "If you were to try the Memex out for yourself, that might clear up a number of questions. I don't want to spoil things by telling you too much."

Chad couldn't believe it. Did she really think he would try the machine?

Seeing his hesitation she pressed on. "It's quite safe. I've logged a lot of hours and I feel perfectly fine."

"No memory loss, depression, headaches?" he asked.

Brooke laughed. "Nothing like that. The Review Board had it all wrong. I assure you, it's like nothing you've ever experienced before—at least it was for me. I don't know how it would be for anyone else. But—" a flicker of some dark emotion showed in her eyes—"I have to confess, it's not always comfortable. Things can happen when you're on the machine."

"Come on, tell me more."

"No. Sorry. You'll have to find out for yourself."

Chad was torn. After all, Brooke seemed just fine. The explorer in him was clamoring to try the machine, while the voice of caution was becoming ever fainter. Besides, he didn't want Brooke to think he was a coward. If she could do it... On the other hand, he might jeopardize his position at the university. There were no easy choices.

—∞∞∞—

"Are you ready?" asked Robert. He and Brooke had painstakingly prepared Chad for his first experience with the Memex.

"I'm good," replied Chad. His heart thumped rapidly and his hands were clammy.

"We're going to use the same settings as Brooke used and see what happens." A tingling crept over Chad's scalp, rising slowly in intensity.

The shift was imperceptible. One minute Chad was in the Memex lab and the next he was in an expansive orchard. Trees loaded with apples were laid out in rows that marched off into the distance. Sunshine warmed the scene and there was the nip of autumn in the air. Chad was standing on a ladder resting against a tree, picking apples and tucking them into a cloth bag that hung from his shoulder. Below him a young boy was scrutinizing apples that had fallen to the ground and sorting them into baskets. A large black horse harnessed to a rough wooden wagon stood patiently in his traces.

When had Chad been here before? He didn't remember. The memory was amazingly detailed, complete with chirping birds and the breathless sigh of the wind. What was the boy doing with those worthless fallen apples? He should be up here picking.

Chad examined the scene with a farmer's eye. He saw only two varieties of apple, one a small round red and the other a larger green. The trees were well pruned, with a scaffold structure off a central leader. The apples themselves were not in great shape. Brown spots and wormholes marred many of them, and some were small or misshapen. Most were still on the tree.

"Thomas, how are ye faring?" The booming voice that came from Chad's mouth was not his own. With a shock, he realized that he was not in his own body. He appeared to be a large man, clad in a rough shirt, trousers held up by a rope belt, and wearing worn leather work boots. Many of his back teeth were missing.

"Gut, Pa, but some are only for the swine," replied the boy in an accent so thick that Chad could barely understand what he was saying. Could these be immigrants newly come to America? Chad wished that Brooke had prepared him for this.

A woman in a long dress and bonnet approached the two workers. "Rogell, I brung your supper," she said. She gave Rogell and Thomas slabs of dark bread spread with butter and hard boiled eggs. They tucked in hungrily and washed it down with some sour tasting brew from a jug in the wagon. Chad was sure he had never met these people before. He wondered if they were Amish.

After the meal, Rogell moved his ladder to the next tree and resumed picking. The day was warming up and sweat trickled from his armpits. After scouring the lower branches, he sent Thomas up to the highest reaches, where the branches would not support Rogell's greater weight. The two worked with little conversation. When a tree was picked clean and the apples that could be rescued removed from the ground, Thomas led the horse over to eat up what remained.

After the wagon was filled with baskets of apples, man and boy climbed aboard and rode off down the row of trees.

Chad returned to the lab and was momentarily disoriented. Brooke and Robert were standing beside him.

"So," said Brooke, "what did you see?"

"I was in an orchard, but I wasn't in my own body. It's hard to explain."

"Did you recognize the orchard?" asked Brooke.

"I had never been there before."

A look of triumph gleamed in Brooke's eyes.

"Was there a city nearby?"

"I couldn't tell. I never moved far from the apple trees." Chad described his experience in detail.

"What did it feel like?" asked Brooke.

"It's hard to believe it was only a memory. It felt like real life—full technicolor, with sounds and smells. But I had no control over what Rogell did."

"Wow," said Robert. "Just like your experience, Brooke."

"Did you become Rogell, too?" asked Chad.

"No. I accessed a man named Damian, a goldsmith who lived in Constantinople in the middle ages. For a long time I didn't know where I was, but then I saw a magnificent cathedral that still stands today. After a quick search on the internet, I discovered it was the Hagia Sophia in Istanbul."

"Although I could see, hear, and feel everything, I couldn't tell what Rogell was thinking," said Chad.

"It was the same for me with Damian. You're in his head, but in your own mind."

"I wonder why we're accessing these particular men," said Chad. He had no idea what was going on, and felt a knot of worry in his gut.

"What year do you think it was?" asked Robert.

"I don't know," said Chad. "At first I thought they were Pennsylvania Dutch, but now that you mention it, it could have been sometime in the past. No pesticides were used on those apple trees."

"What language did they speak?" asked Brooke.

"It was some kind of heavily accented English."

"Maybe old English? My host, Damian, speaks Greek. I've gone back enough times now that I understand the language."

"You learned Greek in only two months?" asked Chad.

"When you're on the machine, time stretches out. One minute in the present is like five hours in the past. I had plenty of time."

"How is this going to impact our research on memory function?" asked Chad. Robert looked grim and Brooke folded her arms across her chest.

"We tried a lot of different excitation signals," explained Robert, "but this was the only one that worked. When we change the voltage, Brooke sees Damian at different times in his life. We haven't gone up very high in voltage yet."

"At least something worked," said Brooke. "Even if it's not what we expected. Sometimes surprises are best."

And sometimes they aren't, thought Chad, but he kept that thought to himself.

V

THEFTS

B rooke was ready to revisit Constantinople a few nights later. A tiny doubt had lodged itself in her mind after Chad's experience. Perhaps Damian Balsamon wouldn't be there this time, and she would find herself in the apple orchard or somewhere much worse. She had visited Damian so many times that she fully expected to find him again, but still…

This trip was monitored by both Robert and Chad. Chad had made the point that she could use some backup for her experiments. If something happened to Robert or even if he just fell asleep, she could be trapped for days or weeks in the past. Although Robert scoffed at the idea that he could ever fall asleep on the job, he did agree that the protection of two watchers was wise.

Brooke planned to access Damian in temporal order, from earlier to later times. Jumping around was getting confusing, and viewing his life in the way it was lived was more comfortable. Today she planned to advance a little farther in time than she had been before. She had not had any painful trips since the incident in Damian's youth, and she was becoming more adventurous. At the time, she had assumed the goldsmith was Damian's father, but later she discovered her mistake. The goldsmith had only daughters and he had taken Damian as an apprentice. Eventually, the daughters were married and the brutish goldsmith died. Damian worked for the widow for a while, until she sold him the business and entered a convent. Damian's business was prospering, his family was healthy, and it was a pleasure to watch him live his life.

Brooke, already instrumented and settled into the chair, signaled the men that she was ready to dive in, and they activated the Memex.

The room was dimly lit by torches set in sconces on the walls. The flickering light revealed barely visible tapestries. Damian sat at a wooden table across from a man whom Brooke recognized as the local glassblower. She didn't know his name but Damian had visited his shop a few times. He was partially bald, with the fringe of hair left to him streaked with gray and melding into his neatly clipped beard. His lively eyes were set in an unlined face that suggested the late thirties.

"Are you ready to lose again, my friend?" he asked.

"Marcus, your memory is going. It is you who should fear defeat," replied Damian. Before them on the table was a chessboard, and they were arranging their pieces in the starting position. The board was set with inlaid wooden squares, alternating dark and light. The pieces were of blown glass, each individually crafted, the white king beardless and cloaked in a flowing garment pinned at the shoulder, the black king wearing furs and hefting a crude bludgeon. Clearly, the white side were the Byzantines, led by the emperor, and the black their enemies from the North. The white knight rode a magnificent steed, while the black was perched on the back of a donkey. Damian was playing black.

Marcus pushed out a king's pawn as his initial move, and Damian followed suit. In the next few moves, the players struggled to deploy their pieces and gain the upper hand. Brooke had played chess on the internet and knew the standard openings. These competitors were amateurish by comparison.

"How is business these days?" asked Damian.

"It's increasing, praise God. There is more and more work for my son to do. He has good eyes and can see the work well. I hope mine last a few more years."

Marcus drove a bishop halfway across the board, pinning a knight against an unfamiliar piece—a tall, slender man in a toga. This set had no queen, her role usurped by the toga-clad figure. Damian challenged the move, bringing forward a pawn to cover the knight. Marcus brought more firepower to bear by advancing his knight into the fray. Damian paused and became thoughtful, running his fingers through his beard.

"Did you hear what happened to Lecapenus?" asked Marcus. "Last week, he awoke and found some gold solidi missing from the till. He swears he had counted them at day's end, as usual, and half were missing. It's a blow for him. Since the new tailor moved in a few blocks away, he has been losing customers, and now this."

"Was the door forced open?"

"That's just it. Doors and windows were all secure. It makes you wonder if someone in his family is guilty."

Damian grunted and returned his attention to the board. He exchanged a bishop for a knight and relieved the pressure at the center of the board.

"Do you know Donus, the blacksmith?" asked Damian. "He told me an odd tale about losing some tongs. Just two weeks ago, he was starting his day's work and reached for them, but they were missing. A hammer had also disappeared. His house had not been broken into either."

"Maybe he just misplaced them," offered Marcus.

"I doubt it. Would you misplace your blow pipe? Why would you take it from the workshop?" Damian and Marcus exchanged several more pieces, and Damian ended up with a one-pawn advantage.

"I tell you, I'm worried about these thefts. I don't want to be the next victim," said Marcus. "Perhaps it's a demon. Something that can turn into vapor and infiltrate under your door."

"In that case, you'll need a priest to ward it off. But what would a demon do with a pair of tongs and a hammer?" Actually, Brooke could think of several things that a demon might do with such implements.

The endgame of the chess match was drawing near. Both sides had exchanged ministers and Marcus was down a bishop and a pawn. His position was weak and, against a competent opponent like Damian, he had little hope. Nevertheless, he was not of a mind to concede and stubbornly searched the board for a good move. Damian ate a few dates from a small bowl near the board. He had ignored them while concentrating on his game, but now he was quite relaxed, certain that Marcus would have to yield.

Damian pushed forward a rook and checkmated Marcus.

"Ah well, you were lucky that time," said Marcus.

As if on cue, Brooke found herself back in the Memex lab.

"So, did you find Damian again?" asked Chad.

"Yes," she replied. "He's still there. He's a pretty good chess player."

⎯⎯◦⚬◦⎯⎯

As long as all three students were together in the lab, Chad decided to visit Rogell again. He wanted to use fewer pick-ups and probes, but Brooke insisted he apply them all, including those that led to the EEG. He prepared himself with help from Robert, who was now quick at that job, and drew the helmet over his head.

Chad found himself at a scarred kitchen table in an overheated room. Rogell's wife sat across from him, stitching pieces of dark brown cloth together. The last light of the day shone in through the room's only window, giving her just enough illumination to work by. She drew the needle in and out with a practiced rhythm.

A blackened pot hung in the fireplace and a small door in the brick stood open, revealing an oven within. A reciprocating pump with a long metal handle and a spout directed into the sink was built into the counter top. Chad could believe that this was a long time ago. Without modern appliances or electricity, the room hardly felt like a kitchen. How long ago it was, he couldn't say.

Rogell had a toothache—a big, nasty toothache that throbbed in time to his pulse. "What did I do to deserve this?" he asked his wife. Chad wanted to know too, since he shared Rogell's pain.

"It will get better. You should go ask the barber to pull it out," the wife replied.

"So you say, Elinor, but I didn't see you going to him last fall when your tooth was aflame."

Elinor raised her eyes from her sewing and scowled at him. "It will just keep getting worse, you know."

Rogell took a swig of bitter beer from the mug in front of him, and gazed at the fire flickering in the hearth. He did nothing for some time but sit and nurse his drink, refilling it from a cask in the corner when it was empty. A log gave way and fell into the center of the fire, sending sparks flying, and pushing the remaining logs away from each other. Rogell hefted himself out of the chair and, grabbing a poker, proceeded to rearrange the logs in a triangular pattern. The beer had dulled his coordination and he struggled with the simple task. Flames licked up and Chad felt the heat strong on his face.

"That was a shame about how Brandon's horse ran out of his traces last week. He's a careless lad. I feel sorry for Daisy's daughter being married to him," said Elinor.

"Aye, he'll never amount to anything. He should keep his harness in better repair, but he's a lazy one and prone to..." Chad couldn't get that word. The accent was strange. "He's goin' to kill that horse one day, and then he'll be sorry. I've seen sores on her mouth from a badly fitting bit."

The husband and wife went on for some time about Brandon's bad habits, which were numerous and stretched all the way back to his childhood. Chad had the impression this was well-trod ground, and they had each said these same things many times before. He wished he could leave. Between the toothache and the boring conversation, he was yearning for the 21st century.

Rogell became more inebriated. When he moved his head, his eyes were slow to follow. Chad hated the feeling of being drunk, but he had to admit that the toothache had lessened.

"I'm going to have a chicken for dinner tonight," bellowed Rogell.

"Are ye daft, it's not even Sunday."

"Don't cross me, woman, or it'll be your neck I wring." Rogell rose and steadied himself as best he could before lurching out the door. The chicken coop was a foul place, with two rows of nests along one wall, and years of chicken droppings on the floor. Chad's nose wrinkled and his eyes watered in the stuffy space.

Rogell flailed about trying to catch one of the birds, who flapped around desperately, kicking up even more noxious debris. Rogell, his hand clutching a chicken foot more by chance than plan, stumbled out of the coop with the unfortunate creature struggling noisily. He shoved the barn door open with his shoulder and the smell of fresh hay wafted out. Stumbling to the back of the barn, Rogell retrieved a hand ax from a nail on the wall, all the while clutching the frantic chicken with an iron grip.

Out in the barnyard, Rogell approached an old stump whose stained and weathered top was etched with ax blows. Setting his ax aside, he tried to grab the chicken's head and was pecked at. With an oath, he redoubled his efforts and, avoiding the pointy beak, finally captured the head. Even when he twisted the hen's neck, she still struggled. He laid her body on the stump and hacked at it with the ax, missing the first few times. At last, he severed the neck and lost his grip as blood spurted out in a wide arc, like water issuing from a moving hose. The headless chicken flapped her wings and took a turn around the barnyard before finally collapsing in death.

Chad was relieved to see the Memex lab around him. He sat up and looked for his friends, who were nearby, Robert sitting at the monitor and Brooke peering over his shoulder.

"Wow, don't send me back there."

"Did you have a rough time?" asked Brooke with a worried expression.

"Rogell had a hell of a toothache and I wasn't spared."

"Ouch. Let me look at the measurements and see if that came through." Brooke examined the records of Chad's brain waves, his temperature trace, his pulse and his respiration. If only she could find some small indicator, some hint, that the operators could use, but there was nothing. All readings were normal.

Fortunately, Prof. Hunter rarely visited the Memex lab. She was more of an action-at-a-distance manager, and she never came in the evening. This gave the students plenty of opportunities for their experiments. Brooke could not figure out the date on her visits to Constantinople. She had the months worked out based on the many feast days that the populace celebrated, but the year still eluded her.

On this Thursday night in July, Brooke planned to revisit the Byzantine capital. Chad raised the voltage slightly so Brooke would arrive a few days later than her last visit. He activated the signal.

Damian was trudging uphill on a sweltering day. Sweat dribbled down the sides of his face and ran from his armpits under his loose-fitting tunic. His legs were bare below the knee and his leather sandals slapped along the paving stones. His daughter, Julia, now newly a woman, walked beside him. She was slim and attractive, with that fresh beauty that is granted only to adolescents. Brooke could only imagine how warm she must be, dressed in a full-length gown, with long bell-shaped sleeves, her blond hair mostly hidden under a head scarf. She seemed not to mind.

"Oh, father, look at this store. Can we stop?" asked Julia. "I need some thread for the trim on my new dalmatica. I've run out of brown and Helena is coming tomorrow."

"Of course, darling," said Damian and they entered a small shop. Bolts of cloth in white, gray, navy blue, deep green, and other subdued colors lined the walls, punctuated by a few bright scarlets and golds. A small table held cups of beads, sorted by size and color. Julia approached the far wall where embroidery thread was wound upon wooden reels.

"Good morning, my lady," said the shopkeeper, a short wiry man. "Is there anything I can help you with?"

"I was thinking to embroider a partridge. I'll need some orange and brown thread."

Julia chatted with the storekeeper for some time before selecting three reels. The shopkeeper measured off the lengths requested, cutting them with spring-loaded scissors. Damian offered a copper coin in payment, and received smaller coins in change. Brooke caught a glimpse of the image on one of the coins, a man's head. If only she could read the words around the periphery of the coin, she might identify the emperor and discover the date. But the coin passed out of her field of vision too quickly. She was slow at reading Greek.

Damian and Julia regained the street and continued upward. At the crest of the hill, a vista of the city opened before them. Vast expanses of rooftops, broken only by narrow streets, were tightly packed within the shelter of the high city walls. The city was crowded enough that the rooftops were a valuable living space, where mothers watched their children at play and idle men took breaks from work. Brooke had become used to the cavalier treatment of the youngest members of the community. It didn't seem as dangerous to her as before.

Beyond the city wall, Brooke saw a stretch of shimmering waterway, dotted by merchant vessels. Constantinople was surrounded on three sides by water, the Sea of Marmara to the south, the Bosporus Strait to the east, and the Golden Horn to the north. By Brooke's reckoning, Damian had been walking more or less north, so this must be the Golden Horn, a sheltered inlet that formed a natural harbor for the city.

They descended the street past a stone retaining wall and came upon a busy square filled with kiosks. Two women were haggling with a rotund merchant, who had an impressive selection of spices on display. Leather bags and shoes hung from another stall, manned by a cobbler ready to make repairs. The aroma of fresh baked bread wafted up from a pastry cart. An outraged vendor at a perfume stall chased away an urchin in a filthy robe. Damian walked rapidly through the marketplace, with Julia in his wake, intent on his destination and not inclined to dawdle. He stopped at a display of locks and keys.

"Sir, come examine these fine locks; this one is the strongest iron and bronze. All our locks operate smoothly without jamming, come try." The locksmith was tall, with a narrow face and dark eyes. Damian picked up a stout mechanism of wood and bronze and turned it over in his hands.

"That is an especially good one, no one can break it open," said the locksmith. "Let me demonstrate it for you."

Damian relinquished the lock and watched as the locksmith inserted an old-fashioned key with a slotted metal plate suspended from its shaft. The lock clicked and opened smoothly.

"May I ask where you need a lock—a front door, a chest—somewhere else?"

"I want to lock a large wooden cabinet in my workshop," replied Damian. "I already have a front door lock. This would be an extra layer of protection."

"Then perhaps this is what you want." The locksmith showed Damian an intricate model that was probably one of his most expensive.

Damian appeared interested. "How do I install this?" he asked.

"Oh, the installation would be our pleasure. This is my son, Origen. He can come to your workshop and fit the lock."

Origen, a handsome youth with wavy black hair and a winning smile, bowed slightly to Damian.

Damian and the locksmith negotiated a price on the cabinet lock. Brooke noticed Origen's eyes straying to Julia, who had modestly covered the lower half of her face with her scarf. Damian concluded the sale and made arrangements for Origen to come the next day.

"You are lucky to catch me. In a few weeks, we will be moving on to Antioch," said the locksmith. "We only stay in the city for three months a year."

As they left the market, Julia asked, "Why are you buying a new lock, father?"

"A few days ago, I played chess with Marcus and learned that two shop-keepers in our neighborhood were robbed. I don't want to be the next victim. The more carefully you plan, the better life works out."

"I'm sure you're right, father," replied Julia.

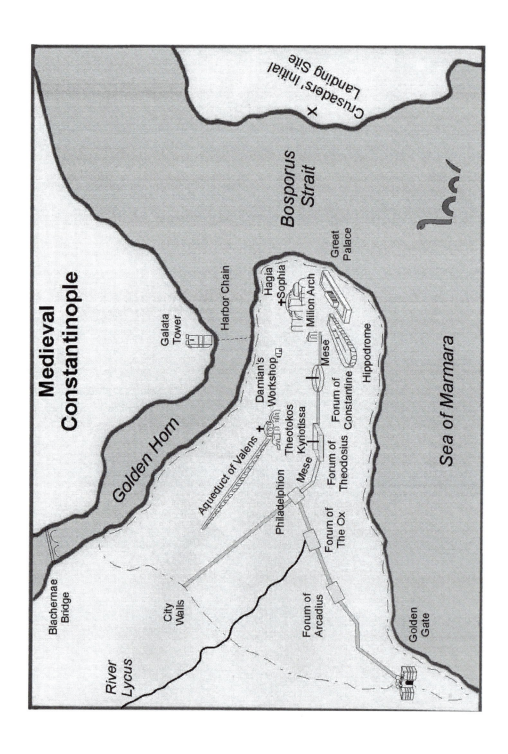

Medieval Constantinople

Crusaders' Initial Landing Site

Bosporus Strait

Golden Horn

Sea of Marmara

Galata Tower

Harbor Chain

Hagia Sophia

Great Palace

Millon Arch

Damian's Workshop

Theotokos Kyriotissa

Aqueduct of Valens

Mese

Forum of Constantine

Hippodrome

Mese

Philadelphion

Forum of Theodosius

Forum of The Ox

Forum of Arcadius

City Walls

Blachernae Bridge

River Lycus

Golden Gate

VI

NEW HORIZONS

Brooke invited Robert and Chad to a strategy session at her apartment so they could think about things away from the lab. The remnants of a pizza sat in a box on the coffee table. Robert lounged in an easy chair, a can of beer in his hand, his dark eyes half-closed behind oversized glasses. He managed to look both scholarly and youthful at the same time.

Chad, his long, lean frame folded up into the chair opposite her, had a thoughtful expression on his face. His features were even, but rugged enough for a man, topped by well-cut chestnut hair and underscored by a distinctive jaw line. When he spoke, his voice was deep and melodious.

"The Memex has turned out to be more interesting than I ever expected. More puzzling, too. I wish I understood how it worked."

"I have a theory about that," said Brooke. "It's a little out there, but this whole thing is out there." She was afraid they might scoff at her idea, but here, on her own home turf, she felt confident enough to voice it.

"At this point, I wouldn't be surprised by anything," said Chad. "Go on, tell us. You always have interesting ideas."

Brooke sat up straighter on the sofa and leaned forward. "What if the Memex is like a radio, picking up signals through the air? The coils might be an antenna and our brains are the receivers."

Chad scratched his chin. "It's possible." To her surprise, he seemed receptive. In fact, he sounded half convinced.

Brooke pressed on. "If you were from an earlier age and had never seen radio before, it would seem just as mystifying as the Memex. Radio waves are invisible and imperceptible."

"But who's sending the signals?" asked Robert. That was a scary thought. Brooke had wondered too and hadn't been able to come up with a plausible idea, at least not an idea she was willing to take seriously.

"I don't know. I can't claim to understand it. But having the receiver might tell us something about the transmitter. I'm guessing that a real person had these experiences and they were recorded. Now we're retrieving the recording with the Memex. That would explain the lush detail of our experiences, like listening to a symphony on the radio."

"But Damian doesn't wear a coil on his head to capture his brain waves," said Robert.

"The recording could be more action-at-a-distance, like a microphone. You can record a symphony with a microphone without anyone realizing what you're doing."

Brooke wriggled in her seat. "Maybe we can work backwards and build a transmitter," she said.

"I wouldn't know where to begin with that," admitted Robert.

"To tell you the truth, I wouldn't either. I've been turning it over in my mind for a week or so, but I can't come up with any concrete plan."

"I think it's more like a narrowcaster than a broadcaster," said Chad. He got up and began to pace around the room. "You and I both got different signals. More like a cell phone than a radio, where each call is individual."

"Good point," said Brooke.

"If it's like a cell phone, there must be other signals out there," said Chad. "Like voice messages from lots of people. We should be able to access more than one person."

"If someone is sending signals, they would have to be recorded somewhere," said Robert. "These signals are from the past. How could anyone in the middle ages have had the technology to send such signals?"

"It looks like my idea has a few holes in it," admitted Brooke.

"Yeah, but it's the only idea we have at the moment," said Chad.

"I know a way to test it," said Robert. "If it's a transmission, there might be dead zones—places where we can't pick up the signal. We could pack the Memex into the back of a van and drive it around to see where it works and where it doesn't."

"I think Hunter would notice if the Memex went missing," said Brooke. "She does stop by every once in a while. But it is something to think about for the future."

"If we're picking up signals, it would make sense to try to find different hosts, like scanning the frequencies on a radio dial," said Chad.

"I agree," said Brooke. "But it took so long to find this one signal that I want to explore it fully before I go looking for another. I would rather go back to Damian and see how extensive the 'recording' is. Besides, I'm on the verge of figuring out the date. I even studied the Greek names of all the Byzantine emperors, hoping to read a name on a coin."

Chad looked skeptical. "That still won't get us a precise date," he said. "At best a fifty year period or so. We need to try something new. Perhaps we can find a more recent time period when people have calendars on their walls. Then we can calibrate the Memex to any time we choose. Or maybe these aren't real people from the past and they just exist in our imagination."

"I didn't imagine my way into learning Greek," retorted Brooke.

"You have a point."

If Chad, who had personal experience with the Memex, was not convinced of the reality of their visits, others were sure to doubt as well. Brooke had set aside the idea of using the Memex to help patients with amnesia and Alzheimer's, at least for the time being, and needed a new focus for her doctoral thesis. If she could explain the mechanism behind the Memex, with supporting evidence, that might do it. It was her best route forward.

"Maybe we can try different stimuli on the mice and see if we can put them under," said Chad.

"I don't like the idea," said Brooke. "It will screw up the test plan. And it will leave a record. I want the data on the mice to be unquestionable. It's a shame we started testing with all of them. If we had just one extra mouse, we could use it."

Chad folded his arms across his chest. "Up till now, we've superimposed two pulse trains of fixed frequency and different duty cycle. What if we superimposed signals of two or three different frequencies. That may open up possibilities."

"The combinations are endless. We could be looking forever," said Brooke.

"That doesn't mean we shouldn't try."

In truth, Brooke did not want to return to sitting in the chair for hours while Robert flipped randomly through possibilities, her scalp tingling and her ears assailed by knocking. Chad had not had that experience, so he didn't know what it was like. Brooke had devoted a lot of time to learning Greek and she didn't want to quit now. All that Greek would be wasted. Besides, she liked old Constantinople. Throughout the middle ages, it had been the largest and most magnificent city in Europe. Tourists came from all over to sample its charms. If she did end up somewhere else, it would probably be at a farm since 98% of people living in medieval Europe were farmers. She didn't like those odds.

"Brooke, how about this," said Chad. "You keep exploring Constantinople and I'll look for new people. There's no reason we can't take both approaches. In the meantime, we can think more about the mechanisms behind the Memex."

"I like that," said Brooke.

<hr/>

After four frustrating days of failed attempts, Chad began to regret taking this tack. He lay for hours under the Memex helmet, occasionally picking at the probes that were plastered on his body, waiting for a breakthrough. He hated the tingling on his scalp and the heat that seemed to penetrate into his brain. After the second day, he suffered a dull headache and almost gave up. On the other hand, Brooke had toughed it out. He had to remind himself that research requires sacrifice; in truth, he had hoped it would be less sacrifice than this.

Brooke and Robert had been trading off with operating the Memex. They had all agreed on a matrix of possibilities and were systematically working their way through them. Robert would sometimes jump ahead to try a setting at random, but Brooke would march ahead one by one, in order.

Chad didn't have much to do while he waited, so he had been spending a lot of time watching Brooke. She was sitting at the monitor now, frowning at the screen. She even looked good with a frown on her face. Today she wore jade teardrop earrings that jiggled every time she turned her head. If only she weren't so single minded in her studies, he might have a chance with her...

The lush green hills rolled away into the distance. Chad walked between rows of waist-high grapevines, expertly supported on wooden stakes. Off to the right, the newly-risen sun washed the scene in soft light. He could smell the wet grass and see the still-green grapes glistening with beads of water. He was wearing a long skirt and carrying a basket. He also felt short. This wasn't Rogell he was in. He felt a surge of elation at having discovered a new person, and a woman at that. This opened whole new dimensions.

There was nothing in his field of view but the vineyard, which seemed to go on for a great distance. The ground undulated in a gentle wave and was covered in damp grass. His shoes were delicate, not what he would have worn into a field and his feet got wet. But the day was pleasant, warm, and mild, and even wet feet couldn't dampen his spirits. His host walked over a hill and made her way to the edge of the field, which was bordered by a forest.

The woman entered the forest and strolled through the underbrush. The trees had well developed crowns and the ground cover was sparse, so the going was easy. Shafts of light from the morning sun slanted through the leaves. The woman seemed to be looking for something on the ground. Bird song filled the air, surprisingly intricate and musical. Chad was enjoying himself.

Finding a funnel-shaped golden mushroom with wrinkled edges poking up out of last year's fallen leaves, she plucked it and dropped it into her basket. Several more were visible a few yards away, and she gathered those as well. No trail was apparent and they were beginning to penetrate deeper into the woods. Chad thought she might get lost, but, on second thought, this was probably near her home in terrain familiar to her. She poked at a small white mushroom, rooting around near its base and examining the underside carefully, then rejected it. By now her basket was half full.

"Rosalina, Rosalina," called a voice from afar. Rosalina turned and saw a young man waving at her from a nearby thicket. He said something that Chad could not understand, but it sounded like Italian.

"Francisco, come sta?" said Rosalina as Francisco approached. She smiled into the tanned face of a tall and well built youth. The two began to converse in Italian. They seemed to know each other well. She said something and he replied with a grin and a raised eyebrow. She touched him lightly on the chest and smiled knowingly. Were they flirting? Chad wasn't sure how he felt about that. Rosalina took Francisco by the arm and they strolled through the woods together, mushrooms forgotten.

The pair entered a more densely forested section of the woods, where vines crept up the sides of the oak trees and ferns dotted the ground. Rosalina turned to Francisco and he stroked her cheek. Francisco touched her lips with his and she sank into the kiss with passion. Alarms were going off in Chad's head. He had never kissed a man before, had never wanted to. He was more startled than repelled, and then he felt ashamed, but these were Rosalina's actions, not his.

Rosalina pressed herself against Francisco and Chad could feel the bulge in Francisco's pants. Francisco's hand wandered down Rosalina's back as she clung to him and his tongue explored her mouth. She pushed him away gently and began to untie her bodice. Francisco nuzzled her breasts, which were full and firm. Despite himself, Chad was starting to grow excited, a diffuse sort of excitement that coursed through his whole body. So this is how it felt to be a girl.

The first thing Chad saw when he returned to the Memex lab was Brooke beaming at him.

"We did it," she said. "Where were you? What happened?"

The abrupt departure left him disoriented, but he managed to spit out "A vineyard in Italy, a really beautiful spot." Chad filled Brooke in on the details of his visit, omitting the passionate conclusion. "What were the settings that got me there?"

"We superimposed two pulse trains, one with a frequency of 972.5 Hz and a duty cycle of 4.22% and the other with a frequency of 1034.5 Hz and a duty cycle of 8.44%."

"How did you happen on that?" asked Chad.

"We tried a hell of a lot of combinations. This one just worked. Dropping the third pulse train reduced the number of variables. Shifting the phase didn't get us anywhere." They both poured over the list of test cases, wondering why this particular case had worked.

"Are you going back to the vineyard?" asked Brooke.

"Not right away. It was fun. I wouldn't mind going back, but I'm more interested in figuring out how to home in on different people than following Rosalina around. I've had enough for tonight. I'm going home."

Brooke was eager to return to Constantinople after the week-long hiatus. The team's efforts had been devoted to helping Chad find new hosts and she had started to miss Damian and the other members of the Balsamon family. She planned a longer trip this time. It was a lot of trouble to get ready for the Memex and she wanted to minimize the prep time. She was impatient with her progress. It was already late July and she still had lots of questions. Brooke lay on the chair at the Memex lab and signaled Robert to get started.

Damian was standing before the smelting furnace in his workshop. A small crucible of partially-melted gold rested on a slab supported by four large stones. Damian's son, Basil, now about thirteen years old, stoked the fire with a large pair of bellows. The gold glimmered with a faintly rose-colored glow. Little slabs of it resting along the inside of the crucible slowly succumbed to the heat and sank below the surface. When the gold was all melted, Damian picked up the crucible with a long pair of tongs and poured the precious liquid into a mold. He hung the tongs back on the wall and man and boy sat upon stools and waited.

Julia wandered into the workshop and sat across from them. "What are you making today, father?" she asked.

"I have an order for earrings from Kyrios Prepundolus. He wants them for his lady." Brooke had figured out that Kyrios meant "Lord" and she was pleased that Damian had attracted such distinguished customers.

"How lucky for her. What's the design like?" asked Julia.

"It's a flat lacework of gold with a single drop-shaped pearl dangling from the bottom. You'll see the gold part soon. It's almost time to remove it from the mold." The part was released, and Brooke, who was something of an earring connoisseur, was impressed with the pattern and workmanship. It was exquisite.

"Father, let me do the etching this time," said Basil. Brooke saw the eagerness in his eyes.

"Well, you have been doing a good job with the waxwork. It might be time to let you try your hand at decorating. Don't forget to use the loupe and take your time. If you mess it up, we'll have to melt it all over again."

Basil got to work scribing small lines in the new earring with a thin metal pencil. The door opened and Origen walked in.

"Good morning, sir," he said. "And good morning, lady," he added, noticing Julia. "I have your lock ready to install."

"The cabinet is over here," said Damian, leading Origen to the rearmost wall of the workshop. They discussed the installation of the lock and Origen laid out his carpentry tools. Damian returned to the workbench to look over Basil's shoulder. The young boy was proceeding with caution, wanting to impress his father. Julia watched them for a while and then approached Origen.

"I hear you're going to Antioch soon," she said. "Have you been there before?"

"Many times," replied Origen. "My father and I make a grand circuit each year to several important markets."

"What's it like?" asked Julia. "I've never been there."

"Oh, it's not as grand as Constantinople—nothing is. But it has a splendid theater. I especially like this group called the Zeno players. They put on a comedy that was hilarious. The whole audience, and there were a lot of people there, was laughing loud enough to raise the dead. And the food. During the performances, vendors bring around little meat pies in such flaky crusts. You can't get them around here. There is also this little shop that sells a dark, bitter, hot brew. The owner is from Keffa."

"I would love to travel. You must see so many interesting things," said Julia.

"I once saw a two-headed sheep," said Origen. "It was in a little town not far from Nicaea."

"So, how is my lock coming?" broke in Damian. "Are you almost done?"

"Yes, sir," replied Origen. "I just have to do the final assembly." He fit the last few pieces in place and Damian inspected the result. Damian slid the key in the lock and tested the action.

"That will do," said Damian. "Thanks for your help."

"If you have any trouble with it, I would be happy to come again," said Origen.

"Don't worry, lad. Go on now. Your father will be looking for you," said Damian.

After Origen had departed, Julia chided her father. "He was interesting. Why did you chase him away?"

"The boy has a head full of nonsense. Two-headed sheep indeed. You shouldn't pay attention to his sort." Julia retreated to a stool and sat there with her arms crossed. Damian returned to Basil and looked at the earring.

"That looks good, Basil. We'll make a jeweler out of you yet." Basil flashed a smile at his father. He set the earring aside and inspected his work area and the floor for any specks of gold that may have ended up there. Even the tiniest bit was precious, and would be retrieved and folded into the next piece.

"Tonight Marcus Gestopian and his family are coming to dinner. I want you to be your most charming self, Julia. His son, Florian, would be a good match for you."

"I can't marry Florian, father. He has a receding chin and his hair lies flat on his head like a mop. Besides, he has nothing to say."

"Watch your tongue—Florian would make a fine husband. He's a talented glassblower, like his father. He has a good business and he would be able to take care of you. Besides, we know the family. They're good people and I won't listen to you say anything against them. Now run along and help your mother prepare for dinner."

Julia left as directed and Damian and Basil continued their work. Damian pounded pieces of gold into thin leafs and set them into the crucible. The crucible was heated and the gold cast into the same mold to produce a second, identical earring. After it had cooled and been removed from the mold, Basil got to work on the decoration.

The door opened and a tall man in clerical garb entered. Brooke recognized him from her first visit to the Hagia Sophia, Constantinople's famous cathedral.

"Good afternoon, Father Scholasticus," said Damian. "Good of you to stop by."

"I was in the neighborhood and thought I would check to see how my reliquary is coming along."

Damian showed Scholasticus a wax form with a partially sculpted handle. Scholasticus examined it for some time and finally nodded his approval. Damian led Scholasticus to a tray filled with packed dirt, and sketched out his ideas for the remainder of the reliquary.

"Looks like you're making good progress," said Scholasticus.

"Your Grace, I will need an advance payment to purchase the gold. It's quite a large piece and I don't carry that much bullion in inventory."

"Ah yes, you did mention that earlier." Scholasticus drew out a pouch that had been hanging around his neck and pried it open. He withdrew several large gold coins and handed them to Damian.

"I know this is not enough, but I'll return later in the week with more," said Scholasticus. Damian examined one of the coins and Brooke saw her window of opportunity. The inscription around the periphery of the coin read Αλέξιος Γ′ Άγγελος. She repeated it to herself over and over, drumming it into her mind. The name was not familiar, but she could look it up later.

The next hour was quiet, with Damian and Basil working on their separate projects. Brooke admired the unhurried approach they used. She could not remember when she had had the luxury to do her work ever so slowly and carefully, without regard for "productivity."

The afternoon was well advanced when Marcus Gestopian arrived at the workshop, with his wife, Sophia and son, Florian. Damian welcomed them with enthusiasm. Brooke could see why Julia found Florian unappealing. He did have a weak chin, like his mother, and his eyes were set too close together. It looked like someone had inverted a bowl over his head and used it as a guide to hack off his hair.

Everyone went upstairs, where the table was set for dinner with pewter plates, silver utensils, and a beautifully embroidered tablecloth. Eulogia, Damian's wife, met them at the door and said, "So glad you could come. Do you know my mother, Ariadne?" The older woman stepped forward and smiled. "Mother, this is Marcus, Sophia, and their son, Florian."

"Welcome to our home," said Ariadne.

Julia appeared in her formal gown and was introduced. She knew the Gestopian family and greeted them politely, if without much enthusiasm. A servant girl bearing a tray of appetizers moved among the guests.

"Did you go to the festival last week?" asked Eulogia.

"Oh yes," replied Sophia, "We arrived early and got a good spot along the Mese for the parade. Were you there?"

"I wouldn't miss it. I enjoy watching the Varangian guard and the jugglers were fun," said Eulogia.

"I liked the guy who swallowed a sword," added Basil. "I don't know how he did it."

The party was seated and the first course served. The men talked about the races at one end of the table and the ladies discussed a new greengrocer who had opened up a store nearby. Julia and Florian, who were seated opposite each other, hardly said a word.

"Florian," said Marcus, "didn't you bring our hostess something?"

"Yes." Florian opened a small sack and withdrew a perfume bottle in blown glass. It was perfectly symmetrical and filled with a pale blue liquid. He presented it to Eulogia.

"Why thank you," she said. "What beautiful workmanship. You must have spent a lot of time on this. I will treasure it." Florian said nothing but just looked down at his hands folded in his lap.

"Florian has a real talent for glass blowing. Good eyes, steady hands," bragged his father.

"I also have something for you, Julia," said Florian. He handed her a small figurine of a dragon, expertly rendered.

Julia turned it over in her hands, curious despite herself, but soon set it aside. "Thank you, it was kind of you."

"Pass it to me," said Damian. He examined the bauble closely. The dragon reared up in an offensive stance, fire belching from his open mouth. Each scale covering his body was marbled with tans and greens. The tail was tipped by a nasty looking spike. Brooke admired the craftsmanship but thought it might have been a better gift for Basil than Julia.

The main course, a roasted goose with carrots and parsnips, was served. It was delectable, and Brooke was delighted that Damian had a second helping. The conversation continued among the parents, but their efforts to draw out their reluctant progeny were largely unsuccessful. Brooke was impatient to get home and use a search engine on the coin inscription.

Her wish was granted. Brooke found herself back in the 21st century. "Robert, I got it." she cried. "I have the name of an emperor." Brooke quickly disengaged herself from the wire harness and removed the probes. She settled into a chair before a computer monitor and pulled up a search engine. After a few tries, she got the spelling right and scored a hit. Most of the webpages were in Greek. She could comprehend spoken Greek with high fluency, but had little practice reading the language. One page was in English and Brooke had her man.

The emperor was Alexios III Angelos and he reigned from 1195 to 1203. The Greek version of his name was Αλέξιος Γ' Άγγελος. The Greek letter "gamma" in the middle was the third letter in the Greek alphabet, hence the III in the English version. As Brooke continued reading, she realized how complex the political situation was in Constantinople during this period, and came to appreciate the meaning of the term "Byzantine." Robert stood over her shoulder, interested in what she had discovered.

"Wow, what a mess," he said.

"It's going to take me a while to sort this out," said Brooke. She spent the next hour perusing web pages and piecing the story together. She grew more interested as she went.

As a young man, Alexios III Angelos had been exiled for conspiring against the emperor. Later, his younger brother, Isaac, grabbed the throne in a military coup. Seeing his chance, Alexios returned to Constantinople and was welcomed with awards and celebrations. But the mood among the nobles was grim—Isaac was not an effective military commander and the empire was destabilized by uprisings among the Bulgarians and Vlachs. Worse still, Isaac lost face when a German army bent on crusading against the Turks openly attacked his troops and forced him to make large, public concessions, including transport across the Bosporus, cheap food, and forgiveness for the German violence.

This did not sit well with the ruling elite, who feared that the emperor's weakness would lead to their downfall. On a hunting trip in Thrace, they conspired with Alexios to unseat Isaac. While his brother rode off on a hunt with a group of soldiers, Alexios pretended illness and stayed behind. With the support of the army and a group of powerful nobles, Alexios marched to the Imperial tent and proclaimed himself emperor. When Isaac realized what had happened, he fled with his small band, hoping to make it back to Constantinople where he could reassert his authority. Alexios pursued and captured his unfortunate brother, confining him to the monastery of Vera. There he gouged out Isaac's eyes.

The Byzantines believed that a blind man was incapable of leadership and unsuitable as an emperor, and many men had suffered this barbarism to render them impotent. Alexios covered his crimes with massive bribes, which drained the already weakened imperial treasury. The outer reaches of the Byzantine Empire were attacked by the Seljuk Turks, the Bulgarians, and the Vlachs. Alexios put up little resistance. Instead, he squandered funds on lavish gardens and palaces and tried unsuccessful diplomatic initiatives on the invaders.

Brooke was disgusted by the actions of emperor Alexios III. How did the people put up with him? Why did anybody trust him, given his actions? She supposed he was no worse than many modern day dictators who held power through fear and the greed of those around them. And then she read about the Fourth Crusade.

"Robert, look at this," said Brooke. "The crusaders attacked Constantinople in 1204."

"I thought the crusaders were supposed to take back Jerusalem," said Robert.

"You're right. They started out intending to capture Egypt as a stepping stone to the Holy Land. But, through a tangled series of events, they ended up scaling the walls of Constantinople and driving out the Byzantines. It was one of the most infamous events in history. The Roman Christians attacked the Greek Christians and sacked the city. Do you know what this means? I have a window into a dramatic historical event. I can be an eyewitness at a crucial moment in time."

"It sounds kind of dangerous. What if Damian gets killed when the crusaders plunder the city?"

That was a sobering thought. Brooke liked Damian and the other members of the Balsamon family. She didn't want to see them hurt. And would she have the courage to watch from inside Damian's head if horrible things happened to him or the others? If Damian were injured or killed, she would feel it right along with him. Brooke put these thoughts aside for the moment.

"We'll have to be careful," said Brooke. "I still don't know the precise year, but I've got it narrowed down. Alexios took power in 1195 and the city fell in 1204, that's only a nine year period. And Chad thought my idea of looking at coins wouldn't work. Won't he be surprised?"

—⁂—

The following morning, Brooke walked between tall stacks of books in the library, looking for her call number. She had learned a lot about the Fourth Crusade and the ignominious history of Constantinople in the late 12th and early 13th century from the internet, but she wanted a more in-depth account. Brooke loved books and had read hundreds of them in her childhood. In college, she had been disappointed to find that she had little time to read. A tremendous amount of time was used to read books required for her courses, mostly dry textbooks or rambling literary classics, but little time was available to explore books on her own.

Brooke located the right section and ran her fingers along a row of books, searching. She found three candidates, one with the call number she held in her hand, and two neighboring books that seemed to be on the same topic. She extracted them from the shelf and piled them into her arms. Continuing along the stack, she noticed two other tomes that might prove helpful. Fully loaded, she made her way to a long table near the window and plopped the books down.

She settled into a chair and opened the first volume. It was a badly written history, filled with unconnected dates, events, and names, altogether confusing and boring. The next candidate was marginally better and Brooke sampled a few pages here and there. An hour passed as she read bits and pieces from her pile of books, hoping for at least one interesting volume.

To her surprise, she learned that the crusades had been initiated at the request of Constantinople. The Byzantine empire was already in decline in 1095, when the First Crusade was launched. The Seljuk Turks were making inroads into the empire, and the Byzantine emperor appealed to Rome for help. Rome and Constantinople had often been rivals and it must have been galling to the Byzantines to have to come begging to Rome. During the hundred years between the First Crusade and the time Damian lived, waves of crusaders had attacked Muslims in the Levant, ostensibly to allow Christians access to Jerusalem. These military adventures had mixed success and left small groups of knights defending tenuous footholds in the Holy Land.

The Fourth Crusade was a complete boondoggle. The original plan was for the crusaders to launch an attack on Egypt. The Nile delta was a land of abundance and whoever controlled it would have enormous tax revenues and a strategic jumping off point for Jerusalem. It would be easier to defend Jerusalem in the long run if both Jerusalem and Egypt were under Christian control.

With these objectives, Boniface of Montferrat and other noblemen contracted with Venice to build enough ships to transport 33,500 crusaders across the Mediterranean. When the crusaders arrived a year later, there were only 12,000 of them, far fewer than promised. Since the crusade was largely funded by the participating knights, the crusade leadership could not pay for the ships they had commissioned.

The aged leader of Venice, Enrico Dandolo, refused to go forward with the attack on Egypt until the bill was settled. The two sides were at an impasse for months until Dandolo conceived a clever plan. He persuaded Boniface to attack a nearby Venetian rival, Zara, to make good his debt. Zara was a Christian city, not a "proper" target for the crusade. Some knights refused and returned home, but most of them followed their leaders and looted the city after a short siege.

Brooke supposed that these crusaders were motivated by the spoils of war rather than by any high-minded ideology. She imagined them as uneducated, rough, and poor. They followed their leaders into battle, hoping to snatch a prize at the end of the day, not caring much about who they were battling. Because they could not read and write, they had not left much in the way of letters and diaries and their lives had gone largely unrecorded. It was a general problem with history. The nobility left records, the commoners did not. The Memex had the potential to change all that, and to give the world a new view of life as it had been.

Brooke sorted through her books and chose two to check out. Understanding the history of Constantinople at the time of the Fourth Crusade was going to take some reading. Luckily, she liked to read.

VII
DATES

It only took Chad and Robert two days to find the third host. Chad had dispensed with many of the probes pasted to his body, since none of them seemed to be giving useful data. He had also decided that one operator was enough. Nothing had gone wrong in the Memex lab while he and Brooke were under the influence of the machine and he didn't expect any trouble. Only Robert was in the lab with him. This streamlined process would allow him to collect more data, and he was hungry for data. Not knowing why these people were the ones accessed gnawed at him like an unsolved mystery.

"Are you ready for the next attempt?" asked Robert. Chad nodded.

The sky was overcast and the street was pockmarked in puddles. Chad felt short as he walked alongside a man dressed in tattered brown pants and shirt. He was wearing a worn gray dress and no shoes. Oh no, Chad thought, I'm a little girl. His heavily callused feet were immune to pain as he stepped on small rocks and sticks. The city around him was awash with pedestrians, most in drab clothing, although a few respectable dames wore nicely tailored dresses and white head coverings. Chad heard the clop of horseshoes, and the crowd pushed away from the center of the street. The horseman that passed wore puffy short pants and a flowing green cape that waved in the air behind him.

Buildings three and four stories high were tightly packed together and generally in poor repair. Chimneys dotted the skyline in what appeared to be a residential neighborhood. Chad felt the girl's stomach contract in hunger and he hoped she would eat soon. At the end of the street, the girl's father turned left and she followed. The pair joined a short line forming in front of an imposing building.

"Maggie, now remember what I told thee," said the father.

"Aye, Da," she replied.

When they came to the front of the line, the father offered an attendant a few coins as an entry fee.

"Not enough," said the attendant.

"Ah, man, the play is half over, I shouldn't have to pay the full fare," said the father.

The attendant scowled, but let them pass. He apparently thought he wouldn't get any more from them. Chad wondered why they were going to see a play. They should be going to lunch.

The theater was round, with several stories rising around the periphery. Box seats held nobility dressed in scarlets, blues, and bright golds. Most of the audience stood on the packed earth in front of the stage. The man and girl insinuated themselves among these commoners. On the stage, a man intoned:

"Aye, lord; she will become thy bed, I warrant. And bring thee forth brave brood."

Another actor answered, "Monster, I will kill this man: his daughter and I will be king and queen—save our graces!—and Trinculo and thyself shall be viceroys. Dost thou like the plot, Trinculo?"

The father continued to ease himself into the crowd, with Maggie in his wake. Chad wished they would stop and look at the stage. But then, Maggie was too short to see much. Her father got a few gruff remarks as he got in the way of the theatergoers, but he continued on, slowing a bit and occasionally stopping. His eyes were more on the crowd than on the stage.

An actor broke into song, singing "Flout 'em and scout 'em. And scout 'em and flout 'em. Thought is free."

Another actor said, "That's not the tune" and Chad heard a stringed instrument and pipe.

Maggie's father caught her eye and flicked his gaze to a heavy-set man with long stringy hair who was absorbed in the production. Maggie ran her eyes over him. When the father jostled the man, earning a rebuke, Maggie stuck her small hand in a purse that dangled from the man's belt. She drew out several coins and quickly slid away. Father and daughter regrouped to choose their next victim. Chad hoped she didn't get caught.

A voice from the stage boomed out "This will prove a brave kingdom to me, where I shall have my music for nothing." Rubbing his hands together in anticipation, an actor replied, "When Prospero is destroyed."

Chad knew this play—*The Tempest* by Shakespeare. The implications spun through his mind. The Memex could let him experience the original versions of Shakespeare's plays. Maybe there were some lost plays, or some parts that were different from what we know. Just his luck to be in such an unfortunate host. Maggie paid close attention to her father and to her marks, and none at all to the action on the stage.

Between one heartbeat and the next, Chad woke up in the lab. Elated at his latest discovery, he told Robert about his trip. Robert didn't seem impressed. In truth, Maggie was not the best platform from which he might experience the Bard's original plays, but there was potential there.

"Is there any way you can tell whether I will end up in a man or a woman? And I don't want to be a kid again."

"I don't know how to select for gender. At the moment, we'll have to take what we can get. The age is related to the pulse height, but I don't have the scaling factor worked out. I went lower that time thinking that your host might be young and healthy."

"You went too low. Up it for the next trip."

"Do you want to go again now?"

"Why not?"

Chad was standing in the bow of a wooden ship. The sun was low in the sky, slightly to starboard, and scattered clouds dotted the horizon. The seas were calm, with an occasional whitecap here and there. Chad had the impression it was autumn. He was happy to note that he was a man, dressed in a red jacket with frilly white shirt cuffs showing at his wrists. Black leather boots rose almost to his knees and some sort of hat rested on his head. Chad's host held a spyglass in his hand and occasionally swept the horizon with it, seeing only the line where the sky met the sea.

The man stood there for some time, his hair ruffled by a light breeze. It was a pleasant place to be, and Chad felt a sense of peace and comfort. There was not much to see, just a hawser coiled up in the bow and a long bowsprit extending over the sea. The ocean seemed to stretch out to infinity, its emptiness powerful and soothing. The man turned and Chad discovered that he was on a square rigged frigate with sails billowing in the wind. His host paced back and forth aimlessly for a while and finally returned to the bow.

The sun dropped lower in the sky and cast a long gleaming stripe on the surface of the water. The man waited until the sun disappeared below the horizon and the stars began to appear. He walked aft and nodded to the pilot at the helm as he entered the forecastle. Sand trickled through a large hourglass, firmly held in a brass frame. As the last few grains slid from the upper half of the hourglass, the man flipped the glass, picked up a circular instrument, and returned to the bow. Moonlight washed the deck and provided enough light to see well. The instrument had a bar that was pinned at the center of the ring. The bar was moveable and a little longer than the ring's diameter. The man raised the instrument and adjusted the bar, sighting Polaris, the north star, through a hole in the end of the bar. Chad didn't know a lot of astronomy, but even he could identify the big dipper and use it to find Polaris. Degree markings were inscribed on the ring of the instrument and Chad saw that the elevation was near 29°.

Chad's host returned to the forecastle and opened a leather bound book. At the top of the page, Chad saw "5th of October, in the year of our Lord 1658." At last, a firm piece of data. Chad's host made a notation in the log book and sat down. When the sands ran out, Chad's host flipped the hourglass over again.

"Nice evening, for once," said a scruffy looking officer as he entered the room. "Wish we had more of these."

"Methinks it won't last," replied Chad's host. "I saw clouds on the horizon and I bet it'll rain tomorrow."

"I can tell you, Henry, I've a bad feeling about this voyage," said the officer. "The food is getting worse day by day. There was worms in the hardtack yesterday and the water has a foul taste. That quartermaster is a weasel. I've never sailed with him before but I hear bad things about him."

"We should make land soon and replenish our supplies," replied Henry. "It's not far now."

Chad found himself back at the Memex lab. He sat up and looked over toward Robert. "That makes four," he said. "If we can find four people, we can find more. And I got a date. I was in 1658."

"That's great. Now we're getting somewhere. Do you want to try again tonight? We have time," said Robert, glancing at his cell phone.

"Do you have a good idea of what might work?"

"Yeah, I think I get it now. I'll go back to the frequency I used with Rosalina and leave the other settings the same. I bet we'll find someone else."

"Let's do it," said Chad and he lay back down in the chair.

Everything was black. Chad's arms were crossed in front of his chest and his legs were tucked up under his body. He seemed to be in some kind of sack. His host was not struggling, and this made Chad think he had been in the sack for a long time. Chad groaned inwardly. This might be his first truly terrible trip. Muffled sounds reached his ears and he strained to make sense of them, without success. At least he was warm and comfortable, despite the confinement. Oddly, his leg muscles were not cramped. Maybe he hadn't been in the sack all that long.

Time flowed past in unknown increments, testing Chad's patience. Without warning, the sack squeezed around him, removing what little range of motion he had. Chad was petrified and longed to push back against the walls of his prison. An image of a boa constrictor flashed into his mind. Had he been swallowed? Would the digestive juices start flowing soon and eat into his flesh? Fluid squished around his body and in and out of his ears. The squeezing stopped. Oh my God, how long was this trip supposed to be? He didn't remember.

Somehow it didn't make sense. How could he be alive inside a snake? How could he breathe? Once he stopped to think about it, he realized that he was not breathing. This had to be a dream, a long, miserable, dream that he had fallen into. Brooke had never mentioned any dream sequences in all her travels, but maybe she didn't think they were important.

The squeezing started again and Chad was immobilized. After half a minute or so, the wall softened and Chad was able to squirm a bit. Chad hoped that was the last of it. Unfortunately for him, the squeezes came one after the other, and seemed like they would never stop. Even after it stopped, he was held tightly, clamped in place, his nose flattened against his face. That was not the worst of it. As time went on, his head was compressed more and more until he thought his brains would pop out.

When he could bear it no more, he felt a cold spot on the top of his head. With each new squeeze, the spot grew in size, as if someone had cracked an egg on his skull and it was dribbling over his scalp. Then, in a sudden shift, his head was ejected from the sack into a cold space. He opened his eyes and saw blurry brightness.

Nearby someone shouted "Vedo la testa."

One of his shoulders was tilted up and the other down. The last push sent him slipping out of the sack into waiting arms. The sudden cold shocked him but his throat was clogged and he couldn't breathe. The next thing he knew, he was upside down suspended by one ankle. A thin wail came from his lips as all the frustration of the last few hours poured out. He heard a woman say "E'un bambino, un bel bambino." Now he understood.

"You idiot, where did you send me? yelled Chad when he awoke in the Memex chair.* Robert looked at him like a child falsely accused of stealing a cookie. "What voltage did you use?"

Robert checked the monitor and sputtered "Ahh, I made a mistake. I used microvolts instead of millivolts."

"In other words," said Chad, "you put me at virtually zero years of age. Now I know what it feels like to be born. It's not something you want to remember."

"I'm sorry," said Robert. "I guess we didn't get anything useful out of that."

Chad had calmed down in the face of Robert's meek apology. "We might have gotten one thing. I think they were speaking Italian. That's twice now I've been in an Italian host."

"It could just be coincidence."

"I don't think so. Italian isn't spoken all over the world. It must mean something." Chad's curiosity drove his mind in circles, but exhaustion chipped away at the edges of thought. He decided to call it a night.

—⊗⊗⊗—

Brooke sat in the stern of an aluminum canoe and dipped her paddle into the water. It was a sunny Sunday in late July and the lake was dazzling in its beauty. The shore was thick with pine trees, their deep green needles hiding dark, mysterious recesses beyond. The pines crept up the low hills surrounding the lake in an unbroken carpet. Chad was paddling in the bow with considerable energy. One of the nice things about sitting in the stern is that the person in the bow can't tell how hard you are working. In addition, you have total control of the direction of the boat. Feng and Robert were paddling in a second canoe a hundred yards ahead of them. Feng had also convinced Robert to take the bow, since that was where the "muscle" was needed.

Brooke trailed her fingers in the water and scooped up a handful, splashing it on her face to cool off. She angled her paddle to adjust the heading of the boat.

"So I saw a coin in Constantinople that helped me narrow down the date," said Brooke.

"Robert mentioned it," replied Chad. Brooke was annoyed. Chad should be more excited about it. Finding the coin was a big step forward.

"This Alexios III was one of the most corrupt leaders I've ever read about," said Brooke. "He and his wife stole the throne from his brother, Isaac II, and blinded him. Then he tried to bribe everybody he could to stay in power. The Holy Roman Emperor, Henry VI, threatened to invade unless Alexios paid him 5000 pounds of gold, so Alexios robbed some imperial graves to raise the money. As it happened, Henry died before he could collect. But the worst threat came from his own family. Isaac had a son, also named Alexios, who escaped from Constantinople and made his way to Europe. There he convinced the crusaders to back him and came back to threaten the city and overthrow his uncle. That's how the crusade got diverted to Constantinople.

"Alexios III came to power in 1195 and the city was plundered in 1204. I figure I'm visiting sometime around 1200. I'll get to witness the infamous fall of Constantinople. I could learn something that historians don't know. This could be huge," said Brooke.

"You're assuming a lot from one coin. Maybe the coin was a hundred years old and you are there long after the fall of the city. Gold doesn't age," said Chad.

Brooke knew he would have objections. He always had objections. She decided to play along with him for a while.

"Somebody would have mentioned the fall of the city. Besides, the coin didn't look worn. It looked like it had been recently stamped," she said.

"It could have been in the church's vault for a long time and not circulated much," suggested Chad. "Then it wouldn't be worn."

"Alexios III was not in power long. What would be the chance that I would find a coin 100 years later from his short reign?" argued Brooke. "Besides, I have proof that I'm visiting before the Fourth Crusade. Damian likes to go to the chariot races at the Hippodrome. I've seen a statue of four bronze horses called the Quadriga that stands on the archway to the Hippodrome. When the crusaders came in 1204, they stole everything of value, including that statue. Doge Dandolo transported it back to Venice and displayed it in St. Mark's square where it stood until Napoleon stole it from Venice many years later. After Napoleon was defeated at Waterloo, the Quadriga was returned to Venice. I actually saw the Quadriga on my trip to Italy. It's in a museum now. So you see, I have to be there after 1195 when Alexios III came to power and before Dandolo took the sculpture to Venice, about 1204."

They had come upon a patch of lily pads near the shore and Brooke steered close to them. "Watch out, we don't want to get tangled in these," said Chad.

"They won't be a problem," said Brooke, relishing her power over the boat's heading. Robert and Feng were still ahead of them, but their lead had shortened. They had come to a narrow section of the lake and Robert's canoe glided through the middle of it, with wilderness on both sides. Brooke examined the nearby shoreline, hoping to glimpse a deer, but without success. Development was restricted in the Adirondack Park and there were no houses, cabins, or docks in view. On this warm summer day, with the water calm and inviting, it was paradise.

They paddled in silence for a while. The narrows opened up and Robert's canoe made for a small island, crowned with a patch of pine trees. Robert made landfall on a thin strip of sand and helped Feng out of the canoe. Brooke steered her vessel alongside and let the bow run up onto the sand. Chad hopped out and grabbed the bow so the canoe would stay beached.

They unloaded a picnic lunch and rested on driftwood and patches of packed sand. Brooke passed around some ham and cheese sandwiches they had bought on the trip up to the lake, Chad produced a canteen, and Feng shared some oatmeal cookies with raisins. Brooke stared at the wind-driven wavelets, sparkling in the late afternoon sunlight. There was no one else on the lake and it was refreshingly quiet.

"It must have looked like this hundreds of years ago," said Brooke. "There's no sign of civilization."

"The canoes would have been birch bark rather than aluminum," said Chad, "but other than that I agree." She couldn't say it out loud with Feng there, but Brooke thought about using the Memex to go back to early America. She was beginning to envy Chad his visits to different places and times. Funny that he never seemed to be in America.

"I heard a report on future water shortages in the Midwest," said Robert. "There's this giant aquifer under eight states called the Ogallala. Last year its level dropped 1.5 feet in the Texas panhandle. They think we'll have serious shortages in 10 to 20 years." Robert was passionate about environmental problems and climate change. Last month he drove to Pennsylvania with the Sustainability Club to be part of an anti-fracking demonstration.

"The same thing is happening in India. Their water table dropped a foot as well," said Chad. "But they'll figure it out. There's a lot of research on farming with less water." Chad was on the "technology will conquer all problems" side of the argument. Brooke hoped Chad was right, but feared that Robert was.

On the canoe ride back, Brooke again took the stern. She watched Chad put his back into the paddling. He had removed his shirt in the heat, and his muscles rippled with effort. Brooke could admire his strong shoulders without anyone noticing. For once, he had set down his white Stetson and it lay protected under the lip of the bow. Brooke supposed it took a certain courage to wear the cowboy hat in the East—a willingness to be different, not to be inhibited by opinion.

"So, I heard you visited three new people last week," said Brooke.

"Yeah, I wish I could figure out what they have in common. So far, there have been two Italians and three British." Chad had a deep and resonant voice, like a bass drum.

"If it were random, I think you would get more ethnicities. Also, they're all Europeans, what about Asia?"

"Good point," said Chad. "I did get one date. My navigator was sailing in 1658. A lot later than your Damian."

"I was also thinking about why we haven't seen any Americans or more recent Europeans. I guess the signal takes us deep into the past. There must be a way to visit more modern people."

Brooke flirted with the idea of doing what Chad was doing—testing many different hosts. But then all her efforts to learn Greek would be wasted. Besides, she was curious about the sack of Constantinople, and although she knew it might lead to intense pain, she was like a hiker walking on a frozen lava field, knowing all the while that the crust might give way and plunge her into molten agony, just so she could get to a river of glowing lava. She had to see, whatever the cost. Brooke would stay the course and go back to Damian.

On Monday morning, Brooke and Robert were preparing to use the Memex. They had gotten bolder of late and used the machine in the daytime. Prof. Hunter traveled a lot in the summer. She was currently in Bulgaria at some international conference, and they didn't expect anyone else to drop by. Even if someone did, Robert would pretend that nothing was amiss, and how would anyone know otherwise? Brooke rested in the chair and signaled Robert to click the activate function.

Damian was walking along a dark and winding street. Torches, set into sconces on the walls of buildings, lit the way dimly. It was quiet, and Damian's sandals slapped on the pavement as he made his way. Constantinople was dangerous at night and there were few people about. Brooke saw a man apparently asleep in a doorway, looking more like a bundle of old rags than a human being. Damian eyed the beggar carefully and gave him a wide berth. The moon was partially obscured by clouds and few stars could be seen. An earlier rain had left the streets wet and the reflections from the torches cast long fingers across the pavement.

Damian turned a corner and came upon a wider avenue, lined with well-shuttered shops. The lighting was better here and he passed a few pedestrians, all men. Damian stopped at an ornate door and rapped sharply. Brooke noticed a drawing of a perfume bottle on a signboard above her head. She heard bolts moving in the lock and the door swung open.

"Ah, Damian, I'm glad you could come. Did Eulogia give you any trouble?" said a short man in his late twenties. He had a stocky build and frizzy black hair.

"She tried to convince me to stay home, said the streets are dangerous, but no woman is going to tell me what to do. I had to get out," replied Damian.

The perfume merchant stepped outside and shut and locked his door. The two friends set off down the street.

"Ignatius, are you having any trouble with suppliers?" asked Damian.

"No," replied Ignatius, "but I hear that silk is in short supply, and prices are soaring. The Turks to the east have been raiding the caravans and some merchants are staying home. How about you?"

"I can't get enough silver for some of my orders, but the problem is not severe. Eulogia couldn't find pepper at the market, and I sorely miss it."

Ignatius glanced around as if looking for spies before he said in a low tone, "I don't have much confidence in the emperor. There are stories about our enemies stealing land from us and he doesn't do anything. We need a strong general, and all he does is build palaces."

"He cut a fine figure in the pageant yesterday," said Damian. "I saw him riding in a magnificent chariot with blue and gold pennants flying, pulled by six white horses. Later in the day, he put in a great performance in the reenactment of the founding of Constantinople. He actually made me feel patriotic." Brooke knew, from her study of Constantinople, that the founding festival was on May 11. She now had a firm lock on the date, although still not knowing the exact year.

"Yeah, he's a real actor. We need a statesman and a leader and we got a wastrel and a fool."

"Be careful what you say." Damian looked around uneasily but no one was nearby. At the end of the block, music was drifting out of an open door. A man lounged on the steps to the door nursing a drink. Damian and Ignatius mounted the short flight of stairs and entered a crowded and noisy taverna. Two long tables with benches occupied the middle of the room. Bottles of various sizes and colors lined a shelf on one wall, and a string of garlic hung from a nail. One patron, sitting near the middle of a table, rose and extricated himself, tossing a small coin on the table as he went. Damian moved in to take his place, climbing over the bench. Ignatius followed, squeezing himself into what Brooke thought of as too small a space. Damian ended up sitting with his hips pressed against those of both his neighbors, but no one seemed to care. Brooke didn't think this would have happened back home.

At the front of the room, a flutist was playing a seductive tune in a minor key to the accompaniment of a slow drum beat. A woman in flowing silks danced languidly to the melody. Her thick black hair was swept up on her head, with long curls dangling to the sides. Her face was unnaturally white, covered with lead-based powders, while rouge set off her slightly pink cheeks. Her eyebrows, darkened with kohl, almost met above her nose but she wore no lipstick. The dancer alternately draped and revealed her lush figure with sheer scarves. Hoots and catcalls accompanied her more audacious moves. A harried waiter in a dirty apron moved among the diners. Damian ordered drinks and food for Ignatius and himself.

"She's good, isn't she?" asked a bleary-eyed man across from Damian. Both his front teeth were missing.

"She's the best thing I've seen all week," responded Ignatius.

Damian swept his eyes from the dancer's cleavage to her undulating hips, while Brooke thought about Eulogia. Damian was faithful to her and looking was all he ever did. The waiter came with their food and set omelets before them. He poured some dark brew into their cups. Damian tasted it and Brooke discovered, to her regret, that it was mead flavored with fennel. Good God, how did he drink this stuff? At least the omelet was tasty. At the end of the table, a backgammon game had attracted kibitzers and a few gamblers.

"Did you hear the news?" asked the man with the missing teeth. "The Bulgarians took the fortress at Varna. And on Holy Saturday no less. Those barbarians."

"Are you sure?" asked Ignatius, alarmed. "Varna is important. We seem to be losing ground left and right."

"Where's Varna?" asked Damian absently.

"Varna is on the eastern shore of the Black Sea. It's only about 300 milliaria from here," replied Ignatius. Brooke knew that a milliaria was almost as long as a mile.

"What else do you know?"

"I just heard that they used a siege tower and the city didn't put up much of a fight."

Ignatius looked ready to launch into an invective against the emperor, but apparently thought better of it. It was one thing to whisper to a friend in a dark street and quite another to speak openly in a taverna, where imperial agents might hear. There were three soldiers at the neighboring tables, although they were clearly not on duty. Brooke was eager to return to the 21st century and check the history books. She had to suffer through two more hours at the eatery and a long walk home before she was released.

The Memex lab appeared suddenly, as always. Brooke, exuberant, told Robert about the fall of Varga. He brought up a search engine while she looked over his shoulder. Varga was conquered by Kaloyan the Romanslayer, tzar of Bulgaria, on Holy Saturday in the year 1201. It was a major blow in the crumbling of the Byzantine Empire. At last she had a firm date.

VIII
BREAKTHROUGH

C had Morgan was a determined man. He was used to applying himself to tough problems and conquering them. If only he visited enough people, he would understand how the Memex worked and be able to direct his explorations instead of flying blind. Luckily, it was summer and coursework wouldn't get in the way. Caring for and testing the mice was a time consuming and boring job, and the illicit excursions into the past broke the tedium. His adventures were both work and play, an ideal combination.

He had a good feeling about today's test. He and Brooke were together in the lab and she was preparing the computer. They had worked out a series of likely settings yesterday, and planned to go through them this morning. He stretched out in the chair and cleared his mind. Whatever happened, he was ready for it.

Chad was sitting on a hard wooden bench atop a moving wagon. Snowflakes drifted lazily down from the sky. A single swayback horse plodded along the road, through an unblemished layer of pure white. Chad's host wore a long dress, a bonnet, and a heavy dark cloak. A blanket covered her lap and lower legs to keep out the chill. To her left, an older man held the reins, while to her right, a young woman sat with a bag on her lap.

"Didn't you notice the way Willie was glancing at Lucinda in church yesterday?" asked the girl. "I think he's sweet on her. Sarah told me he stops by the farm on any flimsy excuse."

"I don't know, Mary," said Chad's host. "I have trouble seeing them together. He's quiet, and you know she's not."

"I don't think that's a problem, Becky. Lots of married couples have a talkative wife and a taciturn husband."

"Still, they just don't seem like a good match to me," said Chad's host, the rather stout Becky. Chad had always been lean and fit, and finding himself in a well-padded body was a new experience. At least he wasn't cold.

"It's not as if there are a lot of men to choose from," said Mary. "Who else would suit her—Harold?"

They both laughed at that. Apparently poor Harold was not a good catch. The girls continued gossiping as the wagon rolled along ponderously. Chad saw a sign that read "Welcome to Roxbury." The name tickled his memory. Where had he heard it before?

Roxbury was a one-street town, with five buildings, including a general store, a post office, an inn, and a smithy. A neat, white church, faced in stone, stood on a square at the end of the street. The wagon pulled up at the general store and the man jumped down. He tied the horse to a rail and helped the ladies descend.

"I'm going to see Benjamin," he said. "When ye are done, I'll be at the inn."

"Yes, Pa," said Becky. "We won't be long."

Mary and Becky entered the shop, a modest one-room affair. A fire blazed in a fireplace on the right wall. Sacks of flour were stacked along one shelf and a barrel of potatoes stood near the entrance. Bolts of calico, linen, and wool rested against the left wall. Household items such as pots, cutlery, cups, candlesticks, and baskets filled two shelves. A stoop-shouldered man with a fringe of white hair circling his bald pate greeted them.

"Good afternoon, Misses Ruggles, how nice to see you both today," he said. Ruggles—Chad was sure he had heard that name before. When?

"Good afternoon, Mr. Read," replied Becky. "How is your wife faring?"

"She's well, thanks. She had a touch of the grippe, but it's passed now."

Mary and Becky browsed the small store. Mary pointed out a small lacy handkerchief. "Oh, look at this. How pretty. Mr. Read, what does this cost?"

"That would be 50 pence," said the proprietor. "We just got it in a shipment yesterday."

Mary set the dainty item aside with a sigh. After the girls had examined the store thoroughly, Mary opened her sack and withdrew two jars.

"We would like a half pound of salt and a quarter pound of tea," she said.

Mr. Read took the first jar, opened it, and set it upon a balance. He added weights until the scale was horizontal. After placing an additional half pound weight, he scooped salt from a container into the jar, rebalancing the scale. He repeated the procedure with the second jar, to which he added a quarter pound of loose tea.

"Here you are, ladies," he said. "Is there anything else?"

"No, thank you," said Becky. "We must be going."

The girls left the shop and walked to the inn. Chad suddenly remembered where he had heard the Ruggles name before. This was Rebecca Ruggles of Roxbury. She was his ancestor. Chad's mother was an amateur genealogist and had mapped the family tree back ten generations or more. She was always telling him about his forebears, but he hardly listened. The name Rebecca Ruggles of Roxbury was so alliterative that it had stuck in his mind. Could this really be his many times great, great, grandmother?

When Chad returned to the Memex lab, he found Brooke absorbed in something on her smart phone. He said, "You won't believe what I learned. I was in the body of my ancestor, Rebecca Ruggles."

"What," said Brooke. "Are you sure?"

"I think so. How many Rebecca Ruggles can there be? And she lived in Roxbury, a small town in Massachusetts in colonial times."

"It might make sense," mused Brooke. "Maybe we somehow inherit the memories of our ancestors."

"I'm going to email my mother and ask her for our pedigree chart. Then we can do some tests to see if the theory has legs. This is great."

Chad had never felt more hopeful. His mind reeled with the implications of what he had learned. It was going to be hard to sleep that night.

⊷∞⊷

Robert removed his glasses, huffed on the lenses, and wiped them with the edge of his shirttail. When he replaced them, the view was clear and clean. He was sitting on the lawn in front of the Fine Arts building, warmed by the August sun. Four Corinthian columns on the facade lent the building an air of dignity and refinement. Not many students were on campus. The undergrads were still away, and even the grad students seemed to be someplace else.

Chad's discovery from last night had invigorated Robert and he had spent long hours going over the data and trying to work out a pattern. Although he had not yet been successful, he was certain that he would eventually figure it out.

Brooke and Chad were stretched out on the grass next to him. Ever since the three had entered into this "conspiracy," they had hung out together a lot more. They were an unlikely group. Chad with his Stetson looked like a displaced cowboy and Brooke with her bejeweled hands and ears might have been a gypsy. No one would have pegged them as scientists.

"I got a chart of my family tree from my mother this morning," said Chad. "Rebecca Ruggles was born in Roxbury, Massachusetts, in 1662. I guess that's why the town was under-developed; it hadn't been around long. Rebecca married Israel Read in 1684, so I was probably there about 1680. The girls called the shopkeeper Mr. Read, and I'm guessing he was some relative of Israel."

"She was your ancestor, but that doesn't mean everyone we access is an ancestor," said Brooke. "I don't think I have any relatives from the Middle East. My family are all from England and France."

"Don't you think it's unlikely that I would just happen upon one of my relatives?" countered Chad.

"Well, the further back you go, the more relatives you have. Think about it, you have two parents, four grandparents, eight great-grandparents, and so on. By the time you get to the tenth generation, you have 2^{10} ancestors, which is…" She pulled out her calculator and ran some numbers. "…1024 ancestors. Actually, that's not that many. But if you go back 20 generations, you have… 1,048,576 ancestors."

"Hum, there's something wrong with that calculation. Following that logic, if we go back 50 generations, we would have more ancestors than there were people on the earth," said Chad. He thought a minute. "In fact, there must be crossovers, especially way back. Some people appear in your family tree more than once. You are descended from them along two different lines."

Why were these two always crossing swords? thought Robert. As far as he was concerned, Chad was right and Brooke was just throwing up flimsy objections. The Memex let you access ancestors. It made perfect sense to him. He idly pulled up blades of grass from the lawn as he listened to their banter.

"As far as Rebecca goes, there are about four generations every 100 years, so between 1680 and today, there have been about 14 generations, which gives 16,384 ancestors," said Chad. "And that doesn't include crossovers. In colonial New England, there weren't a lot of people, but there were probably more than 16,384."

"Wait a minute," interrupted Brooke. "Suppose, because of crossovers, there were only 10,000 different ancestors on your tree in generation 14. The others were duplicates, the same person holding two different spots on the tree. What was the population then? Maybe 40,000? Then there is at least a 1 in 4 chance that you would find an ancestor by accident."

Robert hated this line of reasoning. He wanted the ancestor theory to be true. It gave them something to work on and it was the first theory that made sense. Brooke's skepticism was hardening his resolve to work on the problem until he cracked it. He decided to divert the discussion in another direction.

"Chad, are you related to the famous financier, J.P. Morgan? You have the same last name. Wouldn't that be cool if you could go back to him?" asked Robert.

"Do you think I'd be driving an old wreck if I were descended from J.P. Morgan? My mother doesn't know much about the Morgan line. Our earliest Morgan ancestor crossed the ocean in about 1875, and we don't know who his parents were."

"What about you, Brooke? Any famous ancestors?"

"Unfortunately, nobody has researched my family tree, so I don't know. My last name, Laforge, is not much help. There was a feminist writer, Jean de la Forge, who wrote a book called *The Circle of Women Scientists*."

"When was that?"

"About 1660. But I don't know if he's an ancestor." He sounded like one to Robert. How appropriate for Brooke to be descended from an early feminist.

"The ancestor theory would explain why you guys didn't come upon any Asians or Africans," said Robert.

"We should put you on the machine," said Chad. "That might be a test of the theory."

"Sorry. Not interested. I'm not the explorer type. I would rather sit in the lab, safe and comfortable, and crunch numbers for you two," said Robert.

"If only the damn Review Board would let us test volunteers," said Brooke. "We wouldn't have all these problems. I've had the new form ready for weeks and Prof. Hunter approved it, but we still have to finish all the psychological and memory tests."

"We can try something else," offered Robert. "I'll work on a model that predicts which ancestor Chad accesses. With all the data we have on his trips, we should be able to figure it out. Then we test it."

"Sounds like a plan," said Chad.

Brooke was feeling optimistic the following morning when she entered the Memex lab. Her last visit had pinned down the date as May 12, 1201. This was still three years before the crusaders would storm the walls of the city and she felt it was safe to return. From their previous experimentation, she and Robert had learned that the pulse height was directly proportional to the time of the memory. When she had accessed Damian as a young man of about 13, the pulse height was 220.61 mV. By observing the seasons and the spacing of festivals, she had learned that there were 17.05 mV per year. On her last visit, the pulse height was

683.10 mV, which would put Damian at an age of about 41. Julia looked to be about 16, which was consistent with Damian's age.

Now that they had a well calibrated system of dating, she could select with certainty the date of her visit. For the first time today, she would know exactly "when" she was arriving in Constantinople. After weeks of uncertainty, she felt positively buoyant. She used the new stripped-down prep routine and positioned herself in the chair. Robert set the pulse height at 683.29 mV and clicked a link.

May 16, 1201. "*I'm not saying that he isn't good at what he does, but he has no personality,*" *said Julia.* Brooke was once again in Damian's workshop, apparently in the middle of a conversation with Julia.

"Oh Julia, I know he's not exciting," replied Damian. "I wish I could find someone better. I love you so, and I want, above all, for you to have a good life."

Julia smiled at her father and bowed her head. "I don't think I'll have a good life with Florian, Father. That's what worries me." Julia looked vulnerable, her brown eyes filled with distress.

"Is there someone else?" asked Damian.

"No, no, nothing like that. It's just that I want to be compatible with the man I call my husband. Frankly, I want to be in love, and not in some merely practical marriage."

Damian shifted his attention to his work. He was carving an intricate mold for a spoon out of wax. He set down one tool for another with a finer tip and made a minute adjustment. Brooke had the impression that he had had this discussion before.

"I considered other possibilities, you know," he said. "What about Kosmas, who works at the taverna? His uncle owns the place. His father is a farmer outside of town."

"He's not any better than Florian. He's always talking about gambling and horse racing. I don't understand all that talk about odds and handicaps. He doesn't care what I say. And he's short."

"He may grow yet," said Damian thoughtfully. "On the other hand, his prospects are not good. His uncle has two sons, and his father has three older sons. Kosmas will have to make his own way in life. What about Nicetas?"

"Oh father, can't we just wait a while?" pleaded Julia. "There really isn't a good option."

"Darling, you're almost sixteen. We can't wait forever. We are already a little late. The worst would be if you have no one."

The door opened to reveal a man clad in an expensive silk tunic, exquisitely embroidered. His high forehead and wide jaw, with its tiny mouth, left the impression that his head was shaped like a peanut. The man was of medium stature, with too much flesh on his body.

"Good morning, Kyrios Prepundolus," said Damian. "It's an honor to have you visit my shop." Julia made a small bow and left the room.

"Good morning, Master Balsamon. I came to collect my earrings."

"Just so. We finished them a few days ago. Let me get them." Damian moved to a large cabinet at the rear of the workshop and opened a door. He returned with a small, silk-wrapped parcel. Gently, he unfolded the protective cloth and displayed the contents for Lord Prepundolus to examine.

The nobleman bent over and lifted one of the beautiful pieces. The gold work was a lacy creation of intertwined strands, forming a roughly rectangular sheet. From the bottom hung a single perfect pearl. The two earrings were almost identical. Lord Prepundolus grunted and set the jewelry down.

"About the payment…, I will have to get that to you in a few days. I have had an unfortunate incident and am a little short of cash. I hope that will be all right."

"No problem," responded Damian. "I will just keep them here locked in the cabinet until you are ready to collect them."

"You don't understand. They are for my wife and she celebrates her name day next week. I need them now. Surely my credit is good."

"I'm sorry, but I don't sell goods on credit."

"Are you implying that I am not a man of my word?" asked Lord Prepundolus. A frown creased his high forehead.

"No, no, not at all. It is simply a policy that I must adhere to. See here, what if you select a piece with somewhat less gold in it. I could get it done quickly and have it ready for your wife's celebration."

The nobleman's frown deepened. "If I had wanted earrings with less gold in them, I would have ordered earrings with less gold." There was an undertone of menace in his voice.

Damian held his ground, keeping his face expressionless. Brooke tensed up at this turn of events. Would Prepundolus get violent? Damian was taller and in better physical shape, but he might not choose to defend himself against a nobleman.

"Now, let's be reasonable. Surely you know that I have the means to make good my debts. And don't forget that I have many friends in the church. You *do* often work for the church, I understand." The implications were all too clear.

"I'm sorry, but my business is a humble one. I don't have the resources to supply my clients with jewelry without recompense."

"How dare you stand in my way, you son of a whore. Those are my earrings and I want them now. No low life mongrel like you is going to keep them from me." Brooke saw flecks of spittle at the corner of the lord's mouth.

"Sir, I am sorry, but I must insist. You are welcome to return later. I will keep the earrings for you," Damian replied in a calm voice. He quickly wrapped up the jewelry and set the package behind the counter, out of sight.

"I want them. Give them to me right now." Lord Prepundolus began to sound like a petulant child. "I hope you realize what you've gotten yourself into. Nobody crosses me without paying a price. I can destroy this business. A word in the right ear, and your liturgical commissions will be a thing of the past."

Damian said nothing. Brooke thought he was wise to keep quiet. Prepundolus seemed to run out of words. He turned his back and stormed out of the shop, slamming the door behind him.

Damian's shoulders relaxed as soon as he had gone. He retrieved the precious earrings from their temporary stash and locked them back up in the storage cabinet. Eulogia appeared at the bottom of the stairs.

"Damian, is everything all right? I heard shouting," she said.

"Don't worry, darling, he's gone now."

"It sounded bad. I heard what he said. He threatened you."

"The man has the courage of a flea," said Damian. "I'm not afraid of him."

"Fleas bite," replied Eulogia. "We need to be careful."

Brooke returned to the present day, disturbed by this encounter. She had come to like Damian and worried about him. If Chad's theory was true, Damian and Eulogia were her distant ancestors. Brooke got up and went to talk to Robert.

"So, how's your ancestor model going?" she asked.

"Slow—I know there's something there, but it's eluding me," replied Robert. "I feel like I'm so close."

"Well, keep at it. If anybody can figure it out, you can," replied Brooke. Robert smiled at the encouragement. Brooke thought about undergoing another session that night. But too many Memex sessions had a disorienting effect on the mind. For every minute that she was on the machine, five or six hours went by in the past. She might go under at 2 PM and come back at 2:03 PM. Meanwhile, a whole day had transpired in her mind. When Damian slept in the past, no sensations came to Brooke's mind, not even dreams. On many occasions, she perceived herself to be "awake" for twenty-four hours or more. This led to a nagging sensation that she hadn't had enough sleep and a general lethargy. The more Memex sessions she experienced in one day, the worse the disorientation was.

She wished she knew exactly how much past time corresponded to present time. But it was difficult to measure time in Constantinople. Their "hours" varied in length with the season. Time was divided into twelve hours of daylight and twelve hours of night. In the winter, when days were short, the hours were also short, and in summer, when days were long, so were hours. This certainly complicated calculations.

"I'll see you tomorrow," she said to Robert, and with that, she left.

⁂

It was noon on Friday when Brooke planned her next visit to Constantinople. Chad was running the Memex for this trip. They had worked together that morning on testing the mice. The three students had paid less attention to the mice these last few weeks, beyond routine experiments, basic care and feeding. It didn't make sense to check their health frequently when nothing ever seemed to happen to them.

"So, you're not taking any trips to the past today?" asked Brooke.

"I thought I'd wait until we figure out the math. I needed a break anyway," replied Chad.

"I hope Robert comes up with something. I would rather visit the past than work on that problem myself."

"Well, let's get you back there," said Chad, and Brooke took her place in the chair.

May 27, 1201. It was hot—knock you off your feet hot—and the air was saturated with moisture. Damian squatted in front of a faucet protruding from a marble wall. He cupped his hands and trapped the deliciously cool liquid, splashing it on his face and arms. When he turned around, Brooke saw that he was in a public bath. A shallow rectangular pool occupied the center of the room. A small pantheon of Greek and Roman gods and goddesses graced the walls. Brooke didn't take much notice of the stone figures, however; she was more interested in the flesh and blood ones, resplendent in their nakedness. Her attention fastened on a young man with well defined chest muscles and an ample bush of pubic hair. She could see herself in bed with him, no problem. The scrawny looking kid next to him was not a candidate.

Diverted by her voyeurism, Brooke had lost track of the conversation. Marcus, his bald head glistening with sweat, and looking at a distinct disadvantage compared to the young bucks in the room, was saying, "He's a bastard. You were right not to give him credit. I wouldn't have. I've heard that he never paid Zeno back."

"Really. I'm not surprised. He thinks because he's rich he can muscle me into giving him the earrings. But, in truth, how rich can he be if he can't pay?" Brooke thought about Prepundolus in his expensive finery. All show and no actual wealth?

"He does have extensive estates beyond the walls. When the rent comes in, he's flush with cash. But he likes the horses. And gambling always brings a man down in the end."

"I wish I hadn't put all that work into the earrings. I can't sell them to anybody else. Suppose he comes by with the money and asks for them? By the Holy Spirit, what a bad business."

The two friends sat pensively for a while on a stone bench, and Brooke continued to enjoy the sights. Two men in loincloths approached them and one asked, "Are you ready for your massage?"

Damian nodded and he and Marcus got to their feet. They followed the masseurs into a small room and stretched out on two stone tables. The masseur began by vigorously rubbing Damian's back with warm, aromatic oil, upward along each side of the spine and then downward along the edges. He continued by kneading the muscles along the spine in small localized curling motions with both thumbs. It felt heavenly and Brooke sank mentally into the pleasure of it.

"How is that beautiful daughter of yours?" asked Marcus.

"She is well. She's been embroidering a new dalmatica for herself. A nice design." Brooke knew that Julia had only two dresses, one for everyday and one for special occasions. Her special occasion dress was getting a little short and tight. "She visits the widow Spartenos once a week and brings her a cooked dish. She's a good girl, my Julia."

"That she is. So when are we going to set the date? Florian is ready."

The masseur had moved to Damian's lower back, working lightly in this tender area. He moved on to the large muscles of the leg, digging into one butt cheek and progressing down over the thigh. Brooke was surprised by the touch, more intimate than she had expected, but Damian took it in stride.

"Marcus, you know I'm committed to the marriage, but it's a little early for a firm date. Business is not good, and I need more time to get a proper dowry together."

"I've felt it too, this weakening of trade. We seem to get bad news from every corner of the empire," replied Marcus. "Sales are slow."

The masseur finished both legs while Damian relaxed. He then stimulated the skin with mild karate chops traveling from the top of the back to the bottom of the calves. Upon instruction, Damian rolled over to present his chest to the masseur. There was no modesty towel in this massage. Brooke was thankful, since the air was still oppressively hot and she didn't think she could bear even the lightest covering.

"What if we set a date more than a year into the future?" asked Marcus.

"I don't want to make a promise I can't keep," replied Damian. "Let us trust to the goodness of our Lord, Jesus Christ, and hope for better times to come. Then we can firm up our plans."

Brooke wondered what to think of this. Damian was trying to keep the door open for Florian, while at the same time being unwilling to force Julia into a marriage she didn't want. Maybe he thought she would relent. Brooke thought it unlikely.

The masseur was now focusing on Damian's feet, and Brooke had never felt such pleasure from those extremities. She was going to have to enjoy a massage in her own body once she returned to the future. That was the nice thing about visiting the past—all these experiences that you wouldn't have chosen for yourself, but which open up new possibilities.

Before the massage was over, Brooke was back in the lab. She felt the transition as an abrupt lowering of the temperature. She was sorry to have missed the end of the massage. A small smile of contentment rested on her lips.

"You look like you had a good time," said Chad. "What happened?"

"I just had a wonderful massage," she replied. She told him about the conversation between Damian and Marcus, but did not describe the scene at the pool.

"Is this really taking you anywhere? I thought you wanted to learn about the sack of Constantinople. Shouldn't you leap forward in time a few years?"

Brooke was annoyed that he was challenging her judgment. "They talked about business problems. That's part of the history. I want to see when they really start to realize how much trouble they're in. Part of me is hoping they stay until the crusaders take the city, but the other part worries about them, and hopes they leave. Luckily, I'm not influencing them in any way, so my opinion has no effect on their fate. At least I don't think I'm influencing them."

"I didn't think I was influencing my hosts either. I was simply an observer, with no power at all."

In addition, Brooke wanted to see what would happen to Julia. She was beginning to think of Julia as a little sister, someone she cared about. She knew that Julia's story was probably not important to her thesis, but she was going to follow it anyway.

Robert was hunched over his desk in the Memex lab. Using the settings from Chad's trips as input data, he was trying to build a mathematical model of the ancestor tree. If only he could predict which settings corresponded to which ancestors, the Memex would be much more useful and controllable. In addition, the ancestor theory would be validated. That alone would be a major breakthrough.

It was all about powers of two. Each generation had twice as many ancestors as the generation before. Every model he postulated blew up when he went far into the past. Henry the navigator lived in 1658, which was about 14 generations ago. In that generation, there were 2^{14} ancestors, or 16,384. The settings for Rogell the farmer, Chad's first host, were the same as those for Damian. If Robert was correct, Rogell occupied the same slot in Chad's family tree that Damian occupied in Brooke's tree. Damian lived in 1200, which was about 31 generations ago. The number of ancestors in that generation was an unmanageable 1,073,741,824.

Perhaps the Memex picked out only *distinct* ancestors. He recalled the conversation about crossovers, where a certain person could occupy many places on the tree, and in fact, in generation 31, there had to be many crossovers. The total population of the planet was less than a billion in 1200, so Brooke could not have 1,073,741,824 different people as ancestors. If there was only one setting for Damian, he was screwed. With the data he had, he would never figure it out.

Robert rocked back on his chair and removed his glasses. He rubbed his weary eyes and replaced the glasses on his nose. He glanced around the lab and saw it for the inhospitable place it was. The scarred concrete floor bore the imprint of old spills and dropped tools. Dust bunnies and an occasional dead cockroach had collected in the corners. Cobwebs hung precariously in the high reaches of the ceiling, which was crisscrossed with pipes and ducts. The cleaning staff never entered here because of the parsimony of the administration. They expected graduate students to clean the place themselves. The lab was only cleaned in preparation for a visit from a funding agency, an accreditation team, or a wealthy alum. Sadly, no one of this sort had come by recently.

Brooke was working diligently this afternoon. She was multi-tasking on mouse chores, zapping one on the Memex while cleaning the cage of another. The mice cages occupied one entire wall of the lab, in a stack rising from the floor to a height of about five feet. As Robert gazed at the mouse on the Memex, he idly wondered if the critter were experiencing the memories of his ancestral mouse. Maybe he was being eaten by a cat. Sad thought. Then it occurred to Robert that mice have shorter lives than humans, so the pulse height needed to be lower for mice. This was confirmation of his theory! Of course, there could be many other reasons why the pulse height would be lower for mice, but Robert, like most people, chose to believe what fit in with his favorite theory. He attacked his work with renewed vigor.

Two hours later, he had gotten nowhere. His latest idea had petered out and led to nothing and he felt defeated. Brooke came to his desk and asked, "How's it going?"

"Best not to ask," replied Robert.

"That bad, huh. Well, you know how research goes, three steps forward, two steps back. You'll get it in time."

"I'm not so sure."

"How bad can it be? Just tell yourself that you will work on it for, say, another three days, and if you can't shake anything loose, Chad can go back to visiting new hosts to give you more data. One way or another, you'll figure it out. I really believe that."

Robert smiled. He felt better and was grateful to Brooke for her vote of confidence.

"I'm going to head out now," said Brooke. "I'm going to the movies with my roommate, Claudia. I need a break."

"Well, enjoy," said Robert. He returned his attention to his computer screen and opened a new spreadsheet. He pasted in a summary of the data for Chad's trips and examined it once more.

	Occupation	f_1, Hz	d_1	f_2, Hz	d_2	f_3, Hz	d_3
Rogell	Farmer	700.0	4.22%	700.0	8.44%	700.0	12.66%
Rosalina	Farmer	972.5	4.22%	1,034.5	8.44%	-	-
Maggie	Waif	529.4	4.22%	16.0	8.44%	-	-
Henry	Navigator	529.4	4.22%	8.3	8.44%	-	-
Italian infant	Unknown	972.5	4.22%	8.3	8.44%	-	-
Rebecca	Farmer	700.0	4.22%	4.7	8.44%	-	-

For Rogell, he had superimposed three pulse trains with frequencies f_1, f_2, and f_3. The duty cycles d_2 and d_3 were simple multiples of d_1 and the signals were all in phase. It was probable that Rogell lived earlier in time than the others on the list. It was hard to tell from the technology levels of Chad's visit. Technological change had been very slow in the Middle Ages, and one century was a lot like the next. Rogell's settings were the same as Damian's, so he may have lived around 1200. It was curious that it took three waveforms to get to Rogell, while all the others required only two waveforms.

Robert had a new idea. If you use a simple numbering scheme for members of a family tree, the number for an ancestor who lived long ago becomes enormous. On the other hand, if you select certain ancestors as pivot points, the numbering can be kept more manageable. For example, you might number your father as 1 and your mother as 2. Your four grand-parents would be 3 through 6 and your eight great-grandparents 7 through 14. After 15 generations, the numbers would become unwieldy. But sup-pose you used two numbers to describe a distant ancestor. The father of ancestor 62,350 could be 62,350-1 and the mother could be 62,350-2. This was much better and Robert dove into the numbers to see if he could make it work.

An hour later, Chad showed up. Robert was wrapped up in his calcula-tions, and merely grunted at Chad's greeting. Chad checked the duty roster and began to examine the mice and clean the cages that Brooke had not gotten to. Robert poured himself into the new idea, checking possibilities. Two hours later, his back started to hurt and he decided to get up and stretch. He walked over to the coffee machine and filled the filter with a French roast.

"So, how's the ancestor theory going?" asked Chad.

"I'm checking out a new idea. I think it's going to work."

"I've been searching the internet. I thought we might find a descendent of Shakespeare and send him back to experience the Bard in action. The facts on Shakespeare's life can be written in a few sentences; some people think he didn't even write the plays. But I found out that Shakespeare's only grandchild died without leaving any progeny."

"Wow. You would think that an important man like that would leave descendents. Isn't that kind of the point of evolution? Of course, who lives and who reproduces is a highly statistical process, so blind fate can play tricks on us," said Robert.

"I checked a few other famous people, too," said Chad. "I learned that neither Washington nor Lincoln have any living descendents, but Jefferson does. Jefferson's tree is controversial; many historians think he fathered children by his slaves. I guess the Memex could answer that question for us."

"The Memex is going to put a whole new value on a person's family tree," said Robert. "People who are descended from famous people may suddenly become celebrities. Before the 20th century, actors and actresses were pretty much nobodies, but look at them now. Descendents of famous people might become like them. It just goes to show how arbitrary it all can be."

With that, Robert returned to his desk and resumed his hunt for the key to the tree. Chad left a little later and he was once again alone in the lab. It was getting close to dinner time. He had anticipated that it might take him a long time, and Feng had packed him a dish of rice and vegetables, should he need it. Robert heated his dinner in the microwave and ate it while continuing his search.

Outside, a thunderstorm erupted. Rain lashed the windows, thunder boomed in the distance, and lightning lit up the windows. Robert hardly noticed; he was immersed in math. Just one more calculation… and it all fell into place. He was right, the tree was branched at the tenth generation. If he made that assumption, all the frequencies were multiples of a single fundamental frequency of 0.517 Hz. He had it. Robert dashed off a triumphant email to Brooke and Chad. He also texted Chad to ask him to come in to test the theory, but Chad did not reply. Robert, in a fever of excitement, wandered around the lab restlessly and waited to hear from Chad. He wished he could call Feng and tell her about his success, but Feng still didn't know about the testing. A stab of guilt penetrated Robert's euphoria. At 2 AM, he turned off his computer and headed for home.

IX

TRUE LOVE

C had rose early on Sunday morning, after only six hours of sleep, and gulped down a cup of strong, hot brew. He couldn't wait to get to the Memex lab. He had read Robert's email late Saturday night, and replied to his text, but Robert had already gone. He dressed hastily and drove through the deserted streets to the lab.

When he arrived, Brooke and Robert were waiting for him.

"OK, let's get to it," said Chad. "Dial me into an ancestor."

"I did the calculations to take you to Israel Read, the husband of Rebecca Ruggles," said Robert.

"Yeah, about that, I think I would rather go back to the husband of Rosalina," said Chad.

"But we know more about Rebecca's spot in the tree," protested Brooke. "She was the one that led us to the ancestor theory. Besides, they speak English in colonial America, and you will be able to understand more."

Chad thought about a cold New England winter and stiff Puritanical values and contrasted it with a warm Italian vineyard and the flirtatious Rosalina. "True, but I really liked the Italian vineyard. Look, if it doesn't work out, I'll try Israel next. But last time with Rosalina, I got the names, even though I didn't speak Italian. She had a boyfriend named Francisco. Maybe she married him." Brooke looked at him skeptically.

Robert sat down to calculate the settings for Rosalina's mate, while Chad settled himself in the chair. Robert dialed in two pulse trains, the first with frequency of 972.5 Hz and 4.22% duty cycle and the second with frequency of 1034.0 Hz and 8.44% duty cycle.

Chad's ax bit into the side of a dead oak tree. He was alone in the forest on a bright, sunny day, bare-chested and sweating with the exertion of his labor. He was happy to have landed in a man's body—that supported the theory so far. The oak tree rose above him to a height of about fifty feet. The top had been knocked off by a storm but had not fallen. It hung precariously from the break, lying along the side of the trunk. The lumberjack whose body Chad inhabited had cut a notch into one side of the tree and was now deepening it with expert strokes of his ax. The otherwise quiet forest rang out with each blow.

A horse nickered nearby and shook its head. The horse, a handsome black mare with white patches on her face, was hitched to a wagon on a two-rut path in the woods. Chad's host, having gotten the notch to the middle of the tree, stood behind it and sighted along the trunk, checking the line of fall. The forest was not dense and it appeared that he could drop the oak without it catching on neighboring trees. He began a second notch higher on the trunk and whacked at it again and again. As the tree creaked in warning, the lumberjack stood to the side and gave it a push to help it along, then jumped further away to avoid any kickback. The oak succumbed to gravity, falling in slow motion with a sustained groan and smashed into the ground, just where it was supposed to.

The lumberjack set to work removing lower branches. A woman in a long pale green dress with a basket on her arm approached through the forest. She was mesmerizing, her black curls falling to her shoulders and her brown eyes shining with mischief. A hint of a smile completed the coquettish look.

"Francisco," she said, and the rest was a torrent of Italian that went past Chad's ear. Chad was elated! He was right where he wanted to be and the theory was proven. Francisco replied to the young woman and Chad caught the name Rosalina.

Francisco put his tools aside and turned his full attention to Rosalina. They bantered for a while and he traced the line of her jaw with the tip of his finger. She moved closer and he set his lips upon hers in a gentle kiss. She sank into his chest, and he kissed her with fervor, pulling her slender waist into his body. They became more passionate, hungry for each other.

Chad found himself responding in mind and body to the lovely Rosalina, and almost forgot that he was Francisco. He heard himself murmuring unintelligibly into her ear. His hand moved down and he caressed her taut nipples with his thumb. Before long, the two lovers were undressed and lying on a mossy patch of ground. Rosalina had beautiful, full breasts, with large dark nipples. Chad felt a vague uneasiness at making love outside and unscreened from view. He could still see the horse, who was not interested in them, through the trees. Francisco didn't seem to share his concern; he ran his tongue down Rosalina's belly. Rosalina groaned as Francisco expertly ministered to her desire. At length, she climaxed and grew still.

Chad ached with want. Rosalina stirred and it was Francisco's turn to enjoy the heights of physical pleasure. His orgasm, when it came, was explosive.

In the state of post-coital bliss, Chad idly thought that he still hadn't proven that Francisco was the father of Rosalina's child, but he did have strong evidence. Francisco could be his ancestor through another line, but how likely would that be? Rosalina rose and Francisco helped her brush off twigs that had clung to the backs of her legs and buttocks. Chad thought about coming back to this idyllic forest tryst another time. This opened up a whole new perspective for him on the uses of the Memex.

Rosalina said good-bye and returned to her gathering, while Francisco took up the ax. Chad worked for another three hours before he was called back to the 21st century.

"What happened?" asked Brooke.

"Success beyond your wildest dreams," replied Chad.

She frowned at him, not understanding.

"I was in the forest cutting down a tree. I was Francisco. Rosalina came by and we had a nice chat. I picked up their names," Chad said. "Robert's theory is right."

Robert beamed.

Brooke dared to hope that Chad and Robert were right. If the Memex accessed ancestors and it was possible to predict not only which ancestor, but what moment in the ancestor's life you wished to experience, it would help immensely. She was ready to test the idea by finding out which of Damian's children was her ancestor.

She asked Robert to calculate the settings for Damian's child, which he did rapidly. Like Chad, she had given up on using any probes to monitor her physical state while on the machine, so she just settled herself into the familiar seat of the Memex and relaxed.

June 5, 1201. She walked along a marble-paved avenue on a gentle spring day. A shepherd drove his flock of sheep ahead of her, slowing traffic. She passed under the elegant arches of a tall stone aqueduct that spanned the full width of the street. Beside her walked Ariadne, Eulogia's mother. Brooke wore a long dress and her head and face were partially covered with a scarf.

"Julia, slow down," said Ariadne. "My old legs can't keep up with you."

"I'm sorry, grandmother, I didn't mean to leave you behind."

"It might be best if we rested a bit. This knee of mine is hurting."

"Grandmother, the market is not far from here. I could go the rest of the way on my own. Your friend, Kiria Branas, lives just around the corner. You could stay with her until I get back."

"Oh, no. That wouldn't be right. Who would watch out for you at the market?"

"I'll be fine. There will be lots of people around. No one will hurt me."

Ariadne hesitated. Brooke imagined that her sense of duty was warring with her painful knee. The knee won.

"Well, I guess just this one time. Let's see if Macrina is there." The two women turned a corner and moved down a narrow street. Ariadne knocked on Kiria Branas' door. An old woman answered and welcomed them.

After Ariadne was settled into her friend's home, Julia continued her trek. It was rare for a young woman to walk the streets of Constantinople alone and she got a few disapproving looks and lecherous glances. Brooke was worried about her. Fortunately, the market was only two blocks away.

The avenue spilled out into a large square covered with stalls and kiosks. Colorful awnings shaded the shoppers from the mid-day sun. Business was brisk and the narrow paths between vendors were clogged with people. Julia paused at the entrance and looked around expectantly. A voice from behind her said, "Looking for someone?" Julia turned and saw Origen, the son of the locksmith. He gazed at Julia from under long, dark eyelashes that any woman would have envied.

"There you are," she replied. "It worked perfectly. I suggested to grandmother that she stay with her friend and she leapt at the chance."

"See, listen to my advice and you'll go places," replied Origen. "Come, let's take a walk." Brooke was surprised to see Origen and felt oddly betrayed. She was used to seeing this world through Damian's eyes and knew that he would not want Julia consorting with Origen.

Julia and Origen began to stroll through the market. They passed stalls with leather goods and jewelry. The shelves were not as well supplied as they had been on Brooke's earlier visits. Trade into Constantinople must be pinched by the unrest in the countryside.

"Tell me more about your travels last year," said Julia. "I want to hear everything."

"It was quite eventful. We added a few stops to our usual itinerary, looking for new markets. There is a walled city not far to the east of here where we stopped for two weeks. My father and I went to the local church one Sabbath and listened patiently while the priest talked and talked. An old man next to me pointed out a cat sitting atop one of the side altars. The creature surely didn't belong there. He was coal black with white paws and he viewed the congregation with an air of feline superiority. The man said, 'It's the shade of Bast. A terrible omen. I'm going to leave.' We followed him out and were no sooner outside than the ground began to shake. People screamed in terror. My father was knocked to the ground right before a house collapsed in front of us."

"I would have been so scared," said Julia. "Was your father hurt?"

"He was fine. The streets were starting to fill up with people running out of their homes. Then we heard a low rumble and looked behind us. The dome of the church we had been in was collapsing! The wall on the south side bowed outward and huge slabs of stone fell into the church. I saw a young woman carrying her infant struck by one of the massive falling pieces. They both went down. Then the church collapsed with a deafening crash and a cloud of gray soot billowed down the street toward us. If we had stayed inside, we would have been dead. My father and I hurried to our wagon. Luckily, it hadn't been touched by the quake. We packed up and left the same night."

"Oh, you were so brave," said Julia. Brooke wondered what she could be thinking. In her opinion, Origen and his father should have stayed to rescue survivors. But they had apparently fled, perhaps thinking that they wouldn't make much money in a devastated town. There was nothing brave about that.

"I've never been farther away than my uncle's farm. I hope to see the world someday. Oh look! Isn't this a beautiful scarf?" Julia ran a striped silk scarf through her fingers.

"It would be beautiful if you wore it," replied Origen. "It would bring out the brown in your eyes and the gold in your hair. Of course, even the most humble clothing couldn't hide your loveliness." Julia blushed. Brooke wasn't impressed. No twenty-first century guy could have gotten away with a line like that.

"We have to find a few groceries. I can't return home with an empty shopping bag," said Julia. They selected fresh vegetables, olives, and figs and added flat bread and rolls. A sack of flour rounded out the purchases. Origen stopped at a flower vendor and selected a single perfect rose. He gave it to Julia saying, "A red rose to remember me by. When can we meet again?"

"Three days from now, I plan to go visit my friend, Helena, just after the sixth hour. I will slip out. I'm sure Helena will cover for me. Come and meet me at the back of their house." She told him where to find it.

The rest of the day was uneventful. Julia's grandmother was not at all suspicious.

"*So?*" *asked Robert.* "*Did it work?*" His broad face wore a look of concern and his eyes were open wide behind his dark-rimmed glasses.

"Yes. It worked perfectly. I was in the body of Julia, the daughter of Damian."

"Are you sure?"

"Of course I'm sure. She was with her grandmother, whom I recognized."

As Brooke stood up, a thought occurred to her. "I've been worried that Damian might die in the sack of Constantinople. But Julia *can't* die. I'm her descendent."

"Let's see, you were just there at June 5, 1201. It's still about three years before the crusaders take the city. Do you think she might have a baby before then?" asked Robert.

"Damn it, she could," said Brooke. "Her father wants to marry her off and she has a secret boyfriend that he doesn't approve of. It would be terrible if the only one of my ancestors who survives the assault is an infant. I wouldn't learn much history that way." Brooke's words sounded harsh to her own ear. She cared about the Balsamons and hoped that they survived the coming battle. She felt ashamed to put her need to learn ahead of their need to survive. On the other hand, why worry about something that had already happened?

"It doesn't seem likely to me that the whole family would die and the baby survive," said Robert. "It's possible, I suppose…"

"Well, we'll find out. She arranged a rendezvous with Origen in a few days and I'm going to be there."

⸙

The next day, Brooke was again poised for a trip to Constantinople. Chad was at the Memex console, ready as back-up. He had learned the algorithm from Robert for picking the right ancestor and had homed in on Julia three days later than the last visit.

June 8, 1201. Julia inserted a tiny embroidery stitch in the sleeve of a tunic. She sat in a small room that was unfamiliar to Brooke. From a framed landscape on the wall, a shepherd led his flock down a mountainside. In another painting, a solemn saint, crowned by a solid gold halo, raised his hand in blessing. The single window, framed by a maroon drape, admitted scant light. Across from her, a young woman with long black hair in washboard curls was perched on the edge of a bed. She, too, was absorbed in her sewing.

"Do you think it's time yet?" whispered Julia.

"I would wait a bit," replied the girl, who was probably Helena.

The two continued their work in silence. It was almost as if they wanted to avoid detection by being quiet. Brooke thought it may have the opposite effect. Someone might come to see if they were still there.

"I'm going now," said Julia.

"Let me check to see if mother is in the dining room," said Helena. She opened the door and looked around. "Go ahead."

Julia set her sewing aside and slipped into the next room. The living quarters were on the first floor, and the dining room door led to a courtyard. Julia opened the back door slowly and silently, and slid outside.

She made her way across the small courtyard and through the gate. At the end of the street, she met Origen, who was lounging in the doorway of a wine shop. His handsome face lit up in an irresistible smile when he saw her.

"I hope you didn't have to wait long," said Julia.

"You're worth waiting for," replied Origen. "Come, let's get away from here."

They walked through the streets, which were gray on this overcast day, the threat of rain palpable in the humid air. A priest and three nuns passed them and Brooke thought she saw disapproval in the eyes of one of the nuns. A hawker tried to sell them pastries sweetened with honey but they pressed on. The street opened into a small square with a weather-worn statue of Neptune in its center. Origen led Julia to the statue.

"Come, touch it. We'll see the future," he said. Julia was hesitant, but reluctantly reached out to the arm of the statue. Origen, resting his palm on Neptune's chest, closed his eyes and said, "I see us walking through a fabulous grove of pear trees. We are dressed in the finest silk and have fat purses. We pluck pears from the trees and enjoy their juicy sweetness." Julia giggled. She offered no prognostication of her own.

Beyond the square, the street looked less prosperous. Origen said, "This way. I know a short cut," and he led her into a narrow alley. This was a view of the city that Brooke had not seen before. Dilapidated houses crowded together in haphazard order. A pig snorted as it rooted in a malodorous trash heap. Barefoot and dirty children sat on the doorsteps or played in the street. The children looked at them warily, their eyes too old for their small bodies.

Julia asked, "Are we going far?"

"Don't worry, this is just a short detour, I'll protect you."

True to his word, they passed the slum quickly and came upon a prosperous avenue. Origen brought them to a small taverna and they went inside. In the dim interior, Brooke's eyes adjusted slowly. At this hour, the taverna was half empty. Most honest men were at work and the few clients included a group of soldiers and a sad-looking drunk. Origen and Julia sat at one end of a long table, he on one side and she on the other. Origen entertained Julia with stories about his visit to Tarsus. The owner came by and gave them plates of salt pork with garlic and a bottle of dry red wine.

"I'd like to show you something," said Origen. "See this coin?" He laid a small gold solidus on the table. "I can make it disappear." He slid the coin to the edge of the table and folded his fist around it. "So, it's in my hand, right?" he asked. Julia nodded. With a flourish, he uncurled his fingers to reveal his empty palm.

"Where did it go?" asked Julia. Origen opened his other hand and revealed the coin. "Oh," she said in surprise. "How did you do that?"

"I'll never tell," teased Origen. Brooke thought it was a pretty simple trick. After Origen slid the coin to the edge, he let it fall surreptitiously into his lap while making a big show of closing his fist around it. As Julia was watching the closed fist, he retrieved the coin from his lap with the other hand. She had to admit he had been pretty slick about it.

Origen was a girl's dream, with his lush black hair and even features. He had a boyish charm that was hard to resist. Brooke began to worry that Julia would fall in love with him. A relationship with Origen was sure to lead to tears.

The couple left the taverna and ambled down the street. Origen led Julia towards the city wall and stopped at a set of stairs leading to the battlements.

"Let's go up," he said to Julia.

"Are you sure? I don't think we're supposed to."

"I've got it covered. Come on, it'll be fun."

They climbed the steep stone steps and arrived on top of the wall. A soldier lounged a dozen yards away.

"Ho, Origen," said the soldier.

"Vincentius, how are things?"

Origen approached Vincentius and passed him a small coin.

"We just want to enjoy the sights," he said. "We won't be long."

Brooke had to admit the view was breathtaking. The sky had partially cleared, and the sun poked through here and there. She could see the blue expanse of the Golden Horn below her, and the verdant countryside beyond it. The harbor was dotted with small boats, their white sails bowing out in the wind. A trireme made its way around the point, the three rows of oars dipping into the water with perfect synchrony, like a giant mechanical centipede. Each oar left a tiny swirling wake behind it, and a line of foamy white streaked out behind the vessel.

Looking into the city, they caught site of a lush garden, hidden behind a high stone wall. It must belong to one of the elite nobility who ruled the empire. Two women, sitting on a stone bench in an open part of the garden, laughed together. Before them walked a peacock, with his multicolored tail flared out, followed by his harem of peahens.

"Oh, I've never seen a bird like that before," said Julia.

"The rich have some amazing things," replied Origen. "I'm going to have a garden like that one day. I have a plan."

"What plan?"

"I'll tell you about it in time. It's still forming in my head."

Julia set her hands upon the warm stone ledge. "It's so beautiful. Thanks for bringing me here."

"If you spend more time with me, I can show you many things," said Origen. "I know that you would enjoy traveling. Come with me and my father when we leave in August and I will show you the world." Alarm bells went off in Brooke's head. What if Julia ran away with Origen? Maybe that's how she escaped the sack of Constantinople.

"I couldn't," said Julia.

"Think about it," said Origen. "You would love it."

When Brooke returned to the present, she was in a bad mood. Julia was so naive she just might fall for Origen. Then where would Brooke be? Brooke was tempted to jump ahead in time to see what happened, but that would be a little like jumping ahead in a book to see how it ended. The idea offended her. No, she had come this far, she would stay the course.

—<small>◦◦◦</small>—

Brooke wondered what Damian was doing while Julia was sneaking out to see her boyfriend. She was disappointed in him for not keeping a closer eye on his daughter. She decided to skip a couple of weeks ahead in time and return to him.

June 25, 1201. Damian and Basil were working in the courtyard behind the workshop. The skies were cloudy and the air smelled of rain. A bunch of violets overflowing the edges of their pot looked like they could use a drink. A vegetable patch held onions, leeks, kohlrabi, and some greens that Brooke could not identify.

Damian was holding a wooden piece in his hand. "And now we need to drill a hole here in the head of the bellows," he said to Basil. He picked up a hand drill and started to rotate it. Curls of wood spun out of the hole as the blade bit.

"So, how are things going with Master Dalassenos? asked Damian.

"It's fine," replied Basil.

"What are you reading?"

"Nothing much."

"You must be reading something. I pay the schoolmaster a tidy sum to educate you." Damian finished drilling the hole and said, "Now get me that ram's skin."

Basil unhooked the skin from a stretcher and gave it to his father. "It's Virgil."

"I think Virgil is better than Cicero," said Damian. "I know Cicero's Latin is supposed to be superb, but I just didn't like him."

"Uh-huh," said Basil.

Basil had grown into a compact, short young man. The scar on his cheek had faded, but would always be with him.

Damian continued to assemble the bellows, joining two wooden pieces together and preparing to stitch two others to the skin. A bell rang in the workshop, and Damian left the courtyard, followed by Basil.

The unwelcome figure of Lord Prepundolus stood before the counter. This time, he was not alone. The shorter of the two men with him stood six feet tall and was built like a barrel, solid and broad. The taller one towered over Damian by a full head and a half. His ears struck out straight from his head, which sat on a thick neck, and his nose had a pronounced hook. But the most unusual feature of the two was their beardless faces, the only that Brooke had seen in all her visits to the city. After a moment's thought, it struck her. They were eunuchs. The cruel practice of castrating boys had largely died out in medieval Constantinople, but a few nobles still kept eunuchs.

"Goldsmith, I have come for my earrings," said Lord Prepundolus.

"It would be my pleasure to deliver them to you," said Damian.

The nobleman opened his purse and counted out six coins. Damian glanced at them and then looked directly in his face.

"What about the rest?" he asked.

"This is enough."

Damian pulled out an account book and began to leaf through it. "Let me show you what we agreed on," he said.

"Look, I don't care what it says in your book. This is what I intend to pay and this is what you will accept."

"I couldn't do that. It's much too little." He set down the account book.

The air of menace in the room was palpable. Brooke was torn between annoyance that Damian was so stubborn and respect for his willingness to stand up to pressure.

"No cursed merchant is going to stand in my way. Your prices are exorbitant. You won't get away with this. Are you sure you want to cross me on this?"

Damian glanced at the two eunuchs, who were watching him carefully. At that moment, Father Scholasticus entered the workshop.

"Good afternoon," he said. All eyes swung to him.

"A million welcomes," said Damian. "We were just finishing up our business here, Father. We won't keep you waiting long."

Prepundolus looked from Damian to Scholasticus and back to Damian again.

"I'll be back," he said in a cold voice, and he and his servants left the workshop. Brooke inwardly relaxed as the crisis passed. Previously, Prepundolus had threatened Damian with his ecclesiastical connections. Brooke wondered if he had been bluffing.

"What did you do to him?" asked Scholasticus.

"Ah, he doesn't want to pay his bill. It's an old story," replied Damian.

"I've heard about him. That's Prepundolus, isn't it?" Damian nodded. "A bad sort. You would be best off not doing business with him."

"I wish I had known that earlier," said Damian. "But I'm afraid I'm involved now."

Brooke was transported to the lab at that moment. These transitions were often abrupt and she never knew exactly when they would take place. She was disappointed that she had not seen Julia. But there was always tomorrow.

⸺∞⸺

Chad stood at the back of the dojo, posture erect, eyes hard, mastering the urge to fidget and pace. Sensei Nakamura was talking with a few black belts and had not yet assembled the students. Sensei was tall, with thick black hair and piercing eyes. The black belt that he wore around his waist was so worn with age and use that it was almost white. Today Chad would take the black belt exam, and he wished Sensei would just get on with it.

"Line up," ordered Sensei, and the brown belts arranged themselves in three neat rows at the front of the dojo. Chad was in the second row. He took comfort from the familiar shrine at the front of the class. A banner with the dojo's motto in Japanese hung above a photograph of Shihan Tanaka, the founder of the style of karate that Chad practiced. Three samurai swords mounted in a black lacquered holder completed the tableau.

The class bowed to the shrine, to the instructor, and to their fellow students. Black belts stood on all sides as observers. The exam began with each student, in turn, coming to the front and giving a three minute talk on some aspect of karate. For Chad, this was the easy part. He knew that some of his fellow martial artists were more afraid of public speaking than of any other part of the exam, but he had a lot of experience with presentations and excelled at them.

After the first two talks, Chad began to zone out, thoughts of Brooke surfacing from some hidden corner of his mind. He shunted them aside and tried to concentrate on the drone of the current speaker. Karate usually sent him into a state of flow, where stray thoughts never intruded. He had thrown himself into the sport with great fervor in order to escape from his painful longing for her.

After the talks, the floor exercises began. Sensei marched the class up and down the dojo, ordering punch and kick combinations. It was late August and the air was sweltering and heavy with unshed rain. The dojo was not air conditioned. An hour into the exam, Chad's gi was plastered to his back with sweat. His face was red and sweat dripped from the tip of his nose.

"Stepping forward in zenkutsu dachi, right chudan zuki, left chudan zuki, right mawashi geri. Hai," barked Sensei. The class stepped forward and executed two middle punches followed by a roundhouse kick. Chad was panting with exertion and having trouble processing the Japanese instructions. He saw a student to his left collapse on the floor. Everyone stayed motionless in position while a black belt tended to the fallen student, giving him water and leading him off the floor. Chad was glad for the temporary respite, and then felt ashamed of benefiting from his fellow student's distress.

After the floor exercises came the kata—long sequences of memorized moves against imaginary assailants. As he whirled, punched, and kicked his way through twelve kata, Chad got his second wind. He knew his kata cold and was enjoying showing off his skill. The black belts lounged on the edges of the class, looking bored. Finally, the kata were done and Sensei ordered the class to a relaxed position. Chad was relieved that this part was over. Abruptly, Sensei called for 50 pushups. Chad dropped to the floor and dug deep. After 45 pushups, his muscles began to tremble. He powered on, heedless of the pain, and made it to 48. A brief rest, and he attempted the 49th, almost falling.

A black belt yelled "Go, Chad, you've got this." Chad completed the last pushup and rose to his feet, exhausted.

Sensei said, "Ten minute break, drink water, then put your gear on."

The toughest part of the exam was yet to come—sparring against the black belts. Chad gulped half of the gallon bottle of water he had brought with him. He put on headgear, a mouthpiece, and padded gear for his hands and feet. The student who had collapsed earlier had recovered and rejoined the class in the middle of the kata.

Sensei approached and said, "Remember, this is training. Don't hurt anyone." Surprised at these words, Chad looked again at the black belts preparing to spar with him and saw some who were shorter, lighter, and less accomplished. In addition, a third were women and one was a twelve year old boy. Sensei was telling them not to go crazy. It calmed Chad.

Chad had to spar with fifteen different black belts in two minute long matches. The black belts were fresh and outnumbered the brown belts three-to-one. By design, it wasn't a fair fight. Chad readied himself for his first match. He bowed to George Hopper, a gangly young man who had become a black belt just three months earlier.

George came in with a lot of energy, jabbing left and right. Chad easily parried the blows and returned a front kick. The two danced lightly on the balls of their feet, trading offensive and defensive moves. They were evenly matched, and the sparring went smoothly. The bell rang for the next bout before Chad expected it.

The next five bouts were also uneventful, although Chad was beginning to tire. He had blocked one kick to his head on the knife-edge of his hand and had somehow sprained it. He was relying on his left hand and feet as weapons.

"Next bout, brown belts line up against each other," said Sensei.

This was unexpected, but Sensei was known for surprises. Chad found himself across from Zack Mitchell, a strong young man with a red face and desperate eyes. When the bell rang, Zack came at him and Chad parried. Chad attacked with a feint to the left followed by a kick from the right. The ball of his foot lightly touched the front of Zack's gi. Zack scowled and retreated. Ten seconds later, Zack got through Chad's defense with a side kick that hammered into Chad's ribs, knocking him backwards. Chad waited until Zack thrust forward, then danced to the side and caught the edge of Zack's heel with the bottom of his foot. Chad simultaneously pushed Zack's chest backward with the side of his arm and swept his front foot forward, and Zack crashed to the floor.

"Fuck," muttered Zack.

Chad stepped back while his opponent recovered. Sensei approached them but said nothing. The bout was over before they could recommence.

Chad moved through the next seven bouts in a haze. His right hand throbbed and his ribs hurt, but he pushed the pain away and continued fighting. On the last bout, he was up against an eighteen year old boy who had placed fourth in the world in his age group at last year's international karate championship. He was tired beyond belief and could hardly raise his arms to block the attacks. The champion let him off easy, adjusting his play to Chad's current skill level and evident exhaustion.

Chad heard the last bell with immense relief. The brown belts lined up once more at the front of the dojo, three hours after the exam had begun. Sensei invited them to sit and gave one of his homilies on the warrior spirit. Chad listened gratefully. He thought about how much easier it would be to listen to his professors lecture, if only he had exercised vigorously first. After the talk, Sensei began calling up the students one by one. At his name, Chad scrambled to his feet and approached Sensei. He removed his brown belt, and Sensei tied a stiff new black belt around Chad's waist. The class clapped and Chad moved down the receiving line of black belts, shaking each hand in turn. Each firm grasp shot pain into his injured hand, but he didn't care. He took his place at the end of the line, feeling elated.

The ceremony proceeded until Zack was the only student left sitting on the floor. Sensei looked him in the eye and turned away. The black belts began to disperse. The exam was over and Zack had failed. It took Zack a moment to interpret what had happened to him. Once he did, he rose and left the floor quickly. Chad guessed it was the swearing. He was enormously grateful that such public humiliation had not happened to him.

After the exam, Chad drove to the lab. He had promised Brooke that he would run the machine for her, since Robert was not available. As weary and battered as he was, he felt the warmth of a dream realized and the afterglow of intense exercise. He had never experienced such euphoria before in his life, and he wanted to share that feeling with Brooke. He rehearsed in his mind some casual ways of announcing his achievement, and daydreamed about her delighted response.

He got to the lab twenty minutes early. Since he had extra time, he decided to check the mice. He called up the duty roster to see where they were in the rotation, and moved to group B. The first cage needed cleaning and he ran through the routine mechanically. He progressed to the second cage and the one after that, working his way to the last cage in B Group.

Mouse 116 was dead.

X

TEST RESULTS

Brooke sat stiffly in the uncomfortable wooden chair. Chad and Robert, who were seated next to her in Prof. Hunter's office, looked as unhappy as she was. She had been dreading this meeting. She had hardly slept for the past two nights, and was only on her feet because of a massive caffeine boost. When they had reported the dead mouse to the professor, Hunter had asked a colleague to perform an autopsy. Brooke desperately needed to know and equally desperately didn't want to know.

"Prof. Antipov told me the results of the autopsy late yesterday. The mouse died of a brain tumor," said Hunter.

The reaction of the students was palpable. Everyone moved and shifted as if they had heard of a major catastrophe. Robert pushed his glasses higher on his nose and squirmed in his chair. Chad sat up straight and his mouth fell open. Brooke could not avoid a look of horror on her face.

"What's the matter?" said Hunter. "Brooke, you look pasty white. Do you feel sick? Are you going to pass out?" Brooke felt tears prick at the edges of her eyes, but she used all her willpower to hold them back.

Hunter looked them over, waiting for someone to say something. Robert lowered his eyes at her scrutiny and Chad ran his fingers through his hair.

"There's something you're not telling me," said Hunter with a suspicious look in her eye. "Out with it. I will learn sooner or later. Have other mice died?"

"No," said Chad. "The other mice are fine."

"Then what are you keeping from me?" pressed Hunter.

After a pause Chad said, "I've been testing myself on the Memex."

"You've been doing what?" said Hunter. Anger burned in her eyes as she stared at Chad. He dropped his gaze. "Are you out of your mind? You know the Review Board did not authorize testing. They had their reasons."

Hunter's voice was low and dangerous, perfectly controlled but oozing menace.

Brooke had never liked her thesis adviser, but they had got along. Now, at this moment, Brooke hated her. Just a few months ago, Hunter was denigrating the Review Board's decision. Now she was supporting it in a stunning display of hypocrisy. Brooke's opinion of Hunter would be forevermore damaged.

"I've been testing myself on the Memex, too," she said.

Hunter looked at her in alarm. "What about you?" she said to Robert. He shook his head rapidly in negation. Hunter rose from her chair and paced back and forth in the small space available in her office. She turned and faced them, fury in her eyes.

"I can't believe you would betray my trust like this. Unauthorized use of the machine—reckless experimentation—foolish secrecy. I have imbeciles for graduate students." Hunter towered over them.

"You have all lied to me. Do you know what this means? How can I trust you in the future? What's next—falsifying lab results? I'm not sure I even want to do research with you three any more. I supported each one of you, getting you grants and assistantships. I believed in you." Brooke winced at the use of the past tense.

"I've never had such treacherous students in my entire life. And now we have a crisis—the dead mouse. Normally, it wouldn't be a big deal to lose just one mouse, but the manner of death is significant. Very few cancerous tumors start in the brain. Most brain tumors originate from cancer that has spread from other parts of the body, but this mouse had only a brain tumor—no other organs were involved. This points to the Memex as the likely cause of death."

Brooke became paler still as she absorbed the professor's words. "Now tell me some good news," continued Hunter. "How much time have you been exposed? Chad, you first?"

"Uh, I don't remember exactly. I would have to look it up."

"Once, twice?—out with it."

"I'm afraid it was more like seven or eight times."

Hunter shook her head as if she pitied Chad. "And you, Brooke?"

Brooke bit her lower lip. She could feel everyone in the room staring at her. "I've spent a lot of time on the Memex—a lot more than Chad."

The professor snorted in disgust and turned away. She gazed out the window for a long time, leaving the students to stew in their fears. Her thin form was silhouetted against the bright summer day. Brooke wondered if she was going to be kicked out of school after all. It seemed like the least of her worries.

"This is what we'll do," said Hunter. "I'll call Dr. Fischer in the Student Health Center and ask him to order MRI scans of your heads. Chad and Brooke will go see him right away. When we get the results, we'll go from there."

She sat down again and said, "This was really a foolish stunt. It could set the whole program back." Anger bubbled up in Brooke. Didn't the professor care about them at all? Was the stupid research program more important than Brooke's life?

"On the contrary," said Chad. "We made a lot of progress." Brooke couldn't believe he was talking so calmly.

Hunter arched her eyebrow and narrowed her eyes. "What did you learn?" she asked.

Brooke broke in. "When we're on the machine, we don't remember our own lives, we remember the lives of our distant ancestors. It's like being in someone else's body and seeing what they see and feeling what they feel. It's a form of time travel."

"Time travel..." Hunter's voice dripped with sarcasm.

"Brooke is right," said Chad. "Robert worked out a way to set the signal to a particular ancestor. I've visited several of my ancestors, including a many-times-great grandmother who is documented in my family tree. One minute on the Memex is like five hours in the past. It's an unbelievable experience."

Brooke filled Hunter in on her excursions to Constantinople. She described how she was hoping to witness the sack of the city during the Fourth Crusade and what a difference that could make to historians.

Hunter glanced at her watch. She said, "I have to go. My class starts in five minutes. In the meantime, no more human testing. Do you hear me? But do continue with the mice." As if they were going to do any more human testing, thought Brooke darkly.

Chad and Robert left first, and Brooke started to follow them.

The professor called her name and Brooke turned, wondering what extra torment she might dole out.

Hunter looked straight into her eyes. "I didn't know you had it in you," she said in grudging admiration. Brooke took that as a compliment, all the sweeter for being so rare. She left with a smile on her face.

———✲———

Brooke stared at a coffee stain on the floor. This lab was a dump. Somehow it hadn't bothered her much in the past when she was full of hope and excited about the research. But today, every dust bunny, every cobweb, every window pane covered with grime, offended her. Her nose wrinkled up at the acrid smell of rodents. Robert was standing in front of the racks of cages that covered one wall. He was feeding, cleaning, and testing the mice. He had stepped up his contribution to the care of the mice given the stress that Brooke and Chad were under. Brooke had planned to work today, but she just didn't have the will to do it.

"I think the brain tumor is a coincidence," said Robert. "You're going to be fine."

"Oh Robert, how can it be a coincidence? We've been zapping their brains and they get a brain tumor. What could be more plain?"

"That's not logical and you know it. If five mice had brain tumors, you would have a point. But it's only the one mouse. Even if it were more mice, it could be something else, a genetic flaw or something in their food that caused the tumors. And even if the Memex causes tumors in mice, it might not cause them in humans." Brooke wanted to believe him.

"Every morning since the meeting I've been checking the mice, and they're all fine," continued Robert. "Besides, we're zapping them for much longer than we put you and Chad under, both in single tests and cumulatively over the last year. It may be that there is a threshold of exposure that needs to be reached before the effects set in."

Brooke hoped he was right. It was easier to believe that than the alternative.

"I'm having a hard time with this. I'm really scared. I'm too young to die. I want to fall in love, get married, raise a family, and make great scientific discoveries. If I die now, I won't do any of that."

"You're not going to die," soothed Robert.

"In the last few days, I've been noticing old people with white hair and envying them. They got to see their children grow up and they get to play with their grandchildren. I'm not sure that will ever happen to me."

"Look," said Robert, "Do you have any headaches?"

"No."

"See. You're fine. If you had a brain tumor, you would have headaches." He had a point. "When are you going for the MRI?"

"Tomorrow." Brooke had waited five long days for the appointment, and she knew it would be several more before she got the results. It felt cruel of them to make her wait like this. They could see her right away, do the test, and have the results, all in a few hours if they wanted to. But instead, she had to suffer in an agony of suspense.

"Just take it step by step. It's easier that way."

"Oh Robert, I'm sorry I dragged you into this. I should never have tested the Memex on myself."

"On the contrary, I helped you because you inspired me. You said that there had been enough testing, and I agreed. You were very brave to be the first person to try it. I admire you for that."

Brooke smiled for the first time in days. "You're such a good friend. I would never be able to get through this without good friends."

⸺ ❧ ⸺

Brooke had stripped to the waist and was struggling into the hospital gown. The unfamiliar tie was annoying. Feeling vulnerable, she stepped out of the tiny changing booth and sat in the small inner waiting room. A newscaster droned on about a flood in Arkansas from a monitor set high on the wall. Brooke's neck hurt from watching it, but she wanted the distraction.

A nurse came for Brooke and led her to the imaging room. The space was dominated by an MRI machine, a massive hollow tube with thick walls. A padded gurney extended from the monster machine like a hungry tongue. Brooke was surprised to see how many technicians and nurses were in the room, slaves to the demanding beast.

"Please take off all jewelry and set it in this bin," the nurse said. Brooke removed ten rings from her fingers, one by one, and unhooked the earrings from her ears. It felt like she was being stripped of her last line of defense.

"Put these earplugs in, the machine is rather noisy," the nurse said. Great, thought Brooke. A noisy monster. The nurse clipped a small microphone onto the front of Brooke's gown. "We will want to communicate with you while you're in the machine. You'll be fine. Don't worry." These words raised Brooke's anxiety level a notch.

Brooke lay on the padded table, head toward the machine, and felt it slowly draw her into the hole. The walls were close, too close. When the table stopped, she saw a small screen above her face. It was hooked to a camera that gave her a view out the end of the tube. Doctors and nurses moved about, preparing for the test. The screen was a welcome claustrophobia-fighting enhancement.

"How are you doing in there? Are you OK?" asked a technician.

"I'm fine," said Brooke, although perhaps that was an exaggeration. "I haven't panicked yet," might have been more accurate.

"Good. We're going to start now. Hold very still. There will be a lot of noise."

"Rat tat tat tat tat," came in a burst of staccato pulses that arced around her head. They were loud despite the earplugs. Brooke was used to the sound of magnetic clacking from using the Memex, but the Memex was a pipsqueak compared to this behemoth. A pause. Another burst of "rat tat

tat tat tat." Brooke wanted to move, but forced herself to stay still. Her anxiety was rising. She felt a desperate desire to bend her knees, but knew she could not. It was like being upside down in a kayak, and needing to keep your legs straight in order to jackknife out. Better not think about escaping from a kayak just now. She could breathe. All was well. She gazed at the screen and watched the goings-on in the room, deliberately pretending that they were fascinating. She tried to ignore the continuing racket from the machine.

"How are you doing?" asked the nurse.

"I'm good," replied Brooke.

"Excellent. You're half done," said the cheery voice.

Only half, thought Brooke. She wasn't sure she could take any more. But the logical part of her brain knew how important this test was. If she quit now, she would just have to do the test all over again. No way. If she didn't take the test, she would worry endlessly about a tumor growing in her brain. She had to make it through. Another round of "rat tat tat tat tat" assaulted her. She decided to think of lying on the deck of a yacht, warming herself in the healing rays of the sun. In her vision, the sky and sea were achingly blue and calm. The "rat tat tat tat tat" made it hard for her to keep her focus, but she persevered.

"OK, all done," said the nurse.

Brooke was relieved. They couldn't get her out of there fast enough.

Chad gazed into the shallow pool and followed the golden koi's slow, lazy glide. The fish lived in such a small and protected world, his main problem was probably boredom. The pool was broken up by elegant rock formations, but they were more for the viewer than for the inhabitant. Chad tried to relax the tense muscles in his upper back. He couldn't bear the thought of Brooke with a brain tumor. Before the mouse died, he had tried to put her out of his mind and occasionally succeeded. But now, little icy thoughts of her sick, of her dying, stabbed him at all times of the day, a torment that he could not avoid. He glanced out the window anxiously, and seeing no one, returned to his examination of the fish pond.

A voice, one he knew well, said, "I hope I didn't keep you waiting. It's hard to find a parking place now that classes are in session."

Chad turned toward Brooke, searching her face for the answer to his question, without success. "No problem. I just got here."

A waiter showed them to their table in a warmly-lit corner of the restaurant. Chad removed his Stetson and settled into his place, fidgeting with the chopsticks and napkins. Brooke ordered immediately, but Chad spent a fair chunk of time perusing the eight page menu before deciding on shrimp tempura.

After the waiter had gone, Chad looked into Brooke's eyes.

"So what did the doctor say?" he asked.

She smiled. "I'm completely normal. What about you?"

"I'm OK too." He relaxed for the first time in days, settling down into his seat in relief. When he had gotten the good news from his physician, he had dared to hope that Brooke would be all right as well, but she had spent more time on the Memex than he had.

"I have to admit I was scared," said Brooke. "I can't believe I did that. And I dragged you into it, too." She covered his hand with hers. "I'm so glad that you didn't get hurt." Her touch was warm and it sent all his nerves jangling, but the contact was all too brief. He noticed that she had done something with her hair. It looked great, but Chad couldn't figure out why.

"Finding that mouse was a real shock," he said. "I was on top of the world that night, and then to come upon that little critter—it was like plunging into ice water. I completely froze up."

"That was the day you took the black belt exam, wasn't it?" asked Brooke. "How did the exam go?"

"I passed," said Chad with a smile. "But, I'll tell you, I didn't know what I was getting into. This week, I went to two black belt classes. I thought it would help me take my mind off things. When somebody is trying to kick you in the head, you don't think much about anything else. The black belt exam was hard, but that was only a hint of what black belt classes are like. Tying on my new belt is an act of courage each and every time."

"Sounds like you're enjoying it," said Brooke.

He smiled. The waiter brought their order, laying a spider crab roll with a selection of sushi a la carte in front of Brooke and the golden crispy shrimp tempura in front of Chad. She delicately lifted a single slice of fresh ginger with her chopsticks and consumed it as a prelude to her meal.

"Here's a toast to the bravest grad student in Cognitive Science," said Chad as he lifted his glass of saki.

"Here's to the two bravest grad students," replied Brooke as she raised her glass. They clicked glasses and took long drinks.

"This whole experience has inspired me to pick up painting again," said Brooke. "Life is a gift and I want to immerse myself in the beauty of it. I started a seascape, a lone galleon in a choppy sea with the sun just breaking through the clouds. It's all done in blue, black, and white."

"Sounds pretty," said Chad.

"I used to be a fussy painter," said Brooke. "I wanted to get the color just right and every line just so. Then I took a class at a local art store where we did a still life from start to finish in under two hours. It really liberated me. To keep up with the teacher, I had to loosen up and stop trying for realism and perfection."

"Another thing I like to do is travel," continued Brooke. "I'm going to miss all these visits to Constantinople. You know, the Memex could be great for tourists. If it turns out to be safe, people would pay a lot of money to visit exciting places in the past. Maybe watch the building of the pyramids, for example."

"Yeah, if they're lucky enough to have an overseer as an ancestor," replied Chad. "They won't like it if they have to haul the stones themselves."

"Seriously, these visits have been mostly fun. For me, it's an escape from the humdrum routine of research. It's like reading a novel or watching a movie, only a whole lot better."

"I spent so much time learning Greek," continued Brooke. "Lately, I've been practicing reading the language. It's weird to sound out words with Greek letters. I know all the names of the letters, of course, from all these years of studying science, and I understand spoken Greek. It's actually not a big step to reading. I'm pretty slow, though."

"Well, you probably won't need that now that the testing is over," said Chad.

Brooke didn't say anything, and Chad grew alarmed.

"You aren't going to use the machine again, are you?" asked Chad.

"I guess not," said Brooke unconvincingly. "I've been trying to decide."

"Well, it's ridiculous to even think about it," said Chad. He instantly regretted saying that. It was sure to put her back up.

She gazed at him coolly, all the earlier warmth vanishing. "Rationally, I have nothing to fear. There was not even a tiny tumor on the MRI. Tumors don't just spring to full size in a few days—they grow slowly. If I'm clean now with all the exposure I've had, I should be fine."

"You don't know when one might start. There could be a threshold of exposure beyond which the tumor begins to form. You can't have MRIs every day to see how you're doing. Suppose you did find a small tumor—would you want brain surgery?"

"All this drama over one dead mouse. I don't think the Memex has anything to do with the mouse's death. After all, Transcranial Magnetic Stimulation is used for other purposes without anybody getting hurt. Even MRIs expose the brain to magnetic fields. I, for one, am not jumping to any conclusions."

"You're deluding yourself."

"You're overreacting."

They finished the meal in silence and Brooke signaled for the check. When the waiter arrived, Chad offered to pay the bill, but Brooke insisted on paying her share. Chad felt rebuffed.

Monday morning at 9 AM was a terrible time for a meeting, but Hunter was a busy woman and this was their only opportunity. Brooke, Robert, and Chad were sitting on the floor outside Hunter's office. It was already 9:20 and Brooke's patience was waning. Robert sat with his back against the wall and his knees drawn up to his chest. His head nodded forward from time to time.

"Looks like you had a rough night," said Chad.

"Emily kept waking up and crying. She slept through the night last month. I don't know what's happening now." He sighed.

At that moment, the door opened and Hunter appeared.

"Come on in," she said.

The students filed into the office and looked for seats. A stack of papers rested on one of the three chairs.

"Can I move this?" asked Chad.

"Let me have it." The professor took the pile and set it on the floor.

"I'm glad to hear that you're both all right," said Hunter. "You gave us quite a scare." She pulled out a pad of paper and prepared to make notes.

"Now then, I wanted to talk to you today about the plan going forward," she said. "We're going to have to adjust our test protocol in light of the incident. I've been thinking that we should increase the exposure time for the remaining mice and see what happens."

"We could do that," said Brooke, "but it might backfire. When I use the machine, I sometimes get disoriented by the time difference between the real world and the memory state. A few minutes of real time becomes a whole day in the past. This gives me a sort of mem lag, similar to jet lag. It's not as bad as jet lag, but it still can be hard to take."

"If we expose the mice too long, they might have the mouse equivalent of a nervous breakdown," said Chad. "They could get depressed, not want to socialize with their cage mates, something like that."

"Well, we don't have a lot of other options," said Hunter. "I don't have any money to buy more mice. We'll have to make do with the ones we have. Besides, have you seen any signs of depression in the mice?"

"No," replied Chad.

"How are the mice doing overall? Do any of them look like they might die on us?"

"The mice are all fine," said Brooke. "It's been two weeks since mouse 116 died, and there are no other problems. Maybe it was just a coincidence," said Brooke.

"You could be right," agreed Hunter.

"I doubt it," interjected Robert. "I think the mouse was killed by the Memex."

"That's not what you said before," challenged Brooke. "You told me it was a coincidence."

"Well, I just wanted to make you feel better," said Robert. He looked miserable.

"And what about all your other arguments? It could be something in their food, a genetic flaw, some random event. Don't you believe that either?" Brooke continued.

"I just think we need more time to see what happens to the mice," cut in Chad. "Clearly, this death should give us pause."

"When you think about it, we have a total of 620 mice," said Brooke. "The chances of just one dying are pretty large. Mice only live about two years."

The professor looked from one to the other speculatively. Brooke wondered which side of the argument she would come down on. Brooke decided to go bold.

"I want to continue using the machine," she said.

"No," said Robert, "that would be a terrible idea."

"I agree," said Chad. "We need to wait before anybody else is exposed to the Memex."

They all looked at Prof. Hunter who gazed back at them impassively. Finally, she said, "If you want to continue testing, Brooke, that's up to you. I can't sanction it, given the circumstances. I also can't stop you, unless I kick you out of the program. My advice, and it's only advice, is that you wait. On the other hand, you have a good argument for ignoring the one data point—the dead mouse. After all, people always throw out the outliers."

"Not when the outlier might kill you," said Chad in a growl. Hunter scowled at him.

"Look Brooke," said Hunter, "if you do decide to test again, I would insist that you get another brain scan in three months."

Brooke thought about the difficult test. Maybe it would be easier the second time.

"All right," she said. "It's a deal."

XI

INTIMIDATION

It was a tense group that gathered in the Memex lab that Tuesday afternoon in September. Robert was perched stiffly in front of the computer. Chad was huddled at a desk with his arms crossed and his hat pulled down to obscure his eyes. Brooke lay on the tilted chair, ready for the Memex to activate. Hunter stood behind Robert, with her tall, lean form hunched over him and her palm flat on the desk near his. Robert had said he did not want to be the one to "push the button," and he was showing Hunter how the machine should be set up. He expected her to make the final click.

"All you have to do is click this link and it will start," said Robert.

"I see," said Hunter, but she didn't move to take the controls. "I could start it this time, but do you really expect me to come to the lab every day to do this? It's your job, not mine."

Robert was silent. He pushed his glasses up his nose. Hunter moved her lips closer to his ear.

"Brooke is willing to do this of her own volition," she said. "We are merely helping her. There's no reason you can't do this, Robert. I'll take responsibility." She could ruin him. She could delay his degree, stop his funding, or even fail him in his candidacy exam. Robert caved.

"I guess so," he mumbled as he activated the machine.

July 1, 1201. Julia and Origen were wandering through the market. They stopped at a stall where eight varieties of dates were displayed in open bins.

"You'll love this one," said Origen, selecting a fat, reddish-brown date and holding it to her mouth. Julia giggled and took a bite. She nodded approvingly. They sampled two other specimens and paid the vendor.

"I have something else I want to show you," said Origen. "Come with me." He led her through the narrow aisles of the bazaar, past shops selling leather goods, silks, spices, foodstuffs, artwork, and shoes. Striped canopies covered the walkway in places to shield shoppers from the fierce noon sun. They came to a small store selling baskets, where an elderly man with a deeply wrinkled face sat weaving straw, twining together individual blades that stuck out from the edge of a half finished bowl.

"We would like to see the dwarf in your back room," said Origen. The shopkeeper held out his hand and received the small coin that Origen offered. Origen led Julia behind a drape into a little room filled with baskets of all sizes, the smell of hemp infusing the air. It took a while for Brooke's eyes to adjust to the dim light. A man sat on a stool next to a pile of straw, weaving. He rose to greet them with a tight smile. He was no more than three feet tall and chunky in the way that little people often were, with short stubby legs, and a long torso.

"Oh," said Julia. "I've never met a dwarf before." The dwarf kept smiling rigidly and Brooke felt compassion for his plight.

"It is my pleasure to make the acquaintance of so fine a lady as yourself," said the dwarf. Julia couldn't seem to find anything else to say.

"Well, we'd best be going," said Origen. At the next stall, Origen purchased two ripe pears and suggested that they eat them while sitting in the front of his wagon.

"What about your father?" asked Julia.

"He's taking the day off. He went with a friend to a taverna and I don't expect him back till the tenth hour." They arrived at the wagon, climbed up, and settled on the bench. Brooke watched the people go by. She spied a man and woman making slow progress as they shepherded four small children along and a collegiatus, an officer of the peace, eying some urchins.

"It would be better if we go inside the wagon," said Origen. "You don't want anyone to recognize you."

Julia agreed and they pulled aside the flap to the back of the wagon. Through the dimness Brooke could make out two narrow beds, one on either side, a basin, and a low chest. The rear wall held crates filled with trade merchandize. Origen lit a candle and closed the shutters of a small window in the rear of the wagon. The walls held a variety of tools, pots and pans, and clothing hung on pegs. Brooke hoped that Julia would think about where she would sleep if she chose to run away with Origen.

Julia settled on one bed and Origen sat facing her.

"You have such beautiful blond hair," said Origen. "In all my travels, I have never seen a woman more attractive."

"Oh, you flatter me," responded Julia. "You must have seen many beautiful women."

"None like you," said Origen. "I have never met anyone like you." He rose and sat next to her. "And your mouth is so delicate and fine, like an angel's." He played with a strand of her hair, running it through his fingers. "Since I met you last summer, I have thought of you every day."

He took her face in his hands and kissed her, a long lingering kiss that went on and on. Julia ran her fingers through his hair. Origen slid his tongue between her lips and she opened her mouth in welcome. They kissed passionately for several minutes. Brooke thought they would never come up for air. Origen's beard was starting to irritate her skin, but Julia didn't seem to mind. She was transported by love.

Origen raised his hand to Julia's breast and cupped it in his hand. Brooke felt the thrill pass through Julia's body. Then Origen moved his hand below her waist, and Julia stiffened. She took hold of the hand and moved it back to her breast. Origen made a second attempt and Julia again rebuffed him.

He pulled away. She opened her eyes wide and said, "Don't stop."

"It's clear that you don't care for me," he said.

"That's not true, it's just…," she replied.

"Ours is a true love, we were meant to be together. If you loved me, you would let me touch you."

"Origen, I do love you. I really do. But why can't we just kiss?"

"That's not what lovers do, my darling," said Origen. "Let me show you." He moved close to her again and drew her to her feet. Holding her in a firm embrace, he kissed her harshly, almost punishingly. He released her and slid his hand beneath the hem of her dress. Slowly, slowly, he ran a finger up her calf, past her knee, and along the inside of her thigh. She seemed paralyzed, as if charmed by an evil spirit.

He removed her undergarment and she didn't resist. Brooke was alarmed. The last thing she wanted was for Julia to get pregnant.

"Lie down," said Origen, as he gently pushed her onto her back. He lowered his pants and his engorged member sprang forth. Julia stared, apparently fascinated. Origen bunched Julia's dress up around her waist and suspended himself above her. He covered her mouth with one last kiss.

"Let me in," he whispered into her ear.

As he entered her body, Brooke felt a brief stab of pain. Then he was pumping hard and they rocked up and down on the narrow bed, threatening to collapse it. He came quickly and plopped down on top of her. Brooke felt more bruised than excited by this maladroit coupling. Julia squirmed under his weight and he rolled off her. The bed was so narrow, he almost knocked her onto the floor. In time, Julia rose and smoothed out her dress.

"No man has ever felt such bliss as you have given me, my darling" said Origen. Brooke wanted to slap the silly smile off his face, but Julia just bowed her head in submission.

⸺◦∞◦⸻

Brooke entered the lab the next day in a good mood. She tossed her handbag on a chair and said hello to Robert.

"How's everything?" she asked.

"Well, the mice are still fine," replied Robert, "if that's what you're asking. As for me, I'm worried. Why do you have to take this self-destructive path? No degree is worth this."

"Robert, it's more than just a degree. Someone has to be first to try the Memex. If we won't do it, who will? Besides, I'm going to be just fine—wait and see."

Robert apparently decided not to pursue the point. He turned his face to the monitor and entered the new settings. Today Brooke wanted to return to Damian a few weeks later than her last visit. She had had enough of Julia and Origen.

Brooke settled into position and asked Robert to start.

July 15, 1201. A steady rain beat down on the two men as they staggered along the street. It was night and the doorways and alleyways were obscured by darkness, making Brooke uneasy. There were a few torches set into holders in the buildings, but yawning caverns of blackness stretched between these rare outposts, with the only extra light coming from an occasional window. Damian was guiding Ignatius, who had had too much to drink.

"This is the foulest weather," said Ignatius. "Why are we outside?" His short black hair was frizzier than ever.

"Just keep going," replied Damian. "We'll be there soon."

"These streets are a disgrace. Abominably filthy. Just like our filthy emperor."

"Quiet, someone might hear you," said Damian.

Ignatius stepped in a puddle and almost fell. Damian hauled him upward and shoved him forward. They continued to the end of the street and turned left. Brooke thought she recognized the neighborhood and was relieved when she made out the signboard for the perfume shop. Damian rapped on the door. A bloodshot eye appeared at a peep hole. The door was opened and a woman took Ignatius in, clucking with disapproval.

Damian continued down the street, now unencumbered. The rain had seeped into his sandals, and water squished around his toes. The wind blew raindrops directly into his face. He pulled his cloak tightly around himself and bent his head to avoid the onslaught. His field of vision had narrowed to no more than his feet and a few pavement stones.

Brooke thought she heard footsteps behind her. Damian must have heard them too, for he stepped up the pace. Damian lifted his head to orient himself and turned onto a narrow street. The footsteps followed, growing louder. Damian hurried, and was on the verge of breaking into a run, when someone grabbed his cloak from behind. Damian was hauled up short and almost fell. He pivoted around and Brooke saw two large men. There was just enough light for her to see that they had no beards—Prepundolus' eunuchs.

The tall man with the elephant ears slammed a punch into Damian's face and his head snapped to the side. The other buried his fist in Damian's stomach, doubling him over. Brooke was stunned by the blows and she frantically thought that she must rip free and run away. Of course, she could not take any action, but her mind, in primal response, screamed that she must. A beefy hand grabbed Damian's arm and twisted it behind his back. Damian groaned and bent forward, trying to relieve the pressure.

"When my lord wants to make a deal," hissed a voice, "you accept it. Do you understand?" The pain was starting to build in Brooke's face and stomach, and her elbow joint was on fire.

"Yes," gasped Damian. Brooke saw a collegiatus at the end of the alley. He held a stout cudgel and was supposed to be an officer of the peace, but he looked the other way. At that moment, Damian snapped his head back and struck the man behind him in the face. Abruptly he was released. He aimed a punch at the man in front of him, but was blocked. Damian was punched from behind in the kidney, and Brooke felt a sharp pain in her lower back. A second blow to Damian's face drew blood. It was followed by a strike to the solar plexus and Damian fell to the ground. Brooke couldn't breathe and she thought she would die here on the cold, wet pavement.

Damian drew himself up into a fetal position and covered his head with his hands. He lay helpless on his side on the ground. The eunuchs kicked him mercilessly in the back, legs, and arms. Brooke felt every blow. There was no part of her that didn't scream in pain. The beating went on and on an unbearably long time. She promised herself that if she got out of this, she would never, ever, become Damian again.

The kicks stopped and a rasping voice said, "Just remember what I told you." Then they were gone.

Damian lay on the wet ground in a stupor. He slowly moved to a sitting position, and gently articulated his arms and hands. Nothing seemed to be broken. Brooke's head throbbed, along with many other parts of her body. Damian gingerly rose to his feet, supporting himself on the wall of a nearby building. He wiped blood and rain off his face with the back of his hand. A pedestrian approached and gave him a wide berth.

Damian made his way slowly and painfully down the street. His back hurt and he bent over slightly. When he arrived home, Brooke felt a surge of relief. Damian quickly unlocked the door and slipped in. He rested a moment on a stool in the workshop, then made his way laboriously upstairs.

Luckily, they had planned a short trip and Brooke was back at the Memex lab. She pulled off the helmet and looked around with bewildered eyes.

"What happened?" asked Robert. "You look pale."

"Some thugs attacked Damian and beat him up. It hurt so much," replied Brooke. To her dismay, a tear escaped from the corner of her eye and trailed down her cheek.

"Oh Brooke," said Robert, and gave her a hug. She let herself be held as she broke into noisy, wet sobs.

"You're OK now. Nothing to worry about," soothed Robert. He held her tight. For a long time, she couldn't talk. When she finally stopped crying, Robert released her and gave her a box of tissue.

Brooke smiled and started to feel a little better. She decided to leave Constantinople behind her. She would just go about the routine tasks of testing the mice and let someone else take all the risks. But first, she was going to take a few days off. She deserved it.

Brooke sat at a card table and dabbed paint onto her canvas, filling in the outline of a hull. She was attempting an ambitious seascape, a frigate tossed on the waves. The motif was blues, blacks, and whites, with shafts of light piercing the clouds in an otherwise stormy sky. It was Sunday afternoon and she had indulged herself all weekend. On Friday night, Jose had invited her to a party at his place and she had danced for hours. Brooke loved hip-hop, rock, heavy metal, anything with a beat. On Saturday, she and Claudia had gotten their nails done and gone to a movie. The movie was a wacky romantic comedy, pure fun and no danger. Today, she was absorbed in her painting project.

Brooke's thoughts drifted to Constantinople. The Queen of Cities, as it had been named in medieval times, called to her. The wide avenues paved in marble, the lovely churches, the elegant aqueducts, the open plazas graced with statues, gave the city a unique character no longer seen in the modern world. She also thought about Damian. What had happened to him? Would he give in to Prepundolus, or would they come after him again? It was the last question that kept Brooke away from the Memex. She wanted to be brave, but the beating had shaken her.

Brooke took a small brush, wet the tip, and dabbed it in an almost black color. She sketched in the outlines of the rigging and spars. The painting was going well and she was pleased with her efforts. There was no one home at the moment. Claudia had a test tomorrow and had gone to the student union to study with some friends. The painting did not provide enough distraction to quell her mind, which wandered from topic to topic. It had been fun to be with Julia and Origen as they toured the city, up until they got intimate. Julia was definitely a chancy host.

Brooke had already applied a dark blue background for the ocean, and now added waves in a lighter color. It was possible Julia would have a baby by Origen or run away with him before the crusaders got to Constantinople. Then Brooke's chance to observe an historical event might be gone. But Brooke doubted that Origen would take Julia with him when he left. If only she had an ancestor like Henry, the navigator that Chad had accessed. She loved the idea of sailing the ocean, despite the possible challenges, and at least she would be spared vicious customers and dubious boyfriends.

There was one route open to her. Perhaps she should access Eulogia. Prepundolus might visit his wrath upon Damian, but he wasn't likely to attack Damian's wife, at least Brooke hoped not. And if she accessed Eulogia, she could find out how Julia was doing. Eulogia was her ancestor as well, and it would be easy to adjust the settings to get to her.

Brooke considered the idea. As far as she knew, Eulogia was in good health, with no major aches and pains. At least she never complained about any. It was a good compromise. She could go back to the family without putting herself at risk.

Brooke highlighted the crests of the waves in white, giving them definition and power. Setting her paintbrush in a bowl of water, she went to wash her hands. She pulled out her cell phone and texted Robert, hoping he planned to go to the lab on Monday. He answered quickly that he would be there in the afternoon and Brooke was set upon her new course.

"So you're determined to go back again," said Robert, as he cleaned his glasses. He held them up and peered closely at them.

"It's a good plan. I'll be perfectly safe as Eulogia," replied Brooke.

"I've been thinking about you. Have you been feeling OK? Any nightmares or flashbacks?"

"I'm fine. I'm tougher than you think," replied Brooke. "And I'm not suffering from post-traumatic stress disorder, if that's what you're hinting at. You've been spending too much time on that human volunteer consent form."

Robert looked unconvinced but said nothing. He turned to the Memex screen while Brooke positioned herself in the chair. She took a deep, cleansing breath and relaxed as best she could.

July 16, 1201. Brooke sat across from Damian at the dining room table, taking in his ravaged appearance. His round face was disfigured by a black eye and a massive bruise on his other cheek. A cut on his eyebrow had scabbed over. Brooke did not remember being hit there. The background behind Damian was fuzzy and indistinct. Eulogia seemed to be nearsighted.

"You must do it," said Eulogia. "There is no other way."

"I will not," said Damian.

"Kyrios Prepundolus is too powerful. He will get his way in the end. If not tomorrow, then the day after that, or two days hence. We can't stand up to him."

Damian looked stubbornly at her.

"My husband, I know you are brave. I married you knowing that you have strength of character that few men can match. But there is a difference between bravery and foolhardiness. What if his servants attack you again and do grievous harm? Think about your family. Without you, we can't survive. The jewelry isn't worth it."

"Darling, we can't give in to him. He'll just come after us again and again. Once he knows we can be intimidated, he will harry us like the jackal that he is. We will be forever beset by him." Damian shifted in his chair, wincing as some injury was reawakened.

"What about the collegiati? We could ask for their help," said Eulogia.

"Them," said Damian scornfully. "When I was in that dark street and the filthy eunuchs were attacking me, I saw one watching us. He looked away and did nothing. Either he was a coward or Prepundolus' goons paid him off. Besides, if I approach the collegiati, it's my word against the word of a powerful noble. Who do you think they're going to believe?"

"There must be something," Eulogia pressed.

Damian slumped a bit in his chair and a flicker of pain showed in his eyes. He stroked his long black beard.

"There is one thing," he said. "Maybe I could ask my nephew, Theodoret, to come and stay with us. He's a powerful young man and the two of us would be a match for the eunuchs."

Eulogia looked skeptical. "Those eunuchs are trained in combat. You and Theodoret aren't."

"I forge my own tools and have the arms to prove it. Theodoret is a farm boy who specializes in shoeing horses. We can whip them. I'll go to the market tomorrow morning and get a ride to my brother's farm. This is going to work out, don't you worry."

"Maybe you should look at yourself," said Eulogia. She handed him a polished copper plate that served as a mirror. Damian's eyebrows rose as he observed his face.

"Hum. I might have trouble getting anyone to take me to the countryside."

"And you might scare Theodoret away," added Eulogia.

"Next week, then. I'll make the trip next week.

XII

JUMPING AHEAD

B rooke walked past the stately brick buildings on the west end of campus, dodging students on their way to class. It was late September and a few leaves had already begun to turn color. Brooke had a hard decision to make. She wanted to follow Damian into the countryside. She had not been outside the city yet and her curiosity was piqued. On the other hand, she was still worried that Damian might be severely injured or killed by Prepundolus.

It wasn't very interesting to follow Eulogia with her impaired vision. She could do close-up tasks like cooking and sewing, but everything more than four feet away was a blur. How sad that Eulogia had to live like that.

Brooke arrived at the Wilson building and climbed the steps to the front entrance. There were few students here, since this was primarily a lab building and not part of the between-classes rush. Before entering, she turned and looked back over the campus. An abstract sculpture with sweeping curves drew her eye skyward. The grass was still green but the promise of a new season was evident in the chilly air. Brooke hesitated, not sure if she wanted to go in. It would be easier to just forget about her experiments and stay out of danger.

With a sigh, she entered the building. Chad was in the lab today and had agreed to help her. He asked her what settings she was going to use.

"I think I'll jump forward in time," said Brooke, "much as I hate to. My new plan is to access Eulogia a month before the city is sacked. Then I can see how Damian is doing."

"Makes sense," replied Chad. "I'll get it set up."

Brooke sat in the chair, put on the helmet, and waited.

Mar. 15, 1204. Early morning light shone in through the window in Eulogia's bedroom. A cock crowed outside, announcing the dawn. The room was small, with an icon of the baptism of Jesus on one wall and a large chest at the foot of the bed. A rug in muted orange, yellow and brown covered the floor. A chamberpot was hidden beneath a small bedside table on which a water pitcher rested.

Eulogia ran her fingers over Damian's chest, as he stirred from sleep. She snuggled against him, pressing herself along his length. He opened his eyes and smiled at her. They made love with the ease of long practice, like a dance in which each player knows their part and each takes satisfaction from the reenactment of a beloved script. When Damian had finished, he lay on his back in a state of evident satisfaction.

Neither said anything for a while as they lounged under the soft coverlet until Eulogia broke the silence.

"Darling, I'm afraid. The Franks scare me."

"Don't worry. It's going to be all right. They won't hurt us," said Damian.

"What if they get into the city?"

"The walls have held back invaders for hundreds of years. Sure they got in last year, but the Varangian guard drove them off."

"But they're still out there. I wish they would leave."

"They will, eventually."

"Damian, I think we should leave town." Brooke was alarmed. She might miss the last, bitter, fight after all if the Balsamons left the city. She should have realized that they might do that. On the other hand, these were her ancestors, and, given what would happen in Constantinople, they should leave.

"If we leave town, we might be waylaid by thieves on the road. Many people are running away now, and the thieves know that they have valuables with them. We're safer here. Besides, I don't want to lose the house. Leaving is a bad idea."

"But we could have another fire. That would be horrible. We really need to leave."

Damian sighed and threw the covers off his chest. Brooke noted that he was whole and complete. No missing fingers or dramatic scars indicating terrible suffering. He propped himself up on his elbows and looked at Eulogia.

"Even if the barbarians get into the city, they'll attack the nobles, unseat the emperor, and put one of their own men on the throne," he said. "It's the aristocrats that need to fear. Not common people like us."

"It would be horrible to have one of the Franks in charge. They are greedy beyond belief and will take everything we have."

"Darling, we just have to wait and see. Our own emperor is exacting all the taxes he can get, just to pay the Franks off. It may not be that different if they take over. We've made it this far. This crisis will pass and good times will come again."

Damian got out of bed. Before he moved out of Eulogia's limited field of vision, Brooke could see that the rest of him was scar-free.

Not long afterward, Brooke was back in the 21st century.

"How's Damian?" asked Chad.

"He looks fine. Whatever happened to him in the years before the city falls, it didn't do any permanent damage," said Brooke.

"Why don't you just go forward from this point?"

"Oh no, I want to observe events leading up to the sack of the city. They might have historical significance."

"But Brooke, your degree is in Cognitive Science. How will historical discoveries help you?"

Brooke had been asking herself the same thing, but was annoyed that Chad had brought it up. "It's better than doing nothing. I can't speed up the animal testing program and I'm having trouble figuring out how the Memex works." She stopped abruptly. She hadn't meant to reveal so much. Damn Chad and his reasonableness.

"OK, what's next?"

"I want to go back as Damian, a few days after the eunuchs attacked him."

"Tonight?"

"Why not?"

July 24, 1201. Another dawn in Constantinople, but this one three years earlier. Damian walked briskly along the patchwork of worn stones, whistling tunelessly. A strap ran across his chest and ended at a sack nestled against his hip. As he crested a low hill and began to descend, Brooke caught sight of the Sea of Marmara extending off into the distance. On this cloudless day, the water was placid and deep blue. A small group of people was climbing towards Damian, clearly a noble and his retinue. The noble was dressed in a brilliant silk robe studded with precious gems and clasped with golden buttons that glinted in the early morning sun. His wife wore a stunning scarlet gown, a drum-shaped hat, and a curly white wig. Brooke thought briefly about the vagaries of fashion.

Damian passed the group, and turned a corner into a narrow alley. Brooke doubted the wisdom of this shortcut, but the alley was deserted at this early hour, and if you could stand the smell and avoid the piles of rodent-infested garbage, you could save a lot of time. The alley debouched into a large market square, already busy with vendors preparing for the day. Some were setting up their wares for display and others were hitching up their wagons in preparation for departure. Damian approached one farmer and inquired about his destination, but the man was heading northwest, not what Damian wanted. A second farmer seemed reluctant to carry a stranger. The third farmer, a lean man with a gap-toothed smile, knew Damian from his occasional visits to the market, and was heading southwest. He would pass near Damian's destination and agreed to take him on.

Damian climbed up onto the wagon's hard bench seat. Brooke enjoyed the ride as the mare plodded down the street, her hooves clicking rhythmically on the pavement. After a while, they turned right onto the Mese, Constantinople's main thoroughfare. Although it was only an hour past dawn, the street was already busy with pedestrians and vehicles. They passed a man pushing a handcart filled with lettuce. A young child jumped into the street ahead of them, but his mother, covered from head to foot in gown and veil, snatched the toddler out of the wagon's path.

They came upon the Forum of Theodosius, a broad, open expanse ringed by public buildings. Brooke was reminded of downtown Washington D.C. In the center, a Roman triumphal column more than eight feet in diameter pointed skyward. Battle scenes and victory celebrations were carved in relief on its marble surface. A basilica flanked by two larger-than-life bronze statues dominated one side of the square. They exited the forum under the rightmost of three soaring marble archways. The columns here had a curious looped pattern and looked almost modern to Brooke's eye.

The farmer was a talkative fellow, and kept up a one-sided conversation with Damian. He complained about his chilblains, his lazy son, the price of cotton, his neighbor's dog. Poor Damian was paying a high price for this ride. Brooke happily tuned him out, since she would not be required to respond. When the Mese divided into two major branches at the Philadelphion plaza, they chose the leftmost route. This was as far as Brooke had ever been on foot in the city, and she was eager to see what lay beyond.

As they rode along, Brooke caught occasional glimpses of the harbor to the south. They passed the Forum of the Ox, where they stopped at a fountain to water the horse and slake their own thirst. The day was beginning to heat up. Beyond the forum, the shops gave way to upscale residences, with broad sweeping staircases leading to sheltered porticoes. Soon they reached the old city walls, which were in a state of general disrepair. The city had expanded farther than these walls, and they were no longer an important line of defense.

They passed the walls and entered a region less densely populated than the inner city, where Brooke saw estates with fields and pastures. She was beginning to grow tired of the slow pace of the trip and the yammering of the farmer. She had grown accustomed to the generally unhurried pace of life in Constantinople, but this was even slower than usual.

At last, they arrived at the golden gate that pierced the massive outer walls. True to its name, the gate was decorated with an unbelievable quantity of gold inlay, drawing every eye to its beauty. With its trumpeting elephants and triumphant emperors, it appeared to be a cross between artwork and fortification. As Damian watched, soldiers ambled along the top of the wall, guarding against thieves as much as against potential invaders. The walls themselves were constructed of alternating strips of red brick and limestone blocks, topped by octagonal towers.

Traffic was heavy here and the wagon progressed in fits and starts. Taking advantage of the situation, a beggar stretched a skeletal hand up to them. Damian tossed him a small coin. With the next lurch forward, the wagon cleared the bottleneck and traversed a bridge over the moat. The city spilled out even here and the road was lined with homes and occasional businesses. Brooke had her first look at the countryside a half hour later, a rolling meadowland dotted with poplar trees. The farmer had finally tired of repeating his woes to the largely unsympathetic Damian and they rode along in silence.

At an intersection, Damian took leave of the farmer. He walked along a rutted path past cow pastures and farms, sweat dripping from his temples into his beard. About noon, he stopped by the banks of a stream and pulled some cheese and bread from his sack. The cheese was pungent and the water deliciously cool. Brooke wondered how much further they had to go, but she couldn't even ask. There must be a way to modify the Memex so you could fast forward. Real memories worked that way. She idly wondered if the pitch of voices would rise as you accelerated the memory. Doubtful.

Damian walked another few miles before turning up a narrow lane leading to a farmhouse. A tall man working in the field caught sight of him and shouted. Damian replied and started toward the distant figure. The men met and Damian was enveloped in a crushing hug.

"It's a great day when I get a surprise visit from my brother. How is everyone?" said Zenobius. His voice was deep, appropriate to his barrel-chested physique. His beard was streaked with gray and his face was leathery from long exposure to the sun.

"They're all fine. They send their love," replied Damian.

Zenobius led Damian into the farmhouse and summoned his daughter, Palatina. She was about fifteen years old, short and pudgy, with a bad complexion. Zenobius directed her to run to the far field and tell her brothers their uncle had arrived. Then she was to pick fresh vegetables and kill a chicken for dinner.

Zenobius poured wine mixed with water for Damian and they settled into the small sitting room. A wooden bench was softened by a scattering of decorated pillows. Palatina had left a hand spindle on the bench and the half finished thread wandered over the edge of the seat to a mass of raw cotton on the floor.

Two young men, so alike they might be confused for twins, joined them. Both of Damian's nephews were broad of shoulder, with powerful arms and bushy eyebrows. Nilus, the elder, had a prominently hooked nose, while Theodoret, the younger, had inherited a less dramatic version of the family trait.

"So, Nilus, I hear that wedding plans are in the works," said Damian.

"Yes, uncle, she's all I could wish for. My father made a good choice," replied Nilus. "We'll be married in three months."

"It'll be good to have a woman around the house again," said Zenobius. "Palatina does her best, but I fear she is lonely since her mother died."

The men launched into a long discussion of a mysterious disease that was threatening the equine population, causing lameness. Theodoret had formulated a poultice to apply to the stiff joints, but it had limited effectiveness. He suggested the farmers keep their afflicted animals separate from healthy ones, in case evil spirits jumped from one beast to the next.

Dinner was served and they all moved to the kitchen. The smell of fresh baked bread advertised an excellent meal, and Brooke was not disappointed. The range fed chicken and the just-picked vegetables were of a quality rarely available in industrialized America. Palatina poured milk from a bucket into serving glasses and placed them on the table. When Damian tasted the milk, Brooke would have gasped if she could have. It tasted truly terrible. Milk, still warm from the cow, was nothing like the modern, de-fatted, cold, pasteurized version. Brooke considered adding a new hazard to the review form.

The men brought Damian up to date on the doings of local families. It appeared that he had grown up in this house, the younger of two brothers. When Zenobius inherited the farm, Damian had been sent to the city as an apprentice to a goldsmith. Now Nilus was about to marry and Theodoret needed to find a place for himself in the world.

After the meal, Palatina cleared the table and left the men alone to talk.

"As you may have guessed, I have something important to tell you about," said Damian. "Last week, I was attacked in the street by the hired men of a client who owes me money. His name is Leo Prepundolus, and he is of noble rank, but less than noble character. In short, I need help to defend myself and my family. Basil is a scrappy lad, but still too young to be a great help."

"Of course we'll help you," said Zenobius. "We can all go into town and show this miscreant what the Balsamon men can do."

"I'm not inclined to go after him like that. If I escalate the disagreement, he will eventually win. He has a lot more power than I, and probably has the collegiati in his pocket. I just want to wait him out and not look like easy prey."

"Are you sure?" asked Zenobius.

"I'm sure. What I had in mind is inviting Theodoret to come and stay with us. His skills as a farrier will be useful in the city. He can earn a living by shoeing horses in our courtyard, and also be there in case Prepundolus comes after me again."

Theodoret looked thoughtful.

"I don't want to minimize the danger that Prepundolus represents," continued Damian. "He is a vicious, small-minded bastard. He left me pretty badly bruised and beaten last week."

"I'm not afraid of bullies," said Theodoret. "I can be there for you, but we do have to think of the harvest."

"This hasn't been the best year," said Zenobius. "The harvest won't be as big as all that. We can get help locally to bring in the crop. You go with your uncle. Family is everything."

"What about next year?" asked Theodoret.

"We need to leave one of our fields fallow in any event, and we aren't going to need as much food after you leave. I doubt Nilus' new wife can eat like you do."

"That settles it," said Theodoret. "I'll go with you to the city, uncle." Brooke was surprised at how easily Theodoret accepted this drastic change in his life. She suspected that he loved the idea of living in the city, far away from dull farm chores. Also, since his brother was getting married and would someday inherit the farm, Theodoret needed to get out on his own. Looking at his solid body and confident demeanor, Brooke felt protected. She would not fear using the Memex again.

⚬⚬⚬

"These so-called memories that you experience, are they complete? No gaps or distortions?" asked Prof. Hand. Hand was a heavy-set man with a full white beard and long gray-white hair tied in a loose pony tail.

"They're complete. It's just like being there, in full color and perfect detail," replied Brooke.

"Memories don't work that way. They're always altered by personal feelings and edited by our brains into a manageable size."

This meeting of the University Review Board was not going as well as Brooke had hoped. It was late September and the board had finally consented to review their application again. Prof. Hunter had insisted that they tell the board about their Memex experiences as part of the review process, so Brooke, Robert, and Chad were all at the meeting.

Besides Prof. Hand, there were eight other committee members seated around the table, some, like the small bird-like woman from the History Department, paying close attention to Brooke's every word, and others, like the bald, jowly, man from Biology, doodling aimlessly on his notepad. The best-dressed members were George Brashley, the university lawyer, and Beverly Aimes, vice president of the Mohegan Trust Company, the obligatory community representative. Brooke found the group intimidating, especially given their skepticism of her work.

"Do you have any evidence of historically verifiable events?" asked Prof. Porter. "That may help to establish if these 'memories' have any relation to the real world." Porter was an older woman with salt and pepper hair and prominent bags under her eyes.

"I came across my ancestor, Rebecca Ruggles, in the right town and the right time period," said Chad.

"I had in mind something like a wedding or a birth. If you observed a wedding and noted the date, and later checked it in the genealogical records, that might be convincing evidence," said Porter.

"It's hard to observe dates in the past. People don't talk about them much and there are no calendars on display," said Chad.

"How do you select a given ancestor anyway?" asked Porter.

"I worked out an algorithm that selects the person at a given spot on the family tree," said Robert. "For example, I can find your maternal grandmother's paternal grandfather."

"And how does the Memex work, exactly? What are the physical or biological principles behind it?"

None of the three students wanted to answer that one, but Brooke jumped in with, "We have some theories, but we need more time to investigate. We know what it does, but we don't have the mechanism worked out yet."

"I think we're getting off track here," interrupted Prof. Urbanowitz, the chair of the committee. "The key issue is the health risks that volunteers would be taking, not the ultimate value of the experimental results or the inner workings of the machine. If indeed, test subjects might experience anything their ancestors saw, heard, felt, tasted, or touched, then the risks are extreme. You do warn about everything from disease and torture to actual death, as well as the possibility of post traumatic stress syndrome. I personally think you'll have trouble getting volunteers. This experiment is so filled with possible peril that we'll need legal help to draft appropriate language." He looked at Mr. Brashley, the institute lawyer.

"Certainly," said Brashley. Brooke doubted that a lawyer would help. Protect the university, perhaps, but not the test subjects. Her mood darkened further.

"I think people will have trouble believing this," said Porter. "It's virtual time travel. There will be skeptics who will accuse us of perpetrating a hoax."

"We're in an odd position," said Urbanowitz. "We have to tell people what might happen, or we would be remiss. On the other hand, we could be accused of sensationalizing things. If only you hadn't tested it on yourselves. Doing that created a whole new pile of problems."

"From my point of view," said Prof. Hand, "the real issue is the death of the mouse." Brooke could see a few heads nod around the table. "I think we need to extend the animal testing period further." Brooke wondered if Prof. Hunter, who was supposed to be on their side, would step up to the plate. She had given the opening presentation and then retreated into silence, letting the students field all the hard questions.

"What I suggest," said Urbanowitz, "is that we refer the consent form to George for review. In addition, we require at least nine more months of testing with animals. How does that sound?" Brooke thought it sounded terrible, but no one spoke against the plan.

"That's settled then," continued Urbanowitz. "And there's something else I'd like to say. I insist that you students stop testing the Memex on yourselves. It's rash and irresponsible. You need to develop a professional distance from the work, and not dive in like amateurs."

Brooke bristled under the scolding. She said nothing. But Urbanowitz was looking at her and awaiting a response.

"You have a good point," she said. Any thoughts she had about quitting had just been squashed. She was going to redouble her efforts.

Aug. 5, 1201. Damian sat back in his chair with a contented sigh. A few crumbs of bread and a small wine stain on the tablecloth were all that remained of the evening meal. The entire household was present, including the newest member, Theodoret. Eulogia had been subdued this evening, unlike her usual self and Brooke wondered what was troubling her.

"Basil, you can be excused now," said Eulogia. Basil left, looking perplexed, but recognizing the steely tone in his mother's voice.

"I'm afraid we have a problem," began Eulogia. "Mother, please tell everyone what you told me earlier today."

Ariadne sat up straighter in her chair, as if to reinforce her words. "I went to the market today and stopped to visit my friend, Macrina. She told me that she saw Julia in the marketplace alone with the locksmith's son. They wandered around together, acting most indecently, laughing and talking. Then they went to his wagon and disappeared inside."

"What?" yelled Damian. "Is this true?"

Julia looked like she had been cornered by a snake. Her eyes filled first with fear and then with guilt. Stunned, she did not respond to her father's insistent question.

"Well, say something," he thundered. "Did you consort with the locksmith's son?" Theodoret looked thoughtfully at his cousin, Eulogia clasped her hands together tightly in front of her, and Ariadne watched Damian cautiously.

"Yes," said Julia in a near whisper. She hung her head and cast her gaze downward.

"I can't believe you would do that. Have you no sense?" The volume of Damian's voice was rising. Brooke was sure that Basil could hear, wherever he might be in the house.

"You have dishonored the family. You will drag all of us down. After all we've done for you, you go off and behave like a common harlot," roared Damian.

Julia began to cry and started to rise from her chair.

"Stay where you are," said Damian. "I have more to say to you. Do you have any idea of all that I have suffered to give you and your brother a good life? When I came to this house as a young man, I was apprenticed to Bardos, a vicious, drunken, bastard." Brooke could attest to that. "I had to cope with his beatings and tongue-lashings and incompetence for years. I had to practically teach myself the trade. When he finally died, I had to put up with the widow and her two brats for several more years until the girls were married and I had saved enough to buy the business."

"After your mother and I married, we had a beautiful baby girl, but she died before her first birthday. Then you came along, and you were the joy of my life." Brooke noted the use of the past tense. "We have had many good years, and now this. Our lives are ruined."

"It's not as bad as that," said Eulogia.

"Be quiet," snapped Damian. "If you had been doing your job as a mother, Julia would never have gotten into this mess." Stung, Eulogia lapsed into silence.

"It's not her fault," said Julia. "I made the choice myself. It isn't fair that I can't marry the man I love. Life is not worth living if you don't have love." True enough, thought Brooke.

His anger dissipating, Damian looked sadly at his beloved daughter.

"Origen can't be a husband to you. He has no house. Where would you live? In a wagon with him and his father? Is there even room for you there? And what if you had children? Where would they live?

"May I leave now," asked Julia in a small voice.

"Not yet. You are forbidden from leaving the house. There will be no more illicit assignations," said Damian.

Julia rose and Damian did not stop her as she made a rapid exit. The others also took the opportunity to hasten away from the toxic atmosphere in the room, leaving only Eulogia.

"Darling, you are right to keep Julia at home," said Eulogia. "I'm sure she will repent and realize the enormity of what she has done. To ease your mind, I am certain she is not with child." Brooke was relieved to hear that. As long as Julia survived the crusade to come, Brooke would have a unique view of events. The view of an infant or toddler would probably be worthless.

"I'm going to go after that damn boy," said Damian. "I'm going to beat him within an inch of his life."

"I wish you could," said Eulogia. "I would cheer you on, but it may be unwise. If you go after Origen, people will figure out why. Julia will be publicly ruined, and we will never get her married. My idea is that we accelerate the marriage to Florian before the Gestopians hear of this."

"Yes. You have a point," said Damian grudgingly.

"And while it's a good idea to keep her inside for a while, we can't do that forever. People would notice. What if we keep her at home for two weeks, but let her think it will be forever. That is a punishment in itself. Then we can let her go out, but only if Theodoret is with her. My mother is too old to keep up with Julia."

"All right. The plan makes sense," said Damian. He slouched down in his chair, emotionally drained. "I'm sorry I snapped at you earlier," he said. "I didn't mean it."

"It's all right. I understand," replied Eulogia. She rose from her chair and walked around to his side of the table. He stood up and took her into his arms.

The grieving parents clung to each other for a long time. These wounds would be slow to heal.

XIII

MISTRUST

*A*ug. 13, 1201. Damian sat on the hard stone bench, his legs spread wide and his *hands clasped tightly before him.* The courtyard was in full bloom today, with wild roses climbing one wall, finding purchase in the cracks between stones, their delicate pink blossoms a fitting counterpoint to the potted violets. The sun shone intermittently from behind the clouds, casting shadows on the well-worn paving tiles. Damian's face was protected by the shade of a fig tree. Beside him, Julia was spinning thread with a hand spindle, her repetitive motions quick and sure from long practice.

A handsome gray horse, his coat gleaming with good health, was tied to the entrance post, waiting for Theodoret to attend to him. As Brooke admired him, he shifted his stance and lowered his head to lap up water from a nearby bucket.

It was unusual to find Damian just sitting. Normally, he was busy at work or visiting with friends, or in the process of going somewhere. This was a side of him Brooke had not experienced before. The pace of life in Constantinople was slow, but there was always something to do.

"Nice day," said Damian.

"Yes," replied Julia.

Damian couldn't seem to think of anything else to say. He scratched his head and sighed.

"Your work is going well."

"Well enough," replied Julia.

"I have to talk to you about something. I'm going to see Marcus tomorrow and arrange your marriage to Florian. I know he's not your first choice, but I don't see any other way. I love you and want to protect you, but I see now that I can't trust you to control yourself."

"You can trust me, father. I won't do it again," said Julia.

"Trust is like glass. Once shattered, it can never be repaired. You are young and will see things differently in the future. Then you'll understand why I have to do this."

Brooke was annoyed that Julia was not standing up for herself. She should be objecting, voicing all the reasons that Florian was a bad match, or, if that didn't work, at least she should plead and try to change Damian's mind.

"Yes, father," said Julia. Unshed tears welled up in her eyes.

⸎

"The document releases Brackett University of responsibility for all claims of damage to your health, either physical or mental, resulting from the unauthorized use of the Memex. I want to point out that it also applies to authorized use of the machine, in as much as Prof. Hunter knew about your experiments and implicitly or explicitly allowed you to continue," said George Brashley, the university lawyer. He was reviewing the highlights of an eight page document that he wanted Brooke and Chad to sign.

Brooke remembered Brashley from the University Review Board meeting, but, since he had said little on that occasion, she didn't have a good read on him. He was a middle-aged man with prominent widow's peaks and a large nose. His well-pressed black suit, white shirt, and noncommittal striped tie fit perfectly on his large frame. Only his drooping eyes hinted of hidden problems.

Chad sat next to her in the lawyer's spacious office on the fourth floor of the administrative building, an area that Brooke had never seen before. Unlike most of the buildings on campus, which were beaten up and shabby, the fourth floor would have fit in well at a prosperous corporation. Given the tuition rates, she guessed she shouldn't be surprised.

"You don't need to sign this today," said Brashley. "I advise you to check with your personal attorney before affixing your signature. However, I would like you to read through the entire document now so that I can answer any questions." He handed one copy to Brooke and a second to Chad. Brooke began to read the legalese, trying to imagine the implications of what was said and unsaid.

The document specified that there would be no survivor benefits, should she die as a result of Memex use. Pages and pages of disclaimers on every type of possible injury that might result from the use of the machine followed. There was also a section forbidding disclosure or promotion of her invention and any correspondence with the press. If Brooke spoke to the media about the Memex or her "findings while using the machine," without the written permission of the Review Board, she would be expelled from school and sued for damages.

"Isn't this section a violation of freedom of speech?" she asked.

"Absolutely not," said Brashley. "If you report on unconfirmed claims, you could tarnish the good name of Brackett University. In effect, we own the Memex and the laboratory that it is in and you use it at our discretion. The Review Board wanted to forbid you from using it at all, but Prof. Hunter took your side. The result was a compromise: if you sign the document, Hunter could let you continue."

"But what about this?" asked Chad. "It says that we can't make general statements that would in any way damage the reputation, credibility, or standing of the university. That has nothing to do with the Memex."

"Ah, you have to appreciate that in cases like this, students may be inclined to try to 'get even.' Not that you would. We have to include such language as a matter of course."

Brooke was offended by this gag order, but what could she do? She had no money to hire a lawyer of her own.

"And what if we don't sign? I, for one, don't intend to use the Memex again," said Chad.

"I'm sorry to say that if you don't sign, we will not let you register for any more classes or thesis credits."

"How can you do that?" said Chad.

"From our point of view, you're misusing our facilities, and we need to protect ourselves," said Brashley. After a pause, he added "You might choose to contest our decision, but I assure you the lawsuit would drag on for four or five years. Do you really want to interrupt your education for that long?"

Brooke realized that Brashley had all the cards in his hand. They were effectively powerless to resist. She picked up the pen and scrawled her name on the offensive document. Chad did the same. So much for academic freedom.

Aug. 20, 1201. Damian was polishing a silver plate one morning when the door to the workshop opened and Ignatius came in. Ignatius had a smile on his face, and seemed to be bursting with something he wanted to tell Damian. Brooke liked the short perfume merchant with his seditious ideas. He was one of the few people in the city who dared to speak ill of the emperor.

"You're going to be a happy man today," said Ignatius.

"And how would that be happening?" asked Damian.

"Do you remember my friend, Yididyah, the greengrocer on Annia Street? Well he knows a farmer who is one of Prepundolus' tenants, and the farmer is expected to drop off a shipment later this morning. You could talk to him and learn a lot about Prepundolus."

"Yididyah, the old Jew? I did meet him once," said Damian, stroking his beard. Brooke enjoyed the beard stroking gesture, so alien to her normal self. She had found herself stroking her chin lately when in a thoughtful mood. She would have to stop that.

"What would I learn from this farmer?" asked Damian.

"For example, you might find out when he pays rents. Then you could get to Prepundolus before he blows all the money on gambling and whores, or you could be first in line among his creditors."

"You have a point," said Damian. "All right, I'll come."

Damian called up to Eulogia that he would be out for the morning, and left the shop with Ignatius, locking the door behind him. The city was sweltering under a blanket of heat, with no breeze to provide relief. The two friends walked along, catching up on family gossip, but Damian did not tell Ignatius of his problems with Julia. Brooke could hardly blame him.

Yididyah's shop was nestled between a silk merchant and a blacksmith. The shelves looked understocked—perhaps the shipment was coming just in time. Large bags of staples such as flour, dried beans, and millet rested on the floor.

Yididyah welcomed them effusively, and drew up chairs from a back room so they could wait in comfort. The "old man" was probably in his mid forties, mostly bald with stick-thin legs and a protruding belly. He chatted with them, with frequent interruptions to tend to customers. The front door was open to let in the air, and Brooke could hear the clang of the blacksmith working next door.

Ignatius and Damian settled in to wait patiently for the farmer. Brooke was exasperated by this culture without clocks. Rarely did anyone meet at a specified time, it was always, "sometime in the afternoon," or "first thing in the morning." They didn't seem to mind losing half a day's work.

The farmer arrived about noon, in a ramshackle wagon loaded with carrots, lettuce, and scallions. He was a heavyset man clad in a dirty tunic with a ragged hem. Damian and Ignatius helped him unload his merchandise, lugging hefty bags into the shop and emptying the contents into bins. When they were finished, they invited him to join them in a glass of wine.

"I am a goldsmith who has had the misfortune to do business with Kyrios Prepundolus. I understand that you're a tenant of his," said Damian.

To Brooke's dismay, the farmer hawked and spat on the floor. No one else seemed to mind.

"Yeah, I'm a tenant. What's it to you?" asked the farmer.

"He owes me money. I just want to know when he collects rents. Be assured that I would not use your name," said Damian.

"Wouldn't help you much if you did. I don't even know if he knows my name. I've never met him, thank the Lord."

"How do you send money to him?" asked Damian.

One of those eunuchs of his comes to the village every two months and we all give him the rents, which are far too high, by the way," said the farmer. "He's a cruel landlord."

"I can believe that," said Damian. "When will he come next?"

"On the nones of September, I expect him." Brooke groaned inwardly. It looked like she was in for another run-in with the odd way that Romans, and by extension, Byzantines, enumerated things. Not only did they have Roman numerals, which were hopelessly inadequate for even the most basic arithmetic, they could not even count the days of the month sequentially from 1 to 30 or 31. Add to that the varying length of time in an "hour," and you have a recipe for a mathematically challenged culture. It was surprising they accomplished as much as they did.

"Wonderful," said Damian. "You've been a big help. Now I can get a jump on him, thanks to you."

"Any day I can put Prepundolus in a bad spot is a good day for me," said the farmer. "I wish you the best of luck."

Sept. 7, 1201. Damian and Theodoret stood at the base of a wide marble staircase, leading to an imposing front door. Prepundolus lived in a mansion with a domed roof and colonnaded portico, vaguely reminiscent of Monticello, although much smaller. The staircase was paved in green and gold and the base of the banister was a sweeping spiral. Semi-precious gemstones set into the banister sparkled in the sunlight. A dog barked somewhere. Brooke had figured out that the nones of September were on the fifth of the month, so today would be two days after the rents had been collected. Damian was following his plan to collect when Prepundolus was flush with cash. He must have allowed some time for the eunuch to get back to town with the money.

They climbed the steps and raised the heavy doorknocker. A servant in an immaculate white robe opened the door.

"Yes, what is your business?" he inquired.

"We have a delivery for Kyrios Prepundolus," said Damian. "Something he ordered from us."

"I would be happy to give it to him," said the servant.

"I would prefer to speak to him myself," said Damian. "He may wish to ask questions."

The servant scowled at him, but opened the door wide and ushered them into a parlor. This was the most sumptuous room that Brooke had seen in Constantinople. The walls were covered with tapestries, and not the old faded rags that decorated some modern day European tourist sites. These were new, with hunting scenes in vivid colors and dramatic contrasts. Stone seats were softened by silk covered pillows with gold tassels. A large mosaic of a warrior fighting the Minotaur was set into the floor, all the passion of the fight captured in the man's posture. Each tiny bit of the mosaic glinted resplendently, and Brooke thought it was a shame to walk upon such a work of art.

On the side of the room away from the entrance, a double door opened into a hidden garden. From what Brooke could see, it was filled with lush foliage and a spray of bright yellow flowers. She longed to walk into that garden, but of course could not.

Lord Prepundolus entered the room, looking vexed. He was wearing a floor length green silk robe with silver threads. A hefty silver clasp on his shoulder allowed the robe to drape in elegant folds. His small mouth was turned down at the corners and his high forehead was creased in displeasure.

"What are you doing here?" he asked.

"We thought we might do you the service of bringing the earrings that you ordered," said Damian. "To save you a trip."

"So you are here to do me a service," said Prepundolus. Brooke detected an undertone of menace in his words and began to tense up.

"We knew you would want them and we are always willing to oblige," said Damian. Theodoret shuffled his feet a bit, and was perhaps becoming as nervous as Brooke.

"And have you wisely decided to sell at the price I specified?" asked Prepundolus.

"I'm sorry but I can only sell at the originally agreed price," said Damian.

"Get out of my house. You have some cheek coming to my home and bothering me with this. If you need a lesson in understanding your place in society, I have someone who can teach you well."

Damian, recognizing that he would get nowhere while Prepundolus' temper flared, said a curt goodbye and exited rapidly with Theodoret. Their gambit had failed. Even if Prepundolus still had the rent money, he wouldn't pay his bill. At least they left in good health.

Sept. 10, 1201. "Wake up, wake up," whispered *Ariadne.* Damian opened his eyes in astonishment, startled out of a deep sleep.

"I hear someone downstairs," she said urgently. Ariadne's gray and white hair fell forward to obscure her face as she bent over Damian. What few teeth she had were yellow and crooked, giving her a witch-like air.

"What?" said Damian groggily. He sat up and threw off the light cover.

"I heard movement. You have to go look," said Ariadne.

"Yes, all right," said Damian, rubbing his eyes. He got to his feet and stumbled forward. Eulogia was sound asleep and missed the entire exchange. Damian tiptoed through the dining room trailed by Ariadne and paused at the head of the stairs. He motioned his mother-in-law to stay put, and listened intently. A slight noise emanated from the workshop. Brooke thought it could have been anything, but Damian reacted by charging down the stairs at top speed and scanning the dark workshop. In the gloom, shapes were muted and indistinct, but Brooke's long familiarity with this place helped her interpret her surroundings.

The doors to the storage cabinet at the back of the workshop gaped open and a dim figure stood nearby. Upon seeing Damian, the figure turned abruptly and raced for the door. Damian sprinted across to intercept and grabbed a handful of the burglar's tunic. The thief tried to plant an elbow in Damian's stomach, but the blow struck at an angle and glanced off harmlessly. Damian, enraged, lunged forward and knocked the man on his stomach, falling on top of him. The thief wriggled desperately and managed to extricate his upper body. Damian tried to encircle his legs, but the thief was strong and broke the grip. A lucky kick connected with Damian's jaw. Brooke felt her lower face go numb, and the pain slowly build. Damian, unmindful of his injury, scrambled to his feet just as the burglar made it out the front door.

Damian ran outside and caught sight of the thief heading north. It was a moonless night and so late that there were no torches lighting the street. Luckily, Damian had seen no lights since he had awoken and his night vision was at its best. He gave chase, panting with effort, but the thief, propelled by fear, was faster and gained ground. The race continued for more than ten minutes. Just as Brooke thought Damian would have to quit, the thief tripped on something unseen and sprawled on the hard pavement. Damian pushed himself to run harder, ignoring a stitch in his side and his aching jaw. The thief scrambled to his feet and continued his flight, now only thirty yards ahead.

The thief gained another ten yards and turned into an obscure alley. A cat screeched, breaking the late night silence. Damian arrived at the alley entrance just in time to see him take a right into yet another narrow passage. This part of the city housed the poorest and most destitute of its citizens and Damian usually avoided it, but now he plunged down the alley, heedless of the piled trash and the stench of urine. When he came to the next intersection, he saw the thief running ahead, and beyond him, a tall figure loomed.

"Stop that thief," bellowed Damian. The unknown man slammed into the burglar and tried to detain him. The two grappled while Damian ran toward them.

Brooke opened her eyes and saw the brightly lit ceiling of the Memex lab.

"Damn, why did I come back at that exact moment?" she asked.

"What happened?" asked Chad.

"Damian was about to catch a guy who robbed his workshop." She told Chad the details of the heist and the chase.

"Maybe you were lucky," said Chad. "Damian might have gotten into a fist fight with the thief, and that could have hurt."

"I'm getting rather used to being roughed up," said Brooke. Chad could not suppress a smile.

"We can always send you back, if you really want to be in the fray," said Chad.

"I had better not, too much Memex in one day throws my time sense off. I'll try again tomorrow and maybe skip forward a bit. Some things are better to hear about than live through."

XIV

SUSPECTS

B rooke knocked lightly on the door to Prof. Hunter's office. To her surprise, the professor admitted her without delay.

"Brooke, I would like to introduce you to Prof. Papazoglakis. His specialty is classical languages, and he is very interested in talking to you." Papazoglakis was an overweight man in his mid-forties, with dark hair and a full beard going to gray. He sat like a contented toad in one of Prof. Hunter's inadequate chairs. The lowest button on his white shirt was unfastened, and a small area of pale belly showed. He hauled himself to his feet to shake Brooke's hand.

"I have told Prof. Papazoglakis about your experiences in Constantinople, and he is interested in the language that you've learned." Brooke wondered how many people on campus now knew about her research. It wasn't going to be a secret for long at this rate.

"Of course, I would be happy to talk to him about it," said Brooke. She couldn't help but feel shanghaied, given no time or opportunity to prepare for this meeting. With a pang of disappointment, she realized that Hunter didn't trust her and was setting a trap.

Papazoglakis began by clearing his throat. "So, have you ever studied Greek in school or in any formal course?" he asked.

"No," replied Brooke.

"Πώς το λέμε αυτό στα ελληνικά?" he said, pointing to a window.

Brooke was confused. She thought she understood some of what he said, but the accent was strange and she could not be sure. Panic welled up in her. Maybe it *was* all a dream induced by the Memex and not real memories. Then a strong voice deep inside urged her to fight back, and not be intimidated. She decided to reply in the Greek she knew, saying, "I didn't catch all of that."

Papazoglakis' eyebrows rose as he considered her sentence.

"Hum… odd but interesting," he said. "Perhaps you should just tell me a little about your experiences, in Greek of course. Anything you like."

"Well, I'll try. I don't actually speak in the past, you know. I listen to what my host is saying and hear the people around me. So my comprehension is excellent. But I never have to actually put a sentence together on my own."

"I understand. Just do your best," he said. Prof. Hunter, standing by the window, looked at her speculatively. She had never looked more like a vulture than at this moment, with her tall, stooped posture and wrinkled forehead. Brooke resolved to show them both. She launched into a description of the Balsamon family, the workshop, and the local neighborhood, using words that she knew cold. Her speech was halting, in fits and jerks, as she struggled to reproduce the intonations and emphases that she remembered from her visits. After a while, Papazoglakis stopped her.

"Very good. Now let's just focus on one word at a time," he said. How do you say "cat?"

Brooke replied. He continued with a list of other common words such as arm, leg, and table, and she knew them all. When he got to telephone, she protested that there were no telephones in Constantinople at that time.

"Let's work with a few verbs. Would you say, 'I am, I was, I will be?'" Brooke complied. She grew weary as he asked for translations of various tenses of find, eat, drink, walk, and run.

Finally he appeared to be satisfied. "It seems to me that you speak a form of medieval Greek vernacular. Unlike Latin, Greek continued to be spoken by common people during the middle ages. In the Byzantine empire, only Attic Greek, as spoken by the ancients, was considered acceptable for writing and scholarship. The ordinary citizens spoke a so-called 'lower' form of the language. We have no record of it, because it was never written down. It seems to me that you speak something between modern demotic Greek and ancient Attic Greek."

"This could be a linguistic gold mine," he enthused. "Would you consider working with me on this?"

"I'm not sure that would be wise," interrupted Hunter. "Brooke has to complete her thesis in cognitive science before she can take on any new projects. In addition, we can't yet publish any of our findings, because the university insists that the Memex be kept secret. It's afraid of sensationalism. Maybe down the road we can work out something."

Papazoglakis looked disappointed. Hunter, however, looked pleased, as if she finally believed that Brooke was really viewing the past. It's about time, thought Brooke.

Robert ran his eyes over the wooded landscape spread out before him. He was sitting on a warm flat stone on top of Noonmark mountain, eating his lunch. He, Brooke, and Feng had entered the woods after breakfast and made good time to the summit. Emily, who had ridden up the mountain on his back, was now asleep, nestled in her mother's arms.

Robert looked down into the valley below him, which seemed extremely far away. He could hardly believe that he had just been down there earlier today. The mountains were dressed in their autumn finery, brilliant with red and gold against a cloudless sky. It seemed that the mountain range went on forever, with distant peaks in faded colors poking up behind their nearer cousins.

"This is the best ham sandwich I've ever eaten," said Feng.

"That's what a vigorous hike will do for you," replied Brooke. "Feng, how did you hear about our experiments?"

"A graduate student told me. He heard it from a professor. He said you were fighting gladiators in ancient Rome," replied Feng.

Brooke laughed. "Maybe I shouldn't laugh. If I had accessed a different ancestor, I could very well have found myself in the arena."

"I hope you don't mind that I told Feng the truth," said Robert. "It seemed better than letting her wonder about the rumors. I always wanted to tell her, anyway."

"Well, that's honest. Don't worry. I don't mind. A lot of people know at this point. It seems like some professor on the Review Board has a big mouth."

Robert remembered the day they had presented to the Review Board, not one of his best college experiences. Now this day was nearly perfect. Just as he thought that, the wind kicked up and Robert felt a chill. He unzipped Feng's backpack and pulled out jackets for himself and his wife. Emily was already wrapped up in a thick yellow coverall with little ducks on it.

"What are you going to do when your fellowship runs out?" asked Robert.

"I guess I'll interview for an internship in the spring or maybe even a permanent position. Hunter isn't willing to send in any more proposals, not until she has preliminary data. She says it's a waste of time."

"You don't have to use the machine any more. What good will it do?"

"I think I might discover something that will change accepted views on 13th century history. That Greek professor was even excited about the language I learned. He wanted to work with me on a linguistics project, but that wouldn't help me get a degree."

"Well, the Memex is your baby. You were the one with the original idea," said Robert. He had joined the project after Brooke had already laid out the plans and designed the circuits. He had contributed to construction, wiring, and debugging. Lots of debugging. When Chad had joined, he had focused on programming. They all had spent long grueling hours working with the mice. But the real genius behind the project was Brooke.

"I can't leave the Memex now. Besides, what else do I have to do until my grant runs out? More mouse testing?" asked Brooke.

Robert groaned, knowing that more animal testing was in his future. But today, he was going to put it out of his mind. Today, he was a king, a master of the universe, with the whole world spread out at his feet. Conquering a mountain was such a high.

⚬⚬⚬

"What date are you shooting for today?" asked Chad. It was Monday afternoon, and time for another voyage into the unknown.

"I'm going in four days after the theft," said Brooke. "That way, if Damian got roughed up, he should be mostly recovered. Just to be sure, I'm going to make it a short trip." She eased into the chair and stretched out like a cat, supremely relaxed.

"I admire your courage," said Chad as he punched in the last numbers and activated the machine.

Sept. 14, 1201. Damian sat opposite Marcus, who scowled down at the chess board between them, his bald pate gleaming in the light of the torches. They were bogged down in the middle game, with several pieces vying for dominance of the center squares. Few pieces had been exchanged, and the board was crowded with possibilities. Neither side had castled, and both were choosing awkward moves to try to bring their rooks to bear.

Brooke was happy to discover no aches and pains in Damian's body. Damian often played chess with Marcus in the evening, and the normalcy of the scene was soothing. Shadows from the flickering torchlight played over the stationary pieces, giving them a dimension of menace and power. The slightly acrid smell of burning pitch spiced the air. Somewhere in the house, the sound of a flute piped as a simple melody was practiced over and over. In an environment devoid of radio and computers, music was a rare and welcome treat.

"My shop was robbed a few days ago," said Damian.

"No!" said Marcus. "Did they get much?"

"It was a single thief. I caught him in the act and chased him halfway across town. At one point, I was sure I had him. A pedestrian grabbed him for me, but as I rushed up, the thief managed to break free. After that, he disappeared into the alleyways and I lost him for good."

"Bad luck," said Marcus. Brooke noticed that Damian had not told Marcus the extent of the losses. With the delicate negotiations of the marriage of their children in play, such information might be sensitive.

The two friends resumed their chess game. Marcus was taking a long time to decide on his next move. After all his deliberation, he merely pushed a pawn forward. Innocent as that may seem, the move destabilized the board, and Damian considered his next move with great care. The pace of the game was agonizingly slow and Brooke's mind wandered.

"Do you remember me telling you about those thefts last spring?" asked Marcus. "How did your thief get in? Was the door or window forced?"

Damian looked up absently. His concentration broken, he said, "Actually, nothing was broken into, not even the cabinet that housed the stolen pieces."

"Odd," replied Marcus, "but it sounds like the same modus operandi of the burglar who took gold from Lecapenus and tools from Donus."

"You're right. I hadn't thought of that," said Damian.

"What did the collegiati say?" asked Marcus.

"Them," said Damian with contempt. "I didn't even bother to tell them. What good would it do?"

Marcus raised his eyebrow in surprise but said nothing. Brooke could understand Damian's disgust with officialdom. They had not lifted a finger to help him when Prepundolus' henchmen were beating him.

Both men returned their attention to the game. It seemed to take Damian more than fifteen minutes to make his next move. Marcus waited patiently, saying nothing further to distract him. The consequence of all that cogitation was the repositioning of a knight. Brooke inwardly sighed. Still no pieces were captured and the inevitable bloodbath had been, once again, deferred to the future.

Sept. 24, 1201. Damian pushed back from the table with a sigh. Dinner had been a morose affair, with a meager meal of oatmeal sweetened by a tiny dollop of honey, and a fitful and uninspired conversation. He played with his spoon and focused most of his attention on the beautifully embroidered tablecloth. This couldn't have been more different than the happy dinner that Brooke remembered from her first visit to Constantinople. Julia had picked at her food, scant as it was. She had not shown much interest in life since she had been confined to the house and told she must marry Florian. Basil had complained about the oatmeal until his grandmother corrected him with a sharp word about the hunger of the poor in the city.

"I'm afraid I have some bad news," said Damian. "We have to take you both out of school. We need you to work in the mornings to help with our finances. I'm afraid the thief has left us in a tough place." Julia shot a glance at Basil, who looked alarmed.

"Yes, father," said Julia, listlessly. "Of course we will do all we can."

"I like school," said Basil. "What will I have to read if I don't go to school?"

"I'm sorry, son. It's only temporary, just until we can build up our reserves again. We'll get you back to school in time, don't you worry." Basil was hardly mollified but did not protest further.

"I can help, uncle," said Theodoret. "Business is good for a farrier. I could easily take on more horses and work longer into the evening."

"I would appreciate that," said Damian. "It was a gift of God that you came to our household."

The conversation died once again, and, one by one, the family members made their excuses and moved off to other pursuits. Only Damian and Eulogia were left at the table. She had said little during the meal, but her calm attitude had helped diffuse the tensions brought about by the reversal of their fortunes.

"How bad is it, darling?" asked Eulogia.

"We'll be all right in the long run, but the next few months will be rough. I caught him before he had the chance to take more than a few things. Unfortunately, he got some of the gold I was planning to use for the chalice order—a heavy blow. It's a good thing your mother was up and heard him, or we may have been ruined."

"Poor mother, she has a hard time sleeping these days and is often up at odd times. A good thing in this case. Did he get the earrings? Do you think it was Prepundolus?"

"The earrings are still there. Either he didn't have time to find them, or he wasn't specifically targeting them. And I would be surprised if it were Prepundolus. I would have expected him to send two men, not a single burglar. Even if there were only one man inside, another would have been watching the door."

Eulogia looked alarmed at that possibility; clearly she had not thought of it before.

"But don't worry, my dear," soothed Damian. "We'll recover from this. Unfortunately we'll have to put off the wedding till next May or so, when we have more money. I don't think Marcus will object, given the circumstances. He's a reasonable man. Having the children out of school will save us on fees. You'll see—it will all work out."

Brooke hoped so.

Sept. 25, 1201. Damian strode along the pavement with a confident air, Eulogia at his side. A rainstorm had washed the city earlier, leaving it cool and refreshed, and the sun had just pierced the cloud cover, promising a return to warmth. They stopped at a doorway unfamiliar to Brooke and went inside.

The shop was filled with treasures and curios. One wall was covered with icons of Christ preaching his sermon on the mount, Samson pulling down the pillars of a temple, and Peter dying on his upside down cross. The shelves held silver plates and cutlery as well as carvings and statuary in wood and ivory. Brooke was attracted to a cabinet filled with gemstones and jewelry, hairpieces and buckles next to a rack of silk gowns embedded with semi-precious stones. The shop attendant was a slender man with a black beard shaped into two points.

Damian took a statue from his sack and set it upon the counter. It was an image of the Madonna, beautifully crafted in marble. The purple veins in the stone had been worked into the virgin's robe, giving the piece a special luster.

"How much will you give me for this?" he asked.

The shopkeeper lifted the statue and turned it over in his hands. He ran his fingers along the form.

"The best I could do is 35 trikephala," said the shopkeeper.

"Only 35," said Damian. "This statue is worth at least 50."

"Not in my experience. It would be hard to find a buyer who would give that."

"I can't let it go for a mere 35," said Damian.

"Did you want to sell it outright, or use it as collateral on a loan?" asked the shopkeeper. So this is a pawnshop, mused Brooke.

"I intend to redeem it in four months," replied Damian. "I want the loan."

"In that case, I could offer you 40."

Damian looked at Eulogia who did not object.

"Then 40 it is," said Damian.

"Excellent," said the pawnbroker. "I do want to mention that there is also a small storage fee. I would never charge you interest; that is forbidden of course, but to keep it for four months, I will need a repayment of 43 trikephala. If you do not return in four months, I will sell it to recover my loss." Brooke could see that financial innovations had a long history. In her view, there was no real difference between "interest" and "storage fee," but this semantic legerdemain seemed to make the transaction acceptable.

"Agreed," said Damian. He scrawled his name in the pawnbroker's ledger book and received some coins in payment, dropping them into a leather pouch.

Once Damian and Eulogia were back in the street, they headed south toward the marketplace. They were about to enter a greengrocer when Damian noticed a familiar wagon in the marketplace, the one where Origen and his father, Valerius, lived. He paused for a moment and Brooke wondered what he was thinking. The wagon was closed up today and no one was in sight.

"I wonder," said Damian. "We were robbed, but it was as if the thief had a key. He didn't need to break in. All those other thefts that Marcus told me about were the same way. No broken latches or jimmied windows, just a quick in and out. Who could do that but a locksmith? Valerius might be our thief." Brooke was doubtful. The locks of the day had simple warded mechanisms, without tumblers. Anyone with a skeleton key could defeat them. The key might not work on every lock, but the thief could choose the doors it did work on.

"You suspect Valerius," said Eulogia. "But how would we ever prove it? None of our neighbors saw the burglar."

"We could search his wagon," suggested Damian.

"In broad daylight?" said Eulogia incredulously.

"I guess not."

They entered the greengrocer and purchased sacks of flour and dried beans with some of their newly acquired cash, passing by the more expensive fresh fruits and vegetables. As they were about to leave the marketplace, Damian stopped short.

"I have an idea," he said. "We could hire a beggar to watch the locksmith at night. Then if he goes out to steal again, we can catch him in the act."

"That will cost money," said Eulogia. "And you can't be sure it was the locksmith." Brooke hoped Damian would listen to Eulogia and abandon this foolhardy plan.

"Beggars will work for little pay. This is something I just have to do."

Eulogia looked at him with a mixture of exasperation and resignation. She followed as he walked slowly along the street, looking for a likely prospect. The first beggar they came upon was a one-legged man in a tattered robe, and they passed quickly. Brooke also saw a desperate-looking woman with a baby in her lap, who looked up at them pleadingly. Damian walked on, but Eulogia dropped a small coin in her cup. Damian didn't even slow down as they passed a grizzled man asleep in a building entryway. He stopped before a thin boy of about twelve, who was energetically asking for alms. His clothing was less dirty and disheveled than was typical of his kind.

"What's your name, son?" said Damian.

"I'm Cobbo, sir, and I would really appreciate your help."

"Why are you on the street?"

"I came to the city with my mother and father, who were looking for work. But they came down with the pox, and died two weeks ago, one after the other." The boy had an earnest expression on his face, but Brooke thought the story was too pat. Or perhaps the boy had repeated it so many times that it had lost emotional impact for him.

"Would you be interested in taking on a small job for me?" asked Damian.

"What job?" asked Cobbo warily.

"Back in the marketplace, there is an itinerant locksmith named Valerius. He has a green wagon with a white roof. I want you to keep an eye on him tonight. See where he goes after dark. If he enters someone's house, especially after fumbling around a while with the keys, I want you to come and get me. Do you think you can do that?"

The boy nodded vigorously.

"I want you to be careful not to be seen, and don't confront him. He may be a dangerous thief."

They agreed on a price, with Damian promising a bonus if the boy turned up anything interesting. Damian gave Cobbo his address and arranged to meet him again the next day for a report. Brooke was skeptical that this would lead to anything, but you never knew…

XV

A Woman's Fate

The headlights cut through the gloom to reveal a rutted dirt road flanked by an impenetrable pine forest. Brooke expected to arrive at the parking lot at any moment, but they were traveling at only five miles per hour and she had to be patient. Chad was at the wheel of his pickup, and she in the passenger seat, blocked in by a pile of equipment that rested on the bench seat between them. As the front wheel dipped into a deep pothole, she stabilized a laptop that sat precariously on top of the pile.

She and Chad had convinced Hunter to let them try the Memex in a remote location, hoping to test the theory that they were receiving signals from a transmitter. They were bouncing along a one-lane road in the heart of the Adirondack Park, a region far from any town and out of the reach of cell phone towers. If the Memex didn't work here, they might be out of range of the transmitter. Brooke hoped that the rough ride wouldn't loosen electrical connections. The electronics had never been designed for this level of vibration.

Earlier in the day, they had disassembled the Memex and stacked the components into Chad's truck. Brooke had taken a short trip into the past to make sure that the device still worked. It had. They headed north to test their transmission theory. The Adirondacks were at the peak of leaf season, blazing with golds and reds in the late afternoon sun. Exiting past Schroon Lake, they wound their way into the wilderness as the sun set. Now it was fully dark and faintly ominous. Brooke reminded herself that she wanted to arrive just after dark, when the last of the hikers had driven away and the woods were deserted. The last thing she wanted was to attract attention.

A few fat droplets splattered on the windshield.

"Did you check the weather before we left?" asked Chad.

"No, I didn't think of it. At least it's not snow."

"Not yet anyway."

"If it snows we can turn back."

"We'll be alright. My four wheel drive can handle snow."

The skies opened and a torrent of raindrops struck their windshield. Even on max speed, the wipers had trouble keeping up. With near zero visibility, Chad slowed the truck even further until they were almost at walking speed. They crept along for fifteen minutes until they reached the parking lot at the trailhead. The storm's fury was finally spent and the rain abated.

"Who and when are you accessing tonight?" asked Chad.

"I have it all set up. I'm going back to Damian the night after he hired the beggar. I won't stay long." Brooke arranged the helmet on her head and checked that the connection to the signal generator was firm.

"OK, zap me," she said.

Sept. 26, 1201. Damian was wrenched from a deep sleep by a loud pounding on the door. He sat up, disoriented, and swung his legs out of bed. Eulogia woke and asked what was wrong, but he mumbled some words of reassurance and she settled back into the bed. He stumbled to his feet. Moonlight shone through the window, and Brooke could see almost as clearly as in the daytime.

Finally awake, Damian hurled down the stairs and opened the front door. Cobbo stood there, fairly jumping with agitation, his eyes bright with excitement.

"He's robbing somebody. We have to go catch him!"

Theodoret and Ariadne had followed Damian down the stairs and stood behind him in the workshop.

"How far away is it?" asked Damian.

"Not far, we have to go now."

Damian and Theodoret followed Cobbo into the street. They ran along the moon-washed pavement, barely able to avoid potholes and obstructions and a mangy dog who slunk off at their approach. There was no one else in sight at this late hour as Cobbo led them along a tortuous path through winding streets, past dark doorways and dubious tenements. They came out on a genteel street lined with shops and upscale businesses, and Cobbo, breathless, stopped in front of a spice merchant. He signaled them to keep quiet. They arrayed themselves around the door, ready to pounce when the thief showed himself. So Valerius was the thief, thought Brooke, surprised that Damian's astute guess had paid off. Cobbo must have followed him from his wagon.

The door creaked open and a figure emerged, noticed the men waiting, and tried to slam the door in their faces, but Theodoret was quick and he jammed the door with his foot, pushing it inward with a mighty heave. The thief, still holding the doorknob, fell backward and lost his footing.

Theodoret burst into the room and came down on the thief lying supine on the floor, driving a knee towards his exposed stomach. At the last moment, the thief rolled on his side and Theodoret landed on his hip. Although the thief wriggled in an effort to throw off his captor, he was not strong enough and was soon pinned to the floor, face down. Theodoret wrapped a meaty arm around his neck and lifted him, choking, off the ground. Damian stepped forward and landed a blow on the handsome face that, lit by the moon, was recognizable as Origen, not his father. Damian, infuriated, buried his fist in Origen's stomach and struck him again in the face, opening a cut above his eye. Brooke was so surprised to see Origen she hardly registered the pain in her knuckles and hand.

The shop owner appeared in his nightshirt, brandishing a cane. "What's going on here?" he demanded.

"This whore-son was robbing your shop," replied Damian. "We caught him as he was leaving the premises."

The spice merchant looked uncertain, not knowing Damian or Theodoret, who now lay on top of Origen, pinning him to the floor. Origen made an attempt to twist around and toss him off, but Theodoret was much heavier. Theodoret grabbed Origen by the hair, lifted his head back and smashed his face into the floor. Origen groaned and lay still.

The spice merchant picked up a sack that Origen had dropped and looked inside. As the contents shifted, they clinked together faintly. He withdrew a glass jar filled with bright orange threads.

"This bastard was trying to get away with my most exotic spices. This saffron alone is worth a tidy sum," said the merchant. He pulled the neck of the sack open wider and peered at several bottles within. "He also tried to filch cloves, cumin, marjoram, and mustard seed."

At Damian's suggestion, the spice merchant brought some rope and they bound Origen hand and foot. Theodoret turned him over and Brooke felt a pang of pity at his devastated face. Blood had soaked the left side from the cut over his eye and a stream of blood issued from each nostril. Theodoret must have broken his nose when he smashed his face into the floor.

"Cobbo, I want you to go find the collegiati," said Damian. "Bring them back here."

Cobbo ran off and Damian faced Origen.

"So it's not enough that you try to lure my daughter away from her family, you spawn of the devil. You took my hard-earned gold too. I hope you know what they do to thieves around here. I assure you, it isn't pretty. And I will give evidence against you. As a matter of fact, I'm going to gather all the merchants who have been robbed lately and let them all give evidence against you. We only had these thefts when you and your father were in town. I bet we'll find that he sold locks to many of the people you stole from."

Origen said nothing, but looked at Damian with hatred. Brooke admired Damian's restraint. She wanted to lash out in a fit of rage. The past was beginning to change Brooke in subtle ways, and had inculcated in her an acceptance of casual violence. She would have to think about re-civilizing herself.

Cobbo returned with two collegiati bearing cudgels. They untied the rope from Origen's ankles and hoisted him roughly to his feet. Origen was escorted off to prison.

"I can't thank you enough for catching that thief," said the spice merchant. "Here, take this as a token of my gratitude." He handed Damian a small bag filled with spices, which Damian accepted gratefully.

"And you, my young man, accept this coin." Cobbo took the coin from the merchant and stuffed it into a pouch hanging from his neck.

"You did a fine job, son," said Damian, "and I want to thank you as well." He handed Cobbo a silver coin. The boy's surprise was fun to watch. He would eat well for the next few weeks. Brooke hoped Cobbo could find his way in the world. If tonight was any indication, he would make it.

"It worked, didn't it?" asked Chad. "Damn." Brooke nodded her head.

"This is only our first attempt," she said. "Maybe next time we'll find a dead spot." After spending years wanting the Memex to work, it was odd to hope that it might fail. Chad started the engine and turned the truck around. The rain was now a faint drizzle, just enough to dampen the windshield. He steered onto the one-lane dirt road. The moonless night was deepest black, and they saw only what the headlights showed them. The potholes had been filled in with water, and it was impossible to tell how deep they were.

"Be careful. I don't want to get stuck out here," said Brooke.

"I have my camping gear in the back, in case we need it," teased Chad, flashing her a smile.

"Just keep your eyes on the road." Brooke had no intention of spending the night in a tent with Chad.

They jounced along in silence for a while. A dark shape darted across the road in front of them and Chad slammed on the brakes. They missed the creature, whatever it was, but the truck slewed around and came to rest at a sharp angle to the road, one wheel in a deep depression and another suspended above the roadbed. Chad revved the engine, slipping the clutch, but the road was muddy and his wheels couldn't get a grip. The truck strained forward, and then sank back when Chad took his foot off the accelerator.

"Four wheel drive, huh?" said Brooke.

"Doesn't help when all four wheels are in the mud. Look, can you drive a stick?"

"Sorry, I don't have a driver's license."

"Then you'll have to push while I ease us out of here."

"Is that your plan? I think I prefer the tent!" But Brooke opened the passenger side door and slid down into the muck. She felt wetness seep through the holes in her old sneakers as she walked around to the back of the truck.

"On the count of three. One, two, three..." and the engine roared. Brooke pushed, but she might as well have been pushing an 18 wheeler. Mud spit from the rear wheel in a long stream, just visible in the glow of the tail lights. The rear wheel dug itself in deeper.

"Stop!" yelled Brooke. She returned to her seat. "We need a new approach." She pulled out her cell phone to call for help, but had no bars. Of course she didn't. They picked this spot purposely to be out of range. She shivered in her wet clothes.

"Don't worry. I know what to do," said Chad.

"What?"

"I'll find some sticks in the woods and jam them under the wheels. That'll give us enough traction to get out. Hand me the miner's lamp from the glove compartment."

Chad strapped the lamp on his head and left Brooke alone in the cabin. She didn't have much confidence in Chad's plan, and began to feel sorry for herself. Bad enough that she faced dangers in the past every day of the week, but to run into trouble in present-day upstate New York was too much.

She caught glimpses of Chad's headlamp as he scoured the nearby forest. The disembodied light reminded her of every horror film she had ever seen. Five minutes passed before Chad returned to his seat, sopping wet. He gunned the engine and the truck rocked forward, slid, jerked forward a bit, slid again, and finally jumped ahead onto the road. Chad wrestled with the wheel to keep his heading on the bumpy road. Drops of water fell from the brim of his hat onto the electronics, and Brooke swabbed them with her damp sleeve, only making it worse.

"Let's try somewhere less remote next time," said Brooke.

"You don't say."

Two nights later, Brooke and Chad were parked by the side of a road next to a wide fenced-in field. They had driven west into dairy farm country, as far from the university as they could get in a few hours. They stepped out of the truck to admire the stars, brilliant in this dark area away from city lights. Brooke traced an arc along the handle of the big dipper and found Arcturus. Even here in the country, it wasn't dark enough to see the Milky Way.

Brooke caught sight of a star low to the horizon that twinkled red and green. At first she thought it was an airplane, but it never moved.

"What's that?" she asked.

Chad held his iPad up to the sky. A map of the stars on the display mirrored the real thing above them. "I think it's Capella." Another few clicks and he had identified it as a system of four stars in two binary pairs.

"It's the most beautiful star I've ever seen."

Chad pulled up a webpage on Capella. He read, "When Capella is near the horizon, the atmosphere distorts light from the star, splintering it into different colors. The star is normally white."

Brooke still found it beautiful, but the sterile scientific explanation had wrung all the magic out of it.

"Let's get down to business," she said.

They both returned to the truck, checked the connections on the Memex, and settled themselves in for their next experiment.

"What are you doing this time?" asked Chad.

"I want to check on Julia, and see how she's coping with Origen's betrayal."

Sept. 28, 1201. Julia scrubbed the tunic vigorously, working on a particularly resistant stain to the point that Brooke feared the cloth might tear. It was a well-worn garment, and thinning at the elbows. Finally satisfied, Julia dunked it in the now tepid washtub water, wrung it within an inch of its life, and draped it over the clothesline. It was a warm and sunny day, and the rest of the laundry flapped in the gentle breeze of the courtyard.

"Good morning," said a familiar voice. Helena stood in the entryway with a broad smile on her face. She was dressed in a new gown, a luxuriant rust color in the unmistakable sheen of silk.

"Come in, come in. I'm so glad to see you," said Julia. She wiped her hands on a nearby cloth and stepped forward to hug her friend. "It's been ages since you dropped by."

"I'm sorry. I should have come earlier, but I've been tending my sick aunt, and haven't had much free time."

"The new gown is beautiful. It suits you perfectly," said Julia. A new garment was a big event in the lives of the tradesmen and their families. Most people had only two or three outfits, and wore them till they had patches on patches. The girls clucked over the comely dress, admiring its bell sleeves, gold embroidered hem, and the overwrap that hung from one shoulder in long loose folds.

"I don't know if you heard the latest news from my family," said Julia. When Helena looked interested, Julia charged on. "Father hired a beggar to keep watch on Origen. The beggar followed him to a spice merchant and brought my father and cousin Theodoret there. They accused Origen of stealing from the merchant and called the collegiati. I don't know how my father can be so cruel and vengeful. Isn't it enough that he keeps me imprisoned in the house, does he have to go after Origen too? Now he's in prison, and I can't even go visit him or bring him anything. He must think I don't love him."

"Was he really stealing from the spice merchant?" asked Helena.

"I'm sure there was some explanation. Father thinks he was the one that stole from us a few weeks ago, but I don't believe it. Origen wouldn't do that." Helena looked a little skeptical, but wisely refrained from commenting. In Brooke's view, Julia was so smitten with Origen that she refused to see the truth.

"The worst of it is that father wants to marry me off to Florian. He's dreadful. My life will be ruined if I have to marry him. I couldn't bear it, I couldn't. Why was I born a girl?" wailed Julia.

"Don't worry. Things will get better," soothed Helena, patting Julia's hand as the girls sat together on the courtyard bench.

"Every morning, I lie awake in bed and don't want to move. I just want to crawl under the covers and hide there. If my mother didn't come by to cajole and threaten me, I would never get up," said Julia. Helena put an arm around her and made sympathetic noises.

"Maybe I should join a convent," said Julia.

"What, you? You don't even like church," said Helena.

Julia sighed and hunched over on the bench, resting her head in her palm. "I guess they do an awful lot of praying. I wouldn't like that. But as least I would be free of all the men."

"Think of the awful clothes they wear," said Helena. "How could you be a nun?

"I guess you're right," said Julia, in a defeated voice.

"Darling," said Helena, "I know you feel terrible now, but you won't feel terrible forever. Just wait and see, in ten years, this will be a distant memory. Your luck will change, and you'll be the happiest woman in town. That's how life is." This time it was Brooke who was skeptical.

Brooke was momentarily disoriented when she found herself in the front seat of Chad's truck. She had been in an awkward position while under the Memex and her neck hurt.

"It worked again, didn't it?" asked Chad. She nodded.

It was a long drive home.

***

Brooke decided to take a few days away from the Memex. She frequently thought of Julia, and how miserable she was in her terrible situation. Brooke knew what was to come: the capture of the city by the crusaders and the untold suffering that would entail. However unhappy Julia was now, the war was likely to make things worse, perhaps much worse. Julia had been foolish to trust Origen. On the other hand, she was only sixteen and in love for the first time. She wasn't the first woman whose judgment had been clouded by infatuation.

Brooke sympathized with Julia's depression and her desire to hunker down in bed, shutting the world out. Brooke herself clung to the Memex like a drowning sailor clings to a raft. On the mornings when it was hard for her to get out of bed, she thought of the excitement of discovering the past. She knew her choice to continue testing was questionable, and maybe even foolhardy, but if all she had were endless animal tests and no prospect for completing her degree, all hope would drain from her life.

Perhaps Helena was right. In ten years, Julia would forget all the anxiety and emotional pain of the present and be happy and secure. Brooke dared to hope that her own life would be infinitely better ten years hence, this rough patch long forgotten. She was overtaken by a keen desire to know what had happened to Julia, as if her own fate were linked to that of her distant ancestor. She had been plodding forward in a disciplined way for many weeks, following the story in chronological order. Now she wanted to dash forward and see Julia in ten years, long after the sack of Constantinople. If she found Julia well, then she could go back and see the invasion through Julia's eyes.

On a Friday night in late October, Brooke was back in the lab, settled into the reclining chair of the Memex, feeling a new appreciation for its comfort. Robert, at the controls, had entered in a minimum length trip. Brooke didn't know what she would find, but she just wanted a peek.

Sept. 28, 1211. Julia sat on a plush sofa holding a bawling infant in her arms. She cooed soothingly to the baby while unbuttoning her dress with one hand. She slipped the garment off her shoulder and offered her breast to the hungry infant. He clamped down on the nipple as if his life depended on it, which, in fact, it did. Brooke was startled by the vigorous tugging and then felt a wave of relaxation pour through her body. The baby let go momentarily and milk sprayed from her nipple like water from a shower head. The flow quickly subsided and the infant reattached himself and began to suck contentedly.

A little girl with long blond hair sat on the rug, cuddling a rag doll in her arms. In the hearth, a blazing fire warmed the spacious room. Brooke decided this wasn't Constantinople. The floor was constructed of smooth wooden planking and the walls were painted an olive color. The decor was rustic and comfortable, unlike the sophisticated tiled floors and elaborate icons she was used to. A stuffed boar's head protruded from the wall.

"You're such a good little boy," said Julia. "So handsome and strong, just like your father." She stroked his downy head, while he gazed at her from big blue eyes. She looked at him lovingly, enraptured by the tiny person. "I'm so lucky to have you, my little cabbage."

The little girl on the floor began to berate her doll, shaking her finger at the limp form. She wasn't speaking Greek, but Brooke could not catch the language. The doll must have committed some awful crime, for the girl turned her upside down and shook her vigorously.

Julia glanced up as a tall, confident, man entered the room. He had regular features, with piercing blue eyes and a straight nose. A lock of brown hair hung over his forehead, completing the picture of youth and strength. He beamed at the mother and babe with a look so tender that Brooke felt her heart reach out to him. When he spoke to Julia, Brooke was able to pick out a few words, and decided it was French or a closely related language. What a strange accent.

"Papa!" cried the little girl, throwing herself into his arms. He tickled her and a peal of childish laughter echoed through the room. As he tossed her into the air, caught her and tossed her again, she giggled delightedly.

Abruptly, Brooke was drawn back to the present. She smiled, realizing that whatever trials Julia had to face, it would all turn out well for her in the end.

XVI

WAR GAMES

B rooke walked across campus through a flurry of snowflakes. She pulled her jacket tightly closed to shut out the cold wind. The end of October, and it was already snowing. This might be a tough winter. Despite the weather, Brooke was cheerful as she remembered her last Memex session, where she had found Julia in a happy and loving family. She had started following the Balsamons as a way to finish her degree, but it had become more than that. She cared about them, and hoped that they escaped unharmed in the turmoil to come, even if it meant that she didn't discover anything new about the history of the period.

At least she knew that Julia would survive the sack of the city and somehow meet the Frenchman. Brooke had seen Julia with two children, but she couldn't be sure whose children they were. Julia was supposed to marry Florian, and he might be Brooke's ancestor. Brooke wanted to know.

The snowflakes kissed the walkway and expired, leaving no trace. Some flakes clung to blades of grass, attempting a beachhead on the ground, but to no avail. The earth was still warm enough to resist being buried in snow. Brooke climbed the few steps to the Wilson building and entered. She breezed into the lab and said hello to Robert.

"Today, I'm trying something new," she said. "I have to know whether Florian or the Frenchman is my ancestor. I don't know much about Florian and I'm curious about him. I think I'll go back to the time before Marcus and Damian talk about marrying him to Julia and see what he's like. Of course it could be the Frenchman and I have no idea when a good time to access him is. I'll just have to take a chance."

"Should be interesting," said Robert. "I'll set it up."

Oct. 28, 1199. Brooke found herself in a cool, dark room. A young woman lay in a large canopy bed, her hair damp and her face flushed. Brooke's host touched her forehead, feeling the heat come off her body.

"Garnett, please get me a drink," said the woman.

"Of course, cherie, I'll be right back." The French was simple enough that Brooke understood. So her ancestor was a Frenchman named Garnett and she was in his body. Her joy at finding this new ancestor was tempered by the circumstances she found him in.

Garnett went through a hallway and down the stairs to a kitchen, where he dipped a cup in a bucket of water. The house was large and well appointed, much finer than Damian's home. He returned to the bedroom and held the cup to the woman's lips. She only managed to drink a few sips before she fell back, exhausted. The woman was slight of build, with long, straight blond hair and a face that was pretty when she wasn't ill. She bore a vague resemblance to Julia.

Garnett settled into a chair by the bed and sat patiently. From time to time, he dipped a cloth in a ceramic basin by the side of the bed and swabbed the woman's forehead. She appeared to fall asleep, and then was jerked awake by a racking cough while Garnett looked on helplessly.

A matronly woman entered the room carrying a cup.

"Here's the drink you asked for, my Lord," she said. "Hot milk, pepper, and honey."

"Ah, thank you, Agnes. I'll take care of it." She handed him the cup reluctantly.

"Wouldn't you rather I attend to the mistress, my Lord? I could get the doctor to come bleed her."

"No bloodletting. I've never seen that particular remedy help anyone."

Garnett lifted his wife to a sitting position and encouraged her to sip the hot milk. She tried to get it down, draining half, and then waving the cup away. Garnett set it on the side table and gently lowered her back into the bed. At length, sleep released her from her suffering.

As Brooke returned to the 21st century, Robert was waiting to hear the verdict.

"So which one is it?" he asked.

"It looks like I'll be brushing up on my French," replied Brooke. "This opens new doors."

Brooke and Chad were driving down the thruway toward New York City. Once again, they had the disassembled Memex on the seat between them. Last night, Brooke realized that the best place to test her transmission theory would be underground, where the earth might provide shielding from any signals. At first she considered Howe caverns, but it was thick with tourists and she would never be able to bring the equipment underground and use it unobtrusively there. New York City, on the other hand, tolerated all kinds of weirdness. She and Chad were heading for the Lincoln tunnel. No one would remark on a passenger in a stuporous state sitting with a helmet on her head while riding through the tunnel.

Brooke was grateful that Chad had been willing to take her on all these jaunts. She discovered that, like her, he had a taste for hip-hop and they had listened to "Holy Grail" and "Started From the Bottom" as they rolled down the thruway. It was a shame that Chad worked in her lab. Brooke had her rules and was convinced that love in the workplace was too dangerous. What would happen if they had a fling that fizzled out or ended bitterly? She would have to face him every day. No thanks.

As they approached the tunnel, Chad asked her what the Memex was set for today.

"I'm going to see how Garnett and his wife are doing," she said. "That is, if the Memex works."

After waiting in heavy traffic, they finally entered the tunnel. The radio continued even as they penetrated deeper, since the traffic authority had installed their own transmitters. When they were far enough from the entrance to be well shielded, Chad flicked on the Memex.

Nov. 9, 1199. The bishop raised his arms and intoned "Dominus vobis cum." The congregation replied, "et cum spiritu tuo."

Brooke was standing in the front of the church, near a casket covered with flowers. Early morning sun lit the stained glass windows, where Christ walked placidly up Mount Calvary to his death. Throughout the church, people cried openly and noisily. The woman standing next to Brooke was sobbing piteously. The toddler in her arms looked puzzled at the display of adult emotion, her little face wide-eyed and her thumb firmly planted in her mouth.

Garnett, too, was weeping, his face wet with tears that he did not bother to wipe away. The bishop launched into a mellifluous chant that was as comforting as warm honey. From time to time, the choir replied in sweet, young, a capella voices. Garnett's wife had clearly lost her battle with the fever and succumbed. She had been no older than Brooke.

The bishop walked around the casket, waving an incense burner and praying. The sweet smell wafted toward the mourners where it evoked something in Garnett, for he broke into racking sobs, his chest heaving. The bishop picked up his crook and moved to the front of the casket with two altar boys carrying candles. Six burly men arrayed themselves around the coffin and picked it up. The bishop led the funeral cortege down the aisle. A tonsured monk fell in behind the casket, and Garnett and his companions followed.

The procession issued from the church into a cool, autumnal morning. The casket was lifted into a hearse drawn by two sleek black horses. Slowly they walked up the hill toward a cemetery, accompanied by a piper playing a mournful tune. The woman next to Garnett said, "I didn't see Bertram and his family here today."

"There must be something wrong at his house," replied Garnett. "He's a good tenant, and I expect he would have come had he been able."

"Charitable as always, my dear brother. You like to think the best of people. At least the rest of the tenants are here. They ought to be for the funeral of the lady of the manor."

They continued on in silence for a while. At length Garnett said, "I don't know how I'll get along without her. Cerise was the love of my life. I can't image her not being there."

"We will all miss her mightily. She was a sweet person, always ready to help, to soothe a hurt, or comfort a grief. But you must not despair. Cerise is surely in heaven, waiting for you to join her in the fullness of time. She is looking down on us right now, and wishing she could allay your grief."

Garnett took the toddler from his sister's arms. "My poor little daughter will never know her mother, at least not in this world." The child snuggled into her father's chest, hiding her face in his warm embrace.

They reached the grave site, a raw pit six feet deep. A simple wooden cross draped with a garland of roses marked the place. All around, carved stone tablets engraved with the name Renard would keep Cerise company in her final resting place. The thin stones protruded from the earth like crooked teeth, some darkened with age. Brooke surmised that Cerise would have such a stone in time to come.

The bishop read from Psalms and gave a homily, praising the good Christian woman who had been called to her Savior. As the casket was slowly lowered into the grave, Garnett again broke into sobs. He stepped up to the edge and tossed a clump of dirt onto the coffin. This was the cue for the gravediggers to take up their shovels and fill in the hole. Everyone stayed respectfully while they completed their task, then folks drifted away, stopping to say a word or two to the bereaved husband. He remained long after everyone else had departed, his shoulders hunched over in sorrow.

The insistent rhythms of hip-hop jarred Brooke back into the present. They were just exiting from the Lincoln tunnel. Her experiment had failed once again.

Brooke needed a new idea, something to replace the transmission theory. A few ideas were dancing around in her head, but had not congealed into anything meaningful. In the meantime, she carried on with her visits to the past. She and Chad had returned the Memex to the lab and she had no intention of moving it again. Today she wanted to see how Julia was doing.

June 3, 1202. The wedding dress was spread out on Julia's bed. It was made of soft blue silk, with topaz and blue star sapphires sewn into the bodice. Ariadne, Julia's grandmother, and Helena, her friend, helped Julia put it on. Brooke felt the lovely garment mold to her body and drape in long, luxurious folds.

"How does it look?" asked Julia.

"Oh, it's magnificent," said Ariadne, clasping her hands together.

"You look like a princess," chimed in Helena.

Julia picked up a polished copper plate and studied her reflection intently. Brooke saw a pretty face with a tense expression and no make-up. Helena helped Julia into a matching veil of translucent organza.

"Are you ready?" asked Eulogia, entering the room. "Oh darling, you look stunning," she said and gave her daughter a hug, careful not to disarrange the dress. Julia nodded that she was ready. The women left the bedroom and passed down the short hall to the dining room. There, Damian, dressed in a white robe with gold and red embroidered patterns, awaited, his round face animated by a wide smile. Brooke also recognized Ignatius, Damian's drinking buddy, Theodoret, Damian's nephew, and other friends and neighbors among the crowd.

Damian took Julia's arm and led her downstairs and outside. The courtyard had been transformed into a fairyland hung with garlands of myrtle and laurel that twinkled in the noonday sun. Florian Gestopian stood with his parents and best man, looking nervous. Brooke was struck by how unappealing he appeared, with his receding chin and his stooped posture. She wondered about the man beneath the exterior. If he was, as Damian believed, a good man, perhaps Julia would learn to love him in time.

As Julia approached Florian, he handed her a bouquet of delicate white roses, hung with ribbons. Julia took her place next to Florian and Father Scholasticus approached them.

"My children," he began. "On this holy occasion, we have come together to celebrate the sacrament of matrimony. Have faith in the Lord, Jesus Christ, and He will guide and protect you throughout your life together. He is the source from which all life flows, and He will bless you and your progeny for all time."

"A reading from the book of Ephesians: *For the husband is the head of the wife even as Christ is the head of the church, his body, and is himself its Savior. Now as the church submits to Christ, so also wives should submit in everything to their husbands. This mystery is profound, and I am saying that it refers to Christ and the church.*"

Brooke had never heard that particular passage from the Bible before. She would be sure not to choose it for her own wedding.

Damian approached the bridal couple and set a crown of orange blossoms on Julia's head. A second crown, tied to the first by a white ribbon, was placed on Florian's head.

Damian said, "I give you my daughter for a wife, knowing that you will cherish and protect her as I have. Florian, do you wish to wed Julia?"

"I wish to," responded Florian.

"And Julia, do you wish to wed Florian?"

"I wish to," replied Julia in a small voice.

"You are now married forevermore."

The best man came forward and placed rings on their right hands. A stringed instrument began to play a lively tune and the guests chatted happily. Carrying a stick festooned with apples and bits of red wool, the best man led the wedding procession into the street. Florian took Julia's hand with his own damp and clammy paw as they walked side by side. He rubbed his thumb against her skin in a restless circular motion that irritated Brooke.

"It was a lovely ceremony," said Florian.

"Yes. It was," replied Julia. After a brief pause, she added, "I'll never forget this day."

"Nor will I," replied Florian.

Passersby stopped to admire the young couple. A porter with an unbelievably large sack of cress and endive on his back winked at them. Julia glanced up at Florian furtively a few times, but said nothing. At last she broke the awkward silence. "We've been lucky with the weather."

"It's a good omen, I think," replied Florian.

"I want to thank you for the bouquet. It is truly beautiful," said Julia.

"My mother has good taste," replied Florian. They continued on, saying little until they arrived at the Gestopian residence, where Julia would now live with Florian, his parents Marcus and Sophia, and their three younger children.

They crossed the threshold as strangers.

———

Chad watched Prof. Hunter as she paced back and forth in her office, barking short questions into a cell phone held tightly to her ear. There was little enough space to walk in as she maneuvered around stacks of books and papers littering the floor. He could not tell what was making her so agitated, as her monosyllabic comments were unrevealing. As she executed each about face, her long striped skirt swirled around her thin legs and a necklace formed of odd bits of wooden pieces whipped back and forth. The professor was having a bad hair day, with her gray roots showing prominently. Chad had hoped to find her in a better mood.

Brooke and Robert were crammed into two wooden chairs at the edges of the office, suffering the delay along with him. When Hunter finished her phone conversation, she said, "Give me some good news. Have you figured out how the Memex works yet?"

"We've been working on it," said Brooke. "We tried using it at three different locations, north, west, and south of here. The first was in a remote corner of the Adirondack Park, the second in a cow pasture in the countryside, and the third in the Lincoln tunnel. The Memex worked in all these locations, so I'm beginning to doubt that we're picking up signals from some transmitter."

"That's disappointing. Do you have any other ideas?" asked Hunter.

After a short pause, Brooke said, "I've been thinking about monarch butterflies." Chad was surprised by this new topic and a little hurt that Brooke had not mentioned it to him beforehand. Now he was caught flat-footed, unable to contribute to the conversation.

"The monarchs spend their winters in Mexico and migrate to the north each spring, some to the Eastern seaboard and some to California. The migrating butterflies come out of hibernation in February or March, make their long trek north, and lay their eggs when they arrive at their final destination. Then an odd thing happens. The next generation lives only about a month or so, and stays in the north their whole lives. The third and fourth generations are the same, living only a short while, with no migration. Finally, in September or October, the great-grandchildren of the original migrants fly south, miraculously arriving at the same grove of trees where their ancestors lived. This migrating generation lives six to eight months in contrast with the other generations that live only two to six weeks."

"How do they do it?" asked Robert.

"Researchers aren't sure. They know that the butterflies use the position of the sun for navigation. They may also have magnetic field sensors in their antennae. But how the information gets transmitted from one generation to the next is a mystery."

"There must be something in their genes," said Hunter.

"People have looked into that. The California butterflies have the same genetic make-up as the East Coast butterflies, so the flight path is probably not in the genes."

"How does this help us with the Memex?" asked Hunter.

"I'm not sure it does, but there are some parallels..." said Brooke. "The descendents are somehow using information that their ancestor knew."

"You don't know that. It could be that the descendents react to the world in the same way the ancestors did, picking up on subtle clues that we haven't figured out yet," said Hunter. Chad was wondering why he had ever picked Hunter as a thesis adviser. If it hadn't been for the interesting work and the funding…

A short silence descended on the group before Robert said, "I think it's a good lead."

"There's a lot of things we don't know about memory," said Chad. "What about people who have photographic memories? They prove that the mind has greater capacity than we normally think." He wanted to push his point, but he didn't know much about the topic.

"Marvin Minsky claims that photographic memory doesn't exist. It's all a fraud," said Hunter. Chad was left with no defense. He felt like a fool. If only Brooke had shared her theories with him before the meeting, he could have prepared better. But she had left him in the dark, and not for the first time.

"You need to come up with better explanations than these," said Hunter. "Shall we meet again next week?"

Chad never wanted to see Hunter again, but he swallowed his feelings and agreed.

———

When Brooke entered the lab, she found Robert waiting to help her with the Memex. He looked tired and she asked him what was wrong.

"I'm a little discouraged. I was reading about monarch butterflies, but I'm not sure how it will help us. Scientists really don't understand them any more than we understand the Memex."

"I know," said Brooke softly. "But we'll figure it out eventually. We have a lot of exploring to do yet."

"I guess so." He sat up a little straighter in his chair. "Where are we going today?"

"I want to follow Garnett and see how he got to Constantinople."

"OK, get ready."

Nov. 26, 1199. Brooke was perched on the back of a horse, encased in armor and holding a lance and shield. The weighty steel pressed on her and the narrow eye slit left her feeling more claustrophobic than protected. She wanted to reach up and rip off the helmet, but of course, she could not. Her steed was restless, raising his head and shifting a bit from side to side. Before her, a gently-sloping plain covered with long grasses stretched upward to a line of mounted knights. A flash of terror passed through Brooke. The line of opponents stretched wide and menacing. Was there a war in France that Brooke didn't know about?

Through her limited peripheral vision, she glimpsed knights to either side of herself, no doubt her comrades. Horses nickered all along the line, muscles tight and poised to run, held back only by years of training. A trumpet sounded and the knights charged forward in unison, armor rattling and hooves thumping. Garnett leaned forward in the saddle, cradling his lance in one arm, and bracing the elbow of the arm holding his shield against his chest. In that moment, Brooke fastened on details of the attackers before her, their helmets sporting golden feathers, their shields painted with dragons and cocks, and their lances striped with red and white.

As the lines drew ever closer, Brooke was alarmed to see two knights aiming for Garnett. One, with a red and black coat of arms, black armor, and a black mount, was a horse length ahead of the other. Garnett directed his lance toward the forward knight, a better idea than trying to tackle them both. Brooke saw the rearward knight redirect his course, apparently to face an unseen adversary. When impact came, Brooke's arm was shocked into numbness, but Garnett held his seat. As Garnett's lance struck his adversary in the shoulder, the knight twisted precariously in his saddle, but did not fall. The horses passed each other and Garnett pulled hard on the bit. His mount wheeled to face the combat zone again, and he dropped his lance. He drew his sword and raised it high.

The meadow had been churned up by the melee. Most knights were still in the saddle, milling about and seeking targets. Others were struggling up from the ground, drawing their weapons. One man lay on the ground motionless. For the first time, Brooke noticed that each wore a square of cloth, some blue and some white, tied across the breastplate of their armor. Garnett made for a nearby dismounted knight and struck him in the head with the flat of his sword. The knight fell to his knees and Garnett raised his weapon, threatening a second blow. The knight dropped his sword and raised his arms in a gesture of surrender. Garnett dipped his blade and looked about to get his bearings.

A knight decked out in forest green armor galloped towards Garnett, sword ready. Garnett pulled his horse's head about and parried the thrust. The two combatants exchanged blows, each blocking the other's attack. The clank of weapons on steel resounded throughout the meadow, muting the noise of Garnett's duel. Garnett made tight, economical moves designed to get past his opponent's guard, while the green knight was prone to larger, more flamboyant strikes that took longer to connect. Nevertheless, the two were well matched and neither was able to gain a decisive advantage.

Garnett's horse stepped sideways unexpectedly and bumped the flank of the opposing steed, while Garnett slammed his gauntleted hand into the knight's face. Overbalanced, the green knight started to slip sideways. As he fell, he grabbed Garnett's arm and they both tumbled to the ground. Brooke was stunned by the fall, and terrified that the thrashing hooves would connect with a vulnerable spot. Garnett was unshaken. He rose and prepared to resume battle, coming face to face with the green knight, who was also rising to his feet.

The thrust and parry was markedly slower this time. Brooke's arm ached from holding the heavy weapon and fending off numerous blows. Brooke lost track of the rest of the field, her whole attention focused on what was right before her. Garnett was panting and the blood pounded in his ears. Again and again, he attacked, then blocked. Both men were tiring; it was a battle of endurance more than anything else, both mental and physical. Garnett paused, waiting for his weary opponent to make the next move. When the thrust came, Garnett caught the other man's blade in a quick circular motion and sent it flying. Disarmed, the green knight dropped to one knee in surrender.

Garnett nodded, and then scanned the field. Before he had a chance to engage in another bout, a trumpeter signaled a halt to the fighting, and a miraculous silence descended. After the cacophony of metal on metal, the quiet seemed unnatural and menacing. Brooke's ears were ringing, and she was hot and thirsty. Slowly, men gathered themselves and abandoned the field. The knight that Brooke had seen prostrate on the ground did not rise, and Garnett went over to him. With three others, he carried the knight to a nearby barn, where a squire began to remove armor from the unconscious man. The two men that Garnett had defeated joined him near the barn. Both wore white cloth squares; the tie on one cloth had been severed and the square hung limply from the defeated knight's chest.

As Garnett removed his helmet, Brooke drank in the cool air like a drowning sailor breaking the surface of the sea. A teen-aged boy brought cups of some sweet alcoholic drink to the thirsty men.

"Good fight," said the knight in green armor. "I thought I would best you, but the field was yours today."

"It's always a tough fight against you, Phillipe. We were well matched. This is the largest tournament I've ever seen. Sir, I have not had the pleasure of your acquaintance," said Garnett to his other captive.

"I am Evrat of Ecry, and I compliment you on your victory."

Garnett inclined his head graciously. The conversation turned into a negotiation, where the terms of ransom were haggled over, albeit in exquisitely polite language. Phillipe promised four ounces of silver and Evrat offered his saddle as a prize. So this is how knights amass wealth, thought Brooke. She wasn't sure she liked it.

Nov. 27, 1199. On the second day of the tournament, the nobility gathered in the morning for mass. The church rang out with the songs of the faithful, a mix of voices from basso profundo to coloratura soprano. The verse was in Latin, and the melody unfamiliar to Brooke, but words issued from her mouth in a deep resonant tone. The church itself was new to her, of a Spartan and severe architectural style. The nave was uncomfortably narrow compared to the height of the ceiling, in displeasing proportion. The side walls were stark white, with miserly windows high above, leading to a painted ceiling where martyrs and saints suffered their endless tortures.

The hymn ended and a rotund monk in a coarse brown robe took center position in front of the altar. "Heed my word to you, my lords and brothers; heed my word to you! Indeed, not my word, but Christ's. Christ himself is the author of this sermon, I am but his fragile instrument. It is he who grieves before you over his wounds." Brooke was taken aback by this audacious claim. No one else seemed to be; the audience stood as if mesmerized.

"Christ has been driven out of his holy place, his seat of power. He has been exiled from that city which he consecrated to himself with his own blood—the blood he spilt for your salvation. The Holy Land is now infested with the barbarism of a heathen people. Oh the misery, the sorrow, the utter calamity! Jerusalem has been given over to the impious. Its churches have been destroyed, its Shrine polluted, its royal throne and dignity transferred to the gentiles." With each new claim, the monk rotated his considerable belly in a new direction, and the knotted end of his rope belt swayed back and forth like the tail of a cat.

"That most venerable relic, the True Cross, drenched with the blood of Christ, has been stolen by the ungodly and hidden away so that no Christian may know where to look for it. Virtually all of our people who used to inhabit the Levant have been killed or driven out by the infidels. The survivors cling to Acre, withstanding repeated enemy attacks, but cannot prevail much longer."

There were grunts and murmurs from the congregation, and much shuffling of feet. Brooke felt a chill settle upon her, partly from the unheated church, which was as cold as a tomb, and partly from the feeling that the congregation was becoming a mob. The monk seemed to be just getting started with his diatribe.

"And so now, true warriors, hasten to help Christ. Enlist in His Christian army. Rush to join the happy ranks. Today I commit you to the cause of Christ, so that you might labor to restore Him to His patrimony, from which He has been so unmercifully expelled." A man near Brooke shouted, "Yes, brother," and others threw in words of support.

"This crusade is God's work, and whosoever takes the sign of the cross and makes sincere confession will be totally absolved of every sin and when he leaves this present life, no matter where, when, or by what happenstance, he will receive life eternal."

An interesting bargain, thought Brooke. Even if a crusader died of illness on his way to the Holy Land, he would be assured a place in heaven. These people believed that the monk was speaking in Christ's voice, and thus it was Christ himself making the promise. To her, it was a web of lies. The monk probably believed what he was saying, but she didn't. She regarded the entire sermon as manipulation of the gullible.

The congregation, aroused, was becoming boisterous, and the monk raised both arms and stopped talking until they quieted. "Now I shall not even mention that the land to which you are heading is by far richer and more fertile than this land, and it is easily possible that many from your ranks will acquire a greater prosperity even in material goods than they will remember enjoying back here." This crass appeal to greed shocked Brooke, who was not used to such blatant mercenary talk from churchmen.

As the preacher wound up to the climax of his sermon, he raised his voice above the sighs and moans of the people. "Now, therefore, brothers, take the triumphal sign of the cross in a spirit of joy, so that, by faithfully serving the cause of Him who was crucified, you will earn sumptuous and eternal pay for brief and trivial work."

At that point, a young nobleman in lavish costume strode to the front and knelt on one knee before the monk.

"I, Thibaut, Count of Champagne, solemnly dedicate myself and my arms to the cause of Christ. By my oath, I will not rest until the Holy Land is restored to its rightful Master." The monk blessed Thibaut and presented him with a pilgrim's staff and a cross, which he attached to his shoulder. The young count's bold move galvanized the group, already stirred up by the sermon, and the aisle began to fill with knights ready to take the cross. The second to commit was Count Louis of Blois, another high-ranking knight.

Garnett joined the eager knights pushing forward to the front of the church. One by one, they made their oaths and dedicated themselves body and soul to the cause. At his turn, Garnett knelt before the monk and became a crusader.

XVII

PILGRIMAGE

"As you know, I have some questions about the reality of your visions," said Hunter from behind her desk. Her sober stare was cold and unyielding, worthy of a judge about to announce an unfavorable verdict. Brooke sat stiff-backed opposite her, the battered steel desk separating them in distance as well as in spirit. Chad had come to the meeting as well, but Robert had called in sick. Hunter's office was chilly today and Brooke tried unsuccessfully to suppress a shiver.

"They're memories, not visions," said Brooke. "After all, it's the memory centers of the brain that we stimulate. It makes sense that we get memories. Visions are brief and fantastical, not long stories with episode after episode, such as I have experienced."

"I agree," said Chad. "My trips on the Memex were memories. They didn't come from my imagination."

"It would be more convincing if we understood the mechanism by which these so-called memories are generated," said Hunter.

"I've been reading the research literature on monarch butterflies in search of clues, but I don't have anything definitive yet," said Brooke. "They don't understand monarchs any better than we understand the Memex. That doesn't mean that our experiences aren't real. The monarchs keep migrating whether we understand them or not."

Hunter paused and gazed at the two students with wrinkled brow, pursing her lips in a sign of doubt. Did she think they had made it all up?

"Besides," continued Brooke, "Chad has experienced them as well."

"That is hardly conclusive evidence. He could be as deluded as you." This sounded like a conspiracy charge to Brooke, and she blushed despite her innocence. She wished Chad would defend himself, but he remained silent.

"There's one thing I can't make sense of," said Hunter, before Brooke could say anything further. "If you are indeed viewing memories from your forbears, then you must have received them by genetic transmission. It's hard to imagine any other route. You told me about Damian chastising his daughter after her romp with that boyfriend. So you're able to access him after Julia was born. I can understand, at least in theory, how the father's memories could be transmitted to the daughter at conception, but how could Damian's memories formed after she was born possibly get into Julia's head and later, by extension, into yours?"

Brooke had no answer. She had thought of this question herself and shoved it to the back of her mind because she could make no headway with it. She should have realized that Hunter would bring it up.

"The transmission must not be genetic," said Brooke. The statement sounded weak even to her ears.

"Then why are you only getting ancestors?"

Brooke was miserable. This line of thought threatened to unravel her entire thesis. She had wondered why she could access memories throughout the lives of her hosts. It made more sense that she would remember only up to the point where they conceived the next generation. But something odd was happening, something she had no explanation for.

"Many new phenomena are poorly understood when they are first discovered. In time, I believe we'll understand, but right now, we don't have enough data. As soon as we can test other humans, many things will become clear."

"How are the mice doing?"

"No problems. None at all." Hunter looked at Chad for confirmation.

"The mice are just fine," he said.

"Well, *that's* good news at least. All right, let's meet again next Monday at 1 PM." Brooke scribbled the time in her notebook and exited the office as quickly as she could. One more painful meeting finished. Freedom for seven days, until she had to face Hunter again.

Apr. 14, 1202. Garnett stood beside the cart, arms akimbo, and surveyed the packing job that his squire, Peter, had done. Boxes, crates, and barrels were lashed down with thick ropes, artfully arranged to make maximum use of space. Even the curved spaces between barrels were packed with conforming canvas bags.

"Did you remember the spare horseshoes?" asked Garnett.

"Yes, Sir," replied Peter, "and I also brought tools, thread in various gauges, and spare leather for repairs."

"And the provisions?"

"We have two sacks of flour, a side of smoked pork, a barrel of wine, a tent, a cook pot, two blankets, and assorted cooking implements. We ought to be able to buy or trade for other things we need along the way."

"I wish I had been able to collect more money. The 1,500 livres in tithes from my tenants may not suffice. Count Thibaut is lucky—he has more Jews in his dominions, and can squeeze them for double or triple shares." Brooke was upset by her ancestor's attitude to Jews. She wished that Garnett were more enlightened than his fellow knights, but she supposed it was too much to ask of him.

"You did pack the silverware and the jewels? We're going to need them to barter with," said Garnett.

"I did."

"Good lad." Peter beamed under this praise, his long, horsey face taking on a beatific air. Peter had a slim build that masked his considerable physical strength. He understood the horses that he cared for and they reacted to him as they would to kin. Garnett circumnavigated the wagon, pulling at a rope here, shoving at a box there, testing for looseness and finding none. The early morning was foggy and damp, with a chill that reached into Brooke's bones and caused a mental shiver. Although it would be a long ride with no heater or radio, Brooke was by now accustomed to the inconveniences of the past and hardly noticed them.

The front door of the manor house, barely visible through the fog, opened wide and Garnett's sister appeared, looking distressed. "Oh Garnett, it's hard to see you go."

"Don't worry. I'll be back. The Lord will protect me." In a softer tone, he added, "I just can't stay here. Everywhere I look I see things that remind me of Cerise. She was so dear to me and her loss cut deeply into my heart. I welcome the fire of battle to wash away my pain. I also think that God has a plan for me. He took my beloved wife away for a reason, and I must heed His call. It was no accident that I heard the crusade sermon during the tournament at Ecry, just a short while after Cerise died. God wants me on this pilgrimage, and I will fight for Him."

A maid servant exited the house, leading a small child by the hand. Garnett's daughter had grown into a sturdy toddler with curly blond hair and a plump little body. When she saw her father, she ran into his arms. He picked her up and tossed her giggling into the air. He laughed and played with her a long time, while the others, sensing the sweetness of this parting moment, waited patiently.

"Cherie, papa has to go away for a long time," he said tenderly. "Jesus needs my help, and I can't take you with me. You'll be safe here with Auntie."

A frown crossed the little girl's face and she said, "You promise to come back, papa?"

"I do. I'll be back. You probably won't even miss me."

"Does Grumble have to go too?" A mongrel, whose black, brown, and gray coat looked as if it had been painted on by an inept child, looked up from where he lay on the ground at the mention of his name.

"No, Grumble can stay here and play with you."

"Thank you, Papa." With the distractibility of the very young, the girl went to Grumble and patted his head.

"I'll be off now," said Garnett, and kissed his sister on the cheek. A tear ran from her eye, and Garnett wiped it away.

Garnett swung himself up into the saddle of his war horse, waved his arm, and headed off down the road. He looked back once, and saw his daughter in his sister's arms, crying and reaching for him. That image would haunt Brooke's dreams for many days to come.

Brooke leafed through the science and technology section of the Economist, and lit upon an article on weird astrophysics. She was curled up on her sofa and nursing a beer, relaxing after a long day. She read the article with its unbelievable claims on dark energy with an air of skepticism. Of course, if the Economist ever wrote about her work, readers might find her claims equally hard to take. If she ever got to publish at all. At the rate things were going, publication seemed like a distant dream.

Claudia stepped into the living room and plopped into an armchair. "How are things? What are you reading?" Brooke's roommate had skin of a ghostly paleness and flyaway orange hair. She wore a sleeveless top that accentuated her tattoo-covered arms. No one who ever met Claudia forgot her.

"Just some astrophysics." Claudia was an architecture major and not interested in esoteric physics, so Brooke didn't elaborate.

"I heard the strangest thing today. Someone told me there's a working time travel experiment on campus. Do you know anything about it? They said it was in the department of Cognitive Science."

Brooke was genuinely alarmed, not only that Claudia, far away in architecture, had heard about her work, but that she had accurately pinned it down to Brooke's department. Her first impulse was to deny any knowledge. After all, the university lawyer had made her sign a non-disclosure agreement and virtually threatened her with expulsion if she talked. If she were honest with herself, Brooke also wanted to deny the Memex because she didn't want to have to justify her experiments to Claudia. But Brooke was getting tired of all the intrigue. Deception is an acid that eats away at your character, leaving it stunted and disfigured. Brooke longed to return to the honest person she had been before all this started.

"I have to tell you something. You'll have trouble believing it, but I'm the one conducting the so-called 'time travel' experiments."

"Shut up! Seriously, what are you talking about?"

"We're not actually traveling in time—that's impossible as far as I know. But what I can do is remember everything my ancestors lived through. It feels like I'm there, in the past. Of course I can't change anything, and I don't have any freedom of movement. I pretty much have to settle for whatever they saw, heard, or felt."

"This is incredible." Claudia sat up straighter and perched on the edge of her chair. Her forehead was creased in a frown of doubt. Brooke thought she might not be believed. How ironic would that be, to be suspected of lying when all she wanted was to tell the truth.

"What's it like, girlfriend, spill," said Claudia. Apparently she had decided to take Brooke at her word, or at least reserve judgment.

"It's a little like backpacking. You give up the comforts of modern life in exchange for 'roughing it' in the past. Lots of exercise, peace and quiet, a slower pace, but also danger, pain, and excitement. And when you do return from the Memex, you really appreciate your cell phone, your car, and even central heating."

"Doesn't sound like much fun," said Claudia.

"There are good moments, you'd be surprised." Brooke didn't want to get into all the details on this score, so she diverted the conversation.

"Claudia, it's very important that you don't tell anyone. I had to sign papers with the university saying I wouldn't talk about this. I could get kicked out of school if you tell people."

"Don't worry. I don't spread rumors. You can count on me. But you have to tell me more about what happened to you."

Brooke told her about Constantinople and the Fourth Crusade, and all the people she had come to care about. She promised to tell Claudia what happened to her ancestors when the city was invaded, and anything she might discover about the history of that infamous campaign.

"I suppose you got a patent on this invention," said Claudia.

Brooke looked startled, her face blank. "Actually, we haven't talked about that," she said.

"What? This thing has enormous commercial potential. People are going to be lined up to use it. Everyone will want to take 'tourist' trips into the past, especially if they can see famous people or events. Some will just want to see what their ancestors were like. Then there's the genealogists and the historians, who will want to conduct studies. This thing is huge!"

"You have a point. I don't know why I didn't think about it before."

"You could make a lot of money, being the inventor of something like this."

"Knowing Brackett, they'll take most of the profit," said Brooke darkly.

"Even if they do, I bet there will be a lot of revenue to go around. A small cut might turn out to be worth millions."

Brooke took a brief flight of fancy, thinking of herself as a multimillionaire—living on a huge yacht with servants in white uniforms, sipping vintage wine on a sun drenched deck and never having to meet a deadline. The image took hold and she began to want that patent as if it were a key out of prison. All her life, Brooke had dreamed of a fulfilling career with a generous salary. But she had never really believed that she might become outlandishly rich, until this moment. The lure of a lucrative patent aroused a primeval lust for wealth within her. The small flicker of shame that she felt at this impulse was quickly damped down. She started to put together a plan.

May 2, 1202. Garnett ploughed ahead through the driving snow, leading his battle horse, Ajax, by the reins. The ground was covered to a depth of more than a foot, and each step challenged the overworked muscles of his legs. Ahead of him, a wagon piled high with supplies toiled along, leaving a trail from its four wheels and two horses. Although the snow was partially churned up by the group in front of him, Garnett seemed to seek out the deeper, untouched patches of snow and tread on them, like a little boy leaving his mark. Brooke wondered why he would do this, tired as he was.

Garnett glanced back to see Peter behind him, leading two pack horses hitched to a wagon. The uphill grade was steepening as they made their way through a high Alpine valley surrounded by majestic peaks. The light was dim and little gusts of wind blew snow off the sharp edges of drifts, further obscuring vision. Despite the cold, Garnett was sweating with exertion, and he smelled of wet wool and damp socks.

They turned a corner, and Brooke saw a team pulled over by the side of the trail. No one paid any heed to them and they seemed not to be seeking help. As they rested, the fast falling snow accumulated on their shoulders and hats and on the backs of the horses, giving them a white crust. Garnett continued on and the snow was now noticeably less packed down. His heart pounded and he breathed heavily but kept lifting one leg after the other in a measured cadence. The valley was narrower here, and the crags above them traced a jagged line against the gray sky. The higher peaks ascended into the cloud layer and were lost to sight. The mountainside was so steep in places that the snow could find no purchase and the bare rock was exposed.

Garnett was no longer seeking out the deepest snow, but instead followed in the footsteps of those in front of him. Little could be heard except the creak of the harnesses, and an occasional snort from Ajax—the snow dampened other sounds. The snowflakes became smaller and less dense, promising an end to the blizzard. The team ahead of Garnett pulled to the side of the trail and stopped. Garnett passed them and was now faced with an unblemished layer of white—beautiful but daunting. He seemed to get a second wind and broke trail with renewed vigor. Brooke thought he would go on forever—left to herself, she would have halted long ago. It seemed to be a matter of pride to Garnett to spearhead the caravan for as long as possible. Eventually, even he relented and pulled over. Peter followed with the wagon and stood breathing hard next to his master. As they rested, the army marched past, gray and white specters leading horses and carts and moving doggedly forward. It felt like sitting at a railroad crossing and watching a slow moving train rolling along, one car after the other. Everyone was walking except one man, perched on the seat of his wagon, either from exhaustion, injury, or laziness. A large cart carrying a barely recognizable catapult trundled past drawn by four outsized beasts. Several other large wagons followed with heavy equipment—blacksmith and armory tools, a camp cauldron three feet in diameter. At the end of the procession, a group of women labored along. Garnett and Peter swung into position in front of the women and continued their march, now refreshed by their rest. The trail was fully packed and the going was much easier.

The snowflakes tapered off and gently ceased. The light was fading as the day drew to a close. The sun, still hidden behind a thick layer of clouds, would sink behind the mountaintops soon and cast the landscape into the sudden darkness that occurs in the high Alps. Up ahead, the crusaders were veering off the path, spreading out over a relatively flat stretch of land to make camp for the night. When Garnett and Peter had staked out a campsite, they busied themselves packing the snow, assembling the tent, and pulling out dry firewood from the wagon.

Brooke luxuriated in the warmth of the small blaze, feeling a profound sense of comfort. The dance of the flame was mesmerizing, synchronized as it was to the crackle of gas popping from the wood. Garnett looked up to take in the star-splashed sky, now clear of all clouds. Brooke was in awe of the brightness of this sky, loaded with more stars than she had ever seen before. Arcturus and Spica sparkled brilliantly in the tableau and the Milky

Way formed an almost continuous band of light. She thought back to the night she and Chad had tested the Memex by a cowfield, and gazed upon a much less impressive sky. Modern society had obscured one of nature's great panoramas.

A mournful melody played on a pipe drifted over to them from a nearby campsite. Garnett turned his head in that direction and listened attentively. After a while, he rose and approached the musician, settling around his fire. The pipe player was a big man, with large hands that nevertheless managed to cover the right holes and produce a flawless troubadour song. Brooke had never felt so much at peace as she did at that moment. Music was rare in this time period, and more precious as a result.

The pipe player finished his performance and introduced himself as Hugh. Garnett learned that he lived in a village not far from Garnett's home and that they served the same liege lord, Jourdain of Senlis. Hugh came from a family of warriors; both his father and his uncle had served in the crusade to rescue the Holy Land from Saladin. Left to himself, he might have chosen music as his calling, but that was not to be, and he had been trained as a knight.

"I hear we should make it through the pass tomorrow," said Hugh. "It's a gentle walk down to Italy from there."

"I almost wish we were taking the overland route, through Germany and Asia Minor rather than sail the Mediterranean," said Garnett. "I like walking."

"Men starved on that route; it takes far too long. This will be easier."

"Have you been on the sea?"

"No, but I don't have to become a sailor. The Venetians will transport the army."

Garnett fell silent. Brooke guessed that he had never sailed or even seen an ocean, and the uncertainty of the experience gnawed at him. The sea voyage was the least of his worries, but he couldn't know that. The things we fear are often less trouble than the things we never even imagine.

—⚬⚬⚬—

June 15, 1202. The oars dipped rhythmically into the blue-green sea, leaving little trails of swirling foam in their wake. Garnett shaded his eyes from the morning sun as he surveyed the shore from his seat in the middle of the small craft. The island of St. Nicholas, where the crusaders had been camped for several weeks, receded off the stern. Peter was pulling hard on the oars, along with five other men. Hugh lounged beside Garnett, the two privileged knights not expected to join in the heavy manual labor of rowing.

Venice lay before them just a short distance across the lagoon, and Brooke was impatient to arrive. Garnett was playing the tourist today, after interminable days in the flat, sandy camp, with little to do other than train with blunt weapons, exercise the horses, and eat the never ending biscuits and salt pork. Brooke had visited Venice in the summer after graduation, and, like most visitors, was immediately caught in the spell of that most unusual city. The narrow, winding streets, the steep bridges over the gentle canals, the weathered statuary, and the air of genteel decay combined to lull the visitor into a relaxed happiness. Brooke wondered how the city would appear to her today, through the eyes of her ancestor.

The boat bumped up against a short dock, and a sailor jumped out to wrap a rope around a brass mooring. They had alighted at the mouth of a canal that wound into the interior of the city. Here Garnett, Hugh, and Peter hired a gondolier to take them down the waterway. Brooke feasted her eyes on the elegant homes that lined the canal, their stucco walls freshly painted in rose, mauve, and muted yellows, many with arched windows capped by pointed tops and narrow balconies. They passed by a bridge that was under construction and arrived at a wide plaza facing a shipyard.

"Look at this arsenal," said Hugh. "I hear they can build a ship in less than a week." Brooke saw more than seven vessels in various stages of completion, from those with partial hulls and exposed ribs to those fully rigged with sails and oars. "They build so many at once that the craftsmen just move from one ship to the next, performing the same work again and again."

"I would rather build one whole ship than work on pieces of this and pieces of that. What satisfaction is there in that?" asked Peter.

"Gets them built fast though."

The shipyard was active, with men hammering planks in place, hoisting supplies onto the decks, caulking, painting, and weatherproofing. On one vessel, four workers strained to hoist a mast into place, pulling on a thick rope attached to a block and tackle. In Brooke's opinion, the vessels were ungainly, wide and round like a duck, not sleek and narrow like a modern sailboat. These were undoubtedly the craft meant to carry the crusaders off to war.

Garnett paid the gondolier and the three strolled around the square, observing the work in progress.

"I've never seen a manufactory this large," said Garnett. "I didn't realize how wealthy Venice is."

"Wealth breeds wealth," said Hugh. "These vessels let them trade with Egypt, Constantinople, Asia Minor, the Levant, and ports on the Aegean sea. There's no glory in trade, and I would never want to be a merchant, but it's definitely profitable."

The men left the square and wandered into the warren of streets to the west. The homes here were less imposing than those on the canal, but still looked prosperous and well kept. Pedestrians passed them in the narrow streets, bustling off purposefully to unknown destinations. The men they came upon were mostly clean-shaven, unlike the majority of the French and Flemish crusaders. Garnett came to a fork and looked back at his friends for guidance. Peter shrugged his shoulders and pointed to the left. They crossed a steep brick bridge over a small canal that snaked off into the distance. The buildings were arranged to fit harmoniously against the edge of the canal. A jewelry vendor sat at the base of the bridge and offered them her wares, but they passed by. At the next intersection, Hugh stopped and looked left and right.

"I think we should head right."

"St. Mark's is off to the left," said Garnett. They both looked at Peter, who wisely agreed with his master, and the party headed left. A woman dressed in evening attire called to them in a low, throaty voice as they passed. She was perfectly coiffed, her svelte form hugged by a deep green gown, her breasts pushed up to accentuate her cleavage. Brooke didn't understand the language, but the meaning was clear, and the three stopped. When they greeted her in French, she immediately switched to that language.

"Come with me. You deserve a little pleasure—no? I am from the finest establishment in Venice." Brooke doubted that. A call girl from an upscale bordello would not need to solicit on the street. Hugh and Peter wanted to go off with the woman, but Garnett was cool to the idea.

"You go ahead. I don't feel like it at the moment. I'll wait for you in that tavern." He pointed to a dubious looking doorway. Peter looked at him with concern but said nothing. They left and Garnett entered the dark tavern. The place was filled with a lunchtime crowd, every space taken by patrons slurping soup or digging into fresh seafood. The odors of malt, sweat, and fish combined into an unappetizing brew. Since there was nowhere to sit, Garnett stood near the entryway and waited for an opening. Ten minutes later, he snagged a place at a table near the back wall. The others at the table greeted him, but when they learned that he didn't speak Italian or Latin, they lost interest.

Brooke suffered through the next hour, as Garnett consumed a seafood chowder of unknown ingredients and drank a tankard of bitter ale. She supposed it was better than the monotony of the crusader rations, but not by much. She longed to pull out a cell phone or at least read a book to pass the time, but Garnett sat unperturbed waiting for his friends, doing nothing, saying nothing.

When Hugh and Peter returned, they ordered lunch and Brooke thought she would scream with impatience. Usually she was well adapted to the slow pace of the past, but today, a lingering anxiety tickled at her and made her jumpy.

It was midafternoon before the trio regained the streets and started making their way to St. Mark's. They were mostly bewildered by the twisting streets, and lacked either the inclination or the language skills to ask for help. They seemed content to wander around hoping to eventually find the goal. When, by chance, they arrived at St. Mark's, it was late afternoon and long shadows stretched across the square.

As Garnett looked up at the imposing facade of St. Mark's Basilica, Brooke was drawn back to an earlier time in her life when she had stood before this building with Kevin.

The weather was perfect and they had spent a glorious morning together. She and Kevin had walked through the streets, admiring the offerings in the shop windows—the Mardi Gras masks, the pastels of the canals, and the melting timepieces of Salvador Dali. Venice was a city of unsurpassed beauty and uniqueness, and perfect for an art lover like Brooke. They had even taken the obligatory ride in a gondola, and Brooke was surprised to find it every bit as romantic as commonly believed. She felt closer to Kevin than at any earlier time in their relationship, and began to wonder if he could be the one.

They had lunch in St. Mark's square, sitting in plastic chairs tightly packed around tables in the sun. Brooke enjoyed the clock tower, with its giant bronze marionettes that struck a bell every hour on the hour. Kevin had ordered spaghetti with squid ink sauce for them, insisting that she try this local delicacy, although Brooke was skeptical. In her view, black was not an appetizing color for spaghetti sauce, but she had to concede that it tasted better than it looked. The square was filled with tourists in shorts and odd hats, their bored children trailing behind them.

After lunch, she and Kevin waited in an interminable line to get into St. Mark's Basilica, roasting in the heat of the day. Her good mood began to fade. When they were finally admitted, Brooke savored the cool, dark, interior and relaxed as her eyes adjusted slowly to the dimness. The cavernous space was empty of pews, and filled with tourists milling about. Kevin cross-referenced the images in his guide book with what they saw about them, filling her in on the history of the building. Brooke's neck ached from craning it upwards to view the mosaics, bright in gold and bronze, that decorated the high spaces.

A hint of queasiness came upon her, and she tried to ignore it, hoping it would pass. She focused on the multitude of arches and the stained glass windows, trying to distract herself, but it wasn't working.

"Kevin, I'm not feeling so good."

"What's wrong?"

"My stomach—it's roiling."

"You'll be OK in a minute. Here, have some water." He held out a half empty plastic water bottle, but she gestured it away.

"I think we should leave. It's getting worse."

"We can't leave now," he said. "We waited so long to get in, and there's still a lot to see."

Brooke, miserable, trailed along after him, no longer listening to his comments about the Basilica read from the guide book. Finally she turned to him and said, "I have to leave. I'm going to be sick."

"You go ahead. I'll be out soon."

Brooke was hurt that he wouldn't go with her, but she didn't have much time to think about it. She made a dash for the exit, hoping to arrive before she upchucked. She couldn't bear the embarrassment of defiling a church with vomit. She made it outside and around to the side of the building before she couldn't hold it any longer. She retched miserably for several minutes. Afterward, she settled into a nearby table to wait for Kevin. He was taking a long time, and she felt obliged to order something that she wasn't going to consume.

Twenty minutes later, Kevin appeared.

"How you doing?"

"I'm a little better, but I feel weak and my head is throbbing. I want to go back to the room."

"Let's just sit here a bit and see if you improve," said Kevin. Brooke sat unhappily while Kevin sipped a piña colada.

"Kevin, let's go back to the room. I don't have the energy to do any more sightseeing today."

"But we haven't seen the Doge's Palace or the Bridge of Sighs. We have to see those."

In the end, he insisted that she go back alone, and gave her his map. Brooke, feeling vulnerable, navigated the tortured streets. Normally, she was good with a map, but in her debilitated state, she made an error, and had to retrace her steps, adding half a mile to her trek. When she arrived, she threw herself on the hard bed and curled up into a fetal position, feeling abandoned in a foreign city.

Brooke was ill for the next three days. Kevin spent most of his time touring the city on his own, checking in on her and bringing her food at rare intervals.

He seemed to resent that she was sick and blamed her for her "weakness." Luckily, she improved enough to get on the plane home, but their relationship had been wrecked, and Brooke never dated him again after that trip.

Now, as she stood once again before the Basilica of St. Mark as it was in the past, she noted the things that were different. The building was still under construction, centuries after it had been begun, and scaffolding was attached to one onion dome. The highest dome, even impressive in the 21st century, had not been constructed yet. The four prancing bronze horses that stood above the doorway in modern times were missing. She had seen them in the hippodrome of Constantinople when she had accessed Damian as a boy. They would be plundered by the Doge of Venice after the city fell and brought back to the Basilica. The Lion of St. Mark, which would become a symbol of the city for more than a thousand years, flew from a banner that flapped in the wind.

Garnett glanced back over the square and saw a distinctly non-modern picture. No plastic chairs, no swarming tourists. Just residents going about their business. These people were prosperous, and wore clothes that were clean and unpatched. Venice was the mightiest city in Christendom, save for Constantinople. Brooke supposed it was inevitable that the two great cities would clash, although no one could have predicted the bizarre series of events that would lead to the sack of Constantinople.

July 1, 1202. Damian and Basil were alone in the shop after the last customer had left for the day. Damian affixed the lock and turned toward Basil, who was working industriously at the long bench.

"Son, I have something I want to show you."

Basil looked surprised, and, wiping his hands on his apron, stepped out from behind the bench. He followed Damian to the kitchen and over to a corner near the sink. Damian lifted a trap door, releasing a musty odor into the little room. He lit an oil lamp and descended a ladder into the darkness, curling one hand around the rungs and holding the lamp in the other. Basil followed. The light from the lamp played around the small space, revealing boxes, crates, and a broken chair. Dark shadows hid the corners.

"This used to be a cistern," said Damian. "When old man Bardos owned the place, they needed to store water in the dry season. But something happened to the buried pipes and the water came no more. Bardos was too lazy and incompetent to get to the source of the problem, so he made his womenfolk haul water long distances to bring to the kitchen. Later, the city improved the plumbing nearby in a rare show of civic responsibility, and now we have a faucet just down the street. It never seemed necessary to restore the cistern."

Brooke admired the marble tiles that lined this humble space. Admittedly, they were of a lower grade than the marble used in the streets and palaces of the city, but they were still impressive. Damian moved aside a medium-sized crate and picked up a crowbar as Basil looked on quizzically.

Damian pried up one of the tiles with the crowbar, revealing a recessed compartment.

"Here is where I store my gold ingots and more valuable pieces when I'm not working on them."

"Isn't this inconvenient?" asked Basil.

"You can't be too careful in this world. If we had had this system when Origen robbed us, we would have lost a lot less. As it is, I still store some pieces in the workshop cabinet. It can be locked up and made to look like the prime storage place. But in fact, it's merely a decoy. The most valuable items are here, where no thief would ever think to look."

Basil gazed down into the dank hole, and then stepped back. Damian replaced the tile and swept some dirt into the cracks around the edges, making it look like the tarred joints of the surrounding tiles. He moved the crate back into position, and rubbed his hands along his pants.

"Now, you can't tell anyone about this, son. You're a man now and have to bear a man's responsibility to his family. Your mother and sister don't even know about this, so don't be telling your friends. Don't even tell Theodoret. The fewer people who know the better."

Brooke thought Damian was going a little far with this level of security, but she understood. He had sustained a big loss that threatened his way of life and was responding by taking extreme precautions to prevent a recurrence. She could hardly blame him.

July 10, 1202. Ajax splashed through the water along the shoreline of the island of St. Nicholas, his hooves flying and tail twitching. Garnett hunkered down in the slick, wet saddle, chasing Hugh's charger, three lengths ahead. A third knight rode on the seaward side of Hugh in water deep enough to reach the horse's belly. He gradually lost ground as his mount struggled against the greater water pressure and Garnett caught up to him. Brooke enjoyed the mad dash in the churned up surf, feeling carefree and excited.

The knights pushed their tired horses, yelling encouragement and applying spurs. A big wave struck Garnett broadside, and Brooke thought he might be unseated, but he tightened his legs around Ajax, who stumbled a bit and edged toward shore. Garnett pulled the reins hard to force the powerful horse back into deeper water. Ajax continued to nose his way toward the shallows, with his master insisting on staying further out.

Brooke gazed out over the azure stretch of the Mediterranean, sparkling in the morning sunlight. They were on the side of the island away from the lagoon and had an uninterrupted view of the horizon. A few ships plied the waters, the sails mostly flaccid in the calm weather, the oars dipping in a well synchronized rhythm.

The men allowed the horses to slow down and climb up onto the sandy shore. Ajax shook his head and snorted as he left the water, droplets flying off his mane. The knights dismounted and, after securing their horses, stretched out on the sand. Garnett shucked his wet shirt. He said, "I never get tired of looking at the sea."

"I'm going to miss it when we finally return home," said Hugh. "I can see how a man might become a sailor."

"Don't speak so fast," said Jehan, the third knight. "We have yet to go to sea."

"Have you heard any news about our departure date?" asked Garnett.

"Things look bad. There are a lot fewer crusaders than expected. Villehardouin and five others were sent to Venice last year to arrange sea passage for us. They contracted to transport 33,500 men and 4,500 horses to the Holy Land. We were supposed to leave last month, but only about 10,000 men have arrived."

"That's a big shortfall," said Garnett. "How could they have estimated so badly?"

"Truth to tell, many crusaders took alternate routes," replied Jehan. "The renowned Villain of Neuilly marched south from Piacenza and boarded ship at Apulia, bypassing Venice. The Burgundians sailed down the Rhone and set off from Marseille. John of Nesles sailed from Flanders around the Iberian peninsula, and didn't need to stop at Venice."

"If they had been true to the cause, they would have joined us here and not left the army scattered about," said Garnett.

"Maybe, but it's hard to blame them. They just took the shortest route to the Levant, expecting to meet up there. They never agreed to come to Venice."

"It leaves us in a bad spot, though."

"Why can't we just pay our freight and leave?" asked Hugh. "Let the Venetians worry about the loss of income."

"Doge Dandolo would never allow it," replied Jehan. "He claims that the shipyard was employed for a full year building all the ships we would need. They didn't trade that year and forfeited their usual income. He won't leave until he's paid in full."

"We don't have the money," protested Garnett. "We can't pay for all the missing crusaders."

"It's a standoff. I heard that some knights have given up and left, planning to get to the Holy Land some other way."

"Traitors," said Garnett. "We have to stay together. The army can only be effective if we're organized and disciplined and under one leader. The defectors are breaking their vows by abandoning us."

"I don't think so," replied Jehan. "We took a vow to fight for Jerusalem, not to honor some ridiculous agreement that a few deluded knights got us into."

Garnett fell silent, running his hand distractedly through the sand, picking up a shell and gazing at it absently. He lost interest and tossed it aside. Brooke remembered the tough haul over the Alps. If only they had left a month later, they could have avoided the blizzard. Like armies everywhere, it was a case of "hurry up and wait." This was a long wait.

XVIII

PLUNDER

"Can I get you a cup of coffee?" asked Brashley. "I'm fine, thanks," replied Brooke. Chad also declined, but Robert and Prof. Hunter accepted the offer and the university lawyer left the conference room. He returned shortly and said that coffee was on the way.

"How is your son doing, Louise?" asked Brashley.

"He likes Dartmouth. It's his first semester, so a little early to tell, but the signs are good." Brashley and Hunter continued with small talk about their families. Brooke didn't see any way into the conversation. Chad sat up straight in his chair, alert and ready for the meeting. For once, he had left his cowboy hat behind. Robert surprised her by wearing a new leather jacket. He looked good in it, despite the dark-rimmed glasses.

The conference room was well appointed with large, plush chairs fitting snugly against a curved mahogany table. The room bristled with technology, including a state-of-the-art computer projection system with custom console and retractable screens. Internet access ports and power strips were located at each seat. Watercolor scenes of the campus hung upon two walls and a large window afforded a view into a wooded area. The trees were frosted from yesterday's snowfall, branches bending precariously under the weight.

A woman entered with a tray of drinks and coffee was handed out. Hunter and Brashley finally got around to talking business, and Hunter outlined the function and operation of the Memex. She made a strong case for why they should apply for patent protection.

"Brackett University could benefit enormously from this invention," said Hunter. "This is an opportunity that could really put us on the map. The income from licensing the Memex could run to tens of millions of dollars per year."

"I understand there are some significant side effects," said Brashley.

Hunter looked at Brooke, apparently a cue for her to speak up.

"One of our mice died of a brain tumor," said Brooke, "but we don't think it's related to the Memex. None of the other mice show any ill effects, and the human testers, Chad and myself, are fine. Unfortunately, the incident has delayed our approval to test with human volunteers."

"Well, assuming that you do get approval and the machine works fine, tell me why people would want to use it," said Brashley.

"There are a thousand reasons," said Brooke. "Everyone is curious about the past. This is a chance to go on an extraordinary adventure, unlike anything available until now. People want to know what their ancestors were like. Plus you have all the academics, from historians to linguists to…" Brooke floundered, "to anyone interested in the history of their field. Not to mention reporters and writers of historical fiction."

"Descendents of famous people would flock to the Memex," said Chad. "Some of them feel a sense of pride in their illustrious ancestor, and since they would be the only ones who could access the ancestor, they would jump at the chance to prove how 'special' they are. For example, the genealogical tome entitled *Pocahontas' Descendents* lists more than 100,000 people. I'm sure we could find some takers from that group."

"And we shouldn't forget the less high-minded reasons for using the Memex," said Hunter. "Since you have full sensory experience while in your ancestor's head, it could be used for virtual sex." Brooke squirmed in her seat. This meeting had taken an unexpected and unwelcome turn. Chad sat up straighter still, looking ready to take flight.

"Am I right that the Memex could be used for sexual purposes?" asked Hunter, looking directly at Brooke.

Brooke felt a flush crawl up her cheeks, and willed it to abate. "Yes," she said in a low voice. Chad nodded his head in agreement. Robert looked surprised. Clearly this had never occurred to him.

"A lot of new inventions got a major boost because of the pornographic potential. Early movies were funded that way, so was the internet. It's not a pleasant thought, but it's a reality that we must be aware of."

"I see what you mean," said Brashley. "Clearly, the machine has a lot of potential uses. Have you thought about what it would cost to manufacture a Memex?"

Robert sprang into action at this point, pulling out projections and cost estimates. The device required a dedicated computer, a power supply, a signal generator, induction coils, and a padded chair. Similar devices available on the open market ran for about $30,000. Although the price was high, if the Memex became popular, economies of scale could push it down. As it was, the wealthy could easily buy their own machines. Entrepreneurs could set themselves up to sell time on the machine. Since one minute in real time translated to about five hours in the past, many customers per day could be served, and the business was potentially profitable. Of course, there was also a market for research uses of the Memex. Altogether, cost was not expected to be a major problem.

"It's expensive to get a patent," said Brashley. "We want to be sure that the Memex works without any major side effects and is worth patenting. We also have to get the timing right. Patents are searchable one year after they're submitted. If there are problems with the invention, Brackett will have egg on its face and be ridiculed for supporting a time machine patent."

"No, we won't," said Hunter. "People apply for outlandish patents all the time. There's no requirement to prove that the invention actually works—although that's not an issue in our case. The sole requirement is that the idea is original. GE once applied for a patent on a device using a magnetic monopole, even though no one had ever detected one. They wanted to lock in patents just in case a magnetic monopole was ever found. In the early twentieth century, there were so many patents for perpetual motion machines, none of which worked of course, that the patent office finally stopped issuing them."

"There's also a problem with filing too early," said Brashley. "If it takes years before the sale of the Memex produces a profit, then we've wasted part of the patent protection period. We'll apply for both a design and a utility patent, the first to protect the particular implementation of the idea and the other to protect the fundamental function of the device. The design patent lasts 14 years and the utility 20 years. Do you know of any other groups working on this technology?"

"No," replied Hunter. "I haven't mentioned it to anyone and I haven't heard any rumors. At conferences, I spend most of my time in the hallways networking with colleagues, and there's not a whisper of anything like this. I think we're out front on this one."

"Good, that means we might have some time. On another issue, we have to consider the privacy protection under the constitution. Accessing the memories of living people is highly likely to be ruled as an invasion of privacy. Even recent census records are not public. Census records are only available for 1940 and earlier. Can you set the machine to only access memories that are, say, more than 100 years old?"

"Not quite," replied Brooke. "We can't specify a date range, but we can design it to limit the access to, say, great-great-grandparents and earlier ancestors. All we have to do is limit the range of the signal. On the other hand, a knowledgeable person could easily add their own circuits to modify the range."

"But a hacker couldn't," said Brashley.

"No, you would have to get into the guts of the circuitry and bread-board your own design. Not a lot of people could do that."

"Good. Then I think the best course of action is to hold off a while. We'll patent this, but it's better if we file shortly before we start to advertise for test subjects. Meanwhile, keep careful records of your designs and find-ings, properly dated and witnessed. If someone files before us, we'll be able to prove prior invention. Any questions?"

Nobody spoke. Brooke was disappointed that they weren't going to file immediately, but at least Brashley was planning to file later. As long as some-one else didn't get there first...

Oct. 4, 1202. Garnett cradled a statue of St. Sebastian in his hands and kissed it gently before packing it away in a crate. Each night over the long months he had bunked in this tent, he had prayed before the image of the martyr for the soul of his beloved wife. Now he took one last sweep through the tent to be sure that nothing was left behind. The small area had been his and Peter's home while the leadership waited for more knights to join the cause and argued about what to do next. It had been a time of boredom and suffering. Food was scarce on the desolate sandy island and the Venetians controlled their access to the sea. There hadn't been much to do beyond military train-ing and exercising the horses, often with empty stomachs. The early excur-sions to Venice had been stopped. Brooke was grateful that she didn't have to live through most of that. The Memex was great at skipping over things.

Today, the leadership had finally resolved their differences and the fleet would sail. Garnett stepped outside and nodded to Peter who began pulling up stakes. The two men folded up the canvas and packed the tent away on the overstuffed cart.

Jehan came by as they were about to leave. "I wanted to say good-bye. I've enjoyed our time together, but I won't be sailing with you."

"Why not?" asked Garnett.

"Lord Boniface is taking the crusade to Zara, a Christian town. I joined a crusade against infidels, not my fellow believers. It's disgusting." He spat in the sand.

"The Zarans are pirates," said Garnett. "The army of God should smite evildoers, be they Christian or heathen."

"I don't know about that," said Jehan. "It sounds like a convenient excuse to me. Dandolo is greedy like all merchants. He sees a chance to rob from his neighbors and he's using us to get the job done."

"The bishops support the attack. That's enough for me."

"Still, I have doubts. This isn't my war."

"Surely you trust the judgment of the church." Garnett cocked his head speculatively.

"I'm not saying it's wrong, just that I don't want to be part of it. I signed up to fight the infidels and I'll wait until then to unsheathe my sword."

Garnett held out his hand to his friend. "If I can't convince you to stay, I wish you Godspeed and hope that we meet again in Jerusalem."

Jehan returned a hearty handshake and said, "In Jerusalem," and he was gone.

"I liked him," said Peter. "I didn't think he would break his vow and leave the army."

"He didn't break his vow," replied Garnett. "He only vowed to fight the Muslims, not to obey Lord Boniface no matter what. Nevertheless, I think he's making a mistake. The whole army can't get to the Holy Land without Venice. There wouldn't be enough ships in other ports to transport us all to the Middle East. A few knights here and there can find their way on their own, but that won't win the prize for us. A great army is needed to recapture Jerusalem."

"Do you think Doge Dandolo is justified in attacking the Zarans?"

"Who knows? I'm not from this part of the world."

"Where is Zara, milord?"

"It's on the eastern shore of the Adriatic Sea. It won't take long to sail there." The men swung themselves up onto the seat at the front of the cart and Peter flicked the reins. The horses headed for the crowded dock, where sailors busily packed supplies and men into the boat tenders. They stopped at the edge, waiting for an opening, when a troop of Venetian soldiers marched in, bearing a banner with the Lion of St. Mark, patron saint of the city. The crowd made way to let Doge Dandolo pass.

Brooke examined the notorious leader with interest. He was an aged man, tall and erect despite his years, with deep wrinkles in his leathery face and thin white hair barely covering his tanned scalp. He walked forward with a purposeful stride, despite his sightless eyes, trusting his servants to have cleared the way. Enrico Dandolo had fought in a crusade before and had become blind after a blow to the back of the head. He was more than eighty years old, but looked vital and strong. Dandolo had been reviled in the history books; Brooke herself was reserving judgment.

After Dandolo and his entourage had been ferried out to the flagship, Garnett and Peter unloaded their cart, piling up supplies on the side of the dock. They drove the empty cart to a second dock and unhitched the horses. Garnett approached Ajax and stroked his head, murmuring soothing words. The charger gazed at him with big trusting eyes. Ajax was a muscular stallion with a gleaming brown coat and a white blaze on his face. Garnett blindfolded the horse and led him up a gangway to a waiting vessel. When Ajax stepped onto the deck, which swayed slightly, he jerked and looked ready to balk, but Garnett held the reins tightly.

"This will be all right, Ajax. You don't worry now. I won't see you for a while, but the sailors will take good care of you."

Garnett led Ajax down a ramp to the hold and guided him into his stall. A sailor said, "I can take him from here, Sir."

"No, that's all right. I'll stay until he's fully settled in."

The sailor unhitched a length of cloth from a hook on the ceiling and passed it under Ajax's belly. Another sailor took it and, smoothing out the wrinkles, pulled it up alongside the horse and hooked it to a waiting block and tackle. While Garnett spoke to the horse in reassuring tones, the men wound up the winch, gradually lifting the beast off his feet, until he was fully supported in the sling. Now that he was secure against the swaying of the ship, Garnett removed Ajax's blindfold and fed him some oats. The horse gobbled up the unaccustomed treat eagerly, forgetting his unfamiliar situation. Garnett patted Ajax in farewell and made his way back to the dock. Peter had taken care of the pack horses and was negotiating the sale of the cart. From his demeanor, he wasn't getting a very good deal, but the locals had the edge since the market was flooded with carts just at the moment.

It was midday before Garnett and Peter were settled into their own billet on a distressingly small ship. They had a space no bigger than six feet by three feet just aft of the forecastle. Most of their supplies had been stowed below deck, but they retained three crates, securely lashed down. Crusaders occupied every available corner on the deck. The sailors wound around and stepped over them as they prepared the vessel for departure. Garnett was among the lucky; many of the infantry, sergeants, and lesser knights were billeted below decks in dank, cramped quarters. Brooke shuddered inwardly at their plight.

Following the example of other knights, Garnett hung his shield, decorated with a griffin, blue and gold chevrons, and a horseshoe, over the rail near the bow. He hoisted his banner up the mast, where it snapped in the breeze. Brooke caught her breath as Garnett gazed out at the sea. A vast fleet spread out in all directions, flying the heraldic colors and symbols of their occupants, a rare and beautiful sight. Five large warships rose up among the troop transports, led by Dandolo's vermilion-painted ship, dominating the seascape. The vessels were fitted with both sails and oars, a kind of transition between a Roman galley and a square rigger. They carried very little sail as they maneuvered away from land. Brooke counted over 150 ships before she gave up.

Trumpets and drums on the lead warship signaled the launch of the crusade. The music sounded like a lone voice in the distance. Neighboring ships joined in, one by one, amplifying the call to arms. Like a wave, the music spread over the fleet, rising insistently. A trumpet sounded from the forecastle of Brooke's ship, sharp and clear, and a drum boomed. The crescendo, when every musician on every ship played at full volume, stirred Brooke's heart. She felt herself caught up in the pageantry of the crusade, despite what she knew about its sad fate.

The deck took on a gentle roll as they reached deeper waters and a cool breeze washed over Garnett's face. The oars splashed in a hypnotic cadence and Garnett closed his eyes to catch a nap. Brooke was glad she didn't have to live through every minute of this voyage, sleeping on a hard deck, no task at hand, and surrounded by people who talked or twitched or shuffled interminably. Thankfully, the Memex would let her skip ahead.

Nov. 23, 1202. The arm of the catapult sprang upward and launched a jagged boulder into the air. The projectile reached its zenith just short of the battlements and disappeared over the top of the wall, while sailors scrambled to reload. At the next shot, the mast wavered slightly as the ship rocked under the recoil. They had been firing for hours, with mixed success. Most of the stones had breasted the wall and landed somewhere in Zara, but it was hard to say whether they did much damage.

Garnett and Hugh watched from the shore, waiting for orders. The townspeople had hung white cloths painted with huge crosses from the walls, pointedly displaying their Christianity to the crusading army, but to no avail. Brooke saw a badly-aimed stone strike one of these banners and tear a hole in the fabric. The cross was now missing a right arm. The walls themselves were unbroken.

The Zarans counterattacked with projectiles of their own. One boulder splashed within three feet of the port side of the battleship *Paradise*. The next landed on deck and bowled over two sailors. The ship was not carrying much sail, and the Zarans could not bring down a mast. The few shots that landed on the side of the vessel slid off and did not penetrate or damage the oars. Nevertheless, the ineffective barrage from both sides continued sporadically.

Zara was a small city built on a peninsula. The warships of the crusaders attacked on all three seaward sides, but the walls were well built and resisted the assault. The *Paradise* stopped firing and maneuvered closer to shore, coming in line with the *Lady Pilgrim*. When they started tossing boulders again, the target appeared to be a narrowly defined section of the battlements. The two ships worked in synchronization, taking turns battering the wall.

The barrage ceased as abruptly as it had begun, and Brooke noticed groups of men running up to the base of the wall with ladders. The nearest group lifted their ladder into position with alacrity, and a knight scrambled up the first few rungs. Archers appeared at the top of the wall and fired down onto the crusaders. Crossbowmen at the base provided cover for the attackers. The second man up the ladder was struck in the shoulder and lost his footing. He swung out from the ladder, holding on tenuously by one arm until he lost his grip and fell to the sand. The men on the ground fended off the arrows with their shields, and a third knight began the ascent. By this time the leader was halfway to the top and moving fast. He was within four feet of his goal when a defender shoved a broken block over the edge. The block smacked into the knight and knocked him off the ladder. A long, thin scream came to Brooke's ears as the knight plunged headlong to the earth. All along the wall, the crusaders were repulsed and the archers emboldened. The attack fizzled out as the crusaders retreated.

"Before you begin digging, I want to explain what your goal is," said a tall knight as he approached Garnett's group. Brooke was dragged away from observing the battle.

"We intend to undermine the wall. The tunnel starts here, and will run under that stone outcrop up to the edge of the wall. These timbers will be used to shore up the tunnel as we go." He pointed to a pile of rough-hewn logs stacked up next to the tunnel entrance. "Once at the wall, we'll dig out a fair-sized chamber underneath it, all supported by these timbers. Next is the good part. We stuff the chamber with brush and sticks and set it ablaze. The fire will burn fiercely and engulf the support timbers. Once they go— crash! Down comes the wall." He said this with a wide grin on his face.

"Will that work?" asked a young man to their left.

"Without a doubt," said the knight. "Zengi, an infidel, used this method to capture Edessa a few years back. It was effective beyond belief. If an infidel can manage it, so can we."

"But fire can't destroy stone. The fire won't bring the walls down."

"No, the fire doesn't change the stone, but the fire will consume the timbers that hold the mine up. If all the timbers are gone, there will be nothing beneath the wall but a great cavity. That's how we get the collapse. That's what we mean by *undermine*."

"Ahhh," said the young man.

The outcrop provided considerable protection for the diggers. Garnett climbed down into the tunnel with a shovel and relieved a sweaty and dirt-smeared colleague, thumping him on the back. The work was grueling in the poorly ventilated tunnel. Garnett dug into the packed soil with short, sharp, strokes of his shovel. An oil lamp provided a flickering and barely adequate light. Hours later, Brooke's back hurt and her hands were starting to blister, but Garnett, as usual, pushed himself to his physical limits and beyond.

Following the foreman's instructions, Garnett eked out a box-shaped indentation in the soil. He and Hugh manhandled a pre-cut timber into position and jammed it against the soil. They had to widen and deepen the cavity, knocking out the high spots before they could settle the timber into it. They set up a matching timber on the other side of the tunnel and topped it with a lintel. They removed more soil, extending the tunnel beyond the supports.

"Yo, come out!" shouted a voice from above. Garnett and Hugh clambered out of the tunnel entrance. The battle had ended and there was a festive air among the men.

"It's all over," said the foreman. "The Zarans saw that we were undermining the wall and knew they couldn't stop us. The cowards surrendered. Guess they didn't want to lose the wall. Now the fun begins."

⸙⸙⸙

Nov. 24, 1202. A long line of refugees, downtrodden and disconsolate, snaked away from the main gate of Zara. A brisk wind swept through the group, causing men to clutch their cloaks, women to shelter their infants, and children to hang onto their hats and scarves. Dead leaves swirled about, harbingers of the winter to come, one that would be brutally difficult for these newly homeless people. Those at the front of the line were directed to one of several groups of knights, who searched them for valuables and food before allowing them to exit the city. Hugh stood nearby, guarding two piles of confiscated items. One pile bristled with purses, icons, gold crosses, jewelry, and sacks of loot while the other was a makeshift collection of bags of grain, flour, beans, dried meats, and a single barrel of wine.

A wagon pulled up to Garnett's station and he motioned the family to step down. He patted the man down roughly, and fingered the lining of his clothes. He asked the man to remove his boots, and inspected them thoroughly. Finding nothing, he moved his attention to the wife. He searched her with some gentleness and respect, and finished with a quick once over of the two young sons. Meanwhile, Peter rooted around in their wagon and uncovered a sack of oats, which he tossed over to Hugh.

"Sir, shall we take this?" Peter asked. He indicated a hatchet and some cooking pots.

"No," replied Garnett. "We have no need for those items. Leave them for these folk. They're going to need them."

The family, all cleared, departed through the gate. There was a startled cry from the group next to them. Sir Sibold held a distressed young woman firmly by the arm. He felt the front of her dress, running his beefy hands over and around her breast as she squirmed in his grasp. Her husband looked on helplessly, his face reddening with shame and rage. When Sibold thrust his hand between her legs, the husband lost control and launched himself at the knight. Sibold's squire wrapped an arm around the husband's neck and dragged him back.

Sibold drew a dagger from its sheath and shouted, "Attack me, will you? You filthy little peasant." He plunged the dagger into the man's belly and ripped it open in a long jagged gash. At the sound of the scream, all heads turned but no one spoke or moved. The wife, babbling incoherently, tried to support her man as he slumped to the ground, but Sibold pulled her away. Sibold's squire dragged the wounded man off and propped him against a wall. He sat there clutching his stomach and moaning. Sibold chased the frightened young woman out of the gate, waving his bloody dagger at her and laughing.

"Poor bugger," said Garnett to Peter. "He won't recover from that wound."

"He shouldn't have resisted. He's a fool."

"Still, it's a hard fate. He might live for a few days, but after that the fever will get him."

They went back to their work, examining a subdued and frightened family. The wounded man whimpered and sobbed as blood soaked his shirt and trousers. Brooke wished she could avert her eyes.

An old man approached Garnett and said, "Sir, with all respect, please tell me why that poor man was cut? I understood that we were not to be harmed." The man spoke in good French with a slight accent.

"He attacked a knight," replied Garnett. "If you want to help your people, interpret for me. Tell them that they must hand over their valuables and food, and not resist the search. Otherwise, they may end up like him." Brooke was alarmed at the words coming out of her mouth. Sibold had goaded the man into the attack and then brutally slashed him. It was unnecessary and sadistic. Brooke's opinion of Garnett plunged.

The old man posted himself near the front of the line and spoke to the refugees, warning them as they passed. The injured husband moaned and cried for help, but no one dared approach him. More groups came through and the pile of confiscated goods grew taller and broader. Many people were voluntarily giving up their concealed items. A wagon with a young woman, an elderly man, and three small children pulled up. Peter conducted the body search of the five people, while Garnett examined the wagon. In the bottom, he found a ring of cheese wrapped in a horse blanket. Saying nothing, he re-wrapped the cheese and returned it to its place.

The wounded man had started sobbing and crying, babbling words incomprehensible to Brooke. Hugh walked over to him, grabbed him by the hair, and, in a quick, economical motion, slit his throat. There was so little blood left in his body that no jet issued from the new wound. The man gurgled and slumped over, dead.

"Hey, why did you do that?" asked Sibold.

"He was annoying me," said Hugh. "All that whimpering." Brooke was conflicted. On the one hand, it was a mercy since the man was sure to die soon, and on the other, it was murder.

The search became more somber yet, and refugees shuffled by fearfully. A swarm of flies buzzed around the ghastly corpse. Brooke was relieved when the line became shorter and Garnett was released from this duty. He was told to find himself a place to stay and search it for hidden loot. Peter and Garnett walked along a narrow street, whose surface was packed dirt with two wagon wheel ruts. They detoured into a wooden house, coming into a dark kitchen. There were only two rooms, one held three beds and the other a scarred table and four rickety chairs. No other furniture was evident. Passing this one by, they progressed further down the street, poking their heads into the vacated properties.

"Let's see if we can find something more suitable," said Garnett. "After living in a tent for months and enduring the deck of that blasted transport ship, I'm ready for a little luxury." They moved away from the wall toward the center of town and found a cobblestone street that showed promise. Other crusaders were also out looking for spoils and lodgings; 'Better find something quick,' thought Brooke. Apparently, they agreed, for, after examining several candidates, they settled into a neat little house with glass windows and a kitchen garden. They set to work searching the place.

Peter went out to the garden while Garnett tackled the interior. Garnett began by looking behind the few pictures and wall hangings left by the former tenants. He took a broom, turned it upside down, and tapped the floor with the handle, systematically and meticulously covering every square foot of the kitchen floor, finding nothing. He rooted around in the fireplace with the poker, although Brooke wondered what he expected to find there. He tapped the bricks to see if any were loose.

Progressing into the bedroom, Garnett opened an old chest, and found it empty. He examined it for a false bottom or hidden compartment, but the interior dimensions and the exterior dimensions differed only by the thickness of the wood. He rapped on the walls, beginning in one corner and working his way around the room.

Peter entered and said, "No luck outside. There were a few places where the weeds didn't grow that might have been freshly dug up, but I didn't find anything. There wasn't anything in the root cellar, either." Garnett grunted. He continued his stolid search of the wall boards, and suggested that Peter work on the ceiling with the broom handle.

Finally they examined the floor, pulling aside a well-worn rug. They shoved the bed into one corner of the room and tapped on the exposed floor. Brooke heard a hollow thunk, lower in pitch than the sounds from the nearby boards. Garnett probed again; there was something there. He got down on one knee and pried up a floorboard with his knife. Beneath he found a small box filled with coins and jewels. There were more than a dozen gold solidari, a larger number of silver coins, and a few copper pieces in addition to an engraved golden bracelet and a pearl ring.

"Shall we keep them?" asked Peter.

"No. Take them to Count Jourdain. All spoils are to be collected centrally and used for the crusade. We will do our Christian duty."

XIX

RUMORS

B rooke watched Robert insert another unsuspecting mouse into the maze. No ordinary labyrinth for this experiment. The maze was a diabolical construction four feet high with levers, traps, ramps, and slides reminiscent of a Rube-Goldberg machine. Poised at the start, the mouse twitched his whiskers uncertainly and crawled forward hesitantly. The strains of "Grandma Got Run Over by a Reindeer" came from the computer. Robert loved Christmas carols and had his machine set to a radio station that celebrated the holiday season. For Brooke, the carols reminded her that the year was almost over. Her fellowship would end next May and she had to defend her thesis before then. She needed to discover something quick.

"What are you going to do if a mouse gets stuck in the middle?" she asked.

"Hasn't happened yet," replied Robert. "They make it at least to the U-turn. If they can't figure out how to stand on their hind legs and pull down the cord, I can open this little door and take them out."

The maze was made mostly of Plexiglas, so that the inner workings and the progress of the mice could be observed and monitored. The current occupant of the maze had just found the hamster wheel and was running around in it.

"I can't believe you built this," said Brooke, thinking of how much effort it had taken. "We have to document changes in memory and cognition, but this, it's really over the top."

"Bad enough that I had to build it, the least I could do was make it fun. It's cool, isn't it?"

"Yeah," she said and meant it. "Of course, this uber-challenge for the mousey set might, all by itself, give them cognitive problems."

"Well I haven't noticed any yet. There doesn't seem to be any effect of the Memex, either. The mice do just as well, or badly, as they did before they were zapped."

"That's a relief. By the way, I wanted to talk to you about changing our Memex schedule. I think it would be better if I use the machine at about the same time every day and for the same length of time. All the variable-length days are ruining my circadian rhythm. Insomnia's a bitch."

"Makes sense. As long as Chad pitches in, I think we can work it out."

"I thought of one more reason why people would want to use the Memex. It is, in effect, a life extension device. If I use it daily, all my days are about 38 hours long. So it's a little like living 50% longer."

"I just hope that living hard doesn't wear you out quicker," said Robert, refusing to be optimistic about the Memex.

At that moment, the door buzzer sounded. Brooke glanced at Robert but he shrugged, signaling that he wasn't expecting anyone. Brooke went to the panel and released the lock. She opened the door to find an attractive woman in her mid-thirties. She wore a black suit with a silk blouse of a vibrant blue color and low heels. Her blonde hair was perfectly cut in a short, layered look.

"Hello, I'm Mimi Jefferson. May I come in?"

"Sure," said Brook automatically, and stepped aside to let the visitor enter.

"I'm with the Sentinel and I'm doing a story on research at Brackett University." Alarms rang in Brooke's head. The last person she wanted to talk to was a reporter. How could she have been so careless? She should have found out who the visitor was before letting her in. On the other hand, a cold shoulder might have raised suspicions.

"How can I help you?" asked Brooke. "I'm Brooke Laforge and this is my labmate, Robert Chen." The time it took to finish the introductions and shake hands all around gave Brooke a chance to fortify herself. She had to tell this reporter something, but hide the most essential facts. Brooke hated being in this position, forced into secrecy once again.

"Can you tell me a little about what you do in this lab?" asked Mimi.

"We explore memory in the mammalian brain," replied Brooke. "The machine you see over by the wall is designed to stimulate certain regions of the temporal lobe associated with memory functions." Brooke led her visitor over to the Memex. "This helmet contains electrical coils, that, when energized, produce a strong magnetic field. The field penetrates into the brain and induces electric currents there because of Faraday's Law."

"You mean this produces currents inside the brain? Whoa, that sounds dangerous." Mimi's eyebrows shot up.

"Not at all, there are devices on the market approved by the FDA that operate similarly. Transcranial Magnetic Stimulation is used for certain types of major depression, and might also be useful for Parkinson's disease and post traumatic stress disorder. Our focus is on memory function, a new application of the principle."

"We target the hippocampus, a region of the brain that's vital to the formation of new long term memories. It acts something like a switching center, taking in data and distributing it to various storage locations in the cortex. When you repeat something in an effort to memorize it, you basically run it through the hippocampus several times, until it's firmly embedded at a retrievable location in the brain." Brooke showed Mimi a chart of the human brain that hung on the wall.

"So what does the machine do?" she asked.

This was the sticky part. Brooke had no intention of telling her what the machine did, but she had to supply a cover story.

"It's early in our research and we're not sure of the effect of the stimulation." Brooke hoped this temporizing would be enough to bore Mimi and encourage her to leave.

"But what do you hope it does?"

"Well," said Brooke, "it might improve memory function, for example." Then inspiration hit her. "Robert constructed this maze to measure the performance of mice that have been subjected to the machine." The reporter drew closer to the maze and watched as a mouse searched for a way out of a plastic tube. Robert, taking up the theme, explained the inner workings of his creation. The reporter seemed interested. The maze was eye-catching and distracted Mimi from further probing questions about the Memex.

As she was about to leave, Mimi said, "By the way, I've heard that someone is doing time travel experiments here at Brackett. Do you know anything about that?"

"No," said Brooke. "I think you've been misled." Of course, it was Brooke doing the misleading.

"How about you, Robert? Do you know anything about time travel experiments?"

He shook his head.

"Too bad. That would be quite a story. I have to get going. Can you tell me where Prof. Fisher's lab is?" Brooke gave her directions and ushered her out the door.

"That was a close call," said Robert after she left.

"Too close," said Brooke.

Nov. 27, 1202. The dice clacked along the scarred tabletop, coming to rest with double twos. The caster rolled again, and turned up a six. He groaned and passed the dice to Garnett. Coins shuffled over the table as bets were paid up. The room was poorly lit with sputtering oil lamps, fumes mingling with the stink of sweat and the boozy smell of ale. Crickets could be heard outside the open windows.

Garnett threw the dice several times before he fell in the main with a seven. Brooke had finally figured out the complicated rules of Hazard, the hugely popular pastime of the knights and their men. It was a finely-tuned game in which the caster had a little less than 50% chance of winning. As far as Brooke was concerned, they might as well flip a coin, but the hidden probabilities and the vagaries of luck enthralled them.

Three others at the table wagered that Garnett would lose. He blew on the dice, stroked them, and tossed them with elan, getting an eleven. A win! He raked in his prizes and elected to pass the dice to Unroch, a Flemish knight on his left. Unroch rolled first a five and then the dreaded three, losing half of his remaining pile of coins. A Venetian sailor named Leonardo laughed and stacked up his winnings. One of the crusade's dedicated whores placed her hand on Leonardo's shoulder, congratulating him. Unroch shot him a murderous glance.

"Again," said Unroch. He set half of his dwindling pile on the table.

"Make it worth my while," taunted Leonardo, and set out double Unroch's bet. The others at the table watched the tense exchange with interest.

Unroch shoved the rest of his coins forward and rattled the dice around in his hands, shaking and shaking. He tossed them down and got an eight. His next roll took even longer.

"God's wounds," he said as he lost.

Leonardo smirked and drew in his take.

"This wouldn't have happened if I had gotten my fair share of the plunder," said Unroch. The crusaders, who still owed money to Venice, had forfeited any spoils of war from the capture of Zara.

"You did get your fair share, which was zero," said Leonardo.

"Cursed be the bitch that bore you."

"I don't need to listen to your insults," said Leonardo, rising. He brought his fisted hands up before his face and danced lightly on his toes. "Come on, let's see if you can fight better than you can wager."

Unroch hauled his substantial bulk from behind the table and faced off with his opponent, looking like an angry bear. Leonardo came in with a quick jab to the chin, but Unroch blocked. The next punch was to Unroch's stomach, but the heavy fighter hardly registered the blow. He retaliated with a left hook that Leonardo nimbly avoided. An onlooker was offering bets on Unroch, trying to scare up a taker. Before he could close the deal, Leonardo saw an opening and kneed Unroch in the groin, doubling him over.

"Hey, that's below the belt," said a French knight. He came at Leonardo and punched him in the face. Leonardo fell back, holding his bloodied nose, and one of his buddies moved in to avenge him. Before long, fists were flying all over the room. Garnett scooped up his winnings and edged toward the door, to Brooke's immense relief. She had no wish to be embroiled in a brawl. A glass flew past her head and shattered on the wall, but the sound barely registered against the background din. Fists had been augmented by knives, boots, and broken bottles, and blood splashed freely on the floor.

Garnett slipped out of the building into the cool evening air, his way lit by a harvest moon. Others spilled out behind him. Two were fighting in earnest, swords drawn. The animosity between the Venetians and the other crusaders had been building for days and had finally come to a boil. Garnett, keeping to the sidelines, stepped around a man lying motionless on the cobblestones. A passerby joined the fight, weighing in on the side of the sailors. The brawl was becoming a riot, growing like an unchecked fire, and engulfing more frustrated and angry men. A wayward pig ran into the street and wove his way among the combatants, tripping a knight unlucky enough to retreat at just the wrong moment.

Garnett had had enough and left the scene, working his way back towards his captured villa. A few streets over, he encountered Count Jourdain, his liege lord. Jourdain was an imposing man, with heavy features that managed to be commanding rather than ugly.

"What's going on over there?" he demanded of Garnett. The sounds of weapons clanging together could be heard even at this distance.

"The Venetians started a fight and the boys are going at it. Some men are down, injured or perhaps dead."

"Damn. We can't afford to lose men before we even get started. Go suit up and join me back here forthwith."

Garnett obeyed, making his way along the moonlit street. Men passed him, most running toward the sound of battle rather than away from it. When he arrived at his cottage, Peter was curled up in bed snoring loudly. He woke the squire and told him about the riot.

"I knew it would come to no good, this diversion to Zara. Our fellows didn't get to keep any of the loot, and to think that it all went to that Doge Dandolo—well this is what you get." Peter's long face looked more morose than usual. He helped strap Garnett up in his armor, adjusting it to fit snugly over the padding and handed him the helmet. Garnett was back on the street in less than ten minutes. He returned to the intersection where he had encountered Count Jourdain, finding him waiting patiently with another armored knight.

"We have two more coming," said Jourdain. "Then we'll put a stop to this." Brooke felt impatient to get started; just standing there was ratcheting up her fear. The sounds of shouting could be heard to the north and a breeze from the east brought a whiff of something burning. Brooke had not been in a real sword fight before and didn't know what to expect.

The last man arrived and the party headed out. They crossed the plaza at the center of town and found several men on the ground, but no active fighting. A sailor, sitting propped up against a wall, his head covered in blood, was being tended by one of the camp women.

The sounds of blades clanging against each other told them where the action was. They came upon a small group of knights beating back three opponents.

"Desist!" shouted Jourdain imperiously, but he was ignored. Garnett moved in to interpose himself between two combatants. He struck the knife hand of one with his gauntleted fist and deflected the aim of the other. The shorter fighter, startled, turned on him, but the knife thrust glanced harmlessly off the thick steel of his breastplate. Garnett smacked him on the side of the head and the stricken man stumbled away, barely able to stay on his feet. Garnett looked around and saw another rioter slipping away into a dark street. Jourdain's makeshift squadron, well armored, was quenching the battle. Brooke, to her surprise, was enjoying this. She felt invincible in her heavy metal outfit, probably an unwise attitude. Luckily, she wasn't making the decisions, so she could adopt any attitude she liked without affecting the outcome.

It was a long night. The riot had spread to every corner of the town. As the fight was halted in one location, it stubbornly broke out again in another. Brooke felt bone-numbing fatigue replace her initial pleasure in being the strong man. Garnett's moves were becoming slower, but, true to form, he stayed at it and avoided injury. When the sun burst upon the scene, the fight was finally abandoned. Scores of men lay dead in the streets and many more injured would die later. It was a sad omen of what was to come for this ill-fated crusade.

"So the events at Zara were pretty much as the historians describe them?" asked Prof. Hunter.

"Yes," said Brooke. "Everything I've seen so far of the crusade accords with the accepted version." She cast her eyes down at the notebook that lay open on her lap, reminding herself of the facts she intended to mention. Brooke was in Hunter's office, giving her an update on research progress.

"The account of Robert of Clari states that the 'lesser people' from France fought with the Venetians," continued Brooke. "Another contemporary source, the *Devastatio Constantinopolitana*, claims that 100 men died in the riot. That's all consistent with what I observed."

"That's a shame. It would have been nice to have discovered a new twist."

"We did turn up something," said Brooke. "We know how the riot started." Hunter did not look impressed. Her thin lips tightened into a flat line.

"What else?"

"The crusaders stayed in Zara for the winter. Food was plentiful and sailing was more dangerous in the cold season. In December, the crusade leaders received an offer from Prince Alexios of Constantinople. He was the son of the deposed ruler, Isaac II."

"I thought you said Alexios was the emperor," interjected Hunter.

"That was Alexios III. Remember him? He was the man who overthrew his brother, Isaac, put out his eyes, and cast him into prison. Prince Alexios was the son of Isaac and the nephew of Emperor Alexios III."

"Go on," said Hunter.

"Not surprisingly, Prince Alexios wanted to overthrow his uncle and gain the throne. He claimed he was the rightful ruler of the empire. If the crusaders helped him, he promised them an enormous reward—200,000 silver marks and full provisions for the army. He also offered to enlist Constantinople in the crusade and add 10,000 men to the army, which would have doubled its size. To sweeten the deal further, he swore that Constantinople would support a garrison of 500 knights to occupy the Holy Land after it was captured."

"How old was this prince?"

"About 19."

"And they believed him?" asked Hunter, suggesting that anyone who would believe a 19-year-old deserved what they got.

"It was convenient for them to believe him. Dandolo had still not been paid in full and the French desperately needed a source of money to mollify him. Constantinople was the richest city in Europe at the time. Dandolo probably said he would not sail to the Holy Land unless they stopped in Constantinople first. They were counting on the people supporting Prince Alexios."

"But you didn't witness any of these discussions," said Hunter. She was beginning to look bored, slumped negligently into her seat.

"No, unfortunately. What I told you is from the historical record. Garnett heard rumors from time to time, but no first hand information. Other than the riot, his stay in Zara was uneventful. I plan to skip ahead to Corfu."

"That's the next stop on this little pilgrimage."

"Yes. The crusade leadership, including Boniface of Montferrat, agreed to help Prince Alexios, despite heavy opposition from some of the knights. In truth, Dandolo was effectively running the show. He had the ships and the sailors answered to him. The crusade could not advance without his consent."

"You did get a chance to see Dandolo, didn't you?" asked Hunter.

"Yes, I was impressed, although I only saw him from afar. In the history books, he is demonized as a petty, money-grubbing merchant who could not adhere to the "higher motives" of the crusade, namely defeating Muslims. He's blamed for the diversion of the crusade and the attack of fellow Christians."

"And you think otherwise?"

"I think wars of aggression, which this clearly was, are wrong whoever the intended victims are. The crusades were organized theft, plain and simple. But they were not considered wrong in those days; on the contrary, they were considered divinely-inspired. You have to admire Dandolo for joining the crusade at his advanced age and with his infirmity, taking on all the suffering that travel entailed. Despite his blindness, he was arguably the most influential of the leaders and he certainly watched out for the interests of his countrymen."

"So they left Zara and went on to the island of Corfu." Hunter didn't have much patience with ethical discussions. Brooke didn't often talk to her adviser, only the occasional half hour that the professor managed to fit into her busy schedule. Hunter's lack of interest made Brooke want to draw out the discussion.

"I'm not sure what to think of Dandolo. Many crusaders abandoned the army at Zara, not wanting to fight the Christian city of Constantinople. Reynald of Montmirail begged leave to go to Syria, saying he would keep the crusaders there informed of the army's plans. He promised to return to the main force, but didn't reappear at Constantinople until many years later. Just before the crusaders left Zara, Simon of Montfort and his associates abandoned the group and entered the King of Hungary's lands. When Dandolo left Zara, he leveled the town. He ordered the walls and towers to be torn down and the city burned. Only the churches were spared. I understand that he wanted to crush his rival, and that this was acceptable behavior for a conqueror in his time, but I find it hard to forgive him for it."

"Let's move on to your next steps. Are you sure you want to continue to follow the crusade? It doesn't seem to be particularly revealing." Hunter clearly was not interested in Brooke's views. Her callous attitude stung and acted to harden Brooke's resolve. She would follow the crusade through to the end, despite what the professor thought.

"On another matter," continued Hunter without waiting for Brooke's reply, "I ran into Brashley the other day. He's quite interested in this patent. I think he finally recognizes the commercial potential of the Memex and he had a chat with the university president about it. The president knows a few people on the Review Board and is going to talk to them behind the scenes. With any luck, we'll get our go-ahead to test human subjects soon."

Brooke had just about given up on getting approval from the Review Board. Besides, even if she started testing at this point, she wouldn't be able to finish her thesis before the funding ran out. Brooke was deeply enmeshed in her visits to the past. The lives of her ancestors seemed more real than her own life as a graduate student. At least they were living and making progress of a sort, while Brooke's life was in stasis. But she couldn't tell Hunter that. She just had to go along.

―――⁓――――

May 5, 1203. A line of men stretched ahead of Garnett as he stood waiting in the early evening gloom. Hugh was by his side, looking bored and tired. A few words were exchanged up the line, and then it was quiet again. After a year on the trail, the crusaders were beginning to show signs of their ordeal. Their clothes had been patched with oddments of cloth, the rips sewn together with puckered stitches, and the shirts held together by mismatched buttons. The levies on the crusaders had been heavy to pay the Venetians and money was reserved for true necessities.

After all this time, they had only progressed as far as the island of Corfu, just off the western boundary of Greece. Brooke felt a kinship with these adventurers; she too had been stymied this last year, making little progress toward her degree. Like them, she had been a victim of poor leadership, and could only extricate herself by paying a heavy penalty.

The line shuffled forward steadily. A pleasing aroma wafted toward them as they approached the camp kitchen, where a cook ladled out soup from a waist high cauldron. Garnett held his bowl out and it was filled with a creamy liquid. Steam rose off the surface of the soup in thin wisps and was absorbed by the cool air.

Garnett and Hugh made their way to a nearby campfire and settled in to enjoy their dinner of carrot soup with wild onions and herbs. After months of shipboard rations, it tasted heavenly. A haunch of deer roasted on a spit over the fire. From time to time, juices dripped off the meat and sizzled into the blaze. The wind shifted direction and smoke blew into Garnett's face, hot and fragrant. He retreated leftward, nudging Hugh in the same direction. A pale young man got up to turn the spit, protecting his hands with a piece of leather. He set an open glass jar at the edge of the fire and gentled it inward with a forked stick, positioning it right under a drip.

"I hear we sail again tomorrow," said Garnett.

"I wish it were to a different destination," replied Hugh. "We already attacked one Christian city, should we be going after another?"

"We're not going to attack Constantinople. We just want to reinstate their rightful ruler."

"And you think the sitting emperor will just step aside?"

Garnett was silent. He ran his finger around the inside of his bowl, mopping up the last drops of soup.

"It all depends on what the people want. When the mob in Constantinople gathers, the emperor falls. That's how they change government."

"Sounds barbaric to me," said Hugh.

A log collapsed in the fire and sent sparks dancing upward toward the evening sky. A welcome wave of heat washed over the two men. The roast sizzled, its surface becoming ever browner and more appetizing. Hugh poked at the fire and added a log, rearranging things to improve circulation.

"I just want to get to the Holy Land. All these diversions are sorely trying," said Hugh.

"I hear that Constantinople is guarded by enormous walls," said a red-bearded man sitting nearby. "They make the walls of Zara look puny by comparison. No one has breached those walls in hundreds of years. And the city is huge, almost as big as Baghdad. It makes Paris look like a provincial town. The people better support us, because taking Constantinople by force is impossible."

"God is with us and will guide our crusade," said Garnett. "He was with the Israelites when they faced the walls of Jericho, and look how that turned out. If the people of Constantinople are wicked enough to stand in the way of the crusade, God will smite them. I'm sure of it."

He was right, too, thought Brooke. The people of Constantinople would soon feel the wrath of the Almighty, or at least the wrath of these frustrated crusaders. Nothing could prevent it, since it had already happened.

XX

BEFORE THE STORM

May 30, 1203. Garnett stood in the prow of the transport ship, gazing out over the rippled sea. The sun laced the water with white slashes that glimmered in the heat. Brooke felt at peace just standing here, having nothing she needed to accomplish or tend to. A small island covered with trees was visible on the port side, growing imperceptibly larger as they made modest headway. The fleet had been plying the waters of the Mediterranean for many days, hugging the shore line cautiously. Brooke could name many of the larger ships by this time: the *Pilgrim Lady*, the *World*, and *Paradise*. Her vessel was under sail, with masts six stories high and sweeping yardarms, but the fleet included many galleys powered by oarsmen. The galleys slowed them down and forced a halt every night while the rowers rested. Each ship in the fleet was trailed by two or three smaller boats, like ducklings following their mother. The ship designers had little appreciation for streamlining and reducing drag, and the fleet lumbered rather than flew.

The prow rose and fell in a gentle rhythm, soothing Brooke's fatigued spirit. She had been accessing Garnett at sea for many days. The numbing mindlessness of the voyage was somehow relaxing, even though the ship was overflowing with people. In truth, she was delaying her arrival at Constantinople. She knew rationally that she would not be killed or seriously wounded in the coming conflict, but that primitive beast who lived in the deepest recesses of her brain would not listen to reason. She approached the city with a mixture of fear and fascination, as if she were watching a tornado and was mesmerized by it, unable to take cover. She had enough experience with the Memex to know that it could deliver acute pain and real distress at times, a sort of mental torture that left her physical body intact.

Garnett stepped down from the prow and made his way aft. The helmsmen were leaning hard on the massive oars that were used to guide the ship. Garnett settled himself down in his spot just aft of the forecastle and pulled out a half-carved block of wood. Without haste, he turned his attention to the dog that was slowly emerging from the piece. The sails snapped overhead as a sudden gust billowed them and the boat rocked to one side.

Brooke told herself that she might learn something historically significant by closely examining this voyage. Little was known about it from contemporary records; maybe she could uncover a telling incident, a shipwreck, a freak storm, something... But the real reason she spent so much time on it was the coming conflict that loomed ahead. Even if she did not get hurt herself, witnessing the death and maiming of others was going to be dreadful. The murder she had watched in Zara haunted her dreams. Sometimes she could hear the voice of the dying man, moaning and pleading for help. Her tender heart was not made for this martial madness.

Garnett, whose thoughts were hidden from Brooke, seemed unperturbed by what would come. If only she could tell what he was thinking, but perhaps that was asking too much. It was amazing enough that she had access to his perceptions. He calmly worked at his whittling, turning the piece to and fro in his hands. Out of the wood rose a mastiff with a noble head, floppy ears, a thick neck, and a heavy, well-muscled body. He looked alert and ready to do battle. A fitting dog for a warrior like Garnett.

The vessel creaked as they came around to the wind and a breeze ruffled Garnett's hair. Brooke wasn't sure why she was continuing to follow Garnett. Even if the Review Board approved the testing of human subjects tomorrow, there wouldn't be time for her to get her degree before her funding evaporated. She might as well give up now and start looking for a job. She liked research and discovery, but felt bitterly disappointed by the lack of support. Her work was excellent, groundbreaking even, but she was left hanging in a precarious position. Despite it all, she was not ready to give up. Perhaps tomorrow she would skip forward in time. But for now, this peaceful, unhurried voyage was a relaxing break from all her troubles and she wanted to enjoy the feel of the sun on her face a few days longer.

—⟨∞⟩—

June 3, 1203. Damian had been working his way patiently through the crowd, greeting an old acquaintance here and introducing himself to a new one there. The room was packed with party-goers, gentlemen in their embroidered robes, raising their voices to be heard in the general hub-bub, ladies with up-swept hair and glittering jewels, fanning their faces in the oppressive heat. This was not Brooke's favorite sort of social gathering, but she supposed she must put up with it.

Damian came upon Donus, the blacksmith, who seemed to want to tell him everything about his wife's illness. He sympathized as best he could, not caddish enough to cut the old man short. When he finally extricated himself, he wove through the throng, avoiding eye contact until he reached the dessert table. He consumed three small pastries, packed with nuts and soaked in honey.

"These are delightful," he said to Sophia, who approached him on the left. She was dressed in a flowing lavender gown with small pearls sewn into the bodice. Her long gray-streaked black hair was done up in a complicated-looking arrangement, with a few wisps of curls trailing down.

"Can you believe that our children have been married an entire year?" asked Sophia.

"It was good of you to host this party for their anniversary," said Damian as he picked up a fourth pastry. "Quite a lot of people came." He mopped his sweating brow with the back of his hand.

"You know Marcus, he's always talking to people. He collects friends the way some men collect coins."

"He clearly knows which is more valuable."

"There you are," interrupted Eulogia. "Sophia, you must let me take him. I'd like to give Julia and Florian their present."

Eulogia led Damian away by the arm to a large group of people across the room. At the center of the group, Julia was chatting amiably with the guests, receiving their congratulations and thanking them warmly. When she saw her parents, her eyes lit up. Brooke had the impression that they were rescuing her from boring company.

"Happy Anniversary, darling," said Eulogia, handing her daughter a red bag. Julia withdrew the present from the bag, a forest green ceramic bowl with pale yellow roses in a ring about the rim.

"Oh mother, it's lovely. Where did you ever find such a piece? I shall think of you every time I use it."

"Many thanks," said Florian.

"You wouldn't have any good news for us?" asked Damian. A look of distress darted into Julia's eyes, but she quickly erased it.

"I'm afraid you must wait a bit longer. These things happen in their own time," she replied. Florian shuffled his feet. Eulogia deftly changed the conversation and the two women went on about cooking. Brooke wished she could reassure Julia, her many times great-grandmother. She wanted to say, "Look, I'm here. Don't worry—you'll have children," but of course she could not. She wondered if Julia would become pregnant by Florian, and if so, what would become of the child. This line of thought worried her, and she let it go, preferring to focus on the moment.

Damian drifted away, trying to find a mooring in this restless sea of faces. He was jostled about in the crowded quarters, until he came upon a familiar figure with curly black hair and a tankard of ale in his hand. Ignatius was talking animatedly to a group of men; as usual, the topic was politics.

"They say the fleet is enormous, at least 200 vessels heading this way," said Ignatius.

"That can't be," protested an elderly gentleman. "They have wantonly exaggerated."

"Prince Alexios is with them, and is, no doubt, vying for the throne."

"If he's their guiding spirit, they have reason to despair. The people will never accept him," said Damian.

"They may be forced to. It's not as though our current emperor is well-loved," said Ignatius. "I see a battle coming."

"They will never get past the walls or the Varangian guard," said Damian. "Constantinople will brush them off like a stallion rids himself of an annoying fly with a mere flick of his tail. Our walls have stood for hundreds of years, and will stand for hundreds more. We have no need to worry."

Brooke knew otherwise. Constantinople had been limping along on the legacy of its former glory for many years. The navy was in shambles, with hardly twenty ships. The emperor was an inept leader who cared only for his own pleasure, and was too foolish or debauched to keep the empire strong. The elite Varangian guard was stuffed with mercenaries from Scandinavia and England. But the palaces and churches and noble estates still glittered with gold and made a tempting target. Soon the people would pay for the mistakes of their leaders.

───❧───

Chad strode down the hallway of the administrative building, past portraits of wealthy or illustrious alumni. Chad did not often come here, the last time being the meeting with the university lawyer, George Brashley, at which they had discussed the possibility of applying for a patent. Now Brashley had called him and Brooke to another meeting, and Chad didn't know why.

He opened the door to the lawyer's office suite and was greeted by an attractive young receptionist. She directed him to a waiting area—a sofa and two comfortable armchairs arranged around a mahogany table. Brooke was already there, settled into a chair and flipping through a magazine. He felt a flush of pleasure as she looked up and smiled at him. Her auburn hair shone as it fell over her shoulders in loose curls. For the hundredth time, he thought about asking her out, but he knew it was hopeless.

Brooke set the magazine aside as Chad sat. "Here we are again," she said.

"Most students go through school without ever coming to this office," said Chad. "I guess we're special."

"Did he give you any idea of what he wanted?"

"None."

At that moment, Brashley appeared and invited them into his office. From his tepid greeting Chad guessed that the news wasn't good.

Brashley sat behind his oversized cherry desk and directed Brooke and Chad to two chairs that stood before it. He pulled out a file folder and gazed at them unsmilingly.

"I was very disappointed when I read the Sentinel this morning. I thought you understood how important discretion was in this matter of the Memex."

"What are you talking about? I didn't read the paper this morning," said Chad.

"I'm talking about this article by Mimi Jefferson in which she claims Brackett is operating a time machine. Do you know anything about it, Brooke?"

Brooke shook her head as Brashley handed them a copy of the newspaper. The article, which began on page 6, read

Is Doctor Who at Brackett University?

Long the darling of science fiction and fantasy stories, time travel may now be a reality. Researchers at Brackett University have invented a practical time travel machine and are using it to explore the past, according to informed sources within the university. The implications of such an invention would be far-reaching and would change our world in unexpected ways.

The scientists have visited the Middle Ages and tracked the history of the Knights Templar, a mysterious sect that was persecuted by the church establishment in the early fourteenth century. In particular, they have examined the life of Jacques de Molay, the 23rd and last Grand Master of the sect. De Molay was accused of heresy and confessed under torture. He later recanted and was sentenced to death by fire. At his execution, he asked to be tied to the stake facing Notre Dame with his hands in a position of prayer. As the flames engulfed him, he warned that God would send a calamity to smite Pope Clement and King Phillip, his accusers, and both were dead within a year. Throughout the Templar persecution, so many knights were accused of heresy and stripped of power that medieval Europe was left with a leadership crisis.

Tom Crawford, the Vice President for Research at Brackett, was contacted for information on the time machine experiments, but declined to give a statement. Other sources told this reporter that scientists are already operating the machine and expressed concern about whether they will alter the past by their presence there...

The article concluded with references to popular novels and TV shows and a call for the university to make details of the experiments public, implying that they might pose a threat to society.

"This is nonsense," said Brooke. "They have it all wrong. We're not investigating the Knights Templar or changing the past. I don't know who fed them this line."

"You didn't talk to Mimi Jefferson?" asked Brashley.

"No," replied Chad. "I never heard of her."

"And you, Brooke?"

Brooke hesitated, then said, "Actually, I did speak to her. She dropped into my lab unexpectedly and started asking questions about my research."

"That is expressly forbidden by the terms of the agreement that you signed with us. I can't tell you how serious this is. You are risking your good standing at this university." Brashley looked grim and unyielding.

"I spoke to her but I didn't tell her anything about time travel. I pretended that the Memex was only used to enhance memory function in mice. Would you rather I told her that I was forbidden to talk to the press by the university administration? Don't you think that would have raised her suspicions? Besides, she didn't ask about time travel until the very end of the interview, and I just said I didn't know anything about it."

"Brooke is right. She had no choice but to go with the flow," said Chad.

"Nevertheless, she violated the terms of the agreement and will have to pay the consequences," intoned the lawyer sanctimoniously. Brooke looked pale and said nothing.

"You might want to think about that a bit," said Chad. "If Brooke leaves the university, she will have no reason to avoid the press; on the contrary, she would have every reason to contact this reporter and tell her the real story, including how you kicked her out. Do you want Brackett to be remembered as the university that kicked out one of the greatest geniuses of the 21st century?" Brooke's eyes widened in surprise to hear Chad speak of her in this way. Brashley scowled, not used to being challenged by a student.

"How did the press get wind of this if you two didn't tell them?" asked Brashley.

"The entire Review Board knew about these experiments," said Chad. "One of them might have mentioned it to a colleague. Something this shocking is hard to keep secret. I'm sure the board members took notes at the meeting. Suppose someone made copies and left the original on a photocopy machine, or threw a bad copy in the trash next to the machine. It could have been picked up. Or a student could have hacked into a prof's computer and read about it. There are a dozen ways the info could have leaked out."

"This badly garbled story didn't come from us. Look how inaccurate it is. Brooke has accessed a knight from the Middle Ages, but not a Templar and not in the 14th century. And we certainly can't change the past. Rightfully speaking, there is no time travel, just the illusion of time travel."

Brashley sat back and looked at them stony-faced. He held a pencil by its end and tapped it slowly on his desktop. Chad and Brooke sat tensely, waiting to see what he would do.

"I have another appointment," he finally said. "Don't let me see any more articles in the paper."

Brooke and Chad left. In the hallway, Brooke asked, "So are they going to kick me out?"

"Not today."

<hr />

June 9, 1203. After weeks at sea, Garnett glimpsed the walls of Constantinople off in the distance for the first time. He hung on the port gunwale, shoulder to shoulder with other knights, as the sailors worked to guide the vessel into the Bosporus. The fleet had tightened its formation upon approaching the city and Brooke could make out details of the activity on neighboring vessels. Knights hung their shields off the sides of the ships and hauled banners up the mast, putting on a dramatic martial display. Drums banged and trumpets blared, voicing the collective enthusiasm of these crusaders who had finally arrived after their long voyage.

The fleet labored north against a strong current as it entered the narrow straights of the Bosporus and its advance slowed. A following wind pushed them northward, giving them an edge against the southerly current. The walls grew larger as they approached, and the knights had their first close look at the task before them. Brooke wondered how they could dream of scaling those walls, so tall and mighty, and topped by well-fortified towers. The knights had been noisy and excited earlier, but seemed more subdued now that the full power of the city was on display.

Although they were imposing, the walls were not flawless. Here and there stones had collapsed and gathered in rubble heaps at the base of the wall. Sections had been hastily patched over and were showing signs of degradation. The overall image was of a genteel lady fallen on hard times. Greek onlookers lined the ramparts, taking in the extraordinary procession of warships—a once in a lifetime event for them.

A French knight, Sir Caspar, had previously visited Constantinople on a pilgrimage, and was pointing out the sights to those near him. Garnett pressed close to the knight beside him so he could listen in on Caspar's explanation.

"That long structure just beyond the wall is the Hippodrome where the chariot races are held," said Caspar. "And next to it is the Grand Palace. I couldn't go inside when I visited, but the outside alone is more magnificent than any other place in Christendom. That column poking up was erected in Justinian's time, a monument to his martial victories. The church beyond is the Hagia Sophia. That means 'Holy Wisdom' in Greek. The mosaics inside are the most beautiful I've ever seen. You could spend two days there and not see everything."

The city was certainly impressive to behold. Beyond the large public buildings, villas and churches nestled on the hills, surrounded in some cases by verdant gardens. Constantine had chosen the site for his city well, surrounded by water on three sides. It was no accident that the peninsula boasted seven hills—"New Rome" would be just like old Rome.

"Where do you think we're going to attack?" asked a young knight near Caspar.

"That's hard to say," said Sir Caspar. "We're to the east of the city now. To the south, we have the Sea of Marmara and to the north, there's a well protected harbor called the Golden Horn."

"What about the land side?"

"The walls are truly immense on the western side. I don't think we're heading there. We've passed them already. If Sir Boniface planned a siege from the west, we would have landed by now."

"We may not have to attack," said Garnett. "If the people accept Prince Alexios, there won't be a battle. The mob has deposed emperors before in Constantinople."

A small Greek boat that had set out to cross the Bosporus turned about and headed back to shore upon seeing the fleet. An overeager archer loosed a few arrows at its retreating stern. Scattered cheers went up. A few vessels were making landfall ahead and their own ship began to take in sail and lose speed.

When Garnett set foot on solid land, it seemed to heave under his feet, an artifact of weeks at sea. This disorienting feeling was one more trial for Brooke to suffer through. Garnett pushed ahead and he and Peter found a suitable site for their tent. A half hour later, the tent poles were firmly anchored, the canvas was tautly stretched, and the men stowed their supplies within. Peter arranged a few blankets for their bunks and unfolded a camp stool.

Hugh poked his head into the entrance. "Did you hear about the pile of stores that we found? It looks like there was a good harvest this year. We'll eat well tonight," he said. Brooke thought about an emperor who would leave food just sitting around for an invading army to capture.

Garnett unpacked one crate with care, removing the cotton swaddling from a small statue that he placed on an altar he had erected in a corner of the tent. It was a depiction of St. Sebastian, the patron saint of athletes and soldiers. Sebastian was tied to a tree and pierced by a flock of arrows; nevertheless he looked perfectly at peace. Garnett struck a flint and lit two small candles on the altar. He and Peter knelt before it and began the Lord's prayer:

"Our Father, who art in heaven, hallowed be thy name…"

Garnett had prayed unfailingly every day of this crusade, his faith never wavering. He concluded with a special appeal for the soul of his departed wife, and touched his forehead, breast and each shoulder in the sign of the cross. Although she had died young, Cerise had known true love.

XXI

AGAINST THE WALLS

July 5, 1203. The belly of the transport ship was filled with mounted knights, their steeds jumpy, dancing sideways a bit and snorting, but the knights had trained them well and kept them under control. Garnett was among them, sitting erect in the saddle, his body enveloped in armor. He wore a blue and gold surcoat over the metal for protection against the summer sun, which could be blinding in these latitudes. Brooke could sense the tension in the hold, a cough here, a snuffle there. The ventilation was not adequate for all the bodies, both human and equine, and the air felt hot and heavy. The faint creak of the ship's timbers and the slight sway of the deck told her that they were underway.

Brooke felt an itch just behind her left knee and suffered with it, trying fruitlessly to will it away. Garnett absently tapped his leg with the point of his shield, in a parody of scratching. Count Louis of Blois, the leader of the Fourth Division to which Garnett had been assigned, was posted near the exit. He was magnificently attired in a surcoat of silver and green, with a dragon emblazoned on the back. The Count's steed was caparisoned in a thick cloth that covered his back and flanks and protected the horse from arrows. An alternating pattern of herringbone patches and red and white squares decorated the cloth. All the knights were decked out in their finest and most colorful battle raiment, looking more ready for a parade than a life and death struggle.

Over the past several weeks, the crusaders had exchanged envoys with the emperor in a vain attempt to seat Prince Alexios on the throne. Even more disappointing than their talks with the ruler was the unenthusiastic reception that the young prince had received from the populace. There would not be a mob clamoring for him to be leader of the vast empire. Faced with the political reality, the crusaders had resorted to a military solution. They were crossing the Bosporus, heading toward the Golden Horn, the harbor that guarded the north flank of the city. The entrance to the Golden Horn was blocked by a huge iron chain, strong enough to stop even the largest Venetian warship. Across the Golden Horn from the city lay the suburb of Galata, and this was the target of today's action.

By a subtle change in the feel of the deck, Brooke knew that they were no longer underway. An order was given to don helmets. A sailor threw open the hatch to the hold and daylight streamed in, temporarily blinding Brooke. The knights waited, tense, expectant. Then came the call to arms—hundreds of trumpets sounding the simple melody, becoming louder on each repetition as more musicians joined in. Count Louis, followed by his honor guard, charged out of the hold. One by one, the mounted knights followed, Garnett near the front of the pack.

On deck, Brooke caught sight of the Greek army, numerous and menacing, lined up in battle formation on the shore. Their swollen ranks were set back about ninety yards from the waterline, with archers in front and foot soldiers in the rear. The enemy let loose a barrage of arrows, but the distance was great, and most splashed uselessly into the sea. The crusader fleet, led by Doge Dandolo, was arrayed to their right and left, in close formation. The prows were stuffed with archers and crossbowmen, ready to offer covering fire for the amphibious assault. But the enemy cowered far from the waterline, out of range of the arrows. Instead of wasting projectiles, the archers streamed into the water, which rose up to their armpits, and waded towards the shore, carrying their bows above their heads. Foot soldiers joined the archers plowing through the viscous water as best they could.

Count Louis led the knights into the sea with great splashing and churning. Brooke felt the cold water seep under her armor and grip her legs and chest. The trumpet blasts were now augmented by the deep throated boom of the drums and the higher-pitched rapping of the tabors. A lucky arrow from the enemy struck a horn player in the throat, and his melody was brutally cut off in mid note. Another arrow landed just to Brooke's left, doing no harm. The powerful warhorses raced through the water, closing the distance to the shoreline. Through the spray, Brooke saw a foot soldier shot in the face and thrown backwards. He sank underwater, leaving only the shaft of the arrow upright, and then only the feathers, and then nothing. Brooke felt trapped, propelled forward into the fray and unable to exert any control. She had not expected to be so abjectly afraid, so viscerally terrified. The pounding of Garnett's heart was loud in her ears.

The first knights had made it to the beach and their leaders shouted at them to form lines. The Greeks were still shooting from too long a distance and did little damage. Brooke saw one arrow graze the helmet of

Matthew of Montmorency, who led the Fifth Division, but he was unhurt. The knights stood dripping while their comrades joined them from the sea. Garnett took his place in the front row of the Fourth Division.

When all seven divisions were formed up, the command to drop lances was passed from group to group. Boniface of Montferrat, the military leader of the crusade, dropped his sword in a signal to advance. In a well practiced and choreographed movement, the crusaders loped forward, accelerating as they went. Garnett stayed centered between the two knights that guarded his flanks. The individual faces of the Greeks, with their long beards and turbaned heads, came into focus.

As the knights reached the halfway point to the enemy, a section of the Greek line caved in. Men turned and ran in disarray and desperation. The retreat spread like fire down a fuse, and soon the only section of the line still standing was that opposite Garnett. As Brooke thundered down upon them, they too realized their predicament and turned to flee. For one soldier, it was too late. Garnett's lance caught him in the lower back and smacked him face down into the dirt, scraping him along several yards. Garnett dropped the lance and drew his sword, making for a second straggler. He easily caught up with the running figure and slashed his weapon down onto the man's head. All about, knights were chasing down the slowest of the Greeks and killing them mercilessly. The dead and wounded lay bleeding on the battlefield in the one-sided struggle. Brooke now felt powerful, invincible even, and found herself relishing the prospect of more victims. A small voice of regret tried to break through, but was quashed in the heat of conflict.

The retreating enemy was gaining ground and Garnett spurred Ajax on to close the distance. As he reached the summit of a shallow rise, Brooke saw the enemy's camp laid out before her, a vast field of tents and pavilions. The camp was abandoned and the crusaders rode through it gleefully. The place was richly appointed, a valuable prize to the attacking army, filled with food and equipment to fill their every need. There were enough provisions to feed an army, just not the army the emperor intended. The crusaders lost interest in pursuing the enemy and instead staked out claims to the spoils.

Garnett slowed and trotted between the tents. Hugh came up alongside him and said, "That was easier than I expected. The Greeks ran like women. If this is the best they can do, it'll be a short siege."

"Looks like we'll eat well tonight," said Garnett pointing to a cage filled with squawking chickens. Beside it Brooke noticed a tub of salt fish and a basket heaped with loaves of bread. Garnett dismounted and removed his helmet. Brooke suddenly realized how thirsty and tired she was, the aftermath of pent up anxiety and exertion. Garnett found a full wineskin and drank greedily before passing it to Hugh.

Brooke reflected on the Greeks' dilemma. Their cavalry was weak and poorly trained, unprepared to counter the well-disciplined and coordinated forces bearing down upon them. Their army was led by an emperor who had more interest in self-indulgence than in warfare. They had little experience in combat and the army was dominated by mercenaries. Despite their overwhelming numerical superiority, the Greeks were in a difficult position, and would suffer for it.

July 6, 1203. Sparks flew off the edge of the blade as the servant pressed it against the grindstone. Garnett stood waiting for the sharpening to be finished as he chatted with Hugh, who was next in line. It was a bright, clear, morning, with a gentle breeze off the Golden Horn. Both men had eaten an enormous breakfast, thanks to the captured stores, and were in a good mood. Brooke, on the other hand, felt jumpy, waiting for the action to begin. Sometimes knowing the future was a black curse, predisposing one to feel the pain of future events long in advance of their arrival. Yesterday had given Brooke a peek at the inner workings of her mind. She had enjoyed the pursuit and killing of the retreating Greeks, and felt ashamed.

The servant patiently pumped the pedals of the grindstone, keeping it moving. In the distance, the clang of metal on metal came to their ears.

"What ho?" said Hugh. "We had best see what that's about." Garnett agreed, and taking his half-sharpened sword, he and Hugh ran toward the clamor. As they wove among the tents, they came upon Sir Sibold heading in the opposite direction.

"The Greek whore-sons have launched a surprise attack," said Sibold. "We're to take arms and mount up."

Garnett and Hugh changed course and made for their tent. They found Peter and Guillaume, Hugh's squire, standing before the entrance, looking tense.

"Quickly, the shields and the saddles," barked Garnett.

"Can I help you with your armor, milord?" asked Peter.

"No time for that. We are needed now." Brooke's alarm rose. As oppressive as the armor was, it did offer security. The men gathered the equipment and hurried toward the corral. Ajax's ears were perked up, his head pointed in the direction of battle. Peter tossed the saddle over his back and cinched it tight, as Garnett spoke to the horse reassuringly.

Soon the knights were in the saddle and galloping toward the fight. They arrived at the scene of a rout. Despite the advantage of surprise, the

Greeks were in full retreat, some heading for shore where their barges awaited and others running uphill toward the tower of Galata. Both groups were pursued by vengeful crusaders. Garnett chose to ride after those heading toward the tower and spurred his warhorse on.

At the gate to the tower, the Greek cavalry made a stand, turning to engage the oncoming knights while the foot soldiers passed inside. Garnett picked out a heavy-set horseman wielding an ax and attacked. His sword was blocked by the opponent's shield. The ax swept downward, but Garnett had anticipated the move and deflected it with his own shield. Ajax skittered sideways, responding to the pressure of Garnett's knees, and Garnett struck again, slashing his sword against the side of the man's head. The chain mail covering his ears protected him, but he was dazed, and could not avoid the next blow. He toppled from his horse. Garnett peered around and saw Hugh in a desperate fight with a cavalryman. Garnett came to his aid and buried his sword in the man's back. The Greek screamed and arched his back before falling to the ground, releasing the sword. Brooke's instinct was to cry foul play, but of course, this was war, and not a polite contest.

Garnett turned about and saw a clear path to the gate, where the last of the foot soldiers were escaping. He urged Ajax on. Man and horse, unencumbered by armor, were fast and agile; nevertheless, the iron pikes of the gate were perilously close as Garnett ducked under the descending grate, Hugh on his heels. Garnett wheeled about and bore down on a soldier pulling desperately on a vertical chain. He slashed down and the blade bit into the man's shoulder. At almost the same moment, Brooke felt a searing pain along the side of her calf. Garnett whirled to face his attacker, but Hugh was already there and killed the soldier.

The last Greek at the gate saw that he was alone and ran across the small courtyard for the tower entrance. Instead of chasing him, Garnett and Hugh dismounted and raised the gate to its highest position. Crusaders trickled into the courtyard, having defeated the rear guard. Brooke steeled herself for an assault on the tower that loomed menacingly above her. Her leg throbbed and she wanted to examine the wound, but Garnett was focused on the windows of the tower. As more crusaders filled the courtyard, a Greek opened a window and waved a white flag of surrender. A ragged cheer went up and Brooke relaxed.

Shortly, the Greeks opened the door at the base of the tower and Garnett climbed the spiral staircase, followed by Hugh and others. At each story, enemy soldiers were sitting cross-legged on the floor, their weapons in a pile at the front of the room. The crusaders posted guards on the prisoners, but Garnett continued his climb to the top, heedless of the burning pain in his leg. He arrived at a circular room with a wooden post in the center that extended from floor to ceiling. Wrapped around the post was the end of the great iron chain that blocked the harbor. The chain was at its highest position to keep the crusaders from sailing into the harbor.

Garnett rose one more level and came out upon the top floor into a spacious circular room ringed by windows that offered a panoramic view of the surroundings. Constantinople lay like a jewel to the south, the spires of its churches stretching to the sky. Brooke had never seen the city from this vantage point before and admired the sight along with Garnett.

A massive wooden mechanism squatted in the center of the room, spokes protruding in every direction. Sir Ragenard examined the device and called Garnett over to lend a hand. The two men looked over every piece with care, working out its function. Ragenard found a ratchet, cautiously released it, and began to pump the handle up and down so that the great wheel slowly rotated. He sent Garnett out onto the balcony to observe the results of his action. Foot by foot, the iron chain that stretched across the Golden Horn sank towards the water. A foot soldier relieved Ragenard and he came to stand beside Garnett.

From the balcony, Brooke could see the entire sweep of the harbor and the city that lay beyond. The center of the chain was now touching the water. Several Venetian warships were sailing into place, ready to breach the barrier that had so frustrated them earlier. When the chain had sunk deep below the waves, the *Eagle,* one of the tallest ships of the fleet, majestically passed above it. Other warships and galleys followed.

The Greek navy and merchant vessels caught in the harbor scrambled to defend themselves. It was an uneven battle, with the Greeks commanding fewer than twenty warships to the crusaders' fifty. Brooke could see several of them already hauling up a white flag. But one captain was determined to take a stand against the intruders and set course to intercept a galley. The galley changed direction to lay alongside. As its prow came near the Greek vessel, two Venetian sailors grabbed a hose and directed it toward their opponent. A thin stream of liquid issued from the end, fed by a tank set up on the forecastle. To Brooke's astonishment, a Venetian sailor ran forward with a torch and, as he touched the metal nozzle at the end of the hose, a great gout of fire issued forth. The flamethrower bombarded the Greek vessel as the ships slipped by each other, splashing burning goop on the deck. Greek sailors scrambled to douse the flames, but water was not effective. One man's shirt caught fire and he ran madly about until someone tackled him and suffocated the flames.

Brooke was seeing the medieval equivalent of napalm. Ironically, this "sticky fire" had been invented by the Greeks and used to great effect in earlier times when their fleet was strong; now, they could not even muster their most famous weapon against the invaders. Instead, it had been turned against them. A line caught fire on the beleaguered ship and the aft sail was quickly engulfed in flames. Brooke saw men jumping overboard to escape the inferno. The oarsmen no longer rowed and the ship glided aimlessly. The Venetians stayed well clear as the vessel burned.

On the other side of the harbor, a Venetian galley rammed its metal reinforced prow into the side of a Greek ship, taking out half the oars. Grappling lines were cast and the ships hauled into close proximity. A furious battle erupted in which both sides took severe casualties. Brooke was distracted by the throbbing in her leg. Garnett had never even examined the wound, so Brooke could not tell how serious it was. The blood-soaked sock in her left boot squished as Garnett shifted his stance.

The battle on the water was winding down. One captain chose to scuttle his ship rather than let it be captured, but most of the Greek vessels were in the hands of the Venetians. Brooke had mixed feelings about this conflict. After all, she had relatives on both sides. She liked Garnett, with his attention to duty, his bravery, and his drive. She also liked Damian, a gentle artist and devoted father.

If she considered the opponents on their merits, the picture was decidedly murky. There was nothing to admire in Emperor Alexios, the wastrel who had overthrown his brother and blinded him. The emperor had so neglected the defense of his city that it was at the mercy of a small band of crusaders, a wounded Goliath before a determined David.

His nephew, Prince Alexios, was no better. To further his own ambitions, he was willing to pauperize his people. He had promised an enormous reward for the help of the crusaders, one that would be hard to deliver on, even for the most wealthy city in Christendom. He pushed his agenda without popular support and with no demonstrable leadership ability.

On the side of the crusaders, Boniface of Montferrat had done little to distinguish himself. Although he was the designated leader of the crusade, he had been conveniently absent at the siege of Zara, perhaps to avoid the wrath of Pope Innocent III at his attack of a Christian city. Boniface was the kind of general who led from behind, not the one who stood at the head of the army.

Indeed, the whole concept of a crusade was repugnant to Brooke. It was nothing more than an unprovoked attack on a group of people from another culture. She realized, though, that the crusaders were convinced that they were serving God, that they had to serve God, that they were doing the most noble and valiant thing in all the world. In her time, Muslims who did the same would be called terrorists.

And then there was Doge Enrico Dandolo, past eighty years old, blind, and nevertheless the driving force behind the westerners. It was he who had orchestrated the amphibious attack on Galata, towing the transport ships with galleys so that they would all arrive together, and not be separated by the vagaries of wind and waves. Dandolo was protecting his people from financial ruin brought on by the disorganized crusaders.

Long after the battle was over, Garnett lingered on the tower balcony, gazing out at the city across the water. Its seven hills rose gently beyond the walls, some covered with villas and palaces where the rich lived in comfort and luxury, others lined with close-packed tenements where the poor lived in hunger and despair. The dome of the Hagia Sophia glistened in the early evening light. Garnett stayed till after sunset, a calm end to a turbulent day.

———

July 9, 1203. Three days later, Damian and Basil stood upon the battlements on the other side of the Golden Horn, watching the western fleet. The attack had been the most dramatic political event in Damian's life, his version of 9/11. The crusaders had sailed their entire fleet into the harbor and most of the ships were anchored at the Galata suburb across the harbor to the north. The once busy docks next to the city walls were empty, as all the Greek warships and merchant vessels had been sunk or captured.

"Does this mean we won't get shipments by sea?" asked Basil.

"No, nothing as bad as that. We still have the docks on the Sea of Marmara," said Damian. "The crusaders look strong, but they're only on one side of the city. A strange sort of siege if you ask me."

"They'll never get past the guard," said Basil. "They'll be cut down and destroyed, eliminated like the vermin they are."

"I hope so, son," said Damian.

The two men continued to scan the harbor. Despite their bravado, they must have felt some tingle of fear. The forest of masts from the Venetian warships, surrounded by the many war galleys, each with their own more modest rigging and sails occupied the full breadth and length of the Golden Horn. Such a great fleet had never been assembled before, and to be on the wrong side of it was daunting. A few galleys were patrolling the harbor, ready for any eventuality, the oarsmen rowing languidly while the sails flapped in the light wind.

At length, they descended the walls and headed for home. Basil had just turned sixteen, and he was starting a growth spurt. He had lost some of his roundness, and now sported a sparse beard. City life continued around them as usual, uninterrupted by the threatening presence of the Franks. An old hag called to them from her seat under a portico as they passed, begging for alms, but Damian was too distracted to notice. They stopped to buy two small loaves of warm bread from a street vendor. Damian broke off a chunk and ate it as he walked. The aroma and taste of the just-baked bread was a treat for Brooke, child as she was of the industrialized food economy.

When they arrived back at the workshop, they discovered that Eulogia and Theodoret had gone shopping, while Ariadne was taking a nap.

"This is our chance," said Damian. "Come with me." He locked the front door and led Basil into the kitchen. Lighting a torch, he descended into the cistern under the floor and set the torch into a bracket on the wall. The place was damp and dingy, thick with cobwebs.

"Help me shift this crate," said Damian. The two men pushed the large crate aside and Damian searched for the crowbar.

"Do we really need to do this?" asked Basil.

"Yes, we do," replied his exasperated father. "I was robbed once, and I'll never be robbed again."

"But you said the barbarians could never get into the city."

"I said they almost certainly would never get into the city, but there's still a chance, however small. Now stop arguing with me."

Damian found the crowbar and pried up the cover over the secret stash. The hole was only half filled with items. Damian removed them and set them aside. He dislodged the thin bricks that paved the side of the hole and handed them, one by one, to Basil. Working steadily, he enlarged the space, tossing the dirt into a bucket.

"Take this out to the courtyard and distribute it among the plants," said Damian. "And bring back more bricks to line the hole."

Basil sighed, his whole body settling into a dismissive slouch, but he did as his father requested and returned with the bricks in hand. Damian filled the bucket twice more and sent the reluctant Basil back and forth. Finally, the small space had been enlarged and again lined with bricks, the cover secured, and the crate shifted over to hide the cache.

"That should do it," said Damian. "Between the decoys in the cabinet upstairs and the difficulty of finding this spot, our valuables will be entirely safe. You do remember that you can't tell anyone about this, don't you—not even your mother or your best friend?"

"Of course, father. You say that all the time," replied Basil. "I've never told anyone."

"Good. We can't be too careful."

⸎

Brooke perched on the edge of her chair, back straight and hands resting gently on her upper thighs. Her eyes looked without seeing at a point on her living room rug. She drew all her attention to breathing in, imagining the air swirling into her nose and filling her lungs. On the exhale, she felt a wave of relaxation warm her body. She held her focus for several more breaths, cocooned in a safe place, free of worry and fear. Julia's face swirled into her mind, as she had looked at the anniversary party, pinched and fretful. Brooke let the image sail away, and returned to a peaceful place. The walls of Constantinople stood before her, tall and impregnable, but Brooke calmly returned her attention to her breath. Her breath was in the present moment, not in the past or future.

Brooke had been suffering from insomnia for the past few weeks. As the situation in Constantinople got close to boiling point, her anxiety mounted. Thoughts raced through her mind like unruly children. She preferred meditation over medication as a way of dealing with the problem and spent ten minutes every day in calming practice.

The alarm sounded on her cell phone and she rose from her chair and turned it off. Gathering her things, she set off for the campus. It was a brisk day in mid-February, with wispy clouds scudding across the otherwise clear sky. The feeble sun was dipping behind the buildings and would set soon. She had decided to walk to save on gas money and get some exercise. It hadn't snowed in several weeks and the piles of snow at the side of the street were crusted black from dirt and exhaust fumes. Brooke looked away.

By the time she arrived at the Memex lab, she felt refreshed, clearheaded, and ready to work. Uncharacteristically, Chad and Robert were both there waiting for her. Chad had a pained expression on his face. Robert, who was seated at a long table, took off his glasses, tossed them down, and rubbed his eyes with his knuckles. Then he replaced the glasses.

"What's wrong?" asked Brooke.

"Another mouse died yesterday," said Chad. "Robert discovered it after you left last night and I autopsied it this morning. It was a brain tumor again."

Brooke was startled, as if she had looked up and seen an asteroid aiming for her head. She had put the dead mouse out of her mind and never expected to deal with it again. But then her rational mind kicked in. She had nothing to worry about.

"Last week I went for my follow-up MRI. You remember that the professor would not let me continue experiments unless I promised to get routine brain scans. I was perfectly normal—no tumors."

"That's a relief," said Robert, smiling broadly. Chad visibly relaxed, his shoulders slumping as he leaned against a table.

"You got lucky this time," said Chad. "Now I hope you'll stop exposing yourself to that machine. I'm convinced it's dangerous."

Brooke bristled at his words. "I don't intend to stop. I think the brain tumors have nothing to do with the Memex."

"But why would you take the chance?"

"Maybe some of us have more courage than others," she said, and instantly regretted it.

Chad looked angry but said nothing. He picked up his Stetson, clapped it on his head, and left the lab.

Brooke sighed. His protectiveness invariably pushed her to greater recklessness. She wondered if he was right, and she was being a complete fool.

Turning toward Robert, she said, "We have to get to the bottom of this mouse problem. There must be a reason these mice are dying, and I hope it's not the Memex." Robert looked a little confused at her admission that the Memex might be responsible, but wisely refrained from commenting.

"Let's review what we know. How much exposure did the first mouse to die have compared to this recently dead mouse?"

Robert pulled up a file on his computer.

"The first mouse was a male who was exposed for a total of 6172 minutes over a period of seven months. The average exposure for his cohort was 5001 minutes. The mouse that died yesterday was a female with an exposure time of just 5216 minutes. However the average exposure time for her cohort is longer, since we've been testing longer. It's now crept up to 7711 minutes."

"If exposure were to blame, I think we would see more cases," said Brooke. "Let's take a look at the last batch of mice that Chad sacrificed and autopsied. They were all negative for brain tumors. What was their average exposure time?"

"That'll take me a minute," said Robert.

While he worked, Brooke thought about the ordeal to come. She knew, in broad outline, what would happen today in Constantinople, but she had no idea what would happen to Garnett. Of course he wouldn't die or be permanently maimed. But other than that, she would have to explore the memories that somehow were lodged in her brain. The team had not advanced very far in understanding how the Memex worked and that bothered Brooke. She had never faced such a vexing problem before, one that left her so few avenues to explore. But she was determined to keep trying.

"I have the number. The average exposure time for the sacrificed mice was 5938 minutes. Chad must have chosen them because they had logged a lot of time. That would make sense."

"That supports the idea that exposure is not the cause. Let's step back a bit. These mice are all from the same inbred strain, DBA/2, subline 3. Their lineage goes all the way back to C.C. Little who first bred them in 1909. Their genetic similarity has been maintained by mating brothers and sisters ever since. We bought them from Pimpleton Laboratories, who got the original stock from the National Institute of Health in the sixties."

"I think we need to find other researchers who are using our strain and see if they have seen any tumors. What's the maximum life span of the males of this strain, by the way?" she asked. Robert pulled up the website for Pimpleton and clicked through a few screens.

"It looks like the mean male life span is 825 days with a standard deviation of 142 days. Our male died after only 280 days."

"Of course, we can't draw any real conclusions with such a small sample size. We really need to network on this one," said Brooke.

"OK. I'll search for recent journal articles that use our strain and capture the email addresses of the authors. Then I can send out feelers and see if they've seen anything. We could also call the company."

"Good idea. Let's do it."

Robert pulled out his mobile phone and dialed a number from the company website. Brooke waited impatiently while he made his way through an annoying phone tree. Surprisingly enough, they got a representative fairly quickly.

"Yes, we are interested in purchasing some DBA/2, subline 3 mice. Before we choose this strain, we would like to talk to some researchers who have experience with it. Can you give me names and contact info?"

He waited while the voice on the other end replied.

"I understand that you can't divulge the names of your customers." He paused a moment and gave his email address.

Robert turned off the phone and said to Brooke, "He said he would ask them to contact me. Who knows? They might."

"We can't count on it." Brooke ran her fingers through her long hair, sweeping it back from her face. Then she went over to the Memex and settled herself in position for the day's journey.

"I'm ready." Robert turned to the computer and hit a button on the screen.

July 17, 1203. Garnett stood on the hill with the other knights of the Fourth Division in full armor and surcoat. Before him, across a small river, lay the northwest corner of the city. The Blachernae Palace, one of the emperor's sumptuous residences, was nestled into this corner, its outer wall forming part of the city's defenses. It was early in the day, and birds sang their morning greetings, oblivious to the coming conflict. A scaling ladder lay on the ground nearby, one of many scattered among the troops. Brooke could see walls stretching off into the distance in both directions, facing the land to the west of Constantinople and the sea to the north.

Behind Garnett lay the crusader's encampment, set up beside the castle of Bohemond. Six days earlier, the army had crossed the Blachernae bridge over the Golden Horn, and was now within shouting distance of the city itself. In one of the more unenlightened war maneuvers in history, the Greeks had destroyed the bridge, but had done a shabby job of it. It only took the crusaders one day to make repairs, and the enemy had sat idly by while they worked.

The crusader's encampment had been harried several times a day by Greek sorties, but the knights held on tenaciously. Now, reduced to eating wormy flour, almost rancid bacon, and the meat of their fallen horses, they had to either move forward or backward, and their code of honor would never allow a retreat.

Brooke heard faint sounds of battle off in the distance—the clink of metal, the thump of stones striking the earth, and faint shouts and screams. Garnett looked about expectantly, barely able to restrain his eagerness to be on with it. Brooke knew that the Venetians were striking from the sea, softening up the city's defenders in support of the major assault by the French. They had constructed covered passageways that they suspended from the tops of their highest masts, through which their knights could reach the top of the wall. To build the floors of these ingenious structures, they laid two yardarms parallel to each other and nailed down a plank walkway. The sides and top of the passageway were covered with hides and canvas liberally doused with vinegar to shield the attackers from flaming arrows and other missiles. Brooke wished she could see the vessels bristling with these ungainly tentacles, but as always, her point of view was limited to what Garnett could see.

The knights in front of them started to move forward at last. A knight in an emerald surcoat picked up the front end of the scaling ladder while others picked up the rear, and Garnett joined in, lifting the middle. The army walked down the hill, four divisions strong. The remaining three divisions, headed by General Boniface, never one to be in the front lines, were left to guard the camp. Garnett's shoulders strained under the weight of the ladder as he picked his way through the bramble and stones. They came to the river Lycus and hoisted the ladder over their heads, balancing it on their broad shoulders. As they splashed in, Brooke felt the chilly water seep into her metal boots and rise slowly up her legs. There were still no Greeks in sight, and the army crossed the river without opposition. Count Louis, mounted on a magnificent white stallion, stood on the far bank, scanning both the ground ahead and the progress of his troops at the ford.

At its center, the river rose to Garnett's waist, and the water inside the armor reaching his groin, its frigid touch sending a spasm through his body. He lumbered up on the far bank. Here the army halted and the knights set down their ladders. Water was slowly draining from the suit, but the chill had spread up into the iron breastplate and back piece, and Garnett shivered. They waited while the battle to the east intensified.

Things were not going well for the Venetians. Their ships were lined up facing the wall, and the cantilevered passageways brushed against the battlements, sometimes coming close enough so that blows were exchanged, but to little avail. Other Venetians had landed on the shore and, amid a rain of missiles from both sides, attacked the wall with a battering ram. They managed to break open a hole and both sides fought fiercely to control this pinch point. The Venetians, who had seemed to be making progress, now faltered and fell back.

At that point, Doge Dandolo, who had been standing in the prow of his vermilion warship, ordered his men to take him to shore. He advanced with a full color guard, the banner of St. Mark flapping in the breeze. When the sailors saw their beloved leader—aged, blind, but forever brave—leading the charge, they streamed from the ships to the shore and ran like madmen into the fray. Their ardor was unstoppable and they pushed back the defenders amid heavy casualties, pouring through the hole into the city.

While the Venetians were pushing their attack, Brooke waited impatiently for the French divisions to be deployed. With every passing minute, her fear kicked up a notch. Garnett's heart beat quickly, and he opened and closed his gauntleted fists spasmodically. A wisp of smoke rose over the city near the walls; the Venetians had set some buildings ablaze. Every eye was diverted by a horseman galloping toward them at full speed. He asked where Count Baldwin was, and finding the good leader, relayed the news of the Venetian victory.

Baldwin gave the order to advance, and, with trumpets sounding, the men took up their positions, picked up their scaling ladders, and moved forward in haste. Garnett loped along in a slow run, positioned again at the middle of a ladder held parallel to the ground, toward the impossibly high walls. The Varangian guard held the battlements and poured missiles of every kind upon the French—deadly crossbow bolts, flocks of arrows, and giant stones. A bolt struck the knight at the head of Garnett's ladder and lodged in his leg. He collapsed, and the front end of the ladder bit into the earth, its momentum carrying it forward to dig a shallow groove. Garnett was jarred to a halt and waited while another knight stepped in to lift the ladder's leading edge. The line of attackers had become ragged, with a few groups out in front and most falling behind under the onslaught.

Garnett pressed forward, breathing heavily, the weight of the ladder increasing with every step. Brooke could make out individual faces at the top of the wall, grimly determined. They ducked now and then when French arrows came close to the mark. As she looked up, she spied a huge stone hurtling toward her and her brain stopped in mid-thought. It smashed into the ladder just ahead of Garnett's position and broke the side rail in two. Garnett dropped the now worthless ladder and, heart pounding, took his bearings. Smoke to the east billowed beyond the wall in a great black smudge, as the city burned fiercely. One group of knights had succeeded in reaching the base of the wall and were frantically raising their scaling ladder. Another group was almost there. Garnett ran forward to assist his comrades, zigzagging to evade arrows sent from above.

A knight had reached the top of the only ladder up against the wall when he was dislodged by a blow from a battle ax and fell screaming to the ground fifty feet below. Another valiant fighter took his place but was no more successful. A second ladder was partially raised when the Greeks dumped several large stones on it, knocking it aside and injuring several knights. Garnett rushed to help the men make another attempt to set it up. But the ladder snapped as they lifted it, and Garnett threw it aside in disgust. The Greeks seemed to sense that they were winning and redoubled their efforts to drive off the invaders. An arrow glanced off Garnett's helmet, knocking his head back. Pain erupted in his neck and lanced up into his brain stem, but he stayed on his feet. The French were in retreat, having given up on going over the wall. Garnett followed them back toward the river, running with what strength he had left, head aching as the blood pounded in his skull.

It was a disconsolate group of knights who trekked back towards the camp, walking wearily once they were out of range of the Greek archers. When he arrived, Garnett removed his helmet and drank deeply from the buckets of water that the servants provided. A commotion rose up on the far side of camp as a herd of captured horses were driven in. Dandolo had anticipated the needs of the French knights, many of whom had lost their mounts in battle, and sent these captured animals. His forethought would prove to be critical in what was yet to come that day.

Garnett rested and ate some hard biscuits, avoiding conversation. The fire still raged within the city, fanned by a southerly wind that drove the flames deep into the interior, and sent smoke billowing up to dizzying heights. Brooke shuddered to think of what was happening to the citizens, and felt relieved that she was not there. She was supposed to be observing history, to augment or overthrow the prevailing viewpoint. As such, she had studied the many eyewitness accounts of the Fourth Crusade and compared them to her experience, finding that the old documents were largely accurate. If she were in the city now where the great fire raged, she could check the historical record, but, lucky for her, Garnett was safely outside the walls.

A shout went up to prepare for battle. The Greek army had finally decided to engage their tormentors, and was issuing from the city through three gates, led by Emperor Alexios himself. The French rushed into formation. Six divisions of knights were arrayed in front of the encampment, with archers and foot soldiers in front and mounted men in the rear, while one division was left to guard the siege engines.

Garnett was poised on Ajax, lance tucked under his arm, his headache reduced to a mild background sensation. The Greek army was forming up in a long line parallel to the river. Three fat columns of soldiers snaked across the field from the gates to the Greek position. They came like water pouring from a bottomless jug, slowly filling the field with a vast crowd of combatants. As the Greek lines grew deeper and wider, the French position looked more and more hopeless. They were isolated, without back-up, and outnumbered by more than two to one. Many of the French knights had lost their horses and others were mounted on unfamiliar captured beasts. In desperation, Count Baldwin ordered that the stable boys and cooks be decked out in blankets as makeshift armor and be capped with iron pots for helmets. They carried butcher knives, ready to go down fighting.

At last, the Greeks were in position and the moment had come to advance. Both armies edged toward each other, like wolf packs creeping in for the strike. The Greek line was longer than the French and a competent general might have wrapped his troops around their flanks, but Emperor Alexios took no such action. Brooke, finding herself in the middle of the French group, watched as Baldwin of Flanders led the charge, followed by Hugh of Saint-Pol and Peter of Amiens. The leading edge of the French line became a little ragged, and Baldwin dropped back. Hugh of Saint-Pol rushed forward to keep the troops moving, and the net effect was a speed-up of the French army. The Greek troops moved forward at a more measured pace, and halted just across the Lycus river. Here both sides paused.

Then, in a stunning display of cowardice, the Greeks began an orderly retreat. Like a movie running backwards, the assembled troops filed back into the city, retracing their steps. It was true, thought Brooke, the emperor had no stomach for a fight. Even with every advantage, and a heavily armed guard protecting his person, he was unwilling to endanger himself, and would go down in the annals of history as one of the most incompetent military leaders of all time. The French maintained discipline, and eased forward in formation, resisting the temptation to chase a vulnerable retreating army that could have turned on them and overwhelmed them by sheer force of numbers.

The last of the Greeks disappeared behind the walls. The crusaders had won the day.

XXII

A HEAVY BURDEN

*A*ug. 3, 1203. Damian sank back in his chair and peered across the table at his *tired wife*. The dinner had been a modest affair, a step down from the delicious meals of former days, when life had been more hopeful. Eulogia looked every minute her age, the dark circles under her eyes betraying the strain she had been under and the sleepless nights she had endured. The others, Basil, Theodoret, and Ariadne, had all retired for the night, leaving the husband and wife a rare opportunity for private conversation.

"How was the work at the convent today?" asked Damian.

"It started well enough. When we opened in the morning, there was already a line of people that stretched far down the avenue. I couldn't see the end of it. People were so grateful when we gave them a bowl of soup and a crust of bread. The nuns were well organized and everything went smoothly."

"If you could have seen some of these unfortunates," she continued. "Most of them lost their homes in the great fire and have nowhere to sleep. Half have a desperate look in their eyes and the rest are merely resigned. There was one little girl whose face was so badly burned I doubt she will ever find a mate."

Damian picked up his flagon and sipped some mead. It was his third cup, a rare indulgence for him, and an indication of his troubled state of mind.

"After serving all morning, I was assigned to the dishwashing detail," continued Eulogia. "No sooner had a pauper finished his meal than I washed up the bowl and sent it to the servers for reuse. We could barely keep up. The worst part, though, was the end of the day. Father Potamius had to close the doors when there were still hoards of people to feed. They begged him piteously, but he told them they would reopen in the morning.

After he shut the door, many just sat on the pavement, intending to spend the night there."

A look of concern crossed over Damian's face. "Did you have trouble getting out?"

"No, not really. We exited by a back door. There were a few beggars there, but they didn't touch me."

"Are you going back tomorrow?"

She nodded and Damian picked up his flagon again. Eulogia sat folding and unfolding her napkin with her long straight fingers.

"I had lunch with Ignatius today," said Damian. "He has friends who have friends who work in the palace and he told me a strange tale. The night after the fire, when Emperor Alexios fled the city like a common thief, he took with him a big chunk of the royal treasury. Some say it was a thousand pounds of gold." Brooke did the mental arithmetic. At the current price of gold per ounce, 1000 pounds would be worth about $30,000,000. Quite a haul.

"I still can't believe we've fallen so far that our emperor would sneak away in the night," said Eulogia.

"He was finished after the debacle on the plains outside the city. When he retreated before the western army without exchanging a blow, even his supporters realized he was unfit to rule. Had he stayed, the mob would have torn him apart in a slow and disgraceful death."

"I can't help feeling pity for his wife, being left behind. Where is she now?"

"Ignatius thinks she was imprisoned in the Blachernae Palace," replied Damian.

"At least he took his daughter with him."

The conversation flagged and the two sat disconsolately. It was already dark outside and the single candle flickered as the wick burned low.

"Why are the barbarians still here?" asked Eulogia.

"It's hard to say. I thought they were waiting for Prince Alexios to ascend the throne. His old blind father, Isaac, wasn't fit to rule. Now we have them as co-emperors." Brooke mused over the irony of Constantinople being ruled, even if only for a few weeks, by a blind emperor. The Greeks had a long tradition of regarding the blind as incapable of leadership, stretching all the way back to Oedipus Rex. Alexios III, the recently departed emperor, had blinded his brother, Isaac, so that there would be no question of setting him back on the throne. Now the unthinkable had happened. Not only were the Greeks led by Isaac, but the crusaders were led by Dandolo, the real force behind their actions. It was a case of the blind fighting the blind.

"I wish the Franks would leave. We won't be safe until their fleet sails off," said Eulogia.

"Don't worry. They'll be gone soon. They have what they want. The prince has become the new emperor, Alexios IV. Why would they stay?" If only you knew, thought Brooke. The worst was yet to come.

※

"Pretty naive, your Damian, isn't he?" asked Prof. Hunter. Brooke bristled at the implied criticism of her many-times-removed great-grandfather, whom she had come to think of as a member of her extended family.

"I suppose it's a lot easier for us to figure things out, since we know what happened. Damian has never been interested in politics," Brooke said in his defense. She was seated in an uncomfortable chair next to Prof. Hunter's desk. The weekly research meeting had gone smoothly enough, as Brooke told Hunter about her latest trips to the past. Hunter had taken to meeting with the students separately over the last few weeks, for a reason of her own without telling them why.

"Still, he had to think that the crusaders wanted something. They didn't just set Alexios on the throne out of the goodness of their hearts."

"Some of the crusaders did. Garnett is a devout Christian who believes that the monarch is a divinely appointed ruler. He thought that Alexios III was a usurper who had broken God's law and that Prince Alexios was the rightful heir."

"Another naive relative of yours." Hunter said this as if it were a judgment of Brooke's character, since she was descended from both of them. "What was Prince Alexios like, anyway?"

"I haven't gotten close to him, only seen him in passing. Garnett has never talked to him, but I can give you an impression. He's immature, interested only in gambling and drinking, hardly emperor material. He also has trouble inspiring anyone to support him, especially in this era."

"Why do you say that?"

"Alexios is gay, and he is, let us say, on the feminine end of the gay spectrum."

"I see. That would be tough."

"Worse than that, he isn't very smart. He made enormous promises to the crusade leadership. I have to wonder if he even realized how much he was giving away. He committed 200,000 silver marks and 10,000 soldiers for the crusade. Besides that, he promised to keep 500 fully equipped knights in the Holy Land after it had been conquered. As a final stroke, he also agreed to make the Greek church submit to the Pope in Rome."

"What does that mean, 200,000 silver marks?"

"I wondered about that too, so I did an estimate. The contract that Venice signed with the crusaders specified that they would transport soldiers to the Holy Land and supply them with nine months of food for two silver marks per man. Say it costs $15 a day to feed a soldier and $4000 to transport him across the sea. Then 200,000 marks is equivalent to about 800 million dollars."

Hunter arched her eyebrows at this impressive sum. "And could Constantinople afford that much money?"

"They certainly didn't have it in the treasury. Both Isaac and Alexios III had raided the treasury for their extensive building projects. When Alexios III skipped town, he took half a ton of gold with him, all that he could carry. Constantinople was mostly broke. The common citizens had no idea how bad things had gotten."

Hunter didn't seem to have any sympathy for the people caught in this disaster and no regret about what had ultimately happened to them. Instead, she changed the subject.

"On another matter, I had a conversation with a friend of mine on the Review Board."

Brooke looked up hopefully.

"I'm afraid the news isn't good. It seems that Brashley, the university lawyer, got the president interested in our project. Normally this would be a good thing, but our president doesn't understand faculty. He called Review Board members one by one into his office and made a badly-concealed attempt to influence them. As soon as they realized that he wanted them to expedite the approval of our project, their position hardened. They see it as an attack on intellectual freedom."

"But can't the president override them?"

"No, no, no. There's this little thing called tenure. The president can apply pressure of course, with subtle threats to anything from salary actions to lab space, but the board is composed of older faculty who are well-positioned to defy him and they can't be fired. This president isn't very forceful, so it's easy to stand up to him. They see his overtures as crass and greedy—putting financial gain ahead of the health of the test subjects—and they're feeling righteous about their position. I'm afraid it's a setback. To make matters worse, they're concerned about the second unexplained mouse death."

"Robert is working on that," said Brooke. "He's tracking down other researchers who are using our strain and seeing what he can learn."

"It can't be too soon," said the professor. "This whole debacle is ruining my reputation on campus. I've never had so much trouble getting approval for a project. While we languish, rumors are flying around campus, multiplying like rabbits."

Brooke thought about her own troubles and what the delays meant to her. At the end of the spring semester, she would run out of money, and at the moment, she had no plan to cope with the problem. She knew she should take steps—interview for jobs, look for alternative support, etc.—but she just couldn't face all that. Once she was allowed to recruit volunteers and they saw for themselves what the Memex could do, she would have a thesis. It wasn't too late.

Dec. 11, 1203. Julia had been ignoring the knock on the door, not wanting to see anyone, but the visitor was insistent. With a sigh, she walked across the kitchen, released the latch, and swung the door wide. Helena stood there in a long cloak of speckled gray wool, cheeks ruddy with the winter chill.

"What happened to you?" she asked as her eyes opened wide in surprise. She laid her hand on Julia's cheek in a gentle caress. Brooke wondered what was going on. She felt just fine in Julia's body.

"It's nothing," said Julia. "It will heal."

"A black eye isn't nothing."

"Really, don't worry about me. Come, sit down and chat while I work on the baking." Helena removed her cloak and looked around for a place to set it, but the kitchen was in disarray, with dirty dishes and pots occupying every horizontal surface. Julia, seeing her hesitation, took the garment and hung it up on a hook behind the door. There was already another cloak there, and Helena's cloak fell off. On the second try, it remained.

Helena took a seat at one end of the workbench while Julia attacked a batch of dough.

"I'm sorry about the mess. I just can't keep up with things. My mother-in-law doesn't help much. We're lucky that she went to fetch water, or she would be hovering about, telling me what to do." Helena made sympathetic noises.

Julia sprinkled some flour on the board, folded the dough in half, and sank her fingers into it. She repeated the action—fold, sprinkle, knead, turn—again and again.

"I would take you into the bedroom," said Julia, "but the bedbugs have gotten bad." As she said it, she scratched her forearm, where a trail of angry red bumps ran past her elbow. Brooke could also feel intense itching in her back, although Julia ignored it.

"Don't fret about it," said Helena. "Everybody has bedbugs."

"That's true, but not everybody has as many as we do. My mother used to take the mattresses out often and beat them, and sweep the bedroom floor daily to keep the bugs in check, but not in this household."

"Tell me what happened to your eye," said Helena gently.

Julia looked down and hesitated, ignoring the dough for a moment. A blush crept up into her cheeks. Brooke thought about how lucky she was not to have been around when Julia got hurt. She was interested in hearing what Julia had to say.

"You shouldn't worry about it."

"Is this why I haven't seen you lately?" asked Helena. Julia said nothing. "Was it Florian?"

Julia cast an anguished look in Helena's direction and said, "He came home from the taverna one night and wasn't himself. He and his buddies had had a lot to drink. He's angry because there's no child on the way."

"Oh, Julia, I'm so sorry." Helena came to her friend and hugged her, heedless of the flour on Julia's apron. "Don't worry. The Lord will help you, and, with His blessing, a child will come."

"What if the Lord is punishing me? What if this is because of Origen? I acted shamefully and…"

Helena looked at her friend tenderly. "Darling, the Lord Jesus Christ is a merciful God. He forgives us our transgressions if we are truly repentant. You can pray and ask for His forgiveness. I am sure He will come to you and help you in your struggle. I will pray for you, too, every night before I go to bed."

Brooke wanted, not for the first time, to step out of her bodily prison and talk to the women. If only she could tell them that Julia was fully capable of conceiving and delivering a baby and would do so in the future. Either Florian was infertile or they had just been unlucky. The vengeance of an all-seeing deity had nothing to do with it.

As if Helena could read her thoughts, she said, "How long have you been married? These things sometimes require patience."

Julia thought for a moment and replied, "It's been 18 months."

"Kiria Eustatius didn't have her first child until three years after she was married. It can happen."

"I can't wait that long," said Julia. A tear spilled from her eye. "I'm so afraid."

"It could be sooner. You have to keep trying."

Julia looked doubtful. "I've been doing everything I can think of. I even went to the pharmacist and bought a nostrum that will increase my fertility. I've used most of it up."

"He does lie with you, doesn't he?"

"Every night," said Julia in a flat tone. She didn't seem to be looking forward to it. Brooke wanted to chastise Damian for putting his daughter in this terrible position. She knew he loved her, but this wasn't what you do to people you love.

Julia laid a hand over Helena's. "You've been such a good friend to me. I don't know what I would do without you." The two women rested quietly in that bond of sisterhood that has sustained women throughout the ages.

Dec. 20, 1203. "Over here is our next destination, the church of the Holy Apostles," said the scruffy young man. He was a Pisan who had lived in Constantinople all his life. His fluent French made him the ideal tour guide for the small band of crusaders. Garnett scanned the Greek church, an imposing, blocky structure with five domes, each topped by a golden cross. A beggar draped in tattered brown rags squatted on the entrance steps, but he fled when he saw the armed group approach.

Brooke was surprised that Garnett would enter the church with his sword and dagger. He was usually the first to follow all proprieties to the letter, especially in a house of God. But the people of Constantinople were decidedly hostile, and it would be unsafe to move about the city unarmed. The interior of the church was dominated by an altar of gleaming silver, studded with precious gems and adorned by a pyramidal canopy of marble. The tour guide stopped before a golden reliquary, one of many that extended to either side of the altar.

"Here we have the finger bone of St. Thomas, the very same finger that he placed in the wound on Christ's side." As Brooke remembered the story, doubting Thomas said he would not believe in Christ's resurrection until he placed his finger in the wound, but he never actually did it. Seeing the risen Christ was enough to make him believe. The tour guide next pointed out the skull of St. James, the brother of Jesus. Brooke was skeptical.

The guide droned on, intent on introducing them to each and every relic. After hearing about St. Andrew the Apostle, St. Luke the Evangelist, St. Timothy, St. John Chrysostom, and St. Gregory the Theologian, Brooke stopped listening altogether. The crusaders, however, paid rapt attention, frequently crossing themselves and exclaiming in awe.

Finally they moved to a side branch of the church and viewed the sarcophagus of Emperor Justinian the Great. Two hours passed before they regained the street. The sunlight felt unnaturally bright after the dark nave of the church, but Brooke was happy to be outside again. The crusaders remained in a tight group as they followed their guide, careful to scan the streets for threats. To Brooke, the people looked more weary than threatening. The knights were unmistakable, in their western garments with crosses sewn on their shoulders, and pedestrians gave them a wide berth.

The next tourist attraction was the Aqueduct of Valens, two rows of arches that soared seven stories above the street. Garnett forgot about watching for hostiles, and gawked like a child. Brooke had seen it many times before and waited patiently for the crusaders to take it in. After the aqueduct, they walked eastward toward the center of town.

Garnett was now in a business district not far from the Balsamon's home. The streets were busy with morning shoppers. Brooke scanned their faces anxiously, searching for Julia. She often came this way, usually with a male escort. Was this the day that Garnett would finally meet her? As usual, there were few women on the street, and each wore a veil that obscured her face. Of course Brooke would recognize Julia by her gait and carriage if nothing else. Garnett tried to make eye contact with one tall woman, but she quickly looked away. Brooke noticed a woman in a green gown out of the corner of her eye, but she was too heavy to be Julia.

They approached within a block of Florian's house and Brooke recognized the local baker, standing in the doorway of his shop. She both anticipated and dreaded the event that would finally bring Garnett and Julia together. Garnett was a good man, honorable and brave. Unfortunately, Brooke could not imagine a scenario that would pair him up with a married woman in any kind of honorable way.

The crusaders stopped by a street vendor's cart and bought sticky buns. The sweet taste of the honey soothed Brooke's overwrought mind. The group continued eastward, leaving the business district behind. Brooke felt both disappointment and relief. They came to the edge of a fire-blackened zone that stretched into the distance. The city had suffered two great fires, one in July while the crusaders were storming the walls, and the other a month later, after the crusaders had taken over the city. No one knew how the second fire had started, although the Greeks firmly believed the crusaders were to blame.

The devastation was widespread, with large flat areas that looked as barren as if the fire had happened yesterday rather than four months ago. Two walls of a large villa rose from the rubble, the stones charred and black. Blistered roof timbers had fallen into the vacant building. Brooke saw no signs of rebuilding. There were a few tents and shanties, with open air fires, but no masons or carpenters trying to put things right. Her heart ached to see her beloved city in this state. Until this moment, she had not realized how attached she was to the majestic imperial capital, with its lavishly decorated villas, palaces, and government buildings. To see it thoughtlessly destroyed made her sick with grief.

Garnett walked along a well-traveled roadway that had been cleared of debris. The tour guide, who had kept up a steady stream of patter for hours, had now fallen silent. Hugh walked up to Garnett and said, "You could fit all of Paris in just this burned part of town."

Garnett nodded. "This city is unbelievably large. It's hard to understand why they can't defend themselves."

"Greeks are cowards, that's all." This was a widely held view among the crusaders.

At last they traversed the burned zone and reached the center of town, where the Mese, the broad central avenue, was paved with marble and flanked by elegant buildings. The crusaders marveled at the selection in the marketplace, but Brooke found it meager compared to earlier and better times.

The tour guide led them to the Hagia Irene, a church that Brooke had never visited before. The relic collection within was extensive. Its centerpiece was a magnificent icon of Jesus with the Virgin Mary and the apostles. More than thirty individual relics were set into this icon, including a milk tooth that Jesus had lost in childhood, a splinter from the lance that pierced his side while he was on the cross, and a scrap of his burial shroud. Brooke was saddened by the gullibility of the worshipers. Did they really think that Mary had kept one of Christ's baby teeth to preserve for all time and that this relic had come down through a thousand years of history? Apparently they did. The clergy couldn't display Christ's bones, since He had risen from the dead, so they had to make do with whatever they could. The crusaders also admired a thorn from the crown of thorns, a belt of the Virgin Mary, and a vial of Christ's blood, still liquid after all this time. These were some of the treasures that men would spill blood to gain. It made Brooke want to cry.

⸺

Jan. 7, 1204. Damian turned the picture frame over and examined it carefully. He took up his polishing rag and touched up the delicate silver filigree in several places. Unlike the icons Brooke was used to, this Virgin Mary had a slight smile on her lips as she looked serenely at a point in the distance. She was dressed in red and had a long nose, but her identity was still unmistakable.

The bell rang as Ignatius entered the workshop, bringing a puff of cool air with him. There were new strands of gray in his curly black hair and his forehead was creased with a frown. The two old friends exchanged greetings.

"What a pleasant surprise to see you at this time of day," said Damian, coming out from behind the workbench. "I'll call Eulogia and ask her to bring refreshments."

"Don't trouble yourself, my friend, I can't stay long. There's a lot I must do today." Brooke wondered why he was stopping by for a casual chat if he had a lot to do. The answer came quickly.

"I wanted you to be the first to know. I've decided to leave town."

"What? Why? How can you leave?" sputtered Damian.

"These new taxes are more than I can bear. Last month, I could hardly pay the grocer and replenish my stock of perfume. I fear this month will be even worse. Customers are scarcer than nuns in a whorehouse."

"But tough times have come before. Things always get better if you wait it out," said Damian.

"I'm not sure about that. This time is different. The refugees from the fire aren't in a mind to buy perfume. How long will it take them to rebuild? In fact, many people are cutting back, and luxuries are not selling well. The crushing tax burden has changed people. I'm surprised your business hasn't been affected."

"I've felt the pinch, to be sure, but half of my business is with the church, and I have a number of long range commissions."

Ignatius looked even more dour at the mention of the church. He said, "I was outside the Pantocrater monastery last week when I saw a group of our own soldiers enter. I got curious and stayed to see what might happen. They came out a short while later with something wrapped up in a cloth. It was a fat cylinder about four feet long. The wrapping slipped and I got a glimpse of a jewel-encrusted golden candlestick. I think it was the one they use for the Pascal candle."

Damian's eyes opened wide in surprise. "They were raiding the monastery?"

Ignatius nodded. "Looks like it. I also heard rumors that soldiers are robbing the graves of wealthy citizens. The new emperor must be desperate indeed to risk the wrath of the nobility and the clergy at the same time."

"It must be the Franks," said Damian. "They'll leave in the spring to continue their crusade and then everything can get back to normal. Where are you going?"

"I have a cousin in Antioch. I was planning to sell the shop and head there. At least there is some demand for real estate. I can thank the fire for that."

"It's a long journey to make in the winter," said Damian. "Perhaps you should wait a month or two."

"In a month, my children will be hungry. Things are that bad. I'm afraid I have to go now."

"May the Lord go with you," said Damian. He clasped his friend in a fierce farewell hug. After Ignatius left, he stared at the closed door for a long time.

Uncertain about what she wanted to explore next, Brooke poured over her lab notebook. She was a careful researcher and made a habit of documenting each visit as soon as possible upon her return, avoiding memory lapses and mistakes. She was equally curious about the fate of her family members and the accuracies or inaccuracies of the historical accounts. Unfortunately for her, none of her forebears were placed in the upper reaches of the power structure in either of the opposing camps. Nevertheless, she persisted, hoping to turn up something of interest.

Her watcher this afternoon was Chad, who was lounging in a chair before the Memex, turning the pages of a magazine and waiting for her to decide what to do next. He was annoyingly attractive in his tight blue jeans, well-worn leather boots, and big silver belt buckle. She finally made up her mind.

"I'm going to go back and see how Julia's doing."

"Doesn't her husband beat her?" asked Chad.

Brooke shrugged. "It goes with the territory. I've been through worse. Maybe I'll be lucky and avoid that part." Chad looked skeptical, but closed his magazine.

"Besides, I need to discover when Julia met Garnett. Maybe she ran away from Florian and went outside the city." Brooke regretted saying this as soon as it left her lips. She shouldn't have to explain herself to Chad.

"Whatever you want, Brooke." He moved to the computer and asked for the date.

Brooke told him. She went to the Memex like a gambler to a slot machine—hopeful beyond reason for that big jackpot. Chad activated the machine.

Feb. 3, 1204. "Oh my God," cried Sophia. "Help, help!"

Julia ran into the kitchen to see two men stumbling in through the courtyard door. Florian, his right arm drenched in blood, his left wrapped over the shoulder of his friend, Phocus, who supported most of his weight, was on the verge of collapse. For a moment, Julia just stared. Marcus entered, and, taking the measure of the situation, directed Phocus into the bedroom.

"What happened?" he bellowed.

Florian just groaned as Phocus laid him awkwardly on the mattress. "There was a fight at Athos taverna," said Phocus, "and things got rowdy. I'm afraid Florian was caught in the middle of it. He was slashed by a soldier with a broken bottle."

Sophia lingered in the doorway. "Is he going to be all right? How bad is it?" A small black head peeked around Sophia's skirt, but Florian's little sister did not venture in.

No one answered. Julia, finally mastering her shock, went to Florian's bedside and examined the injured arm. The cloth of his tunic, sodden and stiff with dried blood, obscured the wound itself. "We have to clean this up," said Julia. "Get me some water and a cloth."

For once, her mother-in-law went to do her bidding, eager to be away from the dreadful sight. Brooke caught a whiff of Florian's breath, yeasty and smelling of alcohol. His unfocused eyes traveled over her, but did not stop.

Sophia brought a basin of water and a rag, but left as soon as she deposited them by the side of the bed. Julia gently soaked the arm in the cool water, sopping up the excess with the small rag. As she worked, the water in the basin became pink, then bright red. Marcus looked on with a deep frown.

"We have to remove the cloth," said Julia. She grabbed the edges of the torn fabric and yanked hard, tearing the sleeve from wrist to shoulder. Florian groaned and tried to turn away. Phocus gently pressed his shoulder back unto the bed. As Julia continued to dab at the flesh and wipe away dried blood, the extent of the injury became clear. The arm was cut in two places. A long jagged gash ran from the shoulder, across the deltoid, and just short of the inside of the elbow. Worse was a deep cut in the forearm, which still oozed droplets of blood. The sides of the wound had separated, revealing the layers of fat and tissue underneath. Brooke felt a wave of nausea at the dreadful wound, and wished she could turn her eyes away.

"We need to stitch this up," said Julia in a calm voice. "Do you want to get a physician, or have me do it?"

"You have experience with this?" Marcus asked in surprise.

"I do," said Julia.

"It may be best to do it now, while he's still inebriated. Besides, wounds heal best if they are tended quickly."

Julia went to her sewing kit, and removed a hefty curved needle meant for leather work. She threaded it with a stout twine and approached the bed. Brooke was alarmed that she neither cleaned the needle, nor dipped it in alcohol, nor ran it through a flame.

Florian mumbled incoherently, not aware of what was to come. Julia said, "Florian, I need to work on your arm and it will hurt a bit. Take this piece of leather and hold it between your teeth. You can chomp down on it to ease the pain."

Florian looked at her with puzzled eyes, but he took the scrap of leather in his left hand and put it in his mouth. His father and Phocus moved nearer. Julia directed Phocus to hold Florian's wrist, then she pinched the wound together and deftly jabbed the needle into the flesh. Florian screamed, and tried to pull his arm away, but Phocus had a firm grip on his wrist. Marcus pushed down on Florian's shoulders and said, "Take it easy, son, this will be over soon. Just bear it."

Julia continued the first stitch, pressing hard until the point of the needle poked out on the far side of the cut. New blood dribbled out. Florian screamed again and bucked violently, trying to escape the pain. The needle was knocked out of Julia's hand.

"We have to hold him down firmly," said Julia.

Phocus readjusted to immobilize the arm at wrist and shoulder, while Marcus put his weight against Florian's left side. Brooke wished to be anywhere else, not poking the bloody needle into the resistant flesh. So much force was required. Florian screamed again, and Marcus slapped him hard in the face. He was momentarily disoriented and Julia completed a stitch without opposition. On the next stitch, Florian began blubbering and cursing, but some of the fight had left him. Marcus slapped him again, timing the strike with the insertion of the needle.

Finally it was over, and Julia called for clean bandages. Sophia, her face wet with tears, brought in a piece of white cloth. The women tore it into strips and Julia tied it gently around the wound.

"He'll need to rest now," she said. After the others had left, she removed Florian's shoes and socks, and drew the blanket up over his chest. He fell into a mercifully deep sleep.

XXIII
HOMECOMING

Brooke zipped up her jacket as a chill wind blew in off the lake. Ahead of her on the trail, Claudia chatted amiably with Chad. The ground was still covered with last year's fallen leaves and Brooke stepped with care to avoid slippery patches. The forest was awakening to the new spring season, with buds on the bare branches almost ready to pop forth. The overall grayness of the leafless trees was relieved by the happy green of a patch of balsam firs.

When Brooke had suggested geocaching in Grafton Lakes State Park, Robert had declined because of looming deadlines, but Chad was eager to escape from the lab. Although it was only late March, the weather was relatively mild and inviting. On a whim, she had invited Claudia to join them. Her roommate, who was more the movies and popcorn type than the hiking and fresh air type, surprised her by deciding to come along.

Chad stopped and examined his iPhone. "The target is 2,134 ft. in that direction," he said, pointing across the lake. Long Pond was narrow at this point as they neared its southernmost extremity. The actual path to the target would be longer, since they would follow the trail around the lake shore.

Claudia moved close to Chad and peering over his arm at the screen on his cell phone. "How do you know where to go?" she asked.

Chad launched into a long discourse on latitude and longitude, and the several different unit systems that were used to specify them. Brooke hardly expected Claudia to care, but she feigned rapt attention as she moved ever closer to Chad.

Brooke frowned and cast her eyes across the lake, which shimmered in the morning sunlight, its surface broken by only the tiniest of ripples. A woodpecker broke the stillness with a loud rat a tat tat tat, and she searched for it. Despite the clamor it was making, it was totally invisible.

"We should move on," she said, attempting to break up Chad and Claudia's little tête-à-tête. They set off, with Claudia still talking unceasingly. Brooke might as well have gone on this hike by herself.

They looped around the end of the lake past a scruffy zone where the trail was half obliterated by mud and standing water. Claudia called out to Chad to give her a hand in crossing. He turned back, surprised, but dutifully held out his hand. Brooke had an image of him spreading his cloak across the mud to protect the delicate feet of the damsel in distress, but that was unfair to Chad. After Claudia crossed, Chad made eye contact with Brooke in a silent question, but her scowl prevented him from offering her help. He turned away just before she slipped and covered her Nike in mud.

The group walked on through the deserted forest, Brooke's wet sock squishing in her shoe. Chad noted that they were now only 912 feet from the target. He stopped when he arrived at a trail junction and studied his phone intently.

"Which way do we go?" asked Claudia.

"The compass points 38° from north, but neither trail goes off in that direction. One is a little west of north and the other is almost due east. I'm not sure which one will take us there," said Chad.

"Let me see," said Brooke. "The easterly trail will keep us near the lake. I would follow that one."

"It could just be an access path to the shore. The other looks more worn. I think we should head inland," replied Chad.

"Chad is right," said Claudia and walked off down the branch he favored. Chad shrugged and followed, leaving an angry Brooke to bring up the rear. She wasn't even sure why she was annoyed with Claudia. She didn't care if Claudia wanted to go after Chad. Brooke certainly wasn't interested in him. He didn't think women should take risks. On second thought, maybe Claudia was just right for him. Maybe they deserved each other.

Brooke's wet foot was numb with cold and her whole body shivered in sympathy with its neglected extremity. Brooke resolved to ignore it and marched stolidly onward. Chad halted near a fallen tree and consulted his cell. "It's only 21 feet away. We should search the area."

"Which way?" asked Claudia.

"It points that way," replied Chad.

While they picked their way over the uneven terrain, Brooke struck out in an alternate direction. GPS had limited accuracy. When you got this close, the readings became erratic. She examined the forest floor, strewn with fallen logs and hidden stones. The footing was spongy and unpredictable; if she didn't take care she might sprain an ankle. She investigated a six foot high tree stump, rooting around in the interior of its jagged top.

"Now it says 17 feet that way," said Claudia.

"It just means we're close," replied Chad. "If it showed us the spot to within a foot there would be no sport."

The ground was sloped slightly and Brooke clambered up, searching for nooks where a plastic box might be secreted. She brushed away wet leaves from a pile of stones but saw nothing. She glanced back at the trail to orient herself, estimating the point where she had left it. The cache would not be more than thirty feet from a trail, and she was straying too far. Chad and Claudia were as well, but in the opposite direction.

This cache was tough to find, and Brooke wondered if someone had moved it. No one had logged a sighting on the website since last fall, but that was hardly surprising, since fewer geocachers trooped around the forest in the winter. Brooke returned to the path and slowly surveyed the area in every direction. Where would she have hidden the box? Her eye rested on two trees that grew upward from a common base. The notch between their trunks might be worth investigating. As she drew close, she spied a piece of bark artfully arranged to cover something.

"I found it," cried Brooke as she removed the bark and saw a dirty plastic box with a snap on cover. She held it up for the others to see. As they approached, she removed the lid. In addition to the usual log book and pencil stump, there was a prize—a polished stone with the message *Believe in Yourself.* Brooke smiled and felt warm for the first time that day. Chad asked her to pose as he snapped her picture with the booty.

Brooke slipped the stone in her pocket and inserted a replacement prize for the next geocacher to find. It was an unusual coin with lively Chinese characters around the periphery and a hole in the middle. She hoped it would please the next thing-finder as much as the stone had pleased her.

Feb. 6, 1204. While winter in Brooke's world was a time of crisp cold days, leafless trees and snow-covered countryside, in the medieval world, it was often a time of hunger and deprivation. Last year's harvest was all but gone and it would be many months before the new crop would bear fruit. So it was with the crusaders, who, in the late winter of 1204, were camped outside Constantinople with empty stomachs and flagging spirits.

It had been a politically turbulent winter, one filled with the sort of intrigue that would later be called Byzantine. In order to make good his enormous debt to the crusaders, the young Prince Alexios, who was now Emperor Alexios IV, had squeezed the people so mercilessly that a riot erupted in late January. A mob of enraged citizens insisted that the senate elect a new emperor. None of the nobility were willing to serve in this dubious position, until finally a gentle young man, Nicholas Kannavos, reluctantly agreed to take the purple.

Emperor Alexios IV responded by inviting his old buddies, the crusaders, to take up residence in the Blachernae palace. This enraged the beleaguered nobility, and Alexios Ducas, a high ranking noble and confidant of the emperor, betrayed him. The emergence of yet another Alexios on the scene was too confusing even for the Byzantines, and this new usurper was universally known by his nickname, Murtzuphlus, which meant bushy eyebrows. Murtzuphlus had been an envoy between Alexios IV and the crusaders and was privy to their negotiations. To prevent the crusaders from moving into the city, he secured the support of the Varangian guard and, more importantly, the eunuch in charge of the treasury. Then he came to Alexios IV in the middle of the night and convinced him that a mob was after him. He led the hapless young emperor directly to a dungeon, and imprisoned him there.

Murtzuphlus proclaimed himself emperor, and with the support of his fellow nobles, was crowned in the Hagia Sophia. At that moment, four men all laid claim to the throne: old blind Isaac, his son, the imprisoned Alexios IV, the most recent usurper Murtzuphlus, and the popularly-supported Nicholas Kannavos. Such was the instability of the state. Isaac died in his quarters in mysterious circumstances shortly thereafter. Nicholas Kannavos would not negotiate with Murtzuphlus, and the Varangian guard broke into the Hagia Sophia and cast him into prison. Later he was decapitated.

Murtzuphlus had removed two of the three rival claimants to the throne, and only Alexios IV, the darling of the crusaders, had yet to be dealt with. Murtzuphlus simply strangled him in his cell, but pretended that he died of natural causes. The young emperor was only twenty-two years old. So Murtzuphlus, he of the bushy eyebrows, was finally the undisputed ruler of a city that had had five emperors in less than a year. No friend of the crusaders, he had stopped the practice of sending them food, and now Garnett and Hugh were routinely hungry. Despite their military victory, the crusaders were once again locked out of the city, no further along than they had been the year before.

Garnett stared into his nearly empty dinner bowl. Brooke felt the gnawing hunger in the pit of her stomach that the inadequate meal had failed to quench. Garnett ran his index finger along the inside of the bowl to capture the last few gobs of gruel. The stale biscuit that had accompanied dinner was long gone.

"I tried to buy a chicken yesterday, but the vendor wanted twenty sous," said Hugh.

Garnett grunted and shifted on his camp stool.

"Melchior killed his horse and was trading pieces of meat," continued Hugh.

"That's dreadful," replied Garnett. "I'll never be driven to such an act."

"We have to do something."

"Let's ride out after dark and see what we can scavenge."

The sun set early on that cool winter day as Garnett and Hugh slipped into the forest. They avoided the well-traveled roads fearing an encounter with Greek soldiers. The underbrush was thin enough to make good progress, although an occasional branch tore at their clothing or whipped into their faces. The nearly full moon cast long shadows in the black and white stillness of the sleeping forest.

They came upon the edge of a field and cut across at a gallop, not bothering to stop and search it. Farms this close to camp had already been stripped of all edibles. The hooves of their mounts sounded abnormally loud as they traversed the barren land and Garnett glanced around cautiously. They passed through a copse of trees that marked the border between homesteads and continued across the next field. Progress was swift as they cut in and out of the forest, using fields as they could to gain distance from the camp.

Far from the city, the land became more wild. Within the forest again, they happened upon a deer trail that led them deep into the thicket. Brooke felt a surge of hunger, sharp and insistent. This unfamiliar ache was entirely new and unwelcome. It faded in and out, threatening to wipe away conscious thought.

The horses were walking slower now, winded from their run and beginning to tire as the night wore on. They picked their way carefully across a shallow stream, its roiling water gleaming in the reflected moonlight, and climbed up a short incline. The trail led to a lookout over a broad valley dotted with farms. Brooke wondered why the deer came here. Did they have an appreciation of beauty or was there a more practical reason for visiting this spot? Garnett and Hugh didn't pause long, but doubled back and picked up the trail along the ridge. Soon they found a way to cut through the woods and reach the edge of a field.

Tying the horses to a tree, the two men walked towards a barn set away from the farmhouse. Garnett lifted the wooden latch and pried open the door, and an odor of damp hay wafted out. He and Hugh entered the dim space and waited for their night vision to deepen. Brooke heard no rustling, snoring, or grunting noises from barnyard animals. The men conducted a desultory search, but it was abundantly clear that nothing of value was stored in the barn.

Back outside, Garnett crept up to the house and carefully circumnavigated it. No light shone out from the cracks in the shuttered windows. He and Hugh paused at the front door and seemed to be considering how to force entry, when the door opened of its own accord. A sleepy young boy in a long white nightshirt wandered out. Garnett moved quickly and grabbed him before he could shut the front door.

The boy squawked and tried to wriggle from his arms, but Garnett held tight, covered his mouth, and dragged him back into the kitchen, Hugh close behind him. Garnett drew his dagger and set it lightly upon the boy's neck. "Don't move and you won't be hurt," he said in French. Of course the boy didn't understand. He trembled in Garnett's arms and, for the first time, Brooke felt ashamed of her ancestor. Hugh drew his sword.

"What's going on?" shouted a voice in Greek. A grizzled farmer appeared at the foot of the stairs. He stopped when he caught sight of his son in the arms of the brigands. "Let him go! I'll give you anything you want." Brooke ached to translate. The farmer seemed to recognize that words would not work and he held out his open hands in a show of non-resistance.

Garnett caught sight of a crucifix on the wall and glanced away, his cheeks burning. Hugh said, "We need food. Give us supplies and we'll leave you alone." The look of incomprehension in the farmer's face said it all. Hugh began to make eating motions with his hands and the farmer's eyes lit up in understanding. He moved to a cabinet along the wall, opened the door, and drew out a half-empty sack of flour. Hugh took it.

The farmer's wife appeared on the stairs and he barked at her to retreat. She slipped away. Hugh made a "give me more" gesture and the farmer held out his empty hands and shrugged. Just then, Brooke heard a squeal that seemed to come from beneath the floor. The crusaders noticed it too. Resignedly, the farmer shifted the kitchen table and opened a trap door in the floor. A fat hog ambled up a ramp from his musty basement crawl way.

Hugh drew his dagger and slit the pig's throat before the creature could sense its danger. Hugh tried to drag the carcass toward the door, but the pig was massive. The farmer pitched in and the two manhandled it outside. "Stupid barbarian," murmured the farmer. "We could have just let it walk outside." Hugh got the drift if not the words and shot him a menacing look. Garnett still had the boy, but he had lowered the knife.

In the moonlight, Hugh started to butcher the hog inexpertly. The farmer shoved him aside in disgust and completed the job. Hugh left to retrieve the horses while Garnett kept watch. The bloody meat was distributed among the saddle bags and hung off the horses with ropes. Once packed, Garnett finally released the boy and the crusaders headed back.

In the forest, Brooke felt Garnett's stomach send out an urgent appeal for food. During the attack, she had not felt a single pang of hunger, but now it came roaring back in full force. Nevertheless, the knights rode on until they found a suitable campsite near a stream. The weather had been dry and it was easy to gather seasoned firewood. Garnett struck a flint and blew a flame into life. Hugh hacked off a shoulder roast and threaded it onto a sharpened stick.

The two men sat before the fire, taking turns holding the meat over the flames.

"The emperor should never have denied us food," said Garnett. "He drove us to commandeer the pig from that farmer."

Hugh did not reply.

"The Lord will forgive us since we're doing this in His cause."

"Amen," replied Hugh.

"This is a test of faith—all the suffering, the delays, the hardships. He wants to be sure that we are truly worthy when we come up against the Saracen."

"You think too much," said Hugh and the men fell silent. Juices were running from the meat and dripping into the fire, sending up little sparkling fireworks. Brooke felt an intense longing for the pork, exacerbated by the enticing smell of roasting meat. When would they decide it was cooked enough? She would have eaten it already.

At last, Hugh removed the blackened roast from the spit and hacked off pieces for Garnett and himself. The meat was burnt on the outside, still raw in the middle, and unseasoned, but it was by far the most delicious food that Brooke had ever tasted.

Feb. 8, 1204. Julia was perched on the edge of her seat at Florian's bedside. A sickly sweet odor that Brooke could not identify permeated the room. Florian's forehead was covered in sweat and he cried out intermittently in pain. His eyes were moist and darted about like those of a trapped animal. Julia wiped his forehead with a damp cloth.

"I can't bear this pain any more," whispered Florian. "Just kill me. Take a rock and knock me over the head."

"Don't be silly. You're going to get better," said Julia.

Florian looked at her with tortured eyes, as if to assess the truth of her statement.

"I won't get better. Please just help me die. Use a knife." Julia held a cup of ale to his lips and urged him to drink.

She drew aside the sheet that covered his injured arm. A rank smell of decay wafted upward. The upper wound was healing well, but the lower wound was dotted with angry red patches where infection had set in. Worst of all was the hand. The sight assaulted Brooke like no other that she had ever encountered, and she felt a deep visceral revulsion. Florian's hand was deathly black, from the tips of the fingers to a line extending across his palm. The skin looked like plastic that had peeled away in places, revealing more black flesh underneath. A fingernail had fallen off and the flesh near it seemed to have melted away. At the boundary between the dead zone and the healthy flesh, puss oozed from an ugly brown and yellow crust. Mercifully, Julia covered the hand, but not before the image had been burned into Brooke's brain to rest there like an indigestible lump.

"I'm going to get more water," said Julia. "Don't worry, I'll be back." She left the bedroom and its fetid smell behind, taking the basin with her. She emptied the dirty water onto the plants in the courtyard and went to the kitchen. Both Marcus and Sophia were there, looking listless and dejected.

"We have to call the physician," said Julia. "He's not getting better."

"I won't let him amputate," said Sophia. "The physicians are not always right."

"But it's gangrene," replied Julia. "It won't get better on its own." She glanced at Marcus, looking for support.

His forehead was scrunched up in a deep frown, uncharacteristic for him. "He would never be able to work again. What dignity does a man have if he can't work? There must be something else we can do."

Julia sighed.

"He's so weak, the operation itself would kill him," said Sophia.

Brooke could see that Julia was not going to win this battle. Florian's parents, acting from deep love, could not bear to subject their son to an agonizing operation that would cripple him, and preferred to believe that a miracle would save him. Julia said no more. She refilled the basin from a bucket in the kitchen and returned to the sickbed.

Florian was panting, as if he had been running a road race. "I've always loved you, you know. From the time I first met you. You were always so vivacious, so excited about life. I couldn't believe my good luck when my father arranged our marriage. I worked so hard on that dragon that I gave you. I wanted it to be perfect, just like you." Brooke recalled the fierce little glass dragon that Florian had presented to Julia at a long ago dinner. The craftsmanship had been exceptional, with each scale separately rendered and a gout of flame projecting from the dragon's maw.

"All I ever wanted was to win your love," said Florian.

"You have won my love," replied Julia gently. "I will be here for you, my darling husband." A tear rolled down her cheek and Florian wiped it away tenderly with his good hand. Julia began sobbing, unable to hold back. Florian winced in pain and sank deeper into the bed. He sighed and seemed to settle in, a fleeting smile across his lips. Then he dropped into an uneasy sleep.

Feb. 20, 1204. Julia hurried along the street, glancing nervously from side to side. To Brooke's surprise, she seemed to be alone, without even her teen-aged brother-in-law to accompany her. She was dressed uncharacteristically in black and had neither market bag nor water bucket with her.

She passed a cleric in a long black robe with a stiff peaked cap and a prominent crucifix on his chest. He looked speculatively at her, stroking his long, mangy, gray beard. She hurried past before he had the chance to address her and slipped around a corner. It was mid-morning and the birds sang merrily, not sharing in the somber mood of the city.

Julia came to the door of Damian's workshop and went in. He was sitting at his workbench, his head buried in an oversized ledger. When he saw his daughter, he smiled warmly and rose to greet her.

Julia laid aside the black veil that covered her face and kissed her father on the cheek. "Where is everyone?" she asked.

"Basil and your mother went to fetch groceries. They decided to try the greengrocer just east of the Forum of Theodosius. The selection is somewhat limited around here."

"I guess we're lucky to be eating at all," replied Julia, "with those barbarians outside."

"Don't worry about them; they'll be leaving soon. I think they're just waiting for spring, so they can take up their campaign."

"It can't be soon enough for me."

"Darling, why did you come alone? The streets are more dangerous than ever, with so many destitute and desperate people."

"I wanted to talk to you alone. My house is close; the danger was minor. My mother-in-law is hinting that I should join a convent now that Florian is dead." Julia cast her eyes down in shame or to avoid seeing the reaction in her father's face.

"I see," he replied noncommittally.

She looked up and met his eyes. "I don't know if I can do it. Of course, I love to pray to the Lord, but to spend hours and hours at it would be so hard. And to wear only a black robe for the rest of my life." She shivered.

"Maybe you can find another husband," suggested Damian.

"Oh father, who would have me? Everyone knows I can't conceive. A child would have made all the difference."

"You might find a widower who already has children. You are still young and beautiful." This suggestion did nothing to mollify Julia.

"I think I would rather go to a convent than be saddled with an old man and his brood. It's just that none of the possibilities seem bearable. If I join a religious order, I'll work hard and never have any fun. I know how saintly that is, but I just don't have the strength to do it."

"It's not as bad as all that," said Damian. "Although I have to say that I can't imagine you in a convent. You love parties and parades and conversations. It's hard to picture you sitting and reading a prayerbook all the time."

"I couldn't do it. There must be some other choice. I'm afraid I don't have much time left. My mother-in-law blames me for her son's death. She thinks that he would not have been in that bar fight if I had given him an infant. And she's right. I am to blame."

Damian hugged her, his familiar scent enveloping and reassuring.

"Darling," he said, "come back home. You are always welcome here."

"Are you sure?" she asked. "What will mother say?"

"It doesn't matter what mother says. I'm in charge here. Besides, she'll be delighted to have you back. Trust me."

XXIV
WITH THE WIND

Robert sat hunched over his desk, frowning down at his papers. He was stuck. He should have been finished with this homework assignment hours ago, but he just couldn't make the calculations work out. The lab was empty and quiet, save for the occasional rustle of a mouse. The late night gloom darkened the far corners of the lab, where anything could be hiding. Robert, though, was unperturbed by his surroundings, all his focus zeroed in on the impenetrable problem before him. He thought of another possible approach.

Ten minutes later, he leaned back in his chair and tossed his glasses onto the paper. Another dead end. He rubbed his eyes wearily. This professor assigned ten long problems per week, five more than the usual homework burden. Robert had put up with it all semester, uncomplaining. Now it was mid-April, and classes would end in a few weeks. He only had a little more to cope with before he could forget this course forever. A rebellious thought welled up in him. Why not just leave the assignment unfinished? Did he have to meet every unreasonable deadline?

Robert rose from the chair and stretched his tired back. He wandered aimlessly around the lab and finally decided to go get a drink. The hallway was deserted at this time of night with not even a glimmer of light under any of the lab doors. At the vending machine, he rummaged in his pockets and came up with a random collection of quarters and dimes, feeding them into the coin slot as he found them. Now what could he afford? Half the selections were too pricey. He drew out a rumpled dollar bill and tried in vain to force it into the bill slot, but the finicky machine kept spitting it out. He gave up and chose a cherry pomegranate flavored Snapple, something he had never tasted before.

On the way back, he sipped the sweet and fruity iced tea and felt soothed. Maybe he should admit to himself that he was completely stumped and move on to the next problem. But when he got back to his desk, he dithered, unwilling to tackle the assignment. Instead, he decided to check his email. The inbox opened, revealing 58 new messages. Robert slumped in his chair. Email arrives like snow—sometimes a few flakes at a time, and sometimes in a blinding blizzard—but, if it is not swept away daily, it will bury you.

His eye caught on a message from an unfamiliar address and he clicked it open. Jim Milthorp from Hargrove Pharmaceuticals had purchased 1,300 mice of the DBA/2, subline 3 strain, the same strain used in the Memex tests. A while back, Robert had asked Pimpleton, the breeders of the mice, to put him in touch with other researchers using the DBA/2, subline 3 strain and now Jim was responding. Robert sat up straighter and read the message all the way through. Jim had only had his mice for three weeks, but he had been happy with the purchase. His group was researching liver disease and testing drugs on the little rodents. Robert quickly drafted a reply. He asked Jim to tell him if any of his mice died, and of what cause. He was careful not to disclose the brain tumors that had killed his own mice for fear of biasing the response.

Earlier, Robert had sent messages to many research groups and been disappointed in the meager response. Besides this email from Jim, he had only heard from one other person, a grad student in Australia with a small research effort. Apparently the strain he was using was uncommon. Perhaps he should try a different tack. He sent an email out to his list of contacts asking if any were using Muripellets to feed their animals.

Satisfied that he had taken a step forward in his research, he felt renewed and able to look at the homework one last time. As he read the problem statement again, he thought of something and struck out in a new direction. It took him three more hours to complete the assignment. He would only manage to snatch a few hours of sleep before he had to turn it in, but it was done and he was satisfied.

Apr. 9, 1204. The creak of the rigging, the sway of the deck, the beating of the sun on her armored body, all seemed unnaturally acute in that brief time before battle. Brooke was jammed in with a pack of sweating knights and sergeants, her ship one of a long line of vessels facing the north wall of the city. The beauty of the scene, with flying pennants and boldly decorated shields, would have been easier to enjoy at a distance. Her heart pounded. Garnett shuffled his feet.

Ahead lay the walls of the city, their tops festooned with hastily-constructed wooden towers. The Greeks, anticipating another attack, had worked to build up their defenses, and these uneven four and five story structures were the result. Brooke was reminded of something from a Dr. Seuss illustration. The underlying stonework, majestic and solid, had preserved a great empire for centuries, while these monstrosities, covered with a shaggy layer of vinegar-soaked hides, looked shabby and temporary.

Beyond the wall, Emperor Murtzuphlus had set up his camp on a prominent hill from which he could observe the action to come. His tents were the same coppery-red color as the doge's flagship. Odd that both sides had chosen the same hue. Of course, they were from a common Christian tradition and shared many cultural elements.

The warships and transports approached the shallows, and men began to splash into the waters. Many carried scaling ladders atop their heads. Greek missiles fell around them, but rarely connected at this long range. The petraries aboard ship lobbed stones high into the air, attempting to dislodge the defenders on the walls. The sailors on Brooke's vessels deployed a ramp from the deck into the surf. Garnett and three others grabbed hold of a siege engine and began to wheel it down the ramp. Its battering ram swung forward as the framework tilted downward, and Garnett stumbled with the sudden shift in weight. When he hit the water, Brooke was shocked at the cold that enveloped her. Garnett was armpit deep in water, with waves crashing over the back of his head. Other ships were disgorging their own "cats," as the siege engines were called. Most groups were ahead of Garnett's and some cats were already rolling up onto the beach.

The mechanism of the cat was protected by a tent-shaped roof that was covered in fire resistant vinegar-soaked hides. The acrid smell of the vinegar tickled Brooke's nostrils. Garnett heaved as he and the others attempted to push the cat over the unseen seabed. The buoyancy of the wood gave them a welcome assist in this effort. A gout of water rose up as a stone splashed nearby harmlessly. But the Greeks had gotten their range, and the next projectile clipped the edge of the cat's roof and took a bite out of it. Miraculously, it missed the crusaders.

Arrows rained down upon the men on the beach, but could not penetrate their armor. The feathered shafts lodged in their chain mail and stuck out like needles in a pincushion. By now, a few scaling ladders were propped up against the wall and the battle was heating up. Garnett clambered out of the water and, muscles straining, put his full weight into pushing the cat forward. Men shouted orders and missiles thumped into the sand. The bravest knights had reached the tops of their ladders and the clang of sword on metal could be heard as they engaged.

An arrow thudded into Garnett's stomach, driving him backward a step. His chain mail held, but Brooke could feel the tip of the arrow scratch her skin beneath the protective padding. Garnett yanked the arrow out and cast it aside, renewing his effort to move the cat, which was now halfway to the wall. More arrows struck from above, and Garnett ignored them as they collected all over his body. Brooke felt pricks everywhere and each step was an exercise in pain.

They positioned the cat against the wall next to one of the scaling ladders. Sir Sibold shouted, "Heave, ho," as the men swung the iron-tipped battering ram against the stone. They struck again and again, slowly chipping out a depression. A crusader fell next to them from a great height with a thump and a clang. He didn't rise.

Back in the sea, the warships were aiming their flying bridges at the tops of the walls. These man-sized tubes were lashed even higher on the masts than they had been the year before, so they could reach the tops of the new Greek fortifications. The crusaders had covered the bridges with grapevines for protection. Brooke was reminded of an elephant with his trunk rigidly extended in anger. Three knights waited in the end of the tubes to jump onto their enemies. But the wind was blowing away from shore, and the great vessels were having trouble closing the distance.

Brooke admired the plan. The crusaders had targeted selected sections of the wall. At each section, they brought a cat to break a hole in the stone, a scaling ladder to harass defenders on high, and a flying bridge to rain warriors onto the ramparts. The Greeks would have to fend off three threats at once. But the wind was strong and blowing in the wrong direction.

A piercing scream jerked Garnett's head to the side. The Greeks had poured burning pitch on the neighboring cat and it had caught fire. A man trailing flames ran toward the water but collapsed before he reached it. He curled up on the ground in a heap as the flames took him. The image of the dying man seared into Brooke's mind, leaving an indelible stain. Her greatest fear was burning to death, and witnessing such a death shocked her to the core.

At that moment, a huge stone fell on Garnett's cat, splintering it and trapping two knights under the collapsed roof. Garnett had been standing on the other side and escaped injury. Garnett and Sibold shifted the broken planks, trying to free the trapped men. One was able to sidle out from underneath but the other was unconscious. The cat was unusable and they abandoned it.

Garnett looked around, taking in the flying bridges that were still only making sporadic contact with the walls, the fallen and broken ladders lying useless on the ground, and the men who could still stand weaving among the bodies of the dead and wounded. Garnett spotted one ladder still active and ran to it. He was halfway up when Brooke heard the trumpets sound a falling arpeggio. Immediately, men began retreating. Garnett hastily descended and ran for the sea. As the crusader's horns continued their mournful call, the Greeks struck up a triumphant tune, drowning out their enemies as they celebrated their victory.

Garnett looked back one last time before he entered the water. Men atop the walls had lowered their trousers and were flashing their bare butts at the crusaders. A jarring end to a jarring day.

⤬

Apr. 10, 1204. "I don't think they'll try again. My brother-in-law was fighting up on the walls and he told me the whole story. They ran away like women. We've seen the last of them." The customer made this declaration with a smug air. He was tall and lanky, with unsightly warts on his cheek and chin.

"I never believed they could win. And now there's even fewer of the bastards," replied Damian. The two men were chatting in Damian's workshop. The attack the day before was on everyone's lips.

"The sand in front of the walls was littered with dead men and broken equipment. They won't be back."

"I can see why they didn't leave in the winter, but now that it's spring and they've lost the battle, they'll slink away in the night," said Damian.

At that moment, the door opened to the tinkling of the warning bell, and Father Scholasticus entered the room.

"How nice to see you Reverend Father," said Damian. "What can I do for you today?" Scholasticus had a grim look to him, not at all in keeping with the gay mood of the day. His long gray beard was more unkempt than usual and his eyes were rimmed in red.

"Don't let me interrupt," said Scholasticus. "Go ahead and help your other customer."

"I can wait," said the customer. Scholasticus looked at him calmly, but said nothing.

"Actually, I think we were finished," said Damian. The customer took the hint and retreated. Once he had left the workshop, Scholasticus got down to business.

"My dear Damian, I have come to beg a favor of you. His All-Holiness himself has sent me on this mission." Brooke was surprised. The patriarch of Constantinople was the head of the Greek Orthodox Church, much as the Pope was the head of the Catholics. The mission must be important indeed to involve him.

"There are some within the church who think the barbarians might attack again. If they get into the city, there's no telling what crimes they might commit, even crimes against the church. They have shown themselves to be no true warriors of Christ, but vicious mongrels barking at the gate.

"I believe that the Lord will protect us; nevertheless, it is wise to take precautions. The ways of the Lord are mysterious," continued Scholasticus. He was having a hard time getting to the point. "In short, I have come to ask for your help. We have known each other for a long time. You have always been an honest man, trustworthy, and God-fearing. Would you be able to secure certain assets temporarily for the Church? Just until this threat passes?"

"Of course, Reverend Father," replied Damian. "I would be honored."

"Do you have a place to keep valuables hidden away?"

"I do. A secure place that no one knows about. No thief could find it."

"Excellent. Before I show you the items, perhaps we should…" Scholasticus glanced at the door. Damian walked over and locked it. After Damian returned to the workbench, Scholasticus drew open a bag that he had been carrying and spread out his treasures. Brooke was enthralled by the beauty and rarity of the items. Scholasticus described each piece in detail with evident pride and Damian showed keen interest. It occurred to Brooke that she was seeing an early version of a safe deposit box. The goldsmiths of the middle ages grew into the bankers of modern times. Then, just as now, citizens relied on bankers to protect their valuables.

Scholasticus was reaching into his bag for more items just as Brooke was pulled back into the present. She resolved to return another day to see the rest of the treasure.

—⁂—

Apr. 12, 1204. Garnett reached upward and grasped the next rung of the rigging. He hauled his iron-clad body higher yet, his muscles knotting with the strain. The deck gleamed far below and Brooke felt a tinge of fear. Luckily, Garnett returned his gaze skyward where the pennant of the warship *Paradise* flapped in the light breeze. Garnett continued upward, his sword clanking against his thigh, the rigging becoming ever narrower. One foot slipped on the thick rope but Garnett repositioned it. Sweat dripped into one eye, and was blinked away. Brooke wished for a sweat band. It was not exactly advanced technology.

Garnett was now near the top of the mast, which swayed back and forth like a pendulum. Brooke felt vertigo mixed with dread coming on. The entrance to the flying bridge gaped like a black hole just above Garnett's position. He pulled himself up by a cleat affixed to the frame and levered himself into the bridge. The sudden darkness was blinding after the brilliance of the morning sun. Garnett rose unsteadily and grasped a barely visible hand rail. Shafts of lights streaked through cracks in the side coverings. He clambered down the wooden tube, jerked this way and that by the pitching and yawing of the floor. Men followed him, the stamping of their feet loud in the confined space. Brooke reeled from the cloying smell of vinegar as Garnett approached the brilliant rectangle of light that marked the end of the shaft.

In the distance, the city walls bristled with Greek defenders. To the right, Brooke saw the opening of another flying bridge, where three knights stood abreast waiting for their moment. Doge Dandolo had conceived a new stratagem to give the outnumbered crusaders an edge. He had ordered two warships to be tied together and their flying bridges pointed in the same direction. The two bridges would clasp the tower, one on each side, like a giant caliper, and spew out knights, six at a time. It sounded good in theory, but as Brooke stood at the end of the passageway and felt, rather than saw, the weight of men behind her, she nearly panicked. She was trapped. Garnett could not retreat. If he stepped forward, he would plunge to his death in the shallows below. When they reached the wall, he would have to advance into a heavily armed contingent of the Varangian guard. There was no good option.

For the moment, the ship's forward movement had stopped. The Greeks were casting huge stones from their catapults, but the ships were heavily draped with vines and impregnable to the assaults. The crusaders, in their turn, sent missiles at the walls, some of stone and some of ceramic. The latter were filled with the mysterious "Greek fire," whose formula was lost to modern science, and even to the Greeks of the day. The incendiaries left a trail of smoke as they arced through the air, but nothing caught fire. The sounds of shouting and hooting could be heard from the troops on both sides. The screaming would come later.

The ineffective barrages continued for some time. Brooke thought back to the scene she had accessed the night before, when the crusaders were preparing for battle. Abbot Simon of Loos had held an inspirational mass for the disheartened crusaders. He told them that their failure to take the city was not evidence of God's displeasure with their mission. It was just that God was testing their faith. The Greeks had surpassed all bounds of civilized behavior when they had murdered their divinely appointed Emperor, Alexios IV. They were no better than Jews and they deserved to be punished. To further mollify God, the clergy sent all the prostitutes out of camp on their own special vessel.

The abbot's speech marked a turning point in history, the moment when the Eastern Orthodox Church led by the Patriarch of Constantinople would forever break with the Holy See in Rome. The schism would become too deep to mend and the two Christian sects would be at odds forevermore.

The battle continued while Brooke stood and waited. The end of the flying bridge was still far from the towers and the warships could not advance closer to shore. The crusaders were not making progress, and stalemate meant that the Greeks would win. Just at that moment, the wind picked up from the north and filled the sails, driving the warships forward. The deadly walls grew larger as the ship was propelled high up on the beach and the end of the bridge lurched towards the tower. Garnett's heart began to pound and his muscles tensed. A stab of pure terror shot through Brooke.

The edge of the bridge scraped against the tower and retreated with the next swell. The whitecaps far below were visible in the gap. When the waves brought the bridge into contact again, a Venetian warrior grabbed the tower and jumped across. The defenders were instantly upon him, raining blows with sword and ax. He screamed as a blade bit into his neck, nearly severing his head from his body. Undeterred, Garnett bent his knees and leapt across at just the right moment, landing on the tower platform with a thwack. He lost his balance and fell to one knee. Three Greeks struck him on the back and head, but his armor held, and he rose up, unhurt. The burly defender in front of him was awestruck by Garnett's invincibility, and stumbled back in fear. The other Greeks, wide-eyed, also retreated. Soon all the defenders were rushing down the steps of the tower. Garnett did not follow but waited for more of his comrades to make the leap across. Jean of Choisy joined him on the platform, the first of many. Men shouted commands and encouragement, but Garnett's ears rang from the blow to his head, and he was deaf.

A flag was hoisted over the tower to signal victory to the crusaders below. Someone had tied the bridges to the tower and reinforcements poured out onto the platform. Unfortunately, the fickle wind shifted and the bridges were now pulling on the tower, threatening to break either the tower or the bridge. The ropes were cut and the crusaders atop the tower were left without an escape route. In the distance, a flag went up on a neighboring tower as another squadron of men secured the heights.

The crusaders were now at an impasse. The few men on the towers could not take the city alone. Greeks were already advancing on them along the ramparts. As Garnett, armed with sword in one hand and dagger in the other, prepared to meet the attack, he saw a contingent of knights run up the beach far below to a bricked up gate in the wall. Then Garnett's full attention was on the Varangian guard before him, a red-headed giant in a knee-length chain mail coat, spiked steel balls stuffed into his wide leather belt. The enemy swung his battle ax in a wide arc, but Garnett sidestepped the slow move and deflected it with his sword. He countered with a stab to his opponent's vulnerable kidney. The big man collapsed and Garnett stepped around him to face the next fighter. Another crusader was at his side now, protecting his flank. He blocked the next sword thrust with his blade.

Garnett still had not recovered his hearing after the ringing blow to his helmet. It was odd to fight in a soundless void, thought Brooke, as if the audio link had failed in a movie. But there was still that feeling that nothing else existed in the world except the opponent before you. You were totally in the moment and totally engaged, not thinking, just reacting. If you tried to think, you would die. When the swords clashed again, she could hear a faint tinkle, as her hearing started to return. In this silent bubble, she felt no fear, shielded as she was from the screams and clatter of the conflict. Garnett got inside his opponent's guard and cut the man's forearm. He dropped his weapon and Garnett pierced his chest in a fatal wound. The sword was stuck and Garnett stomped on his chest and heaved on the hilt, withdrawing it forcefully in a gout of blood. A few knights had moved past him and were now in the vanguard.

Brooke caught sight of the action below on the beach. Several men were chipping at the bricked-up gate with pickaxes, protected by a canopy of interlocked shields. The Greeks above were shooting arrows and dropping stones on them. Near the edge of the wall, a small flame licked the bottom of a cauldron filled with a noxious brew that would rain death upon the crusaders below. Garnett fought his way to the cauldron and kicked the coals out from beneath it with his armored foot. The flame died. Then he turned to face a heavy man with blood covering one side of his face and matting down his scraggly beard. As he raised his sword to defend himself, the opponent fell to his knees, stabbed from behind. The Greeks were losing the battle at the top of the wall, although they fought valiantly.

Down below, a lone crusader appeared on the inside of the city. He must have crawled through a hole in the brickwork. The Greeks nearby were transfixed as they beheld the unexpected intruder. The crusader raised his weapon and charged and the Greeks fled in terror. Garnett returned his attention to the action on the battlements, but it had petered out, with men dead and dying on both sides. The remaining Greeks still on their feet were in retreat down the staircase, chased by the crusaders.

More men had entered the city through the hole in the wall and a small group formed inside. The Greeks could have easily overwhelmed them, but they seemed leaderless and the few in the vicinity scattered. A knight ran to the inside of a gate and began to chop at the bolts and bars that secured it. Several others joined him and soon they swung the large doors wide open. A horse transport vessel was waiting in the surf and mounted knights galloped down the ramps, across the beach, and through the gate.

Jean of Choisy was shouting commands, but Brooke was still deaf. When knights started descended the steps off the wall, Garnett followed, almost falling on the blood-slick stone. Emperor Murtzuphlus himself appeared on the battleground below with a contingent of Greek fighters. It appeared that a major confrontation was about to commence. The mounted crusaders, lances ready, charged the enemy. The emperor hesitated, and the Greek resistance crumbled and evaporated. Without a fight, the crusaders took possession of the vermilion tents that had so recently housed the Imperial presence and there they remained while masses of their fellow knights, sergeants, and foot soldiers flooded into the city. The sun was low in the sky and the killing was done for the day.

XXV

FIRST ENCOUNTER

Apr. 13, 1204, 9:00 AM. Julia and Theodoret hurried along the marble pavement, eager to reach their destination. The streets were empty, unusual on such a warm and sunny morning and the houses were shuttered. An eye peered out from a crack in one window curtain and darted back and forth uneasily.

"I'm not sure it's wise to go on," said Theodoret.

"We're almost there," replied Julia. "Grandmother is counting on us."

A cart filled with household furnishings clattered past them. The driver urged the lone horse to greater speed, while his wife held tightly to two small boys. Trunks, bedrolls, and cartons were topped by a spindly chair, whose legs stuck up toward the sky. The whole edifice looked unstable and ready to come undone.

"The pharmacist is just around the corner," said Julia. "Grandmother's dropsy is awful; her legs are swollen to twice their normal size. The only thing that helps is ground hedgehog and honey."

"What if we run into the Franks?" asked Theodoret.

"They're on the other side of the city. The butcher assured us of that."

Normally the street would be noisy at this time of day, with hackers pushing their wares, wagons trucking goods, and the footfalls and chatter of many pedestrians, but today was ominously quiet. Anyone who could avoid the streets had done so.

The door to the pharmacy stood slightly ajar, but Julia did not pick up on this subtle signal and flung it wide open. Brooke saw a striking tableau before her. The broad back of a crusader partially shielded the action on the floor, where a second man knelt by the still form of the pharmacist and roughly probed his clothing. Brooke could not tell if the pharmacist was alive or dead. The floor was strewn with smashed bottles, papers, writing implements, and a mortar and pestle. Julia raised her hand to her lips to stifle a cry. A third crusader, who was facing the door, caught sight of her and leered. Brooke did not know these men, although one looked familiar, and hoped that Julia would come to her senses and run.

No sooner had she thought this than Julia and Theodoret exited the shop and fled up the street. Julia looked behind to see if anyone was following her, but no one was. Around the next bend, a knight was breaking down the door of a dry goods shop with an ax while a group of his comrades stood nearby. They had a relaxed air, as if they owned the world and had nothing to fear. They did not even bother to scan the street for opposition. Julia quickly ducked into the portico of a spice shop. The knights had a small wagon hitched to a bored-looking donkey. One of them came out of a neighboring building and threw a heavy sack into the wagon.

"We have to go back," whispered Theodoret, as a thin scream came from an unseen victim.

Julia nodded and they reversed direction, keeping to the side of the street away from the pharmacist's shop. The crusaders were going door to door in this shopping district, scavenging what they could, and did not appear to notice the two. Then five crusaders sauntered into the street a few blocks ahead of them, and Brooke felt trapped.

"Come, this way," urged Julia as she dashed into a small side street. It was quieter here and empty, save for a corpse circled by flies that lay on the street. They hurried on. Julia was breathing heavily and her pace slowed. She could not keep up with the long-limbed Theodoret. He yelled at her to try harder, but she was already running desperately and the words did more to discourage her than speed her up. Brooke was not familiar with this neighborhood, a melange of shops and residences.

They approached an intersection with a wide avenue. Theodoret motioned Julia to stay back while he peered around the corner. She plastered herself against a building and sucked in air. He ducked back in and said, "They're on this street too. We can't take this route."

"What will we do?" asked Julia.

Theodoret looked worried and seemed to have nothing to say. "We can't stay here," said Julia. "The barbarians are busy stealing from the wealthy merchants. We have to leave this district and return home through the Epistex."

"Are you mad? We can't go there."

"We can't stay here. The Franks won't bother with a slum. There's nothing to steal there." Since he could not propose a better plan, Theodoret went along. They waited until the knights were facing away and crossed the broad avenue at a dead run. No one followed them.

The Epistex was an ugly place, with bits of trash everywhere on the ground. The scraggly weeds that pushed through cracks in the broken pavement or clung precariously to the edges of beaten earth did little to relieve the stark poverty. Buildings were drab, with patched or peeling walls and few window openings. Here and there, boards or bricks were missing and roofs sagged precariously. By contrast with the neighborhood they had just left, many people were about, gathered in small groups.

A man dressed in a dirty gray tunic and ragged brown trousers eyed Julia and Theodoret speculatively. They were clearly out of place in this under-belly of the city, too well dressed and clean to be residents. In ordinary times, beggars would have approached them for alms, but today, the air was elec-tric with the tension of great events afoot, and they received hostile looks rather than obsequious ones.

Brooke knew that these slum dwellers could erupt into a mob, as they had done many times in the twelfth century. The mobs had rocked the social structure of the city and toppled emperors. Now the crusaders had interrupted the normal rhythm of life and the collegiati, Constantinople's police, were nowhere to be seen. The night before, Emperor Murtzuphlus had fled the city, although most people didn't know that yet. The army, composed of untrained raw recruits and Scandinavian mercenaries, had followed their emperor and left Constantinople totally undefended.

A wrinkled old woman in a patched and faded dress called out to Julia "Are you coming to live here now? What, the barbarians got your house?" Theodoret turned to answer, but Julia urged him to ignore the taunt and keep going.

"My, my, aren't we brave," said a skinny bald-headed man. The mood was turning sour and Brooke felt a tinge of fear. A group of small children started to follow them down the street. One picked up a clot of mud and threw it at Theodoret, but missed. A mangy cur barked at them, sensing prey.

"Let's get out of here," said Julia. "There's so many of them." It seemed like every resident of the Epistex was on the street, milling about, exchang-ing rumors, and looking for a way to profit from the unrest. Julia altered course, aiming to escape the slum by the quickest possible route.

They navigated a series of narrow alleyways. Brooke did not think Julia knew where she was or where she was going. Brooke had certainly never been here before. At least there were fewer people in these dismal passage-ways, where the morning sun barely penetrated. An old drunk lay sprawled in a doorway, snoring.

At length, they found a better neighborhood, less poverty-stricken and more deserted. Their sandals slapped against the pavement in the relative quiet, sounding unnaturally loud. There was no sign that the crusaders had been here. They turned a corner and came upon one of the loveliest streets in the city, a broad boulevard lined with sumptuous villas and palaces, set well back from the roadway. Gardens spilled over the estate walls, as trees strained to capture more sunlight.

In the air, the acrid smell of smoke drifted by. In the distance, a greasy black cloud stretched skyward.

∞∞∞

Apr. 13, 1204, 10:15 AM. Garnett raised his head and eyed the billowing plume of smoke. The city was on fire for the third time in a year.

"It's not close," said Hugh. "We can try another house on this street."

The two were standing in the roadway with three other crusaders. The wide street was separated into two lanes by a median strip planted with poplars. Brooke knew that Julia and Theodoret could not be far away, but they were not in sight.

Garnett ascended a wide marble staircase leading to the front door of a familiar stone residence. The others followed. One knight stopped to pry out the glittering gemstones that decorated the banisters, but they were solidly affixed to the marble, and he gave up reluctantly, hoping for easier loot inside. Hugh swung an ax against the stout front door, the blade repeatedly biting into the varnished wood carvings. After many blows, the door yielded and the crusaders spilled through it.

Brooke heard a voice call out somewhere that the devils were inside. The front parlor of the mansion was empty, save for its rich furnishings. Garnett pulled a tapestry off the wall and rolled it up quickly. Others followed his lead. Brooke remembered the interview between Damian and Lord Prepundolus in this same room, and despite her dislike of Prepundolus, was sorry to see the walls denuded and the mosaic floor chipped and scratched by the iron-clad feet of the knights.

They passed quickly through the garden, finding nothing of interest, and spread out among the first floor rooms. In the den, Garnett picked up an elegant ceramic vase and upended it, shaking vigorously, but nothing fell out. He pulled open the drawers of the desk and emptied their contents on the floor. Brooke wondered if Lord Prepundolus was still in his house. Garnett eyed the thick woven rug on the floor, decorated with a tiny floral pattern, but decided against. Frustrated, he exited the room and joined Hugh in the hall.

Hugh climbed the stairs to the first floor landing, but stopped when he saw a big man with elephant ears guarding the top. Prepundolus' eunuch was armed only with a knife. Brooke heard Prepundolus shout, "Hold your ground. Don't let them up. If you give way, I will have you executed." She caught a glimpse of the master in the hallway behind the servant.

Hugh drew his sword and ascended slowly. He was protected by a breast plate and chain mail that covered his arms and head. A knife was useless against such armament. For a moment, the eunuch just stood there, as the sword came ever closer. Then, he wheeled around and plunged his knife into Prepundolus' chest. Prepundolus, a look of utter surprise on his face, stumbled backward down the corridor. Immediately, the eunuch tossed the knife away and fell to his knees, holding up his empty hands, palms forward, above his head.

"Don't attack. I can help you find things," he shouted hoarsely.

"Look at these Greeks," said Hugh. "This wretched servant killed his master." Of course, he had not understood the threat that Prepundolus had issued with his limited Greek.

He raised his arm to chop down on the defenseless man when Garnett said, "Wait, I think he might be useful. Just prod him a bit and see if he gets the idea to show us the loot. We can always kill him later."

Hugh hesitated and then asked, "Where's the money?" With his free hand, he made the universal gesture of rubbing two fingers together.

"I can show you," said the desperate servant, nodding his head vigorously.

Hugh motioned with the tip of his sword for the eunuch to rise. They entered Prepundolus' bedroom, a bright and airy chamber with oversized furniture. A life-sized statue of Venus stood in one corner. Filmy curtains billowed in from an open window.

The servant advanced to the dresser and picked up a silver box. The deep grooves in its sculpted exterior were black with tarnish. He opened it, exposing a collection of glittering jewels. Brooke caught sight of a pearl necklace and a gold brooch in the shape of a bird, among other pieces. Garnett took it and stuffed it box and all into a bag. The eunuch then shoved the dresser away from the wall while the knights watched curiously. He slid a panel open on the back of the piece, revealing three sacks carefully tied up with twine. He handed one to Hugh. Each sack was filled with gold coins.

Dagobert, a tall and handsome knight, opened a cabinet and revealed a pile of carefully folded luxuriant robes. He donned one and his companions admired the fine silk, the jewels sewn into the cuffs and the embroidery rendered with golden and silver threads. The garment was too short for him but he didn't care. He pulled a second robe over his head, and passed the remainder around for the others to wear.

Hugh returned his attention to the eunuch. The unfortunate man said, "That's all I know about." He stood with his arms apart, palms upward to show their emptiness and shrugged his shoulders. Then he fell to the floor and lay there prostrate, his chest facing down, his hands above his head, and his face hidden.

Hugh raised his sword, but hesitated. A man in such a humble position, a defenseless servant who posed no threat, is an unseemly target for a noble knight.

"The Lord, Jesus Christ, is a merciful God," said Garnett.

Hugh glanced at him, annoyed. He sheathed his sword and said, "He's not worth the effort. Let's get out of here before the fire catches up with us."

In the hallway, Prepundolus sat slumped in a corner, his sightless eyes gazing into eternity.

Apr. 13, 1204, 11:00 AM. Theodoret licked his finger and held it up in the air. "The wind is blowing from that direction." He pointed up the street. "It will bring the fire to us if we're not careful. Best if we travel this way."

Julia followed him south. They had not gone far when they saw a knot of men standing around a woman who was lying on the pavement. One knight was on top of her, pumping his hips while the others urged him on. Theodoret stepped in front of Julia to block her view and drew her to the side of the street. She looked around desperately. There was nowhere to go. They could not return up the road for fear of the fire and there were no intersections nearby.

Theodoret grabbed her hand and led her into a building past a row of tall Corinthian columns. The hallway was wide and cool and devoid of people. Brooke began to relax.

"Where are we going?" asked Julia plaintively.

"There must be a back door."

They heard a noise and stopped like deer at the sound of the wolf. "Let's hide in here," whispered Theodoret.

He threw the door wide open and rushed in with Julia on his heels. Brooke caught a glimpse of a courtroom, spacious and well-appointed, with carved wood panels on the walls and an imposing upraised seat for the judge. Three crusaders were right inside the door. One turned at the noise. His matted beard hung over a bloody surcoat and his sneering grin revealed several missing teeth. He raised his hand to strike and Theodoret moved to shield Julia. "Run," he shouted. It was the last thing he said before a gauntleted hand smashed into the side of his head and he hit the floor as heavily as a corpse.

Julia fled at a dead run. Brooke could hear the knight chasing her, but he was slowed by his armor and she was pushed by her panic. She ran ever deeper into the building. She came to a broad marble staircase and mounted it at a dangerous speed. At the top, she blindly dashed down the hallway and yanked open a door. Inside, a gray-haired man was slumped over a desk, his broken head resting in a pool of blood. His hand was still touching a hemispherical glass lens used to enlarge the text of the book open before him. Julia retreated and penetrated further into the long corridor. As she rounded a corner, a stitch in her side sent signals of acute pain to Brooke's overwrought brain. Julia pulled another door open and found a sedate library, thankfully empty. She concealed herself behind a desk and huddled there, curled in a ball on the floor, panting heavily.

The library was stocked with more than a hundred books, all lying on their sides stacked on shelves. There was no text on their spines, so it was impossible to tell at a glance what the titles were. The floor was hard, with no rug to soften it. Brooke listened carefully for pursuit, but heard none. The knight must have given up. A half an hour passed. Julia sobbed quietly and rocked back and forth. How long would she stay here? Brooke was impatient, with her twenty-first century sense of time, but Julia came from a slower age and seemed ready to remain in the library indefinitely.

With alarm, Brooke caught the scent of smoke. Julia, her heart quickening, rose to her feet and opened the door. The smell was stronger in the hallway, and tendrils of dirty gray curled up near the ceiling. Julia retraced her steps like a frightened rabbit, sandals slapping the hard floor, robe flying behind her. She barreled down the marble staircase and headed for the courtroom. Inside, she found Theodoret lying on the tiled floor, congealed blood on his head. He was breathing shallowly and his eyes were closed. There was no sign of the crusaders.

"Wake up," she shouted. "The building's on fire. You have to wake up." Theodoret was unconscious and unresponsive. She slapped him hard across the face and shook him so violently his head thumped against the floor. She wept. She begged. He remained impassive.

Finally, Julia lifted his feet and dragged him toward the open door. He was a big man, but she was running on adrenaline, and she managed slow progress. To Brooke's dismay, the smoke in the hallway was thickening by the minute. Luckily, the veil covering Julia's nose and mouth sheltered her from the worst of the sooty air. She heaved, tugging on her cousin's inert body, gaining ground by inches, until she erupted into a spasm of coughing and her progress slowed.

Theodoret groaned and raised his hand to his head. "Get up, get up!" Julia shouted. He managed to sit up and rise, slowly and unsteadily, to his feet. Ahead of them, a wall caved in and bright flames shot up to lick the ceiling. Julia threw Theodoret's arm over her shoulder and led him down the corridor in the other direction, his weight pressing on her thin shoulders.

The corridor was rapidly filling with smoke and visibility was shortening. Still Julia and Theodoret stumbled along. Brooke felt heat on the back of her body and heard the crackle of an open flame. Far down the corridor she spied a second angry red fire. Tears streamed down Julia's face. With a sickening groan, the ceiling gave way and a beam fell upon the pair, knocking them to the hard floor. Julia squirmed forward on her belly and slipped out from under the beam that rested solidly on Theodoret's broad back. With a bellow of rage, he tried to extricate himself, but he was pinned to the floor. The heat intensified. Julia pulled on his arm, pushed on the beam trapping him in place, finally putting her whole weight against it, but it would not budge. Theodoret stared at her from wide-open eyes, glistening with fear, and said, "Don't leave me."

"I won't. I won't," she said as she pushed harder against the blockage, banging into it with her shoulder. The heat reached an unbearable level and Theodoret began to scream. Julia remained until at last, instinct prevailed, and she scampered away from the intense heat of the advancing flame, unable to hold her ground. Theodoret's piteous screams resounded above the whoosh and crackle of the fire as she dashed down the corridor.

Julia ran bent over, coughing constantly. Brooke felt rising panic like a hand clenching her stomach. Intellectually, she knew that Julia would survive this fire, didn't she? Had she made a mistake? One of Brooke's deepest fears was burning to death. She couldn't imagine the level of pain that it must entail. When she was younger, she had read the story of Joan of Arc with horrified fascination. In one account, Joan had screamed for half an hour after they set her ablaze. Theodoret's ragged cries still echoed down the corridor.

Julia was searching for a back door to the building. The fire ahead had petered out and Brooke could see the outline of an exit. Then the ceiling collapsed thirty yards ahead and burning debris clogged the passageway. Julia looked around frantically. She could not return and she could not advance. She spied a door and pulled it open to reveal a stone stairway headed downward into darkness. A hint of coolness and moisture invited her in. When the door closed behind her, Theodoret's screams were finally silenced.

She began the descent in headlong flight, trailing her hand along a rough-hewn stone wall to keep her balance. The sounds of the fire receded and the darkness grew deeper as she sank ever downward. She moved by feel alone at this point. The stairway seemed to go on and on, in endless obscurity.

When her foot struck a flat surface where the next step should be, Brooke knew she had reached the bottom of the long staircase. Julia wandered forward, too excited to be cautious, arms outstretched in total blackness, finding nothing. She had not gone far when the front of her foot sensed empty space and her heel rested on an edge. She lost her balance and fell forward, landing with a splash in frigid water. On the fall, she scraped the side of her leg painfully against the stone. She went under. Kicking her feet wildly, she rose to the surface. Did Julia know how to swim? Brooke didn't think so. How could she have learned? A new fear blossomed in Brooke's mind as Julia waved her arms around. Her mouth and nose filled with water, and she sank to eye level. But she beat down on the water with her arms and flailed with her feet until her head rose once again. She coughed, her throat raw. One of her arms slammed against a hard surface and she grasped the edge of the pool. She clung there, drawing in deep breaths.

We must be in a cistern beneath the Justice building, thought Brooke. She relaxed, feeling a sense of salvation. Small sounds of lapping water soothed her. The chill cooled her overheated body. Then a thought struck her. The fire above would use up all the oxygen as it advanced to the bottom floor of the building. Julia wouldn't burn but she would suffocate. Brooke wanted to cry. A cool draft moved across her wet face. An air current. The cistern was fed by pipes from the aqueduct in a long and intricate network under the city. As the fire used up oxygen, fresh air would be drawn in through these pipes. She was saved.

Time passed, seconds feeling like hours. Her limbs began to stiffen in the chill and her teeth chattered together. The total darkness numbed her senses. Faint sounds came from above where the fire was consuming the building like a greedy ogre. A crack appeared in the ceiling far above, admitting a shaft of achingly bright light. Brooke could see the vaulted ceiling of the cistern far above held up by ornate columns spaced in a regular array. A timber gave way and fell downward, trailing a fiery tail behind it. One end hit the edge of the cistern and the other end sizzled as it touched the water.

Brooke saw a man's head protruding above the surface not thirty yards away from where she clung to the side of the pool. He was looking in her direction, but his face was backlit by the burning timber, and could not be discerned.

Julia screamed.

Apr. 13, 1204, 1:10 PM. Garnett wandered with his band of raiders through the wide halls of the Imperial Palace. He had been exploring them for more than half an hour and had not re-crossed his path, so immense was the labyrinth of passageways. Every surface carried artwork of great beauty and intricacy, in a stunning display of opulence that few modern museums could match. The Imperial Palace had not survived to modern times, and Brooke was now the only living person who had ever seen it. She was as awestruck as her ancestor.

The crusaders entered chapels and audience halls, admiring each, but taking nothing. It seemed that even richer treasure was just around the corner and they kept pushing forward. Garnett stepped into a full-sized church, buried deep within the palace. A mosaic of the Blessed Virgin dominated the wall behind the altar. She was poised on a pedestal with her hands spread open at her sides. Rays of light emanated from her fingertips and shone on a stormy sea, where desperate sailors clung to bobbing boats.

The church was filled with riches, more than any other church that Brooke had ever seen. From golden candlesticks to jewel-encrusted chalices and elaborate reliquaries, the glory of God had never been more gloriously celebrated. The floor was of the whitest marble, perfect and shining. Columns of jasper, bits of glittering stone embedded in their highly-polished surface, rose to support the vaulted ceiling. For a moment, the crusaders just stood and stared. Then Hugh stepped to one of the many side altars and tried to open a silver door set into the altar. It was locked. He drew his sword and smashed at the lock with its hilt.

"What are you doing?" cried Garnett. "You can't rob a church. The penalty is excommunication and death."

"The monk told us that the Greeks were not real Christians, that they were no better than Jews. So this is not a real church," replied Hugh. Garnett had nothing to say to this piece of convenient logic. Hugh pried at the deformed door with the tip of his sword and forced it open. Even the hinges were made of silver, and it was relatively easy to tear it from the altar. From a cavity within, Hugh withdrew a golden box. It was elaborately carved and studded with rubies, diamonds, and jade. Shafts of a clear crystal with sharp points protruded from the top, in an unusual artistic display.

Garnett stood next to Hugh as he lifted the lid. Inside, nestled on a bed of yellow silk, sat what looked to Brooke like an old bird's nest. How odd. Then she noticed the sharp barbs that no bird would feather her nest with. Garnett gasped and quickly knelt before the relic, making the sign of the cross upon his chest. The others followed suit in deference to the holiness and power of the Crown of Thorns, which they believed to be the one and true crown that had rested on the head of the Lord Jesus Christ at His crucifixion.

Hugh carefully replaced the lid on the box and nestled it in his arms. Set loose, the other raiders spread out in search of precious relics, which had more value to them than the solid gold candlesticks within easy reach. They turned up a scrap of the Virgin Mary's gown, three nails from the crucifixion, a vial of Christ's blood, and the head of John the Baptist. Sated, they made their way out of the palace.

Apr. 13, 1204, 1:20 PM. "Don't be alarmed. I won't hurt you," said the unknown man, as the blazing timber sizzled and drifted away. The most reassuring thing about his statement was that it was in Greek. "I'm Paul."

"I thought you were one of them," said Julia. "I was so frightened. How did you get here?"

"I work in this building as an advocate. When I tried to escape the fire, I ran into a pack of barbarians, and hid down here from them."

"Why didn't you say something earlier?" asked Julia.

"I didn't know who you were." More burning debris fell from above, briefly lighting the earnest face of Julia's fellow refugee, until it hit the pool and winked out. A sizable hole had now opened in the ceiling above. It cast a flickering red light that nevertheless failed to penetrate into the furthest reaches of the vast cistern. The fire burned through at a second location, and sparks showered down upon the water. As Brooke watched, a flap of flaming material peeled away from the floor above and hung precariously above Julia's head. Frantically, she slid her hands along the stone lip of the pool, scraping her fingers as she clawed her way to safety. The crackling of the flame and the creak of shifting material resonated ominously in the echoing cavern.

"Go under water," shouted Paul, as he ducked beneath the surface. Julia, however, had no experience in deep water, and was as terrified of drowning as of burning. Brooke wanted to shout at her. Although Julia was wet enough to avoid catching fire, at any moment, a heavy object might fall on her head. She was so petrified that she did nothing other than shut her eyes tightly, as if she could make the danger go away by this childish stratagem. Brooke's fear rose an extra notch now that she couldn't see. Apparently, Julia felt the same, for she quickly opened her eyes again.

Debris began to accumulate on the landing between the cistern and the stairs. Some of it burned away but not everything was flammable. Bricks, chunks of stone, floor tiles, and half-burned beams littered the floor. Brooke had a vision of being buried under this building for days, perhaps injured, with no food or warmth. She kept reassuring herself that Julia would survive this, but that thought was cold comfort. She was scheduled to be in the past for at least four more hours. She should have been more cautious. This was a war zone, after all.

The fire continued to burn as Julia and Paul dodged the deadly rain from above. Miraculously, nothing landed directly on their heads. When the fire's fury was spent, leaving gaping holes in the ceiling above, they hauled themselves out of the water. The staircase was half buried in rubble, and looked dangerous to climb. Smoke obscured the top portion. Julia picked her way through the debris, placing her feet with care on the shifting surface. Paul suggested she be the first to climb, since she was lighter and less likely to dislodge the mound of material that partially blocked their exit. Brooke, less trusting than her ancestor, wondered if he wanted her to test the route.

Julia began the ascent cautiously. Halfway up, a broken tile gave way and she fell to one knee. A small avalanche unrolled behind her. Paul had prudently stood back from the base of the stairs, waiting to see how she fared, and was not injured. Trembling with fear and cold, and bleeding from a scraped knee, Julia began to cry. Her chest heaved in great sobs, as the accumulated stresses of the day assailed her.

"You're almost there. Don't stop now. Look at your right hand. Just grab that big gray slab. It looks sturdy." She calmed and followed his directions. The lingering smoke was thinner now and more could be seen. He talked her up the slope one move at a time, until she found a secure seat at the top. His ascent was flawless, guided no doubt by Julia's explorations, and he soon joined her.

The Justice building had been gutted by the fire, but the bones of the building had withstood the inferno. Navigating the hallway to the nearby exit was easy compared with what they had just been through. Outside, the scene was hellish. As far as the eye could see, the city was in ruins, wisps of smoke still curling up from lingering hot spots. But at least the fire had passed, traveling off to ravage some other neighborhood.

Paul offered to escort Julia home. They encountered a few stragglers, fellow survivors of the blaze, as they passed the blackened stone shells of formerly great structures. Brooke began to worry that Damian's house might have been taken by the fire, but as they advanced, they reached the end of the newly damaged zone. Ironically, the fire had stopped when it came upon an area of the city already burned out by an earlier blaze. They saw no crusaders. At length they returned to a familiar neighborhood that had escaped the fire. The streets were populated by families belatedly fleeing the city, their wagons heaped with possessions. Brooke remembered how the crusaders had blocked the gates at Zara, stripping everyone of their most valuable items. If these folks were lucky, they might escape before the roadblocks were set up.

The door to Damian's workshop stood like a beacon in a storm, and Julia rushed to it. It was locked and she pounded frantically with her fists. No answer. "It's me. Julia," she cried again and again.

"Just a minute," came a muffled voice. The sound of heavy objects scraping across the floor filtered out and then the door was flung open and Julia fell into her father's arms. He was sweaty and hot, but it mattered not at all. Basil and Eulogia hugged her in turn, as Paul said a quick farewell and hurried off.

"Where's Theodoret?" asked Damian. Julia shrank into herself, and a look of such pain and grief crossed her face that they knew. The moment of joy at their reunion crumbled into deepest sorrow, so quickly does the wheel of fate turn. But they could not afford to dwell on his death, for the crusaders were still roaming the streets, becoming ever less civilized as they gorged themselves on the treasures of the wealthiest city in Christendom, their appetite quickened by a year of deprivation. Damian and Basil pulled the workbench in front of the door, and piled up furniture, anvils, boxes, and whatever else came to hand for their barricade.

They were still adding to the pile when they heard a loud banging at the door. Damian told Julia and Eulogia to go hide. Julia set off up the stairs, but Eulogia stayed. Brooke could hear them arguing as she climbed, Eulogia saying that she would stand by her husband and he bellowing that she must obey him.

At the top of the stairs, Julia hesitated. The sound of splintering wood got her moving. She went to the dining room table and pushed three chairs snugly under it. Brooke could not imagine what she was up to. This was no time for housekeeping. Then Julia crawled under the table and up onto the seats of the chairs, lying with her body stretched horizontally along them. The tablecloth spilled over the edge of the table by her side and shielded her from view. It hung low on the other side of the table as well, draping like a protective tent around the frightened young woman. To someone standing in the room, she would be invisible.

Shouts came from the workshop below, along with a thud as something heavy crashed to the floor. Brooke heard Basil yell to watch out. Eulogia screamed and new voices were muttering in a guttural language that Brooke did not understand. What was happening below? A scuffle ensued, sending up a medley of thumps and scrapings and cries. Brooke was rigid with fear, her ears straining to interpret the unseen events. All she could see was the scarred underside of the dining room table claustrophobically close to the tip of her nose as she lay uncomfortably on her makeshift wooden ledge. She turned her head to watch the edge of the tablecloth, her meager protection. A thin wail was brutally cut off.

The struggle was over in less than a minute. The invaders conferred in low, angry voices, and shambled around the workshop, tossing and breaking things with abandon. Brooke feared for her family, and wondered if they still lived. Then her whole mind focused on a footfall on the stairs. The old planks creaked under the weight of the crusader, as he trudged upward step by step. Julia held her breath. She stared at the fringed edge of tablecloth and a small section of the bare tile floor beyond it. Her back hurt where the hard seat of a chair dug into it. She heard light footsteps moving away. Who else was in the room with her? The crusader was still mounting the stairs, not trying to hide his presence.

The man was moving around the room now, and Brooke caught a whiff of his pungent odor. A drop of water fell from Julia's wet skirt to the floor below, and rested as a little rounded hump on the polished floor. Julia stared at the telltale droplet, as her heart thumped madly in her chest. Brooke had never felt such terror. At that moment, she believed that she might die, that she might be literally scared to death.

The edge of the tablecloth was flung upward and a hard face, dirty and scowling, glanced down at the floor. All he had to do was look upward and Julia would be in plain sight as she lay across the chairs. She held herself perfectly still, a rabbit evading the hunter. The tablecloth fell and the man moved off, oblivious. Julia sank into the chairs, her tight muscles relaxing a notch as the footsteps receded.

Muted sounds came to her ears as the intruder moved around the upstairs bedrooms. The man spoke in a harsh voice. Brooke strained to understand, but got nothing. "Please let me be. For the love of God," Julia's grandmother pleaded. More incomprehensible words from the crusader. Brooke was incensed that he would threaten a helpless old woman in her sick bed. A long scream, followed by silence. Julia wept and trembled, but managed to remain silent. Someone called from below, and the crusader replied. He banged around in the bedrooms, searching. At last, he was finished and Brooke heard his heavy tread on the stairway, each step further away than the last.

The front door slammed shut and silence descended. Julia still did not move. Frozen in place, cold as a corpse, she lay. Brooke listened for any sign of life within the house. Her muscles were stiff from tension and from her awkward perch. It seemed that Julia had no intention of ever leaving her hiding place. The longer she delayed, the more uncomfortable and overwrought Brooke became. A small knot of pain erupted in her lower back and grew inexorably in intensity. Julia shifted to her side, and drew up her knees toward her chest. The chair seats were too narrow to support such a move, and Julia ended by dropping to the floor on her hands and knees. Still she hesitated before crawling out from under the table.

There was no one in the dining room, and no sign of any disturbance. In the bedroom, Julia found Ariadne still lying in bed, her eyes open, staring at nothing. The blanket was covered in blood. Julia squealed and then stuffed her hand in her mouth. But there was no response to her cry. Tears came to her eyes and she fled her grandmother's room. She sat at the top of the stairs, weeping, her whole body shaking in shock.

Brooke couldn't tell how long she sat there. But time has a way of pushing us into the future, often against our will. Julia rose and stepped hesitantly down the stairs. The workshop was in ruins, with tools pulled off the walls, benches overturned, and cabinets emptied. Four bodies lay on the floor, unmoving, unnatural. Basil was on his back, arms flung outward, a gaping wound in his neck. He wasn't breathing. A stranger, dressed in western clothes, slumped beside him. The stranger's head had been crushed by a hammer that rested on the floor beside Basil.

"Mama, Papa," cried Julia to her two parents, who both lay face down on the floor. She stepped to Eulogia's side and shook her, as first gently, and then insistently. A trail of blood seeped from under her mother's body. Putting her whole self into it, Julia managed to turn her mother over. Eulogia was dead and Julia collapsed into tears as she cradled her mother's head in her lap, sobbing incoherently.

What about Damian? thought Brooke. He could be unconscious but alive. "Go to him," she wanted to shout to Julia. Julia kissed her mother's cool forehead and released her, as if she had heard Brooke's urgent appeal. She shook Damian. "Father—please, please. I need you. Don't die on me." Brooke held her breath as Julia turned Damian over. One side of his face was wet with blood from a wound near the temple. His eyes were closed. Julia pressed her ear against his chest, but heard nothing. He was gone.

Brooke felt a part of herself die with Damian. She had been him, seen through his eyes, listened through his ears, and traveled with him through his world. Now to see him lifeless was terrible, as if she were gazing on her own lifeless body. She thought of all the goodness in the man. In an age when men were often callous and brutal, he had been caring and nurturing, and had provided for and protected his family. The full agony of warfare fell down upon her. This was no longer just research, this was a tragic moment that would stay with her for the rest of her days, burned indelibly into her memory.

Julia crouched by her father, and lifted his head into her lap, crying softly. She rocked back and forth as she wept. Brooke began to think about the crusader who lay nearby. Would his friends return to collect the body? They must do so eventually. A Christian should be buried in hallowed ground. Brooke felt increasingly uneasy.

At length, Julia had no more tears. She rose and shambled out the front door, empty-handed. The street looked surprisingly normal, if a bit empty, with no crusaders in sight. Pulling a scarf up to hide her face, she walked briskly along, avoiding the main avenues, heading toward the center of town. A few people scurried past, no one willing to meet her eye, and she unwilling to meet theirs. Trust had been shattered, and it would take time to rebuild it.

Julia's destination became clear as the Hagia Sophia rose up before her. Brooke wondered if she was hoping for sanctuary, or whether she just wanted to find solace in the Lord. If so, she would be disappointed. She entered the wide-open front doors into a scene from hell. Several groups of crusaders were savaging the ancient church, the most holy place in the Greek empire. The canopy above the main alter, an exquisite piece of craftsmanship made of a blend of precious metals, had been hacked into pieces and thrown into a cart. A placid donkey hitched to the cart had defiled the beautiful tiled floor with a steaming pile of dung. The cart was filled with candlesticks, crosses, statues, and reliquaries. Not satisfied with looting all the easy-to-hand treasures, two knights were prying the silver inlay from the pulpit gates, destroying a magnificent artwork for its mere metal content.

Father Scholasticus appeared in the nave, dressed in ceremonial Roman vestments, chanting a prayer, and trying to shame the crusaders into recognizing what they were doing. For a moment, they halted and looked at one another. Then a knight stepped up to the priest and plunged a sword into his chest. He fell heavily to the floor and the marauders returned to their evil work.

Julia darted into an arcade, trying to hide behind a pillar. She looked back at the front door, her escape route, but another cart, this one drawn by an ox, was navigating the entryway and she was trapped.

"Look what I found," said a voice in French behind her, as a hand clamped over Julia's bicep. She tried to break free, but was helpless against the crusader.

"Let's see what she looks like." Her captor tore the scarf from Julia's face. "Comely enough, don't you think?"

The crusader spun Julia around to face three knights, and Brooke recognized Hugh and Dagobert. With a start, she realized that the man standing between them must be Garnett. He was dressed in armor from the neck down, his white surcoat emblazoned with the cross. His lively blue eyes were set in a gaunt face, streaked with sweat and soot, the lower half obscured by a neatly clipped beard. A vagrant lock of hair hung over his forehead. His lips were slightly parted in an expression of surprise. Brooke's eyes were locked onto his, and in them she saw tenderness and longing.

"It can't be," said Garnett. "She's the picture of Cerise."

"Who's Cerise?" asked Dagobert.

"His dead wife," replied Hugh. "He loved her beyond reason and mourns her still."

"Let her go," barked Garnett. The knight released her arm but Julia made no attempt to flee. She stood motionless, as if enchanted by Garnett's gaze. After all that had happened to her that day, all the running and hiding, she seemed to be incapable of more fear and resistance, or perhaps she had a glimmering of the underlying intent of Garnett's words and recognized in him a kindred humanity. In any event, she no longer struggled against fate, but waited calmly for it to unfold.

Garnett came closer to Julia, who did not back away. He caressed her with his gaze, a look of wonder in his eyes. He walked back and forth, she following his every move, until he came to rest before her. Time was suspended for a long moment as they stood opposite one another. The sounds of the rampaging knights receded into nothingness.

Finally he said, "She's not afraid of us. I see defiance and dignity in her stance."

"Be careful. She would be a lot to handle," said Dagobert.

Garnett glared at him. "Are you so weak that you cannot master a spirited woman? My wife was strong, God rest her soul, and that made all the difference. Since she died, I've been wandering through life like a shade of my former self, anchor-less, numb, unable to feel pleasure, stumbling through this ugly war that bites into my very soul. But at this moment, I feel awake again, open to life's possibilities. I couldn't save Cerise, but I can save this woman. The Lord has blessed me."

Brooke had never heard Garnett bare his feelings in this way. She had only known him since Cerise died, when grieving had colored everything he did. Now just at the moment when Julia was plunged into grief, Garnett had found his way out of it. Brooke could only imagine what Julia was thinking. She had come to the church in her darkest hour, perhaps to find protection, or at least solace. Like never before, Brooke wanted to communicate with her many-times-great grandmother and reassure her of Garnett's decency and goodness, and tell her she could trust him. But Julia didn't need Brooke's help. Although Garnett's words were unintelligible to her, the underlying sentiment, communicated by a myriad of tiny clues, had come through.

"This woman is under my protection," said Garnett. He rested his hand upon the hilt of his sword to give emphasis to his declaration. The note of command in his voice was unmistakable. Garnett slowly stretched his hand out to her, palm up.

For a long moment, she remained still. The group of knights existed in a small bubble of silence cut off from the general tumult of the ravaged church.

Julia placed her small hand into Garnett's broad one and stepped forward.

And so it was that Brooke's two ancestors met for the first time in the cauldron of war. A moment later, Brooke winked back to the present, the spell broken. She looked around the lab with a sigh. It was some time before she left the Memex.

XXVI

INSPIRATION

O nce again, the campus was decked in its springtime finery. Delicate pink flowers covered the saucer magnolia trees in a look-at-me display. Occasionally a petal would float lazily to the ground, rocking back and forth on the air currents as it went.

Brooke sat on a bench in the morning sunshine, deep in thought. She should be graduating this month, along with Jose and Claudia and several of her other friends and acquaintances. Instead she had not even begun to write her thesis. It had been exactly a year ago that the Review Board had denied her request for permission to test human subjects, but it seemed like an event from the distant past. Of course, all her trips on the Memex tended to stretch out time, making each day feel far longer than it actually was. To make matters worse, she thought that she was no closer to getting Review Board approval now. All the complications of "time travel" had served more to delay than to advance her cause.

The academic propensity to be cautious and study and investigate *ad nauseam* is unfortunately not accompanied by an endless source of funds. Brooke's money would run out by the end of the month, and she had no idea what she would do then.

It was getting near noon, and the campus was filling up with students walking between classes. They wore shorts and T-shirts, even though the air was still chilly. Two women passed nearby, laughing about some shared confidence. An ancient professor, bent with age, crept along the walkway, looking like a rock in the stream of students that flowed past him. The onslaught only lasted ten minutes, until the walkers disappeared down hills, around corners, and into buildings and parking garages. A number of students remained, stretched out on the grass, enjoying the springtime sun, apparently free of obligations. Brooke envied them.

Her hopes of finding some new, enticing aspect of medieval history had evaporated. The Fourth Crusade had unfurled exactly as the ancient documents recorded, right down to the mooning of the retreating French troops by the Greeks on the ramparts. From what she could tell, the emperors had been every bit as cowardly and ineffectual and the Greek army as undisciplined and unprepared as historians believed. It was an unlikely tale, to be sure. At so many points, the crusaders could have been repelled. During the final battle, a brave knight named Aleaumes had been the first to crawl through a hole that the crusaders had hacked in the wall into almost certain death. One man against an entire city. But he terrified the Greeks and no one raised an arm against him. Killing him might have repulsed the whole attack. Instead, other knights swarmed in after him and the city was lost.

Although the crusaders had been courageous in the face of astounding odds, and had succeeded spectacularly, history's judgment had been harsh. Their cause was not seen as a just one, as it pitted Christian against Christian. To be sure, some of their number were brigands interested only in earthly rewards however dubiously obtained, but others, like Garnett, were deeply committed to the ideals of the crusade and thought they were doing the right thing. Once the army was camped outside Constantinople, the knights had few good choices. The Venetians would not take them to the Holy Land, so they could either attack the city, which had been undefeated for hundreds of years, or return home in disgrace. They could not choose disgrace.

And then there was Julia. Brooke had followed her for a while after her fateful meeting with Garnett. He had taken her back to his camp and given her food and shelter. He found a translator and swore to protect her and treat her with respect. She was free to leave at any time, but she chose to stay, trusting Garnett to keep his word. In him, she found first security and later love. Garnett, already a landed noble, had become spectacularly rich from the plunder of the city. He housed Julia in one of the abandoned villas that were plentiful after the sack, and hired servants to care for her. She lived with greater ease than she ever had before. Julia and Garnett were married in the Hagia Sophia three months after their meeting.

Julia never returned to her father's home. The memory of her slaughtered relatives was terrifying and she turned her back on that entire period of her life, rarely speaking of it to anyone. When spring came again, she accompanied Garnett on his return to France and settled there with him. Brooke had not explored too far into Julia and Garnett's future, preferring to believe that they had lived long and happy lives together.

Brooke thought of Damian and the futility of all his preparations. His decision to stay in the city, while understandable, was ultimately fatal for almost his entire family. He had tried to protect his treasure, going to great lengths to hide it from the rapacious crusaders, all for naught. Brooke didn't know what happened in Damian's house after Julia left, since she had no living hosts to access. Someone must have eventually found the bodies and buried them.

As Brooke's mind wandered, a tiny thought winked into existence. Could it be? Was it possible? She turned the idea over in her mind like a shiny new toy. It was outrageous. They would laugh at her if she suggested it. But the little thought refused to give up and kept arguing its case. Brooke rose from the bench and paced back and forth, mulling. At length, she walked briskly down the path towards the lab.

—⚭—

Chad's forehead was scrunched into a deep scowl as he contemplated Brooke's idea.

"But it's been so many years—almost a thousand," he said. He and Robert were looking at Brooke with worried eyes, as if they feared for her sanity.

"I don't think time matters in this case," said Brooke. "Damian was obsessed with protecting his treasure. After Origen stole from him, he became uber-cautious. Only he and Basil knew about the stash in the cistern. The rest of the household were oblivious. They thought everything was stored in the workshop cabinet. The only person outside the house who had any idea what Damian had was Scholasticus, and he died in the attack."

"Scholasticus must have told his superiors where he was hiding the church treasures," said Robert.

"Hard to say," said Brooke.

"In any event, how would you ever find the house?" asked Chad.

Brooke was annoyed that her two labmates were so critical and unsupportive. Chad sat sprawled in a battered old chair in front of the Memex and Robert was perched on the edge of a desk. Brooke had to remind herself that most new ideas are met with skepticism and scorn. The successful innovator needed a thick skin indeed.

"The streets of a city don't change much with time," said Brooke. "Many of the landmarks of ancient Constantinople are still in Istanbul today. The Hagia Sophia stands intact, for example. The Mese, the main street that ran east-west through the ancient city, is now Divan Yolu Avenue. All the old Roman forums along the Mese are still there, like the Forum of Theodosius and the Forum of Constantine. There's also a mosque called Kalenderhane Camii which used to be a church near Damian's house."

"Maybe you should go back to Damian's workshop after the raid and see what happened," suggested Robert. "Someone must have found the bodies and buried them."

"I can't go back," said Brooke. "Julia never returned there so I can't either. Her son, my ancestor, grew up in France. As far as I know, he never made the long trek back to Constantinople. Besides, Julia didn't know about the treasure. Damian kept it even from her. On the day the crusaders murdered Damian, I saw the cabinet door in the workshop hanging open, suspended from one hinge. The raiders took what was easy to find and left for other plunder.

"Of course, someone could have found the treasure over time, I suppose, but it was well hidden. Damian was fanatical about protecting it. Once the items were secured in the hole, he laid a sack full of sand over them and covered everything with floor tiles. I think he didn't want to leave a hollow space that could be discovered by tapping. He knew the crusaders might break into the city, so the night before they came, he mortared up the hole. He spread dirt along the new grout to give the appearance of age. You couldn't tell that spot from the rest of the floor. There would be no reason to suspect what lay beneath. I think that treasure is still there and I think I can find it."

Brooke's enthusiasm failed to move Chad and Robert. "Well, it's all theoretical anyway," said Chad. "We don't have the money to go halfway around the world on a sketchy treasure hunt. Interesting thought, all the same." To Brooke, it was not just an interesting thought, it was her fervent desire, and she was going to make it happen, whatever it took. Great obstacles give birth to great efforts.

Chad stood near the back of Prof. Hunter's office. There were only two chairs for visitors and Brooke and Robert currently occupied them. He shifted restlessly from one foot to another as Brooke told Hunter her wild idea for recovering Damian's treasure. Chad felt sorry for Brooke. He knew she was running out of money and realized she was under stress. But this desperate attempt to rescue her research was a bit much. She would be devastated when Hunter heaped scorn on the idea.

After Brooke finished her story, the professor sat silent for a bit. She ran her fingers through her already disheveled hair. Three pairs of eyes looked at her expectantly. "How would you go about finding the right spot? Surely the workshop is not still there after all these years, even if major landmarks are."

Chad was startled. Hunter seemed to be taking the idea seriously.

"Damian and Julia walked from the landmarks to the workshop on many occasions. I can count their steps and get a good estimate of the distance. I'll have to calibrate their strides, of course. Constantinople is a hilly city. The residents liked to think it had seven hills, just like Rome. The natural contours have not changed over time, and that will also help me identify the right spot. There are a lot of landmarks to start from. I can come from many different directions and zero in on the destination." Brooke explained it so cogently that Chad was starting to change his mind. She might be able to pull it off.

"The distances involved are not large," continued Brooke. "The workshop is less than a mile from the Hagia Sophia. In fact, the whole central part of old Constantinople is only about three miles wide and most of the landmarks I would use are within a mile of the workshop."

The phone rang and Brooke stopped talking. Instead of picking it up, Hunter said, "Keep going. They'll leave a message." Chad couldn't remember the last time the professor had declined to answer the phone.

"The street names all changed after the Turks conquered Constantinople in 1453. It was then that many intellectuals left the city and moved to Italy. Some historians think this exodus was a spur to the Renaissance. The people of Constantinople never thought of themselves as Byzantines, by the way. That name was slapped on later by European writers. They considered themselves to be Romans, the true descendents of ancient Roman culture."

"Back to practical matters," said Hunter brusquely. "Will you recognize the street?"

"Yesterday I looked at central Istanbul using Google Earth and the layout was familiar—not identical, but close. I think there's a good chance I can find the street."

Hunter looked at Brooke intensely for a moment. "You're always full of surprises," she said. "This is the craziest idea yet. Even if no one found the treasure right away, someone must have come across it over the course of time, perhaps when digging a new foundation for a building. To think that you could find it today is delusional."

"But what if it's still there? It would be an enormous discovery," pleaded Brooke.

"I don't have time for this. It's a crazy fantasy, an entertaining idea perhaps, but clearly not practical. Come back when you're ready to talk sense." Stung, Brooke fell quiet. Robert gathered up his backpack and rose from his chair and Brooke followed. Chad felt sorry for Brooke as the three filed out of the office.

Early Monday morning Brooke arrived at the Gifford field, hoping to find it mostly empty. Hunter might not be convinced of her idea, but that could change. Brooke would assail her with so much evidence that she would have to give in. It was the week after finals and the students who were still on campus were probably sleeping in. The field lay green and perfect with its artificial turf, ringed by a dull red track, also artificial. No inconvenient mud or other trace of reality would sully her experiments today. A lone jogger chugged around the track at a measured pace. He was built like a marathon runner, tall and thin. Brooke guessed he would be there for quite a while.

The jogger occupied the innermost lane, so Brooke chose the outermost one. People are a little like electrons. Three strangers in an elevator will not all stand on the same side, but move apart to leave the maximum distance between them, as if repelled by an electric force.

Brooke zeroed her pedometer and slipped it into the pocket of her St. John's Bay jeans. She set off along the track, trying to walk naturally and not think much about what she was doing. The sun shone directly in her eyes, almost blinding her. A few clouds shaped like flattened cotton balls lingered in the sky, moving majestically under the action of an unfelt wind. From time to time, the clouds covered the sun and cast the field into an eerie darkness. Brooke's mood swung from cocky confidence to deep doubt. Surely she would recognize the site of the workshop, no matter how much had changed in the intervening years. On the other hand, Julia and Damian were not consciously pacing off a distance as they walked around the city. As she followed them, they might stop to chat with a friend or be distracted by a street performer or a fruit stall. There would be no pedometer in her memory to help her count their steps. She would have to follow them again and again to verify the count. It sounded tedious, but then again, all research involved some dollop of tedium, often a substantial one.

At the finish line, she pulled out the pedometer and recorded the number of steps into an app on her iPhone. She had traversed 568 steps over the 400 meter track. She re-zeroed the pedometer and set off again. On the second pass, a new runner stepped onto the field, a woman in white shorts with a loose blue tank top over an exercise bra. She took off from an inner lane with great gusto, clearly here to run her heart out. As she flew past Brooke, Brooke felt herself almost imperceptibly speed up. It was irresistible, she couldn't stop herself. Frowning, Brooke willed herself to resume her prior calm walk, but by the time she reached the finish line, her pedometer recorded 554 steps, considerably fewer than before.

There was nothing to do but make another few loops around the track and Brooke settled in for a long morning. Each time she crossed the finish line, she added the data to her app and let it spit out the average stride length along with its standard deviation. As she rounded the far turn on her fifth lap, she could hear the voice of her old statistics professor droning on in her head. The subject had been one of the most uninteresting that she had ever had to study, and the professor's tepid presentation had done nothing to dress it up. Nevertheless, one day he said that you need at least twenty data points to do a defensible statistical analysis. That random fact lodged itself in Brooke's brain, and was now vying for her attention.

Twenty two laps later, Brooke ambled over to the bleachers and sat down. Her average number of steps per loop was 579, which corresponded to a stride length of 0.691 meters. She plotted the stride length data as a function of the lap number, hoping for a horizontal line with little scatter. For the early laps, the data was fairly uniform, if you threw out the second lap where she had been egged on by the runner. But for the later laps, the line dropped downward. Her stride length was shortening as she tired.

Brooke sighed. Even the simplest measurement is harder than you think. She resolved to come back each morning that week and take data for five laps per day. Of course, if she wrenched her knee…, but she stopped herself. You could never control everything.

Robert cast a glance at Brooke's inert form. Many times he had watched her lying in the padded chair in a deep trance state, her auburn hair framing her pale skin. She looked like she was sleeping restfully with no hint of the vivid scenes that were forming in her brain. Today Robert was watching more closely than usual for signs that she was stirring, hoping to save time. They were running a long series of short visits while Brooke repeatedly counted steps that her ancestors were taking and Robert was eager to finish.

Classes were over at last and he was ready to lie in the sun, relax, and accomplish absolutely nothing. Instead, the research project had just intensified with Brooke's latest initiative. In between changing the settings and launching Brooke on new sojourns into the past, Robert was organizing his data on mouse mortality. Since he had decided to focus on mice who consumed Muripellets, he had obtained a much bigger sample population. So far, there were a few tantalizing hints but no firm conclusions. Studying rare events is a statistical nightmare. Many of the studies sacrificed their animals early, before the effects Robert was interested in could manifest.

And of course the mice also suffered fatalities from whatever testing regimen they were subject to and these deaths had to be removed from the equation.

A group at the University of Iowa had been very cooperative, but their experiments had just begun and it would be a few months before anything interesting happened. Robert grumbled. He hated multi-tasking. He preferred to throw himself into a project full force and focus on it alone. Switching back and forth constantly made him jumpy.

Brooke's foot twitched and her eyes opened. She sat up, and without removing her helmet, grabbed an iPad that was sitting nearby. "From the monastery to the first left turn, he took 791 steps, then he detoured to the candlemaker, adding another 302 steps," she said. "After that, he walked 411 steps to Adrianople Road and headed for home." She stopped. "Damn, I don't remember how many paces for the last leg. I have to go back again."

Robert frowned but didn't object. He stoically reset the Memex and waited for Brooke to settle herself in. When she was ready, he threw the switch. She would be under for about a minute. Robert had his doubts about this buried treasure. Surely after all these years, someone would have found it. Perhaps a construction worker digging a basement had turned it up. It was madness to think it was still there. Of course, there was more than one way to conduct a search. If you wanted rare information, there was no better place to begin than the internet. Robert began searching for medieval treasures recovered in Istanbul. Maybe he could end this now.

Brooke was feeling a little unsteady on her feet. A clammy finger of sweat ran down from one armpit. The delay had left her in a state of heightened sensation, every muscle tense, every nerve ready to scream in pain. She didn't know if she could go through with this. Her fevered mind threw up images of herself melting into a puddle like the Wicked Witch of the West. It was like this every time she had to make a presentation. Public speaking was far more terrifying than storming the walls of Constantinople.

Chad sat back in a chair next to the conference room table, looking bored. Robert had his head buried in his smart phone, tapping away. No one else was in the room. The computer projector, its fan whirring gently, cast a pale image of Brooke's title slide onto the screen. It would look better when the light was turned out and the shade drawn.

The door opened and Prof. Hunter stepped in. Without a word of apology or explanation for her lateness, she took the chair at the head of the table and said, "We can begin." Robert pocketed his cell phone. Brooke threw the light switch and drew a deep breath.

"Over the last week, I've revisited Constantinople numerous times through the eyes of Julia and Damian and can now map out the probable location of Damian's shop," Brooke began. "By triangulating from several known locations, and using a map of present day Istanbul, I've narrowed the search to a small area." She flipped to her next PowerPoint slide. "This is a photograph of the Milion. It's the remains of a monument constructed by the Romans in the fourth century CE. They used it as a literal mile stone from which to measure all distances in the empire." The screen showed a scarred, uneven pillar jutting upward. Brooke remembered the graceful arch that the Milion had once been, a distant echo of this sad remnant. "Today the Milion is a tourist attraction that sits atop the Basilica cistern, 150 meters southwest of the Hagia Sophia.

"Both Julia and Damian passed the Milion many times as they walked along the Mese, the main avenue of the old city. Today that same route is called the Divan Yolu, or literally, the road to the Imperial Council. If you walk 700 meters west along this avenue, you come to the Forum of Constantine. The great triumphal column of Constantine stood there in Damian's time and he walked by it many times. Here's a picture of the column today, which the Turks call Çemberlitaş Sütunu." The once mighty column stood upon a crumbling pedestal. The statue was missing from the top; nevertheless, it still exuded beauty and majesty.

"A third excellent landmark is also nearby. If we continue west along the path of the ancient road, which has now changed names to Yeniceriler street, we come to Beyazit Square, which Damian knew as the Forum of Theodosius. There are some ancient stone remains here as well.

"Using these three landmarks, I was able to determine the stride lengths of Damian and Julia as 0.681 meters and 0.622 meters, respectively. These are a little less than average stride lengths of men and women today. Presumably, my ancestors were shorter than people are now, and that accounts for it. The numbers are statistically accurate to three significant figures."

Brooke advanced to her most enticing slide—a treasure map. She had superimposed the routes Damian and Julia took as they made their way home onto a map of present day Istanbul. A small area northeast of the Grand Bazaar where all the paths ended was circled in yellow. "The red lines correspond to Damian and the blue ones to Julia. The solid lines are routes that one could still traverse today. The dotted lines go across obstacles, like the University of Istanbul. It would not be possible to actually walk that route. Nevertheless, the lines all converge on this small area."

"How big is it?" asked Hunter.

"About 120 yards in diameter. I believe I could narrow it down more if I were there and could pace it off myself."

"What's at that location?"

"Unfortunately, I can't tell very well. Google Earth has an incomplete view of downtown Istanbul. It's not like the US where you can zoom in on any street and see a complete 3D rendering of the surroundings. In Istanbul, a few important buildings are drawn and the rest is just flat. There are photographs linked to the map that give an idea of what you can see. I think our target area is mostly two- and three-story shops and residences."

"Go on," said the professor.

"You will notice that I also used a fourth landmark, the former church of Theotokos Kyriotissa which sits on top of the third hill, at the terminus of the Aqueduct of Valens. Today it's a mosque called Kalenderhane Camii. It's only a short walk east from the mosque to the target zone."

"How do you account for hills in your analysis?" asked Hunter.

"I think hills would shorten the stride length, but it's difficult to make that correction from a distance. If I were to walk the routes, I could use the ratio of my stride length to Damian's as a correction factor. Then the hills would probably shorten his stride by the same amount as they shorten mine." Brooke watched Hunter carefully. Was she buying it? It was hard to tell from her face. Hunter rarely smiled even at the best of times. Her squinting eyes and wrinkled forehead could just mean that she was thinking hard.

"That's very interesting," said Hunter. "Wild, but interesting." Robert sat forward in his chair, head cocked. Brooke thought he might say something, but was disappointed. Any support from Chad or Robert was unlikely to influence the professor anyway. Who was she kidding? Her labmates did not actually support her, but at least they had not voiced their doubts.

"As it happens," Hunter continued, "I have a source of funds that I can tap. The money will disappear if I don't spend it. Don't ask for details. I'm not saying that I agree with your highly speculative analysis, but I don't have anything better to do with the money at the moment. Would you and Chad be willing to go to Istanbul and check this out?"

XXVII
DÉJÀ VU

Four days later, Brooke stepped off a United Airlines Boeing 777 jet at Ataturk International Airport. She had not been able to sleep at all on the overnight flight. Chad, of course, had dropped off not long after they left Newark and had not woken up until breakfast. But as they navigated passport control, Brooke was excited and eager to see the city and felt as awake as if she had slept for hours. The professor had surprised her by springing for last-minute visas and a passport for Chad. Hunter could be generous when she was spending other people's money.

Once outside the airport, they found a yellow cab without difficulty and asked to be taken to the center of town. As they swung onto route D-100, Brooke looked around for hints of the city she knew so well, but was disappointed. Everything spoke to modernity, from the six lane highways to the tall, blocky buildings in shades of tan and brown.

"Does anything look familiar?" asked Chad.

"No, we're too far from the center of town. Damian only ventured this way on rare occasions as an adult, and then it was all farmland."

"Well let me know if you see anything."

Brooke was annoyed by his comment. The combination of jet lag and culture clash was already taking a toll on her patience. Then, as if on cue, the road passed between two square towers, parts of the old city walls. Brooke was reassured by the familiar pattern of brick and tan stripes, although now a Turkish flag flew above the turrets. A red double-decker bus passed them in the other direction, and she thought it might be fun to ride on one. Of course, there wouldn't be much time for sightseeing on this trip. That was a shame, since this might be the only time in her life that she visited Istanbul.

Traffic was heavy and their driver swerved around other cars aggressively. "Did you know that this city was once called Constantinople?" the driver asked.

Brooke caught Chad's eye and almost giggled.

"You don't say," said Chad.

"We Turks called it Istanbul for a long time, but the rest of the world insisted on calling it by its old name."

"That must have annoyed you."

"It annoyed Ataturk. In the 1930s, he put his foot down. He told the post office to return any mail that was labeled Constantinople, and that finally worked. Now nobody thinks of it as Constantinople."

Except me, thought Brooke. The name change was the final step in disavowing the old city and its Byzantine culture. She peered out the window at all the signs in Turkish. It was as if she had taken a time machine to Paris in the future and discovered all the signs were in German. She shuddered. Usually she was receptive to new places, new languages and new ideas, but today, exhausted after her long confinement in the airplane, she longed for the familiar. So far, Istanbul had a drab feel to it that disappointed.

As the cab swung onto another multi-lane highway, her opinion changed. In this part of town, construction was everywhere, cranes vying with minarets for space in the sky, and new high-rise buildings growing like giant Tinker Toys. The area was vibrant with change. The cab driver said, "My brother-in-law used to live near here, but they're leveling all the old neighborhoods and building expensive new apartments. I don't know what people are supposed to do."

The cab drove along the southern border of the city, with views of the Sea of Marmara beyond the trees of a city park, past dramatic displays of roses and geraniums that spread like long red carpets along the side of the road. As they drew near the center of town, they passed Cemberlitas square and Brooke caught sight of the column of Constantine. She almost asked the driver to stop, but decided against it at the last minute. They would come back to it later. Now they had to get to their lodgings and drop off their bags. The cab swung around a corner and the Blue Mosque materialized before their eyes.

"That's gorgeous," said Chad. He asked the driver to slow down.

Six minarets soared above the central dome in harmonious proportion. Numerous smaller domes gave an impression of vast spaces within. Brooke felt a surge of pure delight, the kind that only comes from great architecture. Her impression of Istanbul softened and she began to look forward to what she might discover here.

The cab pulled up to the International Student Hostel where they had booked rooms just a few days earlier. It was on a vibrant street, with colorful awnings before well-kept buildings. The area was almost Disney-esque, too quaint and tourist-centered to be real. A motorcycle painted with intricate designs added to the charm. They had traversed the center of town so quickly in the cab. Brooke felt like an adult who returns to her childhood haunts to find them much smaller than her cherished memories.

Brooke and Chad were assigned to a common room with four bunk beds. It was already past two, so only top bunks were left. Brooke tossed her backpack and duffel up on a bed in the far corner away from the window. She thought about theft, but decided not to take any special precautions. She was already wearing her passport in a secure pouch around her neck and her money and tablet computer were in her bag. The freshly made bed, humble as it was, looked inviting to her jet-lagged eyes, but she knew she had to fight the urge to sleep during the day. Walking around outside in the bright sunshine was the best protection against dozing off, and that was what she had come to Istanbul to do anyway.

In a few minutes, they were back on the street and climbing a gentle hill. After a short walk, they came upon a well-kept park where the hippodrome and Imperial Palace used to be. Brooke was saddened that those vast and glorious structures had disappeared so completely. All that was left of the hippodrome was a ruined column and an Egyptian obelisk, etched with hieroglyphs that still looked freshly carved after two thousand years.

Beyond the trees rose up the Hagia Sophia, the magnificent cathedral that Brooke had visited so many times in the past. A stab of alarm coursed through her as she beheld the four minarets surrounding the building. They certainly had not been there in Damian's time. To her, this was a Christian church, and the addition of minarets seemed almost blasphemous. The domed Greek church had been transformed into a mosque.

"How does it look?" asked Chad, as if he could read her mind.

"Familiar but different," she replied. Brooke had been in high school when Osama bin Laden had destroyed the World Trade Center on Sept. 11, 2001. That event kicked the American consciousness up to a new setting, where, almost overnight, Muslim terrorists had become America's most feared and despised enemies. Brooke knew intellectually that the attack had been the work of a fanatic organization, and the whole Muslim world was not to blame, but she sometimes had to tamp down that tribal beast deep in her psyche who was ready to blame all Muslims for the crime. Now this beloved cathedral had been transformed, and it felt like a betrayal.

"When I was there in the past, there were no minarets," she explained.

Chad cocked his head to the side. "It's hard to see places we love undergo changes. Shall we go inside?" They passed through the tourist entrance at one corner of the building.

"I want to walk under the imperial entrance," said Brooke, "something Damian would never have been permitted to do." The portal they sought was close by and topped by a mosaic of an emperor on his hands and knees in a pose of great humility before a benevolent Christ figure. It is said that the emperor was Leo VI, who had sinned greatly in divorcing four wives.

"Clearly the church had the upper hand in those days," said Chad.

"We're lucky we can see the mosaics. After the Turks captured Constantinople in 1453, this building was converted to a mosque. All the mosaics were plastered over, in keeping with the Islamic prohibition on figurative images. In the 30s, Ataturk turned the building into a museum, as it remains today."

"You could get a job here as a tour guide," said Chad.

"Ah, yet another application of the Memex—tour guide training."

They stepped into the main body of the church, where the full beauty and power of its tall marble walls and gilded arches could be felt. The dome, circled by evenly spaced windows, floated high above.

"Pretty amazing for something built in the sixth century, don't you think?" asked Brooke. During the various restorations and rehabilitations of the structure, much had changed. It was like seeing an old friend dressing in odd new garments. Huge round placards with Arabic writing suspended from the ceiling reinforced the impression of strangeness. They wandered around, taking in the beauty of the place.

Brooke turned to say something to Chad, and froze in surprise. He was standing beside a giant pillar, in front of a tall window, the exact spot that Garnett had stood all those long years ago when Julia had met him for the first time. The feeling of déjà vu was overwhelming and Brooke almost stopped breathing. Chad's eyes were soft as he looked at her with a hint of tenderness. Brooke could no more speak to him right now than Julia could have spoken to Garnett.

She observed him with new interest, the tall lanky posture, the strong line of his chin, the rumpled brown hair, the faded jeans with the shiny belt buckle. It was as if she were seeing him for the first time. She had never noticed the dimples in his cheeks before, or the whiteness of his teeth as he smiled at her. He was fit from many hours of martial arts training. Even better, he possessed many of those qualities that Brooke yearned after—intelligence, goodness, and reliability. Brooke waited for him to stretch out his hand to her as Garnett had to Julia, but in vain. The moment passed quickly in real time, but stretched out languorously in perceived time.

Finally she came back to herself and said, "Why don't we explore the upper galleries? In Damian's time, they were reserved for the emperor and nobility and I've never seen them." He agreed and they ascended a peculiar passageway that looked as if it had been blasted out of solid rock, so rough were the bare walls and ceiling. The passageway ramped upward, switching back again and again as they gained height.

On the upper gallery, Brooke approached the railing and looked down upon the nave far below. Although they had climbed a great distance, the dome still seemed impossibly high above. They hadn't made much progress in reaching the top.

"Wow, this place is huge," said Chad.

"The Statue of Liberty would fit inside it," said Brooke. On the whole, the gallery was disappointing, with plain white walls and few exhibits. A tour guide brandishing a neon green patch on a long stick led his charges to an undistinguished corner. Curious, Brooke and Chad sidled up to the group to listen in.

"You see this small area where the plaster has been removed. Set between two blocks is a pane of glass. If an earthquake should occur—you know we have lots of earthquakes in this part of the world—the building might shift. Broken glass would alert the caretakers that the building might need buttressing. No need to worry though, the Hagia Sophia has withstood earthquakes for 1500 years." It was a simple warning system, clever and cheap.

Further along the gallery Brooke observed an area of the floor that was cordoned off with stanchions, and she knew it must be what she sought. At the center of the protected area was a simple engraved stone that read "Henricus Dandolo." She felt herself drawn back into the past, to Garnett's long journey and hard-fought battle.

Chad noticed her interest and asked, "Who was he?"

"The leader of the Venetians in the Fourth Crusade. History has not been kind to him, blaming him for the attack on the city."

"What do you think?"

"I admire him. He was over eighty and blind when he undertook the strenuous crusade. It was his leadership and strategic thinking that won the day for the crusaders. The argument against him is that he perverted the purpose of the crusade by attacking fellow Christians. I frankly don't think wars of aggression against people of your own religion are any more defensible than wars against people of other religions."

"But if he waged a war of aggression, isn't that wrong in and of itself? asked Chad.

"Not in medieval times. Remember that it was the West that first preached a 'Holy War.' Dandolo's whole society glorified such wars."

"So are the Muslim terrorists right today because their society tells them that Jihad is good?"

"Of course not. It's complicated. For one thing, respectable Islamic societies do not support terrorism. The terrorists are a fringe movement, a throwback to the past."

"That they are," said Chad. "Being here in Istanbul reminds me of 9/11. It's not a comfortable feeling."

"So you feel it too, a sort of wariness toward Islamic culture?"

"Unfortunately, yes. It's something we have to fight."

Brooke had been beating herself up for her deep-rooted feelings about Islam, which welled up inside her from time to time despite her attempts to suppress them. To hear Chad express similar concerns was a relief. She was not alone. This trip to Istanbul might help her appreciate and respect what was good in Turkish society, and start to expunge the irrational hatred and fear forever.

"This just became my new favorite food," said Chad as he took another bite of his doner kebab. Served between thin layers of pita bread, the juicy meat woke up all his taste buds. They had watched the restaurant owner shave thin layers of the stuff from a tall inverted cone of meat that rotated slowly before a heater.

"I'm glad we stopped here," said Brooke. She looked a little revived now that she had eaten. A smile played around her lips as she met his eye.

Chad wondered. There had been that moment in the church when she had looked at him intensely. Did she know how he felt about her? Out of pride, he had kept his feelings hidden, not letting her see the raw desire he felt every time he watched her auburn hair swish around her shoulders or her eyebrow rise in a playful question. After all this time, Brooke was still an enigma to him. Her brilliance was both attractive and terrifying, threatening to destroy his confidence even as it drew him in. As much as he wanted to reach out to her, he held back. Chad would wait.

The conversation flowed easily as they talked about recent movies and the latest craziness from Washington. Thinking of home helped to ward off the challenges of this foreign city. Chad had never traveled this far from home before, and he didn't know what to expect.

"Why do you think Hunter sent you along?" asked Brooke.

Chad hesitated before replying. He sensed danger in this question. Brooke, fiercely independent, would not want to hear that he was sent to watch out for her—that she might not be able to manage on her own. He also was miffed that she thought he might not have a place in this adventure. He was a major contributor to the research effort, just like her. He had a right to be here.

"I don't know. Why does the professor do anything? She rarely explains herself." He wanted to retract the remark almost as soon as he had said it. It sounded lame.

"I'll tell you what I think," said Brooke. "Hunter doesn't trust me and she sent you along to verify anything I might discover."

Chad's eyebrows shot up. That hadn't occurred to him.

"Remember when she called in that professor of Greek language to see if I was telling the truth about being able to speak Greek? She didn't trust me then either."

"You have a point." He didn't want to argue with her.

"Of course, maybe I'm just being paranoid. With the Memex, I have no hard evidence to back up what I say and it makes me feel vulnerable. It could be that Hunter just wanted to use up the funds she had. In any event, I'm glad you came." She smiled warmly and Chad relaxed.

After lunch, they searched out the Milion, the ancient Roman milestone near the Hagia Sophia. This was the starting point for Brooke's first calibration run. Chad wanted to suggest that they take a peek at the Basilica cistern that was just below their feet, but he could see she was determined to get to work. She pulled out her pedometer and zeroed it. They set off west along Divan Yolu, which had once been the old imperial highway. The street was well kept and modern, with no hint of its medieval past. They had not gone far before Chad saw the golden arches on a glass-enclosed storefront. He knew he should decry the invasion of McDonald's to this historic district, but he was secretly pleased to see the familiar restaurant, even if he couldn't stop there just now. The weather was pleasant, just the right temperature for a walk in the sunshine. A tram, sleek with its aerodynamically-shaped nose, trundled on tracks along the side of the street.

Oddly, most of the pedestrians were men. The city seemed to have a gender imbalance. It wasn't true of the tourists, who stuck out in this traditional town, but only of the native residents. Chad guessed that Islamic women were less likely to venture out, even in these times. The women he saw were dressed in a wide range of styles. Some wore the ubiquitous blue jeans and casual tops seen in most parts of the world. Others, more traditional, were dressed in long, loose-fitting gowns and patterned head scarves. One attractive woman had on a chic black dress with a hem far above her knees. But the one that gave him pause was a woman encased in purdah—a drab black robe that covered everything, including her head and face, leaving only a narrow slit for the eyes. Incongruously, pale blue shoes poked out from the bottom of her floor-length robe.

When she had passed, Brooke said, "Did you see that? What a shame she has to hide herself from view. That needs to change."

"It does seem abusive," agreed Chad. Five minutes later, a pair of nuns passed them. With their long black robes, and their hair and necks covered by the wimple, they bore a disturbing resemblance to the woman in purdah, but they were quite acceptable to Chad. Of course, these nuns had chosen their lifestyle, not had it imposed on them. Istanbul was the link between Europe and Asia, where East meets West.

They arrived at the column of Constantine, set in a broad open square where hundreds of pigeons pecked and scratched for food. The birds fled before Brooke's purposeful stride. She pulled out her pedometer and noted the reading, entering the data into her tablet computer.

"How does it look?" asked Chad.

"Great. I got the number I expected within 2%. Not bad!" Relieved that their mission was starting off well, Chad turned his attention to the dramatic column as Brooke re-checked her calculation. The column was set on a high, crumbling pedestal. Just getting to its base would be a challenging climb.

"How does it compare with what you remember?" he asked.

"Let's say it hasn't been as lucky as the Hagia Sophia but it was spared the near complete destruction of the Milion. Outside of the column, nothing looks familiar. This used to be a big circular space with bronze statues all around, but they've vanished." A wave of loss swept over Brooke, an aching for the old city, long destroyed. The square was choked with tourists, their white buses parked in a long line, occupying most of the pavement.

"Is it time to go find the treasure spot?" asked Chad. "You have the calibration."

"No way. I have to take a bunch more measurements before I'm ready to do that."

Chad was disappointed. "How can you wait?"

"Look, I want to go there too, but I don't want to be misled. If I don't have an accurate calibration, I could end up in the wrong place. You know that wherever I end up first will seem like the right place. I'll be forever biased toward it."

Chad didn't see that at all, but he knew it would be fruitless to argue. They spent the rest of the afternoon pacing off distances between the Milion, the column, and Beyazit Square, traversing the same street again and again. Bored, Chad began to feel the effects of jet lag. Brooke also looked like she was fading.

"Doesn't your data get corrupted if you're tired?" asked Chad.

"Damn, you're right. We better finish for the day."

They had a leisurely dinner on a terrace overlooking the Bosporus and made their way slowly back to the hostel. Brooke looked totally exhausted and climbing into her bunk even though it was only 9 PM local time. Chad didn't want to think about what time it was in New York. He read for a while and then bedded down. It wasn't easy to fall asleep in the same room as Brooke, so near but so inaccessible. He finally drifted off.

On their third day in Istanbul, Brooke was finally satisfied with her calibration efforts. She now had the ratio of her stride length to both Julia's and Damian's within less than 1%. Chad had grumbled about the repetition, but in the end, had gone along. Now they were standing before Kalenderhane Camii, a mosque that Brooke had known in the past as the church of Theotokos Kyriotissa.

The mosque was nestled up against the eastern terminus of the aqueduct of Valens. Its brick colored walls, desolate windows, and green iron fence reminded Brooke of an abandoned New England factory, with the single minaret resembling a smokestack. Setting aside these uncharitable thoughts, Brooke got her bearings at the entrance and, re-zeroing her pedometer, set off in an easterly direction.

As she and Chad left the area of the mosque, they threaded their way down a pedestrian street no wider than an alleyway, lined on both sides with garment shops. One store was devoted only to buttons and another to zippers. They came out upon a wide street bathed in sunlight with trees and ornamental plants artfully arranged along the center and sides. Brooke continued her determined walking. The path she wanted to take went through the middle of a sidewalk cafe, where patrons smoked Turkish water pipes. She had to make some adjustments, using an alternate route and adding and subtracting extra steps as needed. She hoped the errors introduced by this diversion would simply cancel out, but a niggle of doubt remained.

As they drew near the end of their trek and were achingly close to their destination, Brooke's heart rate rose in anticipation. She feared finding some unanticipated obstacle or worse, an unfamiliar spot. Then she passed a jewelry store, with elegant displays of necklaces and gold bracelets behind gleaming glass display windows. A short distance down the street, she found a second upscale jeweler. This felt like the right neighborhood, still the domain of gold dealers after all these years. Chad halted at a sidewalk vendor standing behind a stainless steel cart. While Brooke waited impatiently, he bought an ear of corn on the cob, burnt on one side, and started chewing on it. They ploughed on.

Brooke began to worry that her pacing would be affected by the throngs of people, both locals and tourists. It was hard to walk naturally in such a crowd. They should try this again in the early morning or late at night when there would be fewer pedestrians. Given her still somewhat jet-lagged circadian clock, early morning would make more sense.

At last they came to the crucial intersection, the last turn onto the street where Damian had presumably once lived. But there was no street there. On the other hand, there *was* an intersection a little distance ahead. Brooke made a note of the extra steps she had to take to reach it. Then she turned left and started up the gentle hill on a narrow street closed to traffic, heart pounding. It certainly looked medieval, paved with cobblestones and no wider than an alleyway.

There were few people here and the neighborhood was mostly undistinguished commercial buildings with a few shops sprinkled in. She glanced repeatedly at the pedometer as she climbed until she finally hit the magic number and stopped. She was in front of a ramshackle house, three stories high. The siding, which had once been brown, was faded into gray. Rough planks had been nailed over one section haphazardly, with no attempt at beauty or dignity. A small shop selling dishes with intricate Turkish designs lay a short way down the street.

"Well," asked Chad, "What do you think? Is this it?"

Brooke was slow to answer. "It could be. The slope of the street is about right. Of course everything has changed." She wanted to kick herself for sounding indecisive. She needed Chad to believe in her. The question was whether she still believed in herself.

"Of course it's changed," said Chad. "Besides, this is only the first data point. If I know you, we're going to do this again and again and again."

His good-natured attitude put her at ease. "True enough. OK, let's record the coordinates of this spot." She pulled out her smart phone and dialed in a GPS app. In seconds, she had the coordinates displayed and saved to a notepad.

"We ought to take photos, too," she said. "It will help to document the exact position."

Chad obliged and pulled out his cell phone. He captured her from every angle, showing her position in relation to the buildings on the street. He also took overlapping photos of all the nearby buildings on both sides of the street.

"Time for data point two?" he asked.

This time they started from the Hagia Sophia and used one of Julia's journeys. Brooke arrived on the same street but about 150 yards further down the hill. She could see the china shop ahead on the left, with its colorful display of dishes.

"Don't worry," said Chad, noting her frown. "This was bound to happen. We just need more data."

Brooke hoped so, but her confidence was shaken.

"It's a funny thing about statistics," said Chad. "You can make some amazingly accurate predictions if you have enough data. For example, think about those big jars of jelly beans at county fairs, where people try to guess the number of beans. Most people guess far too high or too low, but, on average, they get surprisingly close to the right answer." His words were like balm to her soul. She wanted to believe him, and why shouldn't she? He made sense.

"You're right. Let's get started on our next trek." They spent the rest of the day and the following one on walking the routes over and over. Occasionally they ended on a parallel street, to Brooke's dismay. But most of the time, they were somewhere in the vicinity of the china shop, which became a beacon of hope for Brooke. Finally satisfied, they returned to the hostel to see what might pop out of the data.

Chad sat opposite her at a large table in the breakfast room of the hostel. Their plates were empty, looking forlorn under a scattering of crumbs and crumpled napkins. The place was almost deserted, the other guests having taken off to see the town. Brooke felt full and satisfied, the taste of eggs and excellent Turkish coffee still lingering in her mouth. A clang from the kitchen signaled that clean-up was underway, but Brooke thought she would have time.

She pulled out her tablet computer and proceeded to set up the conference call. Chad shifted his chair around so he could look on and be part of the conversation. After punching in an annoyingly long number and waiting patiently for the connection to come through, Brooke finally succeeded.

It was late afternoon at Brackett University, and a haggard looking Hunter appeared on the screen, her hair in an end-of-the-day disheveled state. "Good to see you Brooke. How's Istanbul?"

"We're having a good time," said Brooke, and instantly regretted it. She wasn't supposed to be having a good time, she was supposed to be working. "Of course, Chad and I have spent most of our time pacing off distances."

"How's that going?"

"I have a chart I want to show you." Brooke fiddled with the interface and brought up a detailed map of the target zone. The map was sprinkled with small black dots, each one representing an estimate of the treasure location. "We made thirty separate runs in order to zero in on the workshop. As you can see, the data cluster nicely along this one street. Here is the average of all the locations. Brooke touched the screen and a pre-programmed red dot appeared. "Based on an analysis of variance, there is a 98% chance that we are within 17 yards of the true location. She touched the screen again and a small red circle 17 yards in diameter appeared on the screen.

"What did you find at that location?"

"This," she said as she brought a new image onto the screen. It was a photo of a three story private residence painted a pale melon color. The roof line sagged a bit and the pavement in front was infested with weeds.

"Well, a vacant lot would have been nice, but I guess that was too much to hope for," said Hunter. "What does the rest of the street look like?" Brooke filled her in.

"It looks like you've done all you can," said Hunter. "Time to come home."

"Bummer," said Chad after the call had been terminated. "She could have been a little more excited." Brooke thought so too. She didn't know what she had expected, but not this cursory treatment. As far as she could see, it was all over. The trip to Istanbul had been a lark, not something the professor truly intended to follow up on. She was just curious, not serious. Brooke felt infinitely tired and deflated. This was the end of the line.

XXVIII
FAITH

When Brooke arrived back at Hunter's office, a surprise awaited her. Hunter had a visitor, a thin man in his forties with dark skin and perfectly-cut black hair. His pants were of a rich material and sharply creased while his shirt was a crisp pale blue. When he saw her, his face lit up with a wide smile and his eyes sparkled.

"Brooke, this is Prof. Yogesh Kumar. I asked him to join us today," said Hunter. Wary, Brooke took the proffered handshake, which was warm and firm. Brooke feared another test—someone Hunter had recruited to debunk her story.

"I've heard so much about you," said Kumar. "It's unbelievable what you have done. You'll have to tell me all the details."

"I have taken the liberty of filling Prof. Kumar in on the Memex and your trip to Istanbul," said Hunter. "You don't need to hide anything." What if I want to hide something? thought Brooke. She was angry that Hunter had released such sensitive information without consulting her first.

At that moment, a knock sounded at the door and Chad entered. Prof. Kumar was introduced to him and Brooke learned that Kumar was an archeologist specializing in the Middle East. More alarms sounded in her head. Hunter was surely trying to trip her up.

After Chad was seated, Brooke said, "Our eight days in Istanbul were very successful. We found the site we were looking for. Everything adds up."

Prof. Kumar interrupted her. "Before you tell me about that, let's step back a bit. I want to understand how the Memex works."

Brooke launched into a description of the neural pathways that were stimulated by the Memex, trying to keep the technical jargon to a minimum. Prof. Kumar listened raptly, frequently interjecting questions and comments. His enthusiasm was infectious, and Brooke began to warm to him.

"But why does it work?" asked Kumar. "How are the memories stored in the brain in the first place?"

"Unfortunately, we haven't figured that out yet," said Brooke. "We may get some clues when we start large scale tests with many individuals."

"What's it like to use the Memex?" asked Kumar.

"It's indistinguishable from normal life, except that you are a passenger without volition. You can see, taste, smell, feel everything. It can be over-whelmingly beautiful and a source of deep pleasure. It can also be excruci-atingly painful, just like life itself."

"Unbelievable," said Kumar. "A true virtual journey into the past. The world is going to be astonished when they hear about this. Do you realize what a great discovery it is?" Before Brooke could add anything further, Kumar said, "I understand you have used the Memex as well, Chad. What was it like for you?"

"It was like Brooke said, everything was vivid and real. Sometimes it was disorienting to be someone else. I really had no idea what would happen next. And you can't just stop whenever you want to. You have to wait to be brought back to the present time."

"I've heard of retrocognition before, of course, but never such power-ful experiences," said Kumar.

"Retrocognition?" said Brooke. "What's that?"

"You don't know about it? It's a psychic ability like telekinesis, astral projection, or clairvoyance."

Brooke frowned. This guy was a nut. He was going to discredit her work by linking it to mystics and other charlatans.

"Retrocognition is the opposite of precognition," continued Kumar. "You see past events instead of future events. The most famous case happened in the early twentieth century, when two women were visiting the Petit Trianon in Paris. They met people dressed in the costume of the late 18th century and remembered conversations with them. The Petit Trianon at Versailles was Marie Antoinette's private residence and these two women, who were both university scholars by the way, realized that they were remembering Marie's last days before her death by guillotine. It created quite a sensation."

"We're doing something altogether different here," said Brooke. "We're using science to get our results."

"Of course you are," said Kumar soothingly. "I didn't mean to imply that you weren't. It's possible that many people have glimpses of the past precisely because these memories are buried in their brains. You seem to have found a reproducible way to access the memories. No doubt you have felt that vague feeling of déjà vu in a place that you have never been in before? Most people have at one point or another in their lives. That's a form of retrocognition."

Brooke remembered the powerful feelings of déjà vu that she had experienced in Istanbul. Of course, she was a special case.

"Brooke, show Prof. Kumar your findings from Istanbul," said Hunter. Brooke opened her tablet and showed Kumar the same images that she had shown Hunter, including the map with all the dots pointing to the treasure location. She ended with the photo of the house that she believed stood over the site.

"Interesting," said Kumar. "Not a bad location. We could work with this." Brooke began to feel optimistic. Maybe she had misjudged Kumar. An archeologist could be the perfect team member for what she had in mind—digging up the treasure.

"Of course, I'll need more evidence before I can support this effort," said Kumar.

"I'm not sure what else I can do," said Brooke. She knew it had been too good to be true.

"Actually, I want to try the Memex for myself," said Kumar. After her initial surprise, Brooke found she liked the idea. One more person to confirm her experiences.

"You realize we don't have clearance from the University Review Board to test human subjects," said Hunter.

"Who cares about them? Always too conservative," said Kumar. "Both of you have used the Memex many times, have you not?"

"Yes, we have," replied Brooke and Chad nodded his head. "But…"

"And are there any ill effects?"

"None we can identify, but there is the matter of the animal deaths." She told him in detail about Robert's investigations into the cause of the brain tumors and about her own negative MRIs.

"It doesn't seem like many mice were affected. Mice don't live a long time anyway, do they? Couldn't they have just died of natural causes?"

"Possibly, I certainly hope so," agreed Brooke.

"I am only going to use the machine once. You have used it hundreds of times and are just fine. To tell you the truth, I want to be the third person to try this new invention. For an archeologist to be able to see into the past, I can't tell you how important this is going to be in my field. And I might be in on the ground floor."

"The institute lawyer will want you to sign paperwork," said Hunter.

"Lawyers are always slowing things down. I'm only going to be in town for a few days. We can't wait for some self-important suit to get around to talking to us. It's now or never. I won't tell anyone, it'll be just between us."

All eyes were on Hunter. After a moment, she said, "OK, you're on."

∞∞∞

As Kumar lay in the thrall of the Memex, he looked infinitely vulnerable. He appeared to be in a deep trance, unaware of his surroundings. As with everyone who used the Memex, he occasionally made a few small movements, a turning of the head, a readjustment of a leg or hand. But for the most part, he was inert, empty. Brooke realized that she must look like this when she used the machine. Somehow she didn't like the idea of Chad observing her in such a vulnerable state.

Kumar had pleaded to be "resurrected," as he called it, as his maternal grandmother, a woman he remembered fondly from childhood. Brooke had strongly opposed the idea, citing privacy concerns. Kumar had remonstrated that he couldn't tell if he was accessing an ancestor unless it was someone he knew. Hunter came down on Brooke's side and broke the impasse. Kumar didn't need to prove the ancestor theory. He just needed to know that he could access the past. If they sent him back ten generations, he ought to be able to tell that he was no longer in the 21st century. He had reluctantly given in.

"Do you think Kumar will really help us?" asked Brooke. Chad looked up from a blog he was reading on his mobile phone.

"I think he can't wait to help us. We have a great story, he won't be able to resist it. Especially after he sees for himself what the Memex can do."

"I don't know, he seems a little unreliable. He got enthusiastic easily. He could get bored just as quickly."

"Think about it. An archeologist is a born treasure hunter. Most of the time, he only finds pot sherds and arrowheads and other modest stuff. For him to have a chance at the kind of treasure you've told me about—what archeologist wouldn't jump at the chance?"

Brooke hoped so. Kumar was her last chance. What if the Memex didn't work for him? It could be that the buried memories degraded over time and Kumar was too old. Worse yet, they had only tested it on two people, and it might not work for everyone.

Kumar's eyes flickered open. He caught sight of Brooke and his face broke out in a broad smile. "That was amazing! Unbelievable! I was driving a wagon pulled by a camel, or to be more accurate, I was just sitting on a board at the front of the wagon and the camel lumbered along on its own. The wagon had bulging cloth sides of some rough material. It must have held hay. But I came into a big town, entirely different from today. There were no cars or motorbikes, no plastic or polyester saris. No advertising anywhere. I think it was Pune."

"Where's Pune?" asked Chad.

"It's in the western part of India, not far from Mumbai. I visited the university there once."

"So your ancestors lived near Mumbai. That makes sense."

"That was a fantastic experience. You two are going to be famous, you know. Wait until the world hears about this."

"You're not going to tell anyone, are you?" asked Brooke. "We're not ready to publish yet."

"No, no, no, don't worry. Your secret is safe. What I'm going to do is contact my foundation officer. I have a great relationship with him. I'll tell him that I found some references in an old manuscript that point to an important find, and he'll back me up. He gives me a lot of latitude and I never let him down. I'll look into buying or leasing that house on the site and maybe investigate some of the neighboring buildings as well. You'll see, it will all work out."

Chad climbed the stairs and walked down the hallway, pausing in front of apartment 302. He didn't know what kind of reception he would receive, and it mattered to him. He had thought of calling first, but she would probably say that he didn't need to come. Much better to just drop by. He knocked on the door.

After a pause, he heard her call, "Just a minute." He waited. Seconds oozed by. Abruptly, the door swung open and Brooke stood there, her hair tied back and a fleck of green paint on her chin. When she caught sight of him, her smile was genuine and welcoming.

"Come in," she said, and swung the door wide open. He stepped into the entrance way and noted the neat little kitchen to the left and the large comfortable living area to the right.

"I brought you this. I found it when I was unpacking." He pulled out a small enamel case, covered with hand-painted designs. An image of a peacock, tail feathers flaring, decorated the fitted lid.

"I forgot I bought this," said Brooke, taking the little case. She turned it over in her hands. "There was so much color and vibrancy in Istanbul. I don't suppose I'll ever go back."

"Why wouldn't you?"

"It's a long trip and expensive to get to. Istanbul will always be a special place for me but I feel like it has slipped into my past, never to be retrieved."

"You never know," said Chad. "If a place draws you, you may not be able to stay away." Chad noticed a card table set up in the living room. "What are you painting?" He walked over to take a closer look. The canvas showed a stately dining hall, with high ceilings and a long marble table set for more than fifty guests.

"This is one of the largest reception rooms in the Imperial Palace, where the emperor held state dinners," said Brooke. "The palace is gone now, almost completely destroyed over time. Garnett roamed through it on the day of the sack. I wanted to capture some of its beauty and grandeur."

On the canvas, Brooke had sketched an immense mural of a naval battle. The painting within a painting was almost hypnotic, drawing the viewer into the scene. Chad felt a pang of regret that he could never visit this world so dear to Brooke. On the other hand, maybe he could. All he would have to do is find an ancestor who had lived in old Constantinople. Since the city had more than a million people at the time of the Fourth Crusade, some of them were sure to be his ancestors. The practical problems with finding an appropriate person were, however, daunting.

"This is really good. I didn't know you had so much artistic talent."

"I enjoy painting, but I could never be an artist. I have to see something before I can paint it. I can't just conjure it out of my imagination. I had to go back to the same few minutes in Garnett's life again and again to fix this image in my mind. I may still have to go back to flesh out some of the details. I enjoy reliving that hour he spent wandering in the Imperial Palace. The rooms and hallways were endless, and golden mosaics were everywhere. I don't think anything like it exists in the world today."

Chad noticed several other canvases, some complete, others still in early stages. One showed a statute of a lion and a bull, wrapped around each other in a battle to the death. Another showed a beggar in front of a colonnaded building, his face and body hidden in a drab brown robe, extending a skinny hand in supplication.

"Would you like a beer?" asked Brooke.

Chad accepted and Brooke gave him a cold Molson from her refrigerator. "It's hard to just wait," said Brooke. "Do you think Kumar will come through?"

"I worry that he'll go ahead and we won't hear anything about it. I feel like neither he nor Hunter needs us anymore."

"Did Hunter say anything to you?" asked Brooke.

"She's out of town again. I haven't seen her since that last meeting when you were there." They fell silent, finding nothing encouraging to talk about. The insistent tones of "Don't Let Me Get Me" rang out and Brooke scooped up her cell from the coffee table.

"Hello." Chad watched her face as she listened to the unknown caller. "Really?" She began to pace around the room. "Yeah, sure, I think so. When?" Another pause, longer this time. "He's right here, I'll ask him."

She removed the phone from her ear and faced Chad. "Are you ready to go back to Istanbul? Kumar wants us to participate in the dig."

XXIX

IN THE TRENCHES

The insistent rapping of the jackhammer assaulted Brooke's ears as she swung a thick plastic bag filled with concrete debris over her shoulder. She staggered up a short flight of steps from the basement to a small landing. Opening the door, she stepped outside into the humid summer air. There were still more steps leading to the street, and Brooke doggedly climbed upward. It hadn't been hard to do earlier in the day, but the cumulative effect of repeated trips was beginning to test her endurance and her will.

She told herself things would get easier once the concrete floor of the basement had been completely removed and they could get their hands in the dirt below. When she had signed up for this dig, she had somehow imagined a broad, open site with the sun shining down and an army of archeologists digging happily. Of course, she herself had targeted a building on a narrow pedestrian street, with houses and shops crammed together on both sides. There were no parking lots, gardens, empty lots, or construction zones to be had. Kumar had made a generous offer to the unsuspecting owner of the building and all the residents had been remunerated and asked to leave. Now the building was empty as they began the excavation.

Brooke shifted the load to ease the strain on her back. The noise receded below her as she climbed. At street level, few people were about, just an old woman in a head scarf poking at the vegetables of a greengrocer's display and two young men marching by arm in arm. No one paid any attention to her or the hand cart that was parked nearby.

Hasan, a Turkish student whom Kumar had recruited for this dig, took Brooke's load and hefted it on top of an already overloaded cart, where it rested precariously. Hasan was muscular, with thick black hair, heavy eyebrows, and a prominent nose that gave his face strength and character. His thin gray T-shirt was soaked with sweat and clung to his broad, chiseled chest. He offered her a canteen of water that she drank from gratefully.

Hasan pushed the cart up the street towards a waiting pickup truck as Brooke turned back toward the staircase. She waited while Chad, an enormous slab balanced on one shoulder, ascended. He wasn't even breathing hard as he passed her, a smile lighting up his dirt- and sweat-streaked face. She descended into the bowels of the building, stepping carefully on the narrow treads. The basement gave off that underground smell that was part moisture and part dust, mixed in with the scent of small rodents.

There were still a distressingly large number of black plastic bags slumped on the floor of the basement. Cemile, the other Turkish student recruited by Kumar, was emptying a trowel of loose fragments into an open bag. She was short and clearly the weakest member of the team, so she had drawn the lightest duty. The construction worker had finished with the jackhammer and was winding up the electrical cord in preparation for departure. With great relief, Brooke removed the earplugs from her ears and experienced the world of sound again.

"You must take a break," said Cemile. "You look fagged out."

Brooke smiled at her choice of words but appreciated the sentiment. "I just want to make a few more runs," she said as she hefted several bags. With a pang of guilt, she picked the lightest one and headed back up the stairs. An hour later, Kumar showed up.

"Ah, this looks great," he said. "You guys are quick, very quick." To his credit, he pitched in and helped them haul the last of the debris up the stairs. Chad and Hasan drove off to the dump and Kumar joined the women in the basement.

"Now we must set out our transects in a rectangular grid," directed Kumar. Brooke and Cemile worked together to hammer stakes into the ground and tie nylon cord to the eyelets. They added a length of cord on the northeast corner as a plumb line and took GPS readings. The floor was beginning to look like a dig site and Brooke felt a new burst of energy. Kumar, somewhat slapdash most of the time, was a demanding taskmaster in the serious business of archeology and checked their measurements personally. By the time Chad and Hasan returned, they had just tied off the last line.

"What we should do next is use the ground-penetrating radar to get a reading on subsurface structures," said Kumar. "And we will get to that, but first I want to do something else. This is strictly off the record. We're going to take a quick look with the metal detector. Just sweep around and see what we turn up. We'll get to the systematic stuff tomorrow." Brooke had heard that metal detectors were treated with disdain by some arche-ologists, who associated them with amateur treasure hunters. Luckily, Kumar was as curious as she, and wanted to take a "sneak peek" at their site.

Chad took the metal detector and waved it slowly over the floor, roughly following the transect lines. He chose the All-Metal mode, suit-able for large buried caches. Kumar had brought a detector with a siz-able search coil to penetrate deeply into the ground. As Chad walked, the machine beeped and chirped in a desultory fashion. At one point, the signal sped up and Brooke glanced at Kumar's face for a reaction, but he was unmoved. The machine returned to its baseline pace. Chad continued with his patient scan while the others sat around on crates or boxes or directly on the earth. Camp stools would have been nice. No one spoke, all eyes and ears were on the metal detector.

As Chad crossed the halfway point, Brooke began to feel anxious. She squirmed on her crate, trying to find a better position on the rough sur-face. Still no change in the acoustical signal. When Chad neared the far corner, the machine emitted an explosion of sound. Kumar jumped up and smiled broadly. "Ah, that's what we want. Wonderful." Everyone was on their feet and exchanging encouraging words. The mood had shifted as quickly as fog lifts from a meadow in the morning sun.

Brooke was ready to roll up her sleeves and begin to dig, but it was late in the day and Kumar called a halt. Tomorrow they would collect data sys-tematically with the ground penetrating radar and begin the slow process of removing and sifting the soil. It would be a while before the hidden object lying in wait for them would be uncovered. As the others filed out of the basement, Brooke looked longingly at the spot on the floor where all her hopes might be fulfilled. Then she turned out the light and left.

That evening, Brooke found herself in Beyoğlu, a part of Istanbul she had never explored before. She and the other graduate students followed Prof. Kumar along Istiklal avenue, a wide pedestrian thoroughfare crowned with archways of festive lights. After a long walk, Kumar led them down a nar-row side street past raucous nightclubs and crowded cafes. A woman in a tight black sheath tottered by in red stiletto heels covered with rhinestones. She laughed loudly at some comment from her good-looking companion. The rap blasting from a restaurant sounded both Eastern and Western in an intoxicating blend, making Brooke want to hear more. But Kumar continued on at a brisk pace leading them to a destination only he knew about.

After leaving the dig site, they had gone to their lodgings, a lovely villa owned by a professor at Istanbul University. Kumar had managed to wrangle it for them while the owner, one of his many close friends, was on sabbatical leave. The villa was the nicest place Brooke had ever stayed, with its colonnaded entrance covered in bougainvillea vines, their small purple flowers bursting with color, and its high-ceilinged foyer paved with exquisite gold and brown tiles. Brooke had a large, comfortable room all to herself, with a queen-sized bed and a private bathroom in which she had scrubbed herself raw to remove the accumulated dust and dirt of the dig.

The group had dined at a restaurant serving native Uzbek food. Kumar had ordered six dishes to share without consulting any of his students. Brooke had gamely tried every new offering, enjoying the feeling of surprise in each exotic taste. She could not identify many of the items, but her experience with the Memex had emboldened her. Now, as she trailed along at the back of the group, the accumulated stresses of the day were wearing on her, her energy was dropping, and she wished they could just return to the villa.

Kumar, on the other hand, had boundless energy, and continued up the street at a brisk pace. A block further on, he halted and entered a bar. He led them through a curtain of thick red velvet unto a gleaming parquet floor.

"Wow, look at this place," said Chad. Brooke had to agree. It was sumptuous and beguiling, with an undeniable aura of mystery. The turquoise banquettes somehow fit in with the mustard-colored walls. A three-man band was setting up in one corner. Kumar chose a large round table and they all settled down and ordered drinks.

Before the conversation had a chance to emerge, the band started up and filled the room with sound. Brooke sipped her bitter drink and communicated in short bursts of shouted words, which trailed off as the futility of verbal communication became apparent. A waiter brought a plate of carpaccio and Brooke sampled a thin slice of lemony-flavored raw beef. Kumar urged them to take to the dance floor, which was rapidly filling up. Only Cemile rose and ventured out into the tangle of writhing bodies. Brooke downed more of her intoxicating brew, which was starting to taste a lot better. She sank back into her chair and relaxed, thinking about nothing, just taking in the sights and sounds.

Hasan leaned toward her and invited her to dance. She shook her head, saying she couldn't possibly, she didn't know how to dance to this music, but she wasn't sure if he could really hear her excuses. He persisted, his dark face with the striking black eyebrows and hawk nose revealing that he was not going to give up. After several attempts to decline, she gave in and took to her feet.

The room was hot and the music was fast. She began to get into it, feeling her body find a natural rhythm. The trials of the day slaked off and disappeared, replaced with a feeling that the entire universe was here and now. Hasan had some good moves and Brooke began to copy them. She danced to the edge of exhaustion and then danced some more.

The music paused and they returned to the table. Only Chad was there, looking put out and uncomfortable. Brooke felt so good she did not want to deal with anyone else's unhappiness. She sat down and ignored him. Hasan waved down a waiter to refill their drinks and made small talk with Brooke. Before long, the band struck up a haunting tune.

"You have to try this, Brooke," said Hasan. "It's the Horon, you'll be good at it. It's a line dance."

Brooke turned to Chad and said, "Come on, line dances are always fun."

"Not me," he replied. "You go ahead." His expression was so implacable that Brooke didn't try to dissuade him.

The dance turned out to be much more complicated than she had expected, but she stuck it out and enjoyed herself. When the music stopped and she returned once more to their table, Chad had sunk into a deeper level of withdrawal. She was unsure of the cause. He clearly didn't want to take part in the wild dancing and drinking, but it might be more than that. Was he jealous of Hasan? Brooke was not ready to get into a relationship with either Chad or Hasan, especially at this trying point in her life, but she felt a small frisson of pleasure at the thought of being wanted.

The next morning, Brooke volunteered to operate the Ground Penetrating Radar. She couldn't wait to get the excavation started and the GPR survey was a necessary preliminary. The unit was about the size of a lawn mower, with three wheels and a box containing the antennas nestled close to the ground. She pushed it along between two transect lines, keeping an eye on the small screen that was attached to the handle. Occasionally, traces that resembled diffraction patterns appeared on the screen and Brooke wondered what they meant. It had to be a good sign. Everything was being recorded digitally for later analysis, so her lack of expertise was not an impediment. Buoyed by optimism, she quickly completed the circuit of the basement.

Cemile exported the data to a laptop set up in one corner of the room and ran an image processing routine while Brooke looked over her shoulder. The analysis was slow and methodical, as research often is, and Brooke wanted to encourage Cemile to rush ahead, but she knew enough to remain silent.

"This is interesting," said Cemile. "These nested parabolas indicate a point source under the surface. The radar propagates downward in a conical pattern and reflects off buried objects to give this sort of output."

"Do you know what it is?"

"It could be a lot of things, two pipes crossing, a jar of coins, just a big rock, or even your treasure." Cemile mentioned the treasure with a slight smirk. "As long as the physical properties of the object are different from those of the surrounding soil, we can detect it."

"Where is it?" asked Brooke. She was disappointed by Cemile's skepticism.

"This one is near the southern wall." Brooke frowned. The metal detector had scored a hit close to the northeast corner, and that was the signal Brooke was most interested in. This buried object, whatever it was, was probably not metallic.

While Brooke and Cemile poured over two-dimensional slices of the subsurface images, Hasan ran the radar around the floor one more time, collecting a second set of data just to be sure.

"We got a hit in the northeast corner," said Cemile, "right where the metal detector went wild." Brooke's heart lifted. That could be it—her buried treasure.

"Show me." The pattern of lines was deeply folded, like bunched up cloth. Something big was in that spot. Kumar came over and looked at the output. "Good sign," he said. "Did you see anything else?"

Cemile showed him a few cross-sections that she had trouble understanding. He said they might be a buried wall, maybe the foundation of a building. Brooke felt sure they were the wall of the cistern, but she didn't say so. Cemile's skepticism had put her off.

They all took a coffee break while Kumar fretted over where to stake out the excavation trench. He ended by choosing a large area that covered much of the basement. It seemed that he didn't want to miss anything.

Hours later, Brooke was sifting through yet another tray of dirt. Her fingers were slightly sore from pushing the soil around the screen, separating out small rocks and other uninteresting solids. Her hands looked naked without their usual complement of rings. She knew she should wear gloves, but she liked the tactile sensation of raw dirt, and disliked the feel of the cloth dulling her sensitive fingers. Her nails were outlined in rich dark soil and some dirt had even worked its way into the creases of her palms.

She hadn't found anything of interest. The only object other than stones was a torn bit of Styrofoam cup that she had easily discarded and a coin minted in 1951. They were still working on the first 10 cm layer of soil. Brooke scooped up a sample with a flat-edged trowel and dumped it on the screen, dutifully sorting through it without much interest. To her surprise, she uncovered a bead made of a dark red ceramic, deeply etched with a cross-hatched pattern. It was pierced by a hole where a thread or chain had once held it. Who had worn it? Was it part of a bracelet or necklace? She showed it to Hasan, who told her to catalog it. She dutifully deposited the bead in a plastic bag and wrote down the location, depth, date of find and her name.

Brooke returned to her search with renewed interest. Although she had started this hunt only to find the cache that Damian had hidden, she was beginning to think that archeology in itself was a fascinating pursuit. The inherent fun of discovery was enough to compensate for the long hours of drudgery between finds. Brooke knew that Kumar believed in her treasure, but she recognized that he was hedging his bets. He wanted to have something to show for this excavation even if they never found what they were looking for and he had promised Brooke and Chad that they would be co-authors on one or more publications resulting from the dig. She wondered how a paper on medieval artifacts would fit in her resume. It would certainly add panache.

As her mind wandered, her hands explored in concert. The tip of her trowel jammed against something hard, no doubt another rock. She set the trowel aside and gently brushed dirt away from the unseen object with her fingers. A glint of white made her think this was no boring rock. She grabbed a small brush and began a careful excavation. Kumar came to see what she had uncovered. Bit by bit the object revealed itself to be a white ceramic tube elegantly curved. When it was fully extracted from the ground, Brooke could see a broken edge.

"This looks like the spout of an oil lamp," said Kumar. "Congratulations. It's our first real find." Brooke was surprised at how wonderful a tiny bit of broken pottery could make her feel. Sometimes you're looking for one thing and you find something quite different. Brooke continued to dig.

⸎

A month later, they had fallen into a routine of excavation, classification, and record keeping. Although the trench had grown steadily deeper, they still had not uncovered the tantalizing cache hinted at by the metal detector. One afternoon, Kumar wanted to focus on classification, a task that Brooke and Chad could not contribute to, so he gave them some time off.

A short walk along the hot summer streets took them to the Grand Bazaar, an immense covered market in the heart of Istanbul. As Brooke wandered through the maze of shops, she was overwhelmed by the kaleido-scope of wildly colorful displays of crockery, shoes, jewelry, spices, leather goods, and carpets. One merchant displayed exotic dates by the bucketful, another sold only white ceramic pipes with carved wooden handles. Above her head, an arched ceiling of gold and purple tiles stretched off into the distance. She idly picked up a bowl and examined it closely, running her finger along its intricately patterned surface.

"Funny," said Chad. "If we found something this beautiful in the trench, especially if it was in one piece, we would be so stoked."

"You're right. Here it seems ordinary, one of thousands. But it would eclipse anything we've found so far."

"The stuff we dig out is real, though, not some mass-produced knock-off."

"This is real enough to me," said Brooke. "But I know what you mean about the joy of finding something authentic hidden underground. It's a little like climbing a mountain. When you're the one who sweated and struggled to reach the top, propelled only by muscle power, the view is ever so sweet. But if you drive up the mountain in a car and catch the view at the top, it doesn't have the same punch."

As they continued to wander through the bazaar, Brooke thought about how lucky they were that Damian's shop had not been in this area. There would have been no chance of excavation in that case, at least not the sort of quiet excavation she was involved in. After many turns, she realized that she didn't know exactly how to get out. The labyrinth of alleyways lined with shops and cafes was enormous. She didn't see any exit signs either. The merchants would naturally prefer that people walk around for a long time rather than find an easy way out. It was almost like a lobster trap, easy to enter and hard to leave. She thought about asking Chad if he knew where they were, and surreptitiously glanced his way.

Chad didn't seem worried. He wore an expression of relaxed interest, his eyes roaming over the stalls. Brooke admired his profile, the straight nose and strong chin, giving an impression of rugged individualism. How easy it would be to slip into a relationship with him, to be supported by his strength and intelligence. But Brooke had visited an exotic city once before with a lover and that had ended badly. Her trip to Venice with Kevin had taught her skepticism. Romantic settings can cloud your judgment. She was determined to make it on her own and protect herself from disappointment.

She passed a display of slippers decorated in stripes of five different colors and picked one up, turning it this way and that. Clearly the merchandise here aimed to delight rather than merely fill basic needs.

"I wonder if people ever really wore things like that," said Chad.

"I'm guessing that they did. Most of the designs here came from the Ottoman empire rather than the Byzantine one I knew, but I can still see echoes of the old Constantinople in some of these items."

"People never really forget how to make beautiful things," said Chad. "If something is lost, it's because it was superseded by a better choice. It's an evolution of ideas, where the best ideas survive into the next generation and the worst go extinct."

"I guess that would make us searchers for extinct ideas," said Brooke. "To tell you the truth, I'm rather enjoying all this archeology. I can see why people become amateur archeologists." She would rather label herself as an archeologist than a treasure hunter.

"How does our treasure compare to the stuff we see here? You never really described the treasure in any detail."

"For one thing, our treasure has a number of heavy items of solid gold, such as plates, chalices, reliquaries and necklaces. Real gold has a sheen and solidity that can't be matched by gold-plated nicknacks. It's like nothing else in the world. It mesmerizes you with its rarity and beauty. There's also a large number of precious gems, some loose and some in gold or silver settings. But the largest part of the stash is what came from the church. Father Scholasticus entrusted Damian with two large bags and five clay pots, well stoppered."

"What was in the bags?"

"I don't know. Damian, honest as he was, never opened them. He just dutifully buried the bags alongside his own without ever satisfying his curiosity. I don't know what's in the clay pots, either, but it must be valuable or they wouldn't have gone to all that trouble."

"We'll find out in good time." Brooke felt a flush of warmth at his words. His support and especially his willingness to embrace her wild plan was just the thing she needed to keep her faith strong. No one gets anywhere alone, thought Brooke, and right now, she didn't feel alone.

The trench stretched from one end of the basement to the other, a broad scar on the earth. The team had worked with precision, leaving steep sides and a flat bottom four feet below the surface. Chad was beginning to feel like a miner who never sees the light of day. The dank, rough walls of the basement, unbroken by windows, upper corners filled with cobwebs, felt like a prison. He had a nagging cough brought on by the dampness and his interest in archeology was quickly evaporating. Earlier, the smallest bit of broken tile or antique button had been a cause to celebrate, but now these humble finds were just an annoyance. Another useless artifact to bag and tag.

Not that there hadn't been some interesting discoveries. He fondly remembered the Arabian lamp, which looked as if it could have housed Aladdin's genie, that he had excavated with a small brush. It was scratched and dented, but it was still a marvel. Most of the finds, however, had been more modest—a comb, an iron wedge, old nails, broken cups and dishes, and a few worn coins. All this detritus from the past was carefully cataloged and crated, in the hope that some theme might emerge from these leavings. So far, none had.

There had been some excitement when they uncovered the stone wall. It was deeper than the walls of the current residence and clearly of earlier architecture. It ran almost perpendicular to the trench, and cut across it to the south. Brooke said it looked a lot like the wall of the cistern under Damian's residence, but she couldn't be sure. It was disappointingly ordinary, with nothing to indicate it was the exact wall they sought.

Cemile had worked at dating the finds and estimated that they were now at or below the 1100 AD level. At least they wouldn't have to go much deeper. It was already a chore to lift dirt over the lip of the trench all day long and climb in and out again and again. Any expansion was likely to be in the horizontal direction.

"I've got something," said Brooke. Chad could hear the excitement in her voice. She was working at the bottom of the trench at the "X" spot, the nickname they had given to the location pinpointed by the metal detector. He dropped his trowel and came to stand across from her, watching her gingerly remove soil. Cemile appeared at the top of the trench, face expectant. Hasan soon joined her. All eyes were on Brooke as if she were a surgeon performing a delicate operation that they had come to observe.

The soil under Brooke's hands was discolored, slightly reddish. As she swept it away, the red zone grew in size and darkness. Hasan shot Cemile a worried glance that Chad intercepted. Brooke was focused on her task and oblivious to those around her. Slowly, carefully, she exposed a hard surface, rust colored and pitted. Chad's heart sank. Not gold or silver, but common iron. Brooke looked up with pain and disappointment in her eyes.

"Here, I'll help you finish," said Chad. He retrieved his trowel and worked around the edges of the buried object, going for speed rather than delicacy. Keeping busy kept despair at bay. Hasan walked away, even though this was clearly the largest object they had yet uncovered.

"Tough luck," said Cemile. "I really thought you would find it."

"We might find it yet," shot back Brooke. "Just not at this spot."

By now they had almost finished removing dirt and could identify the find as a rusted anvil. It was cracked and clearly non-functional. Still it was surprising that it had not been melted down for its iron content and reformed into something else. After they had removed most of the surrounding soil, they rocked it and dislodged it from its resting place. Together they lifted it over the lip of the trench and set it on the floor.

Brooke looked at Chad from her sweat-streaked face, eyes dull with disappointment.

"Don't worry," he said. "I have an idea."

XXX

CHANGE OF PLAN

Brooke's cell phone chirped at 3 AM. She emerged from the depths of sleep, disoriented and stiff, wondering what could be happening. As she groped for understanding, the events of the preceding day crashed down upon her. She had failed. There was no buried treasure and she had led everyone on to extraordinary effort and expense for no gain. She didn't know how she would ever recover from this debacle.

Nevertheless, she eased out of bed and set her cell on flashlight mode. There was just enough light in the room so that she could dress in blue jeans and a black knit top. A quick trip to the bathroom to relieve herself and brush her teeth made her feel almost human again. Chad's idea was far-fetched, but what else did she have to go on? Her own ideas had not led anywhere. It was time for a change of plan.

Brooke left the bedroom and walked softly down the hallway of the villa, trying for absolute quiet. Her eyes were well adjusted to the low light level, and she avoided side tables and an old-fashioned coat rack, whose outstretched arms were a bit creepy at this time of day. The front door opened quietly when she turned the knob and stepped out under the portico. Chad waited for her at the base of a short flight of stairs, hands in his pockets, looking relaxed.

The cab they had called pulled up a few minutes later and took them off into the night. Nothing stirred in this residential neighborhood of fine old buildings, not even one of the stray cats so typical of Istanbul. Traffic picked up as they reached a major thoroughfare and crossed the Galata bridge into the heart of the city. Brooke had not seen Istanbul at this early hour before, and found it deeply alluring, rising up on gentle hills before them, the lights of a vessel on the Golden Horn twinkling in the distance.

The cabbie left them at the top of the street, as near as he could get to the dig site. After paying the fare, Brooke and Chad walked down the narrow alleyway, past businesses tightly shut up for the night, their awnings rolled up securely, their windows dark. No sign of life came from the residences. They descended into the basement and rooted around for the metal detector, which, unused for many days, had ended up behind some crates and camp supplies. Brooke led the way up the stairs into the cool night while Chad followed, hefting the detector.

Brooke opened the gate to a courtyard adjoining their building and stepped inside, scanning the environs. Seeing no one, she signaled Chad to join her. The courtyard was a large open space, paved with cobblestones, with a picnic table in one corner and trees and potted plants along the side. Scraps of white paper and discarded tissues clung to one edge, unnaturally bright in the moonlight. Brooke wished the space were larger, so she might have a better chance of finding her treasure.

Chad's idea made sense. Counting steps had inherent inaccuracies and the treasure, while not in the basement, might be close by. They should widen their search to include the area around the house. On the other hand, it would be unwise to draw attention to their activities. If the detector started beeping madly while onlookers were around, they could have some unwelcome company. They might even have thieves trying to get to the treasure before they did.

To Brooke's surprise, Kumar had agreed to their plan without hesitation. While he condoned it, he didn't want to be out here in the deepest part of night himself. Brooke had not filled Hasan and Cemile in. Cemile's skeptical attitude annoyed Brooke and she didn't care to expose herself to any more veiled ridicule.

Chad had taken the lead in the courtyard and was patiently walking back and forth, sweeping the detector head before him. Brooke kept watch, examining the windows of the neighboring buildings and the alleyway next door. A half moon hung just over the rooftops, shedding scant light. It was quiet, and even though Chad had the volume set at a low level, Brooke could hear a desultory crackling coming from the machine, more static than signal. Chad completed the search without a strike, and Brooke's shoulders slumped. She waited impatiently while he double-checked, thinking it was a waste of time. The second pass was also negative and they left the courtyard, snapping the gate shut behind them.

Brooke strode out onto the street, checking for activity. The street was only about twelve feet wide. It was much more likely that the treasure was under one of the buildings that loomed above her than under the cobblestones, if it existed at all. Occasionally, a car would pass the intersection at the top of the hill, its lights alarmingly bright, its motor abnormally loud, but none stopped. Chad came up beside her.

"Time to check the street," said Brooke.

"What's the point? We can't dig it up. I guess this was a bad idea."

"Let's not give up just yet. We're here. We might as well be thorough. Otherwise, when we think back on this night, we may wonder what we missed and regret it."

Chad did not look particularly mollified, but he went along. He covered the area in front of their building and the two neighboring structures with no success.

"We can go further along the street," said Brooke.

"You don't give up, do you?"

"No."

Chad moved further afield, sweeping the detector head back and forth, occasionally glancing up to look for pedestrians. Brooke frowned worriedly. She wondered what insanity had led her to this point, standing on a deserted street in a foreign city in the dead of night, hoping for the impossible. She heard footsteps in the distance and saw Chad stop, lifting his head to listen. A lone man appeared at the bottom of the street, and, to Brooke's dismay, he turned and headed in their direction. He looked like he was wearing a uniform. Was he a cop?

Chad nonchalantly left the street, carrying the metal detector as if it were the most natural thing in the world to be doing at four in the morning. He and Brooke ducking into the courtyard just before the man passed their position. Over her shoulder, Brooke saw him slow, but not stop. He wore a dark uniform, but he wasn't a cop.

When all was quiet, Chad resumed his search. He had covered most of the roadway. Brooke shivered in the cool night air, wanting this to be over. Exhausted, she began dreaming about the warm bed waiting for her back at the villa. Her thoughts were interrupted by the sputtering of the metal detector. She had never heard it sound so strong and rapid. All need for sleep vanished and she was instantly by Chad's side.

"We got it," he said. "We found it, Brooke." The machine beeped madly.

He held out his arms and she moved into his tight embrace. He clasped her hard, crushing her breasts against his chest, and swirling her around. He set her down and smiled like a man who had just won the lottery. Brooke pushed away the tiny doubt the niggled in her head, the demon that told her this was another false lead, and decided on hope. She also decided she liked the hug.

"Let's get our bearings," she said. Brooke was tempted to check the GPS location, but she knew from her geocaching experience how inaccurate that could be. Forgetting about any onlookers, they sighted against a window frame in a building on one side of the street and the doorknob of a greengrocer on the other. Their hit was on a direct line between the two. Brooke paced off the distance from the target zone to each point of reference as well as to the front door of their building. After all, she had a lot of experience with pacing.

"This changes everything," said Brooke. "Time to report back and get going in a new direction. We have a treasure to find."

Although he had only slept for four hours the night before, Chad felt energized and ready to tackle the day. He was finishing up a breakfast of scrambled eggs, sausage, and toast in the kitchen of the villa with Kumar and the other three graduate students. He loved Turkish food, but there was nothing like a taste of home to help ease over the stresses of living in a foreign country. As prearranged, Brooke would tell everyone about the new data when they were in that post-meal relaxation phase and hopefully more receptive to new ideas. Chad sipped his coffee and waited.

"Chad and I discovered something last night," said Brooke. "We took the metal detector outside the building and searched the grounds when there was no one around. We got a huge signal from a large buried metallic object."

"Excellent," said Kumar. "A new lead—just what we need."

"Where was it?" asked Cemile.

"Unfortunately, it was down the hill in the middle of the street," said Brooke. Chad saw the broad smile on Kumar's face dissolve into a worried frown.

"That's complicated," he said. "I suppose we could get permission to dig up the street. It's not that busy. But, to tell you the truth, the red tape around here is stifling. It would take months, maybe years, to get through the process, longer than we have. It may also require generous 'incentives' to local officials. Unfortunately, it's a no go."

"There is another way," said Brooke. She hesitated, letting the pause build expectations. "We could tunnel under the street from the basement. It's not that far."

"Get out," said Cemile. "That's totally crazy."

"No it's not. People dig tunnels all the time. It doesn't take great skill."

"Even if you could dig a tunnel, wouldn't it be illegal to take artifacts from under the street?"

"Just a minute," said Kumar. "We're not trying to find this treasure to sell it on the black market. This is archeological research. Anything we find will end up in a museum, not lining our pockets. I wouldn't worry about the legality, just the practicality. It is a pretty wild idea, but, who knows? It could work."

"What if the street collapses into the tunnel? It could be really danger-ous." Cemile seemed determined to kill the idea. "I once read that the street next to the Berlin wall was in danger of sinking because of all the tunnels drilled underneath it."

"This will only be one tunnel, not like the Berlin wall," said Brooke, "and we can make sure it's deep enough not to undermine the pavement." While Brooke continued to press her case, Chad pulled out his smart phone and searched the internet for info on the Berlin wall tunnels.

"Here, I have something," said Chad. "It looks like they give tours of the tunnels these days. Listen to this:"

> "Altogether, we have counted 71 tunnel projects and 20 per cent of those were successful," said Dietmar Arnold, the head of the Berlin Underworlds Association, which conducts tours and works on opening more subterranean structures to the public.

"I can't find anything about the street being compromised, even after those 71 tunnel projects."

During the discussion, Hasan had been quiet, attending to each speaker, but not taking sides. Now he jumped in to support Brooke.

"It sounds like a good idea to me. We haven't had a lot of luck so far. The stuff we excavated is OK but not outstanding. I think it's worth the risk."

"That's settled then," said Kumar. "We start today."

Brooke raised her trowel to jab at the wall of dirt at the end of the tun-nel. Dislodged soil rained down onto the small pile that she had built up through strenuous effort. The dusty air tickled the insides of her nostrils and she suppressed a sneeze. Now that the tunnel was fifteen feet long, maybe it was time to add a fan. Brooke was pleased with their overall prog-ress, but yesterday they had hit a patch of hard-packed clay laced with stones and now the going was slow.

The tunnel was 2 feet wide by 2 ½ feet tall, small enough to be structur-ally sound and resistant to collapse, but big enough to allow a person to dig while sitting or kneeling. Brooke had grown used to being confined by the rough walls of dirt after many days of excavation, and feelings of claustro-phobia had abated. It was easier for her to tolerate the tight quarters than for Chad, with his larger frame and greater height. Only she and Chad worked on the tunnel. The others were needed to continue the routine excavation. She doubted that Cemile would lend a hand anyway.

The beam from her miner's lamp played over the wall as she moved her head, revealing the surface of a large stone. She hoped it was not boulder-sized, or they might have to veer around it. She scraped the soil away from the stone, prying at it with her trowel, trying to dislodge it. Her back hurt and she longed to stretch out her aching muscles. She moved her backup light, an electric lantern that rested on the floor of the tunnel, to make more space for loose soil.

A few minutes later, she had had enough. She twisted herself around to sit facing the side wall of the tunnel. To her right was the pile of dirt she had just created and to her left was the empty bin they used to haul the dirt out. The bin rested on a flatform truck that Brooke had bought at Carrefour, a local department store. The truck was a low pallet equipped with four large gimbaled wheels. The handle folded into an indentation on the surface of the pallet, a feature ideal for Brooke's purpose, since the handle could be stowed out of the way. She filled the bin with soil and rocks. This excavation was much quicker than an archeological dig since she made no effort to sift for artifacts or protect them from harm.

Once the bin was full, Brooke began the crawl back to the basement, pushing the flatform truck ahead of her. Makeshift knee-pads protected her from the worst of the rocky floor. She passed under several shoring structures made of plywood and two-by-fours that braced the top of the tunnel. It was like crawling under a series of tables, their feet resting on small plywood squares to prevent them from sinking into the dirt floor. The truck's wheels occasionally caught on small projections, or bumped against the plastic air tube that ran along the bottom edge of the tunnel, but she managed to force the wheels around or over and keep making forward progress. It was a feeling of great relief to reach the end of the tunnel and be able to stand again. Brooke stretched her tired muscles and looked around for Chad. He was perched on a camp stool playing a game on his smart phone. When he noticed that she had emerged, he hopped up and helped her dump out the dirt. In no time, he clipped a line to the truck, got down on his knees and crawled into the tunnel, pulling the truck behind him.

As Chad disappeared down the tunnel to take his turn at digging, Brooke tied up the heavy duty plastic bag filled with dirt. Hasan was busy with the box sifter and Cemile was at the computer. It didn't look like anything exciting had been found while she was underground. She hauled the bag upstairs and into the courtyard. She and Chad were distributing the dirt around the house, not overloading any one floor. There was too much of it to leave in the basement. She wasn't looking forward to the clean-up when they either returned the dirt to the tunnel or took it to the dump.

While she waited for her next turn at tunneling, she decided to step outside and enjoy the fresh air. The street was busy today. A family of tourists, a young couple with a small boy in tow, walked uphill, looking lost. They stopped at a sidewalk vendor selling roasted chestnuts and made a purchase. Rain earlier in the day had left the air feeling clean and moist. The little boy aimed for the puddles left behind, managing to hit every one despite his mother's best efforts.

Brooke's eyes were drawn to that magic spot down the street, her goal. It looked so ordinary, nothing special. She imagined Chad under the street, advancing at a glacier's pace toward it, with pedestrians walking over his head. She estimated that he was about two buildings down the street, still five or six feet away from the target. A niggle of doubt struck her. They had been careful in setting the direction of the tunnel, taking compass readings and measuring distances, but even a small error could nudge them in the wrong direction and cause them to miss the target. She had to do something about it.

Back in the basement, all was quiet and routine. She settled down to wait for Chad to emerge from the tunnel. A few minutes later he appeared, hair streaked gray with dirt and face black with smudges. Brooke involuntarily ran her fingers through her own hair, wondering how bad she looked.

"I was just outside trying to imagine how far we've gotten," said Brooke.

"I hope we're almost there," said Chad. "This is getting old."

"Truthfully, I'm not sure. What if we miss it by inches?"

"Then we'll just have to dig to the right and the left until we find it."

"Sounds haphazard. I have a better idea."

For the second time, Brooke and Chad made a nocturnal visit to the dig site. Although it was the deepest part of the night, the area was illuminated by a nearly full moon that cast long, eerie shadows on the empty street. As they exited the cab and walked down the hill, Brooke glanced around at the surrounding buildings. No lights in the windows, no evidence of activity. Good.

Once in the basement, Chad extricated the Ground Penetrating Radar unit from behind some boxes and rolled it over to the exterior door. It was ungainly and heavy. He held the door open with his shoulder as he started dragging it upstairs into the quiet night. Chad pulling mightily on the handle while Brooke pushed the base upward to clear the treads. It took some time, but they managed to arrive on the street without mishap. Two men were advancing up the hill. They looked curiously at her, to her annoyance. She opened the gate to the courtyard and she and Chad retreated inside.

Chad pushed the unit into a far corner and turned back toward Brooke. "What are they doing?"

"Just walking. If we're lucky, they'll keep going." Brooke moved back into the shadows and waited a minute. Hearing nothing, she tentatively advanced to the gate and peeked out. The men were gone.

"Let's take the GPR outside and look for the tunnel. That's what we came for," she said. She wasn't going to be spooked by some strangers. If anybody asked her what she was doing, she would answer in medieval Greek. Not a living soul in all the world spoke the dialect but she.

They maneuvered the unit around to the front of the building and positioned it where they expected the tunnel to be. Brooke turned it on and watched the small screen come to life. Last night, she had searched the internet for information on how to interpret GPR traces. To her surprise, she found a site on using GPR for military and security purposes. There was an image of a hand-dug tunnel along the southern US border, a set of folded lines, not quite symmetric, somewhat uneven. That was what she looked for now on the small screen affixed to the GPR's handle.

Their tunnel wasn't hard to find. Brooke followed it along the street as she descended the hill. It stopped a little uphill of the greengrocer. While Chad stood over the end of the tunnel, Brooke searched for a trace of the treasure and found it without difficulty not six feet away. Its image was also irregular, a good sign. A buried pipe gives a very clean, smooth, symmetrical trace, in accordance with its geometrical shape. But the treasure, a collection of diverse objects in random orientation, should give an irregular signal, and that's what she was seeing. It wasn't proof, but it was encouraging.

The target was offset from the path of the tunnel, just as she had suspected. If they had continued to dig blindly, they would have missed it.

Chad pulled out a compass and oriented on Brooke, who stood directly over the treasure. "If we redirect the tunnel by 28°, we should intersect it," he said.

"Good thing we checked," said Brooke. They lugged the GPR back into the basement and called a cab to take them to the villa. Brooke was exhausted, but pleased. She had a good feeling about this. The reward was within her grasp. Just a few more days to go.

Brooke sat in the basement finishing off her dinner, a sandwich of kaşar cheese that she had bought at the local deli. It was after midnight and Hasan and Cemile had long since left. Prof. Kumar had grown impatient over the last few days and hinted that this would be their last week at the site. Chad was in the tunnel, scraping away at the never-ending wall of earth. Using the GPR a few nights earlier had seriously disrupted her sleep cycle. Now she and Chad were working from noon till two in the morning, pushing hard to finish the digging.

The damp in the basement weighed down on her and she shivered. She put on a windbreaker and zipped it up, stuffing her hands in the pockets. It seemed that Chad was taking longer than usual. She considered pulling out her cell and checking her email, but she didn't feel like writing to anyone at the moment, and email would surely demand writing.

The truck trundled out of the mouth of the tunnel with Chad close behind. He rose wearily and dusted himself off. "I hit a wall, literally. I think this is going to be trouble."

"What do you mean?"

"I uncovered some stones fitted together with mortar. I don't know how big it is yet."

"We didn't see anything on the GPR. It can't be very big."

"If the properties of the wall are the same as those of the surrounding soil, it might not show up on the radar. Why don't you come in and take a look?"

Brooke got down on her hands and knees and crawled into the tunnel, Chad close behind her. She adjusted the miner's lamp on her forehead to point straight ahead. The tunnel now had a slight dogleg where they had altered its direction. The light from the backup lantern was just visible around the bend, a welcome beacon at the end of the musty passageway.

When Brooke arrived, she didn't see anything unusual until Chad pointed out a section near the bottom of the wall. He was right. There were three flat stones that had been chiseled into shape, glued together with a dark mortar. Brooke ran her fingers over the rough contours.

"Damn. Everything was going so well. I guess it couldn't last," she said. "We'll just have to keep exposing it and see how far it extends."

As she spoke, a deep rumble sounded and Brooke felt the earth tremble beneath her. She looked at Chad with alarm. "An explosion?" he said, with uncertainty in his eyes. The next shock was worse. They bounced off the floor of the tunnel and suffered a rain of dirt dislodged by the shaking. They made eye contact and with one mind looked toward the exit. Before they could twist around in the tight quarters, the third shock, much stronger than the first two, struck. Brooke was launched into the air like a flea whipped off the tail of a dog. She struck her head on the roof of the tunnel and blacked out.

XXXI

BURIED

As she crawled up out of unconsciousness, Brooke wavered in that twilight world between sleep and wakefulness. She had suffered a terrible nightmare about the tunnel collapsing. She had just found the treasure but now no one would ever see it. Her old boyfriend, Kevin, was there with a jackhammer but he was ignoring her, too busy sightseeing in Istanbul to care that she was in trouble.

She groaned and her eyes flicked open to reveal the curved wall of soil that formed the side of the tunnel, at once both familiar and startling. Why was she sleeping in the tunnel? Then memory flooded into her like peroxide in an open wound, burning as it went. Bile rose in her throat and fear gripped her belly with an iron hand.

"Brooke, how are you? Are you OK?" Chad's voice was steady and low, a calming influence.

She looked left to find him, face streaked with dirt, a thin line of dried blood along his temple, probing her with his eyes.

"Nothing's broken, I'm OK. How long was I out?"

"Not long. The tunnel's blocked. I've been working on clearing it."

Brooke noticed a pile of dirt by her side and a wall of crumbling soil behind Chad, a frisson of fear electrifying her whole body. How much of the tunnel was blocked? She quickly mastered herself and pitched in, tossing the dirt by her side further back into the tunnel.

"What do you think happened?" she asked.

"Maybe a bomb?"

Brooke wondered if anyone would come to their rescue. It was late at night and no one was in the house. They couldn't count on help. Her whole body shivered as she internalized the extent of their predicament. There was no telling how much of the tunnel had collapsed.

Before her fear ratcheted out of control, Chad said, "Come on, let's dig. We can get this done." He turned toward the blockage and started burrowing. Brooke moved the loose dirt further along the tunnel, forcing her fear-stiffened body to comply. They got into a rhythm of slow and steady progress. Sharp little thoughts floated into her mind, urging her to cry, to flail about, to scream for help in her terror and despair. She damped them down and returned her focus to the task at hand. She listened to Chad's breathing, smelled the not-unpleasant tang of his sweat, and felt the gritty, moist soil in her hands. She stayed in the moment, pushing away the demons that kept trying to shanghai her mind. She had to be calm, logical, contained. It was the hardest thing she had ever done.

Her head throbbed and both arms ached, but she kept going. Chad was a steadying presence, cool and contained in this crisis. If he could bear it, so could she. She thought about losing the light, and a fresh wave of terror engulfed her. Her headlamp was blazing strongly, and so was Chad's. Besides, she had insisted on a backup light, a short fluorescent that sat on the floor of the tunnel and shone brightly. She turned it off to conserve power. Reaching into her pocket, she fingered the two spare batteries that she always carried as a priest might touch a crucifix to bolster his faith.

The digging seemed to go on endlessly. Brooke thought about death. She had so much to do yet in life. For one thing, she had to get her doctoral degree. She wasn't about to let it all end here. Chad paused in his labor and smiled at her reassuringly. He took her hand in his and squeezed. She pressed herself against his side and felt comforted. She could do this. It wasn't over yet.

Chad had been pumping his arms like an automaton, attacking the wall of their earthy prison. A tall pile of loose soil had formed in the passageway beyond where Brooke sat. They should have broken through before now. Chad imagined the entire tunnel filled with debris, all the way from the basement entrance to the point where they huddled near its end. They might never be able to clear it.

He had to keep a positive attitude and banish these defeatist thoughts. He was a black belt, and that identity buoyed him. He visualized himself tying on his belt, crossing one end over the other and forming the knot in just the right way. It was a symbol of his bravery and dedication, qualities that he would need now as he fought for his life. To fortify himself, he began to count to himself in Japanese—ichi, ni, san… How many times had he counted his way through punishing routines—a hundred kicks, a hundred punches, fifty pushups? He had learned how to keep going and go he would.

Having Brooke by his side made it all possible. He shivered to think how hard it would be if he were alone. Those first few moments after the cave-in when she had been knocked out had been a taste of hell. Not knowing if she was alive, he had frantically searched for a pulse, finding it weak and uncertain. He wasn't sure she would wake up and he couldn't bear to lose her. Then she stirred and it was as though he had been given a second chance at life.

The air in their little space had grown hot and Chad's mouth was parched. The heavy labor had left him with a painful thirst. His mind conjured up images of a tall glass of ice water, a slice of lemon on top, the sides glistening with fat droplets that occasionally slid down the sides, leaving sinuous trails. How long did it take to die of thirst? At least a few days. It must be an awfully painful death.

The desire to stretch out seized him and he squirmed unhappily. If only he could stand up and relieve his cramped muscles.

⚭

Brooke lay nestled against Chad's side, his arm around her shoulder. They had taken a short break to catch their breath. Despite his sweaty and dirty state, she was happy to be pressed up next to him.

"It won't be long now," said Chad.

"How close do you think we are?"

Chad pointed his headlamp at the pile they had just created, but it was hard to assess its size in the shadowy light. "Minutes away, just minutes."

Brooke was skeptical, but she beat down a retort. Everything depended on belief—if they lost faith in their own salvation they would stop trying and surely perish.

They got back to work, falling into a now familiar rhythm of dig, lift, toss, repeat. She thought of the odd craze in Victorian England of supplying bells on gravestones. A rope ran from the inside of the coffin to the bell so that a person accidentally buried alive could alert the mourners above. How she longed for a rope to pull to let people on the street above know she needed help. She supposed that the Victorians supplied a breathing tube as well. She looked for the air pipe that ran along the floor of their tunnel, but it had vanished.

"Chad, where's the air pipe?"

"Hunh? Air pipe?"

"Yeah, it's s'posed to be right there."

"God! It's blocked." Chad began to dig in the corner of the tunnel, like a terrier searching for a bone. How long would it be before they ran out of air? Brooke imagined a calculation involving the volume of space around them and the rate of consumption of oxygen per person, but the equation was fuzzy in her head. It was too hard for her.

Perhaps they should abandon the attempt to find the air pipe and instead work on punching a hole through the roof. It was only about seven feet to the surface. The pavement above would be a challenge, but they had a small, hand-held pick that might be up to the task. She wished she had thought of this earlier. If they changed gears, could they dig that air hole in time?

"I found the end, but it's plugged with dirt," said Chad. He ran his finger into the pipe, trying to clear it, but only succeeded in pushing the blockage deeper. He frantically tore away more soil from the top of the pipe.

"Hand me that chisel and lump hammer."

"Whaaat?" Brooke passed him the chisel but couldn't think what a lump hammer was.

"The thing that looks like a small sledge hammer," said Chad.

Brooke handed it over, listlessly. Chad held the chisel to the pipe and bashed it with the lump hammer, a glancing blow without force. He lined the tools up and tried again, this time breaking the seal on the flexible pipe and severing it. He jerked the loose end of the pipe upward. It was clear. He pulled Brooke to himself and, cheek to cheek, they huddled at the end of the pipe, breathing in the cool, life-giving air. Nothing had ever felt as good as the oxygen flowing into her mouth, down her throat, and through her tortured lungs.

When they were sufficiently recovered, they sat in the tunnel, gathering their strength. "That was weird," said Brooke. "I couldn't think straight."

"I wonder if it was oxygen deprivation. Did you ever read about the hikers who climb Mt. Everest? The low oxygen reduces their mental acuity to the level of a five year old. That's probably why one in four die on the mountain."

Brooke didn't want to think about dying. "Let's get back to work."

⸙

They resumed their punishing routine, straining muscles, squashing fears, just getting on with it. Occasionally, they changed position to give Brooke a turn at the wall of debris, clambering past each other in the narrow space, elbows hitting stomachs, and knees poking into faces. At length, Brooke regained her optimism. It was just a matter of time before they would clear the obstruction. They had plenty of air. If they were still here in the morning, their crew would show up and rescue them. She checked her cell phone and saw that it was 4:43 AM. If only she had bars, but cells don't work underground.

"I got it!" shouted Chad. A faint glimmer showed at the top of the plugged passage. As Chad scooped dirt away, the glimmer grew into a dim light, then a gaping hole. Brooke felt a wash of relief and swept away the soil with new vigor. It wasn't long before they had the passage half clear. Chad wriggled forward over the mound of remaining dirt, with Brooke close behind. They crawled into a shored-up section, beneath a plywood-reinforced ceiling. The bend in the tunnel was just yards away when the next tremor struck.

A waterfall of dirt pouring into the space before them as they huddled under the plywood, clumps of unseen debris thumping on the wood above their heads. Before Brooke's horrified eyes, the two-by-four posts holding up the plywood began to shift, creaking under the strain of tons of material. It was like being in an abandoned car about to be crushed to a pancake at the junkyard. Brooke shut her eyes and curled up into a fetal position. With a groan, the framing settled into position, askew but stable, and the tremor abated. The height of the tunnel had been reduced to only two feet, the left side lower than the right.

Panting, Brooke sought out Chad. He seemed surprised to be alive. They stared at each other mutely, until she said, "Where's the air line?" She wasn't about to make the same mistake twice.

"Right here." Chad pulled out a Swiss Army knife and cut the line on the floor.

"Why didn't you use that before?" asked Brooke.

"Give me a break. I was cognitively impaired. I saved you, didn't I?"

"You did," she said with a smile.

They set to working on the new obstruction, a tough job in the squeezed down tunnel. Brooke flashed back to being Julia, hiding under a table to evade her family's killers, afraid, uncertain, and helpless. But Brooke wasn't helpless—on the contrary, she poured herself into her task, refusing to think, resolving to act.

Fifteen minutes later, they had carved out a narrow opening. This time, Brooke made the breakthrough and led the way forward. She could see the light in the basement, framed by the rough end of the tunnel. It was almost within reach. She scurried on her hands and knees, heedless of the stones ripping her flesh, until she covered the last stretch and emerged into the blessedly open space.

At that moment, the earth shifted again, and the roof of the tunnel gave way, catching Chad half in and half out of the entrance. He was knocked flat on his face, his legs buried under dirt and debris, only his torso clear.

"My God, are you alright?" cried Brooke.

"Help me."

Chad could do little to dig himself out. It was all up to Brooke. She worked feverishly, clawing at the dirt with her bare hands, drawing on reserves of strength from her exhausted, overworked, sleep-deprived body. Water gushed from a broken pipe and spilled onto the basement floor, pooling in the excavated trench, ruining it. After clearing the dirt near Chad's body, Brooke could see that he was pinned beneath a broken section of shoring.

"I'll lift. You try to get out." She pushed upward while he wriggled to free himself, but it was no use. She changed tact and dug around the piece of shoring, looking for a way to dislodge it. Water, cold and menacing, seeped into the knees of her jeans as she knelt on the floor. She looked over her shoulder in alarm, and saw that the pit was full and the basement was flooding. She jumped up and turned toward the pipe that was spewing water into the room.

"Don't leave me," cried Chad. His words echoed in her mind, the same words that Theodoret had uttered to Julia, as he lay trapped in a burning building, about to die. An icy finger of fear ran down Brooke's spine.

"I would never leave you. We have to stop the flooding." Brooke ran across the basement, climbed up on a crate that shifted ominously under her weight, steadied herself, tore off her shirt, and tried to stuff it into the end of the pipe, but the force of the gushing water was too great, and she failed. She returned to Chad and slammed her bare shoulder into the shoring, again and again, uselessly.

"The water's rising fast," said Chad. He had propped himself up on his elbows, his back bent, his hips pressed to the ground by the wood and debris above him. His eyes had the wild look of a bear caught in a trap.

Brooke scanned the basement desperately. She spied a length of flexible plastic tubing, cut from the piece they had used to construct the air hose. She brought it to Chad and said, "If the water gets too deep, you can breathe through this."

He grabbed one end of the seven foot line while the other end flopped into the water and started to sink. Brooke needed something to keep the end afloat. A Styrofoam lid from a cooler was floating in the water, near to hand. Brooke seized it and splashed around until she found the roll of twine they had used to mark off the excavation so many weeks ago. She tied one end of the air hose to the Styrofoam and gave the other end to Chad. Now the free end of the air hose would float on the surface, rising as the depth increased.

The rising water might help her, she thought, by increasing buoyancy and dissolving soil. Archimedes flashed into her head. What had he said? "Give me a lever long enough, and a fulcrum on which to place it, and I shall move the world." Where could she find a lever?

Chad watched Brooke as she splashed around the basement. She was his only lifeline. The water was up to his chin and rising fast. He saw her struggle with the rusted iron anvil that they had excavated, lugging it toward him. What was she doing? Water lapped into his mouth. He spit it out and sucked on the end of the pipe, biting down hard, deforming it into an oval, sealing it with his lips. Now he couldn't talk. Brooke deposited the anvil by his side and went back for something else. Water got into his nose and burned its way down his throat. Pinching his nostrils with one hand, and holding himself up with the other, he could just barely keep his eyes above water. The last thing he saw was Brooke coming toward him with the metal detector. Then he slipped below the surface.

He lay flat on his stomach, concentrating on the air line that had become his whole world. He opened his eyes and wished he hadn't, the burning was so intense. With eyes shut tight, he focused on breathing, not too fast, not too slow. He could sense, rather than see, something happening next to him, something shifting and swirling. Water seeped in around his lips and pooled in his mouth. He swallowed and stifled a cough. This makeshift air hose wouldn't protect him for long. He felt doomed.

Abruptly, the weight above him lessened and he scrabbled forward, digging his elbows into the mud. Before he could escape, the weight returned and caught the back of his calves. He lost the air hose before he could draw a deep breath. The weight pressed upon his lower legs, mercilessly. His chest hurt. He needed air. He must not breath the water. He must not. The weight lessened again and he freed himself, rising like a whale breaching in the ocean, gulping in great breaths of fresh air, shaky on his legs, gloriously alive.

Brooke, a jubilant smile animating her face, threw her arms around him. He held her in a bear hug, lifting her off her feet in the waist-deep water. As he let her go, their eyes locked, speaking worlds. Her tousled hair lay on her bare shoulders, her chest covered only by a sassy red bra. The shirt she had tried to stuff into the pipe was nowhere to be seen.

The basement door flew open. "Oh no! Everything's flooded!" cried Hasan.

"But they're alright. See, I told you they would be fine," said Cemile.

Kumar waded through the water to Brooke and offered her his shirt. "Come on, let's get out of here while we can," he said.

Brooke was the last to leave the basement. She looked back at the end of her dreams.

⸙

Three days later, Brooke stood upon the narrow balcony of the Galata tower, the Queen of Cities spread out before her. She and Chad had just enjoyed dinner in the restaurant that now inhabited the top of the tower. On this side of the Golden Horn, in a similar tower closer to the water's edge, Garnett had stood a thousand years ago, a triumphant soldier who had fought his way to the top, literally. Brooke remembered the great chain that had once spanned the harbor, the chain that the crusaders had lowered to allow their fleet access to the vulnerable section of the wall.

Today the northern walls were gone, but the city, every bit as eternal as Rome, lived on. The Hagia Sophia with its added minarets could be seen atop a distant hill, not far from the Blue Mosque, an addition since medieval times. Brooke was saying goodbye to Constantinople and to the ancestors she had come to know so well. Her quest was over. A treasure hunt is a seductive thing, and you have to know when to quit. The turning point had come for her and she was abandoning the search for Damian's stash.

The earthquake that had rocked the city and buried them underground had done remarkably little damage to the city as a whole. It had survived for centuries in this geologically active part of the world and would, no doubt, survive for many more. Brooke thought about the last few moments in the basement, when Chad had been submerged under the rising water. She had tried to use the metal detector as a lever and the anvil as a fulcrum to free him, but the hollow handle of the metal detector had kinked under the strain and become useless. Desperate, she grabbed a long handled shovel and used it to lift the debris just enough so Chad could wriggle out.

At the villa, the dishes had shaken and rattled, and a vase had toppled from a table in the hallway, spilling water and cut flowers across the floor, but only Cemile, suffering from insomnia, was awake to witness these events. She later apologized profusely for not thinking about Brooke and Chad in the tunnel. Her overtired mind had failed to perceive the danger. It wasn't till the others woke that Kumar hurried them off to the dig site to check on Brooke and Chad.

Brooke had forgiven Cemile. As she stood on the balcony, she put thoughts of her ordeal behind her. In fact, she had never been happier than she was at this moment. Life was about the simple pleasures—the kiss of sunshine on bare skin, the fleeting touch of a cool breeze, the majestic beauty of a two-masted gulet on the harbor, sails spread to the wind. Striving after an elusive treasure at the risk of their lives was not the path to happiness that she had previously supposed. Happiness resided in the simplest moments, when she felt alive and open to the glories of the mundane.

Most of all, life was about love, that secret ingredient that elevated any experience from ordinary to magical. Since the accident, she and Chad had been enjoying the city, visiting the museums, the cafes, the Turkish baths, and the ancient ruins. She wanted to be with him all the time and felt diminished when they were apart. He stood next to her now, gazing out over the Golden Horn, his hair ruffled by the light breeze. His hands, broad and strong, gripped the handrail lightly. She wanted to place her hand over his, but was finding it hard to make the first move. They had known each other for such a long time, and she had sent clear signals that all she wanted was friendship.

"What will you do next?" he asked.

"I suppose I'll get a job, like Hunter suggested. I'll have to work nights and weekends to finish my degree, but it won't be so bad. At least I'll be safe."

"I worried about you taking all those chances, but part of me was also secretly curious about what would happen."

"So you didn't really care about me?" she said as the corner of her mouth twitched upward.

"I always cared about you," said Chad with mock seriousness. "But I never really believed you would get hurt. You're like a force of nature, with too much energy and determination to be thwarted. I saw you as invulnerable."

"Well I wasn't invulnerable during that cave-in. If you hadn't saved me..."

"We saved each other."

Brooke realized the truth of his statement. She and Chad had functioned as the perfect team, each had the other's back. But they would leave Istanbul at the end of the week, and the circumstances that had thrown them together so intimately would evaporate. Brooke decided not to think about that. She would just enjoy this moment.

⸙

On another day, all Chad's attention would have been on the harbor before him, but the presence of Brooke by his side was all-consuming. He snuck glances at her hair, falling to her shoulders in lush soft curls, a glint of gold earring peaking through from time to time. He had never seen the light green dress that she wore, its thin straps leaving her shoulders bare and the tops of her breasts exposed. She had always been beautiful to him, but distantly beautiful, like a picture in a museum that you could not have for yourself. Now something had changed between them, something he could feel but not identify.

There was no denying her brilliance, at once both attractive and scary. He wasn't sure he could ever achieve as much as she, and his pride bristled at the thought. It was all very well to admire Brooke from afar and pretend that he wanted her, but when faced with a real opportunity, he was reluctant to take the next step. If he stayed with her long term, would he always be second best—the one who has to take the accommodating job as she found a high profile position?

She had never seemed to be interested in him before, except as a friend. But since the accident, everything had changed. Now she listened closely to anything he had to say, asked questions and encouraged him to elaborate. She was softer, less driven, more relaxed. The last few days of vacationing had been a golden time, thrilling and rewarding, and he didn't want them to end.

Small boats danced on the harbor in the late day breeze.

"Do you like sailing?" he asked.

"I've never had the chance to find out."

"I can see you hanging over the side of a sailboat, balanced on the brink of capsizing, pushing for speed." Chad turned toward her, one hand still on the rail of the balcony.

"And would you be next to me?" She faced him and held his eyes with hers, a slight smile playing around her lips.

"I would be at the tiller. Somebody has to steer."

"You don't see me at the tiller?" One eyebrow rose in a challenge.

"Oh I do, just not all the time. We would take turns."

"I'd like that."

This was his moment. He circled her waist and drew her close, she coming to him willingly. Chad never did anything half way and his kiss was hard and insistent. She returned it with the same level of buried desire and pent-up want. Her soft body was pressed firmly against his, her breasts crushed against his chest, a delicious feeling. The kiss went on for a long time as they got to know each other in a new way. He was not disappointed.

She and Chad ascended the front steps of the villa, hand in hand. Purple bougainvillea, delicate and bountiful, climbed up the white columns of the portico. They were alone in the house, just as Brooke had hoped. The conversation flowed easily, with no need to fill in awkward pauses or plaster over missteps.

Chad took her to his room and Brooke examined it curiously. Inviting someone to your private space is a form of self-revelation, a way to let them get closer to you, and it can be risky. The bed was made, with the light covering slightly askew. A jacket was slung over the desk chair. The only thing on the floor was a pair of shoes, one overturned. No suitcase or other evidence of the temporary nature of his occupancy. The decor, of course, came with the villa, so she couldn't deduce anything from the abstract landscapes in pale colors.

Chad removed his cowboy hat and set it on the dresser, next to a box of chocolates. "Would you like a little dessert?" he asked.

"You seem well prepared."

"I wouldn't want to be without chocolate. That first bite sends a real jolt through you." He lifted the lid and selected a small round candy with a swirled pattern on top. "Open your mouth."

Brooke obliged and let him place the morsel on her tongue. As she bit down, the juice of a cherry exploded in her mouth, and her body responded with a rush of pleasure. Before long she was in Chad's arms again and they continued where they had left off on the balcony. Her passion built as they kissed and explored each other. She ran her hand down his long back and over his hips, pressing herself against him. He began to unzip her dress and slide the straps off her shoulders.

In Brooke's mind, a little tingle of apprehension was mixed in with the urge to continue. It had been a long hot day and she wanted to shower before going any further. The well-appointed villa had a private bathroom off this bedroom. Why not make it part of the dance?

"I would really like a shower," she murmured. "How about you? Want to join me?"

She enjoyed the air of mischief and discovery as they undressed each other. His chest was lean, with well-defined muscles and strong shoulders. She fed the tongue of his belt through the big silver buckle and unzipped his jeans, which strained tightly against his erection.

In the shower, the feel of his soap-slick hands roaming her body was intoxicating. The water poured over his head and dripped in long strings from the ends of his plastered hair. His kiss was rough, and she welcomed the feel of the late day bristles against her face.

"I bet they didn't do this in the 12th century," he said.

"No, they never had the pleasure." Brooke thought that she had never had this sort of pleasure before either, in any century. She had never known it could be this good.

It was a brief shower, since both wanted to move on to the bed. He was a sensitive lover, watching for her reaction as he tried first one thing and then the next. He murmured "Anything you want, baby." So she showed him what she wanted and she got it. Later, after they were both satiated and in a lazy daze, she snuggled next to him contentedly. Nothing could ruin this moment of post-coital bliss, a moment that stretched on and on.

Her eyes fell upon something on his night table. She couldn't believe it.

"Where did you get that?" she demanded, sitting up in bed and letting the covers fall from her chest. He rose up on one elbow, sleepy-eyed, and followed the direction of her gaze.

"Why, is it important?"

"Totally."

XXXII
LAST CHANCE

B rooke sank her trowel into the loose dirt with great energy. She dug rapidly, now that she was near the target zone. The team had judged the old tunnel to be a complete loss and started a new one a few feet away from the first. She didn't know where Kumar had found the funds to keep them going, but she was grateful that he had.

Although the flood had subsided from the basement, two feet of water still covered the bottom of the excavated trench, making archeological work there impossible. Hasan and Kumar had pitched in on the construction of the new tunnel and they made rapid progress. Everything was easier this time around. Brooke and Chad were experienced in construction and in better shape. The new tunnel was straight as a laser beam and tightly shored up all along it's length, reinforced with double-thickness posts set on strong footings.

The tunnel was brightly lit but still exuded an air of menace, at least to Brooke's wounded psyche. It had taken all her courage to go down into this hole again after her harrowing experience, but the pull of the past was strong. For her own sanity, she had purchased a portable compressed oxygen apparatus intended for miners and wore it on her back as she worked.

They had instituted other safeguards this time round as well. Only one person was allowed in the tunnel at a time, and another was always in the basement ready to spring to the rescue if necessary. Aftershocks were still possible even though several days had passed, and who knew how stable the surrounding earth was now that a section of it had collapsed? They had to be prepared for anything.

She and Chad had moved into a bedroom upstairs, sleeping on blankets spread over the floorboards. They worked twelve hour shifts, trading off with Hasan and Kumar, so that there was always someone toiling in the tunnel. Despite the intensity of her workload, happiness infused her in every moment. She and Chad stole the time to make love, against all obstacles of weariness and circumstances.

Seeing the little glass dragon on Chad's bedstand, the fiery breath issuing from its tiny mouth, had jolted her into recognition. This was the bauble that Florian had made for Julia and presented to her at an awkward dinner party close to one thousand years ago. Brooke remembered holding it in her hands and admiring its workmanship. Julia must have taken it with her when she returned to her father's house after Florian's death. Chad had come upon the dragon while they were desperately trying to extricate themselves from the collapsed tunnel and absently slipped it into his pocket. Later he had set it on the end table and forgotten to tell her about it. Ironic that the most significant object they had found had not been carefully photographed in situ, measured, and labeled, as good archeological practice would have warranted, but rather tossed idly to the side and ignored for days.

Now she knew that they were in the right place. This was undoubtedly the site of Damian's workshop. Of course, that didn't guarantee that they would find the treasure. It could have been reclaimed from the earth many years ago.

By her reckoning, Brooke was almost upon the hidden cache indicated by the metal detector. The memory of the anvil occasionally floated to the top of her mind, and she worried about another disappointment. It could just be buried pipes.

Her blade clunked against something hard, and she scraped away at it, probably a rock. But this obstruction seemed flat and without a visible edge. She accelerated her efforts using both trowel and her free hand to wipe away the soil. It looked like two bricks mortared together. As she continued to work, she uncovered a section of wall, old and crusted with whitish deposits. Damian had lined his treasure hole with bricks. These could be the same ones, but she wasn't sure.

She hurried back to the basement to retrieve some tools, pushing the half-filled cart before her. Chad and Hasan were absorbed in a conversation and Kumar was reading a book. She knew she should tell them about the find, but didn't want any interference at this point. This was her show, and she didn't feel like sharing. Kumar might insist that they follow proper procedure, including photographs, measurements, and such, but Brooke had no patience for that just now. She was burning to know.

She gathered up a chisel and hammer as well as a crowbar. Kumar hardly looked up and made no objection, even when she didn't empty the dirt and take the cart back in with her. As she crawled down the tunnel, her heart pounded loudly in her ears. She attacked the wall with as much fervor as any crusader fearing the bite of burning oil from above. The edge of a brick disintegrated under her assault and she was able to get a purchase for the crowbar. She pried out the crumbling brick and loosened its two neighbors. She uncovered some old brownish fabric and paused. If this was really the treasure, she didn't want to damage it. Carefully, delicately, she widened the space and ran her fingers over the ancient material. The fragile cloth tore and Brooke picked up a metallic glint with her head-lamp. Probing tenderly, she withdrew the object still partly entombed in its shroud.

Folding back the scraps of cloth, she beheld a gold tiara, studded with emeralds, looking as clean and polished as the day it was made. She remembered that day, for this was not the first time she had held this treasure in her hands. This was Damian's hoard, preserved and untouched all these centuries, waiting for his descendent to arrive.

The thrill of discovery coursed through her veins. All the effort, the pain, the suffering that she had endured, all the uncertainty and sorrow, had led her to this moment of pure joy. Her fingers wandered over the tiara, feeling it's perfect lines and graceful curves. She longed to tear into the rest of the cache, to hold each precious item in her hands, but she restrained herself. She should share this discovery with her team.

Intending to set the tiara on the cart, she twisted around to look for it, but remembered that she had left it in the basement. Nonchalantly, she set the tiara on her head, where it fit perfectly, and crawled out of the tunnel.

Kumar was the first to notice her when she emerged.

"I found it," she exclaimed, in a voice made hoarse and low by excitement. She lifted the tiara from her head and held it out to Kumar.

For once, he was speechless. He examined the delicate piece with reverence. Chad and Hasan came over and all four of them huddled together, admiring the prize.

"It's gorgeous," whispered Chad. "Do you think it belonged to Damian?"

"I'm sure of it," said Brooke. "I remember him making it." Everyone started talking at once, a babble of happy voices, congratulations, whoops, and cheers.

"I knew you could do it," said Chad, draping his arm around Brooke's shoulder. Brooke broke down in tears, consumed with a bittersweet joy, remembering Damian and all that he had suffered so that she could have this moment. Her vision blurry, she wiped her face, but then gave up and just let herself weep. Chad hugged her and blessedly didn't ask any questions. She was safe in his arms.

Everyone was there, staring at the display spread out on the tables before them. The treasure had been meticulously removed from its hiding place and brought to the basement for sorting.

Brooke was most affected by the items that Damian had made. His elegant style was apparent in the tiny gold bell with the pearl clapper, the golden spoon never meant for eating, and the ring in the shape of two linked hearts. The pendants, bracelets, earrings, amulets, and brooches, all of a style long ago abandoned, were still of universal appeal and loveliness. Kumar had commented on how rare it was to find so many examples of work from the same artisan. In this case, Brooke could tell him how each item was made and who the client was.

More opulent and massive were the items once owned by the church. Brooke ran her fingers over a heavy crucifix suspended on an equally heavy chain. Unlike the examples she was used to, this Christ figure writhed in agony, cords popping out in his neck as he strained his face heavenward. A golden chalice ringed with opals and rubies seemed large enough to hold a quart of wine. But amongst all the candlesticks, gold platens, and precious rings, one piece stood out—an ornate bishop's scepter. It was over six feet tall and weighed more than sixty pounds.

"I bet that belonged to the Patriarch of Constantinople," said Kumar. Brooke tried to remember if she had ever seen him. Damian usually attended a smaller local church and not the Hagia Sophia.

"He must have been stronger than bishops are today if he trucked this around," said Chad.

"Just about everyone who lived then was stronger than we are," said Brooke. "The clothes of the nobility were pretty heavy too, by the time they added all the precious gems and other jewelry. It wasn't easy being a bishop."

Chad pulled out his calculator and plunked away at it for a while. "If we melted down the scepter just for the gold, it would be worth more than a million dollars."

Kumar looked at him with mingled disgust and suspicion.

"Of course, it's priceless as it is," amended Chad.

The sheer amount of gold on display was dazzling, a rare sight in any era. Brooke could feel the deep pull of the immutable metal, its siren song that had led so many to evil and corruption. She knew intellectually that money was not the key to happiness, but it was devilishly hard to believe that. She felt a shiver of apprehension at her own mercenary thoughts.

"When will we open the clay jars?" asked Cemile.

"I called the director at the Istanbul Archeological Museum," replied Kumar. "He is, of course, truly astounded by what I told him. We're going to have full cooperation and the services of his Chief of Restoration. They have a climate-controlled space that we can use to protect the fragile contents. You don't know what's in there, Brooke?"

"Not a hint. I saw the jars looking pretty much the same as they do now. Maybe they're a little duller now. I'll be as surprised as you."

"I bet it's something really big," said the ever-optimistic Kumar. "Something worth waiting a thousand years for."

They waited a thousand years and three days, while Hasan worked with the curatorial staff at the museum. Brooke wanted to be there, felt she had a right to be there, but Kumar overruled her. The museum had strict procedures and Hasan had the training needed to handle ancient artifacts. She had to be content with waiting until he came home each night and reported on his progress.

The jars contained old manuscripts, written on parchment scrolls that predated the Fourth Crusade by many years. Experts at the museum were in the process of using carbon dating to get a better reading on their age. They had promised to push all other work aside because this project excited them. Hasan had taken digital photographs of each page as the scrolls were slowly unrolled. The text was in Latin, a language that he had studied in depth in college, and he was working on the translation. To Brooke's chagrin, he wouldn't give her even a hint of what was in the scrolls. He said he wanted to have a complete picture before revealing anything. To be sure, he appeared to be deeply absorbed and using every available moment on the translation.

When Hasan was ready, he called everyone into the kitchen. As they took their places around the table, little was said. Brooke was tense, her overwrought imagination throwing up daring ideas, but secretly fearing disappointment. Chad looked relaxed, lounging in his chair, limp as an octopus, but Brooke knew him well enough to realize that this was how he dealt with stress. Cemile sat rigidly upright with her hands clasped before her, head forward, expectant, while Kumar faced the situation with a broad grin, unwilling to believe in anything but an exceptional outcome.

"First of all, the manuscript is entitled *Primum Ludæorum Romani Bellum*," began Hasan. "It is a history of the first Roman Jewish War that began in 66 CE, written by one Gaius Andronicus. The document details the unrest that simmered in Judea for many years, and the often brutal actions taken to suppress the Jews. Things came to a head when a group of Jewish rebels attacked Roman officials in Jerusalem and overwhelmed the garrison there. King Agrippa II, a Roman puppet, fled with a small band of supporters to

Galilee. When Rome heard of the insurrection, the emperor sent an army from Syria to put down the revolt and punish the rebels."

"I've never heard of this war," said Brooke. "Is it well known?" She wondered if they might have discovered a new bit of history. Hasan had the air of a performer about to astound his audience. Something must account for his suppressed excitement.

"Actually, we know a lot about it from the Jewish historian, Josephus." Hasan looked annoyed that he had been interrupted. "Just be patient and I'll get to the good part."

"The Romans were defeated at the battle of Beth Horon. Rome reacted as they always did, by sending an enormous army to pound the rebels into submission. General Vespasian and his son Titus led four legions into the Levant. They crushed everyone in their way until they arrived at the gates of Jerusalem and there got bogged down in a siege that lasted for years."

"The Roman engineers dug a great ditch around the city to isolate it and trap the hundreds of thousands of people inside. They ringed the city with an earthen wall just as high as the walls of Jerusalem. Every day, desperate people tried to escape, but most were intercepted by the Romans. Anyone caught was crucified. Their crosses were lined up along the top of the earthen wall where the Jews could see them. On some days, five hundred souls suffered this slow and agonizing death." Brooke imagined a endless line of crucifixes, dark against the setting sun, and shivered inwardly.

"In 70 CE, the Romans breached the walls and captured the city, burning and looting as they went. Titus marched back to Rome triumphantly, bringing with him immense wealth and 40,000 Jewish slaves. Those slaves were put to work building the Colosseum."

"Is that what's new in the document?" asked Chad.

"No, we already knew that," said Hasan. "At least most of us did." He looked at Chad patronizingly. "Wait, it's coming. The most interesting part is the introduction."

"In the years before the war, uprisings against Rome were common. Andronicus cites four different rebel leaders. One was Simon of Peraea, a slave of Herod the Great, who gathered a group of followers and burned down the palace in Jerico. He overran other royal residences until Gratus, the leader of Herod's infantry, opposed him in battle and won. Simon was beheaded."

"A second rebel, named Athronges, together with his four brothers, was only defeated after a long struggle. The third rebel, Menahem ben Judah, the son of Judas, battled against King Agrippa II, but was ultimately betrayed by one of his own people." Hasan paused and glanced around the table, clearly relishing his moment. "Let me read my translation of the next part verbatim."

And there arose a powerful sorcerer, Yeshua of Galilee, who gathered a large following from among the poor and wretched in Judea. It was said he could cast out demons, raise the dead, and turn one loaf of bread into thousands. Unlike the other rebels, he did not openly take up arms against Rome, but officials grew uneasy as the rabble who followed him multiplied, and centurions disguised as Jews were sent to watch him.

In one sermon, Yeshua said, "One day the Word of God will be heard even in Rome." Such sedition could not be tolerated. A military leader who could raise the dead and feed an entire army with one loaf of bread would be a fearsome opponent. Yeshua was arrested, tried, and sentenced to death by crucifixion. His supporters did not raise a hand to defend him.

Brooke was stunned. Here was a Roman author talking about Jesus Christ in the most unflattering terms, as if he was an evil sorcerer planning an armed revolt.

"Whoa," said Kumar. "This is enormous. We're going to be famous. There are very, very few mentions of the historical Jesus outside of the gospels. Some people even believe he never existed. This is confirmation of parts of the Jesus story."

"Are there really people who doubt that Christ lived?" asked Brooke.

"There are a few," replied Kumar. "But they are dead wrong. There is more evidence for the existence of Christ than there is for Alexander the Great, and nobody doubts him. But that aside, we have something really big here. People will be talking about it for years."

Brooke felt a warmth flow through her. This discovery, so unexpected, was just what she needed at this point in her life. Thank you, sweet Jesus.

∞

The air of restrained excitement in the room was electric. The press had been given just enough information to make them hunger for more. Kumar had wheedled the use of a conference room from Istanbul University as a professional courtesy, even though they weren't involved in the dig. Maybe they hoped for some reflected glory from the announcement. Brooke saw CNN, the Associated Press, Reuters, and the Wall Street Journal, along with representatives from local news services such as Hurriyet and the Anadolu agency. The front of the room bristled with microphones, tended by harried technicians running sound tests, and the back was crammed with oversized cameras and over-bright lights.

Erasmus Drake, the president of Brackett University, was preening at the front of the room. He had flown in yesterday with Prof. Hunter to take part in the press conference. Brooke had never met him before today. She frowned at the thought of him stealing credit for her work. The university had done nothing but stand in her way, and now that success was at hand, they acted as if they had been her biggest supporters.

Drake was kitted out in a hand-tailored suit with a red silk tie. His monogrammed white shirt was clipped at the wrist by silver cuff links. From the shine on his Italian shoes to the three hundred dollar hair cut, he was the image of the new breed of overpaid and over-privileged CEOs. Wasn't the university supposed to be a non-profit organization?

At least Hunter looked the part of the dowdy faculty member. Her hair was a flat black color that looked painted on, mostly untamed and too dark for the age of the face it enclosed. She wore an extra long skirt of some coarse material with unflattering horizontal stripes. But she had congratulated Brooke sincerely on her great find. Praise from Hunter was all the more precious for being so rare.

Brooke had some misgivings about facing the press. What if they asked her how the Memex worked? She still could not explain it, or give a reason why she could access memories throughout the entire life of an ancestor, instead of only up to the time the next generation was conceived. It would be many years before she learned the truth. Luckily, she didn't need to know in order to file for a patent. It was amazing how quickly the university lawyer had filed upon hearing about her discovery.

It was ten minutes past the time set for the conference to begin and the audience was visibly edgy. Unable to drag things out any longer, President Drake took the microphone. He ran through a prepared speech on the importance of scientific research and described the discovery in the most general of terms. Brooke could see the Wall Street Journal man wriggling in his seat and the woman from the Associated Press looking at her watch. When Drake finally wrapped it up, he asked for questions. Hands shot up all over the room.

"Yes, the gentleman in the green shirt," said Drake, pointing to a bald guy waving his hand vigorously.

"Can you tell us how much the treasure is worth?" Drake deferred to Kumar, who took the microphone.

"We have cataloged 34 artifacts of various types and sizes—jewelry, gold plates and decorative items, as well as church treasures, all manufactured in medieval Constantinople. Any one of them alone would be an amazing find. When you add in the historical manuscripts, the value appreciates even more. Of course, none of this will be sold on the open market. It is part of our world cultural heritage, but if we did sell it, it would be worth more than 20 million dollars."

Another reporter asked, "Is this the only document that mentions Jesus Christ other than the gospels?"

"Actually, there are a few scattered sources from ancient times. The Jewish historian Josephus mentions him twice and the Roman senator, Tacitus, refers to him as well. Some scholars believe certain passages in the Talmud are about Jesus, but that's controversial. You have to realize that the early church wanted to control information about Jesus. Irenaeus of Lyons, in about 185 CE, declared that there were only four true gospels, those of Matthew, Mark, Luke, and John, just as there were four corners of the earth and four winds blowing over it. All other gospels, of which there were many, were suppressed. This new find is unique in that it gives more than a passing reference to Christ's life and ministry. It describes the miracles of raising the dead and feeding the masses with a single loaf of bread."

The next question came from a heavyset Turkish reporter. "How old is the manuscript?"

"Using carbon dating, we estimate it was written in 122 CE with a margin of error of 16 years. That makes it one of the earliest sources about Jesus. We don't know how it survived but I have my suspicions. Constantine was the first Christian emperor of Rome. In the manuscript, Christ is quoted as saying, 'One day the Word of God will be heard even in Rome.' I think Constantine took this as a prophesy of his reign. When he built his great city in the east, he brought the manuscript to Constantinople and it was kept in the archives all those years. The people of Constantinople regarded themselves as Romans right up to the time the city was captured by the Turks in 1453."

Brooke wondered if she would ever get a chance to say anything. Drake and Kumar seemed to be dominating the press conference and leaving her out completely. She needn't have worried, since the next question was aimed squarely at her.

"What does it feel like to use the Memex?"

Brooke took the microphone and to her surprise, felt no anxiety at all. Whatever had made her fear public speaking in the past had vanished. "It's a feeling of total immersion in the life of another, being inside their body but not their mind. All your senses are alive and you experience a new world, or rather, the world as it once was."

"Are they any side effects?"

"None." Brooke said it without qualification, not wanting to open the door to doubt.

"Have you accessed any famous people?"

"No. We're still in the early stages of experimentation and have not targeted specific people from the past. If we can locate descendents, then we will be able to explore their famous progenitors. But some celebrities, like Mark Twain and Amadeus Mozart, have no living descendents and we will never be able to walk in their shoes." Brooke did not realize that they had indeed accessed one famous ancestor, one they had not recognized, but it would be a while before she figured it out.

"Can anyone use the Memex?"

"Anyone who has ancestors," replied Brooke. A chuckle went through the room. Brooke beamed. There is no better feeling for a public speaker than making your audience laugh.

"Will we be able to send someone back to the time of Jesus? Someone who knew him?"

Here was a question she had to handle carefully. "We have not gone back further than 1173. We don't know yet how far back we can go. The memories might degrade or disappear at distant times. Then there would be the difficulty of finding the right ancestor. In truth, everyone alive today probably has an ancestor who knew Jesus, just because of the enormous number of paths of inheritance in the eighty or more generations since his time. But picking the right one would be an enormous challenge."

Drake stood up. "I think that will be all we have time for. I want to thank you for coming." The group clapped and made haste to leave. This was a great story and they all wanted to get it on their websites.

"Wonderful job," said Chad, coming over and giving Brooke a hug. "You handled that like a pro. I think you may be doing a lot of these in the future." Brooke hoped so. She knew she could do it, and with all the potential uses of the Memex, she would have a lot to say for a long time to come.

On their last day in Istanbul, Brooke and Chad toured the Archeological Museum near Topkapi Palace. An eclectic mix of many eras and cultures, the museum reflected Istanbul itself, a city at the center of history. The Byzantine artifacts drew Brooke in, since she now identified them with her family. She eyed the statues from Greece and Rome and thought of them as people she might visit.

Chad halted at a statue of Apollo surrounded by his four muses and Brooke had to admit it was arresting. The god stood bare-chested in a provocative pose with a garment draped over his legs but not his hips. His arm was raised high over his head to pluck a harp. Brooke wondered whether the feminine posture was her twenty-first century interpretation or the original intent of the artist.

While Chad examined the group of statues, Brooke thought about the week to come, when she would appear on The Daily Show and grant interviews to the Washington Post and the BBC. The international attention had reaped some unexpected rewards. Prof. Hunter had called the National Institute of Health and convinced a program manager to advance funds for exploratory research based on their results. The money would support Brooke for the final year of her doctoral work. Her degree was now within her grasp.

Robert had emailed yesterday with congratulations and some news of his own. Based on data from five universities, he had shown that Muripellets, the food they gave their mice, produced an abnormally high rate of brain tumors. Robert had convinced the University Review Board that the Memex was not the cause of the mortality. With that and the negative results from the psychological testing of the mice, the Board had finally granted approval to test human subjects. Robert had put out a call for volunteers. Sorting through them would be another task awaiting Brooke upon her return.

"Are you ready?" asked Chad. Brooke nodded and followed him into the next gallery, the one they had saved for last.

Spread out before them in gleaming glass cases was the treasure that they had given to the world. A manikin dressed as the patriarch of the Eastern Orthodox Church held the golden scepter in his hand and wore a heavy gold cross on his breast, a dramatic centerpiece to the collection. The manuscript with the history of the First Roman Jewish war was unrolled to the passage about Jesus that had generated so much interest. A placard contained the official translation of the text, which was nearly the same as the one Hasan had produced. The rest of the treasure was distributed around the room in display cases large and small, the ecclesiastical items separated from the secular ones. Brooke recognized herself in a photo of the excavation site and read the short paragraph that described the dig, feeling an odd thrill at being a "real" scientist featured in a museum.

It was fitting that the treasure should be here, close to the place where it had lain hidden for centuries. Brooke ran her hand over a case of jewelry that Damian had crafted. She remembered making some of these bracelets, rings, and necklaces when she was in his body. He had labored in the unhurried pursuit of excellence, an attitude foreign to the hustle bustle of the modern world, but one that Brooke embraced. She resolved to be like Damian, to take something of his ethos into her own life, to be his descendent in spirit as well as in fact.

Brooke felt a pang of remorse that she would never hold these lovely baubles again. Reflexively, she reached up and touched one of the earrings that dangled from her ears. A perceptive bystander would have noticed that it was in the same style as the jewelry on display, a lacework of delicate gold from which a pearl hung like a droplet eternally on the brink of falling. Damian had made them on commission for Lord Prepundolus and had never sold them. He would have wanted Brooke to have them.

She put her arm around Chad's waist and settled in next to his body. Whatever tomorrow might bring, today was perfect. What more can you ask from life?

Acknowledgments

An aspiring author needs all the help she can get, especially for a first novel. Luckily, many people came to my aid, offering comments and suggestions for improvements, as well as catching errors that are beyond the capability of a spell checker. I would especially like to thank those who reviewed the third draft, which was the first one I allowed anyone to see: Sherri Ruggles, Diana Borca-Tasciuc, Wendy Gibson, Linda Schadler, Jane Koretz, Adrienne Lavine, Jean Kirby, Russell de Grove, Jeff Short, Nicole Valicia Thompson-Andrews, and Doyle Goins. Equally important were the reviewers of the fourth draft, including Carrie Kaminski, June Deery, Larry Allen, John Rodriguez, and Naftali Deitsch.

I am indebted to the Critters Writers Workshop, an online forum where writers can obtain unbiased reviews of their manuscript and to Sezai Vardioğlu for his inspired tour of Istanbul.

Most of all, I wish to thank my husband, Chris Kaminski, who edited the third, fourth, and fifth drafts, produced a map of Medieval Constantinople, and designed the cover. He stood with me through every step of the publication process. What a guy.

43069630R00207

Made in the USA
Middletown, DE
29 April 2017